Worlds Known and Unknown

Publications of the North American Jules Verne Society

The Palik Series (edited by Brian Taves)

The Marriage of a Marquis
Translated by Edward Baxter and Kieran M. O'Driscoll

Shipwrecked Family: Marooned with Uncle Robinson
Translated by Sidney Kravitz

Mr. Chimp & Other Plays
Translated by Frank Morlock

The Count of Chanteleine: A Tale of the French Revolution
Translated by Edward Baxter

Vice, Redemption, and the Distant Colony
Translated, with notes, by Kieran M. O'Driscoll

Around the World in 80 Days: The 1874 Play

Bandits & Rebels
Translated by Edward Baxter

Golden Danube
Translated, with notes, by Kieran M. O'Driscoll

A Priest in 1835
Translated, with notes, by Daniéle Chatelain and George Slusser

Castles of California
Translated, with notes, by Kieran M. O'Driscoll

Scheherazade's Last Night and Other Plays
Translated, with introduction and notes, by Peter Schulman

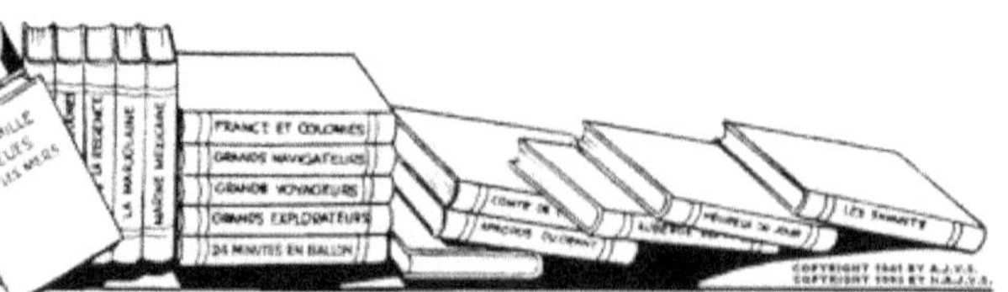

Worlds Known and Unknown

**by Jules Verne
and Michel Verne**

Translated by Kieran O'Driscoll, Edward Baxter,
Alex Kirstukas, Ian Thompson

Edited by Brian Taves for the

North American Jules Verne Society

The Palik Series

BearManor Fiction
2018

Worlds Known and Unknown
by Jules Verne and Michel Verne

For information, address:

BearManor Fiction
P. O. Box 71426
Albany, GA 31708

bearmanormedia.com

North American Jules Verne Society: najvs.org

Typesetting and layout by John Teehan

Published in the USA by BearManor Media

ISBN — 978-1-62933-391-5

TABLE OF CONTENTS

For Robert Florey

Cinéaste *of Jules Verne*

THE "AUTHORS' PAST AND PRESENT"
SERIES OF POST CARDS.

Jules Verne: A Tale of His Works.

BY J. P. MULLINS.

"The Wonderful Travellers" having searched out "The English at the North Pole," who had crossed "The Field of Ice," in emulation of "The Adventures of Captain Hatteras," warmed them by their description of "The Archipelago on Fire" and doings at "Miridiana." Returning to civilisation, all were delighted to hear that "The Begum's Fortune" was theirs, as the result of having purchased "The Lottery Ticket" from "Dick Sands, The Boy Captain." "Five Weeks in a Balloon" of huge size then followed, in company with "The Survivors of the Chancellor," "Martin Paz," and "Godfrey Morgan." Descending, they came upon "The Child of the Cavern," fitting out "The Clipper of the Clouds," from instructions given in "The Mysterious Document." By its aid, said he, we will convey "The Vanished Diamond" to "The Blockade Runners," and get it through to "A Floating City." This they did. "A Voyage to the Moon" proved so entrancing that acting on "Dr. Ox's Experiment" made during "A Winter amid the Ice," "A Journey to the Centre of the Earth" and "Twenty Thousand Leagues under the Seas" was accomplished. Then after "A Voyage Round the World," they prepared for and took "The Flight to France."

Born at Nantes, Feb. 8th, 1828, Died at Amiens, Mar. 24th, 1905.

Jules Verne

Published by MATTHEWS & MULLINS, 3a, Bolt Court, Fleet Street, London, E.C.
(Copyright in Great Britain and United States of America).
[ENTERED AT STATIONERS' HALL].

Verne's Anglo-American renown was established by the early 1890s, as revealed in this postcard.

Foreword

Then and Now—A Personal View of the Palik Series

by Brian Taves

THE 1980S PROVED TO BE the worst of times, and the best of times, for Jules Verne. On the one hand, not since the 1960s and the demise of the Fitzroy Series of Jules Verne had one of the stories not previously translated appeared in English; at best, well-known titles like *Vingt Mille Lieues sous les mers* (*Twenty Thousand Leagues under the Seas*, 1870) received an array of new translations. Yet this was also a time of ferment, for a new network of Verne enthusiasts was making acquaintance, corresponding, and asking some of the pertinent questions that would begin to guide publications in the 1990s.

Most of these active Vernians of the time were collectors, and the key question was being enunciated: precisely what Verne stories had appeared in English? This was not as readily answerable as might seem, since most Verne books either changed the title in translation or in edition, and many had appeared in several translations, but under various titles.[1] In seeking complete libraries

1. *Robur-le-Conqurérant* (*Robur the Conqueror*, 1886) was best known under the title *The Clipper of the Clouds*, but was also titled at one point *A Trip Around the World in a Flying Machine*, and was sometimes included in editions of Verne's *Master of the World*, since both featured the same protagonist. But this was a fairly simple example by comparison with some. His long novel, *Les Enfants du Capitaine Grant* (1867), became, in various translations, not only *The Children of Captain Grant* and *Captain Grant's Children*, but also *In Search of the Castaways*, *The Castaways*, *A Voyage Around the World*, or, depending on the translation, two separate trilogies known as *The Mysterious Document*, *On the Track*, and *Among the Cannibals*, and *South America*, *Australia* and *New Zealand*.

of Verne in English, obscure bibliographic details were gradually reconstructed.

This was occurring in the wake of what had been a golden age. With the fiftieth anniversary of Verne's death in 1905, many copyrights expired, and with steadily increasing interest in science fiction, Verne was a "classic" writer appealing to publishers. Movies, television, and comic books all celebrated "the prophet of the 20th century."[2] Verne books were in print that had not been issued since the 1920s, and stories by Verne not previously in English began to appear. New, improved translations began to appear of many Verne novels that had only previously been hastily (and often poorly) rendered in the late 19th century. By 1970 many of these new editions were also in paperback, and just as important, they could be found in not only college and city libraries, but in community libraries as well.

By the early 1970s, however, the cycle was beginning to wane. A parallel could be seen in the space program; following the apex of global interest with the first lunar landing of Apollo 11 in 1969, subsequent space missions found diminished public attention. Verne, with his reputation as a prophet, had benefitted from much of this attention, especially his novels *De la Terre à la Lune* (*From the Earth to the Moon*, 1865) and *Autour de la Lune* (*Around the Moon*, 1870). In the wake of the accomplishment of man's landing on the moon, Verne's novels, especially those two titles, began to receive less attention.

By the 1980s, the nadir had been reached. Many of the Verne novels whose availability had nurtured the renewed readership went out of print. Libraries placed those "old" 1960s Verne books that had appeared for the first time ever or for the first time in years out for recycling or the nickel-a-book weekend sales. Publishers deliberately chose to reissue poor translations, even when made aware of the problems and when better ones were freely available in the public domain.[3] Filmmakers turned away from the author as well,

---

One of the experiences with the Palik series has involved coming up with fresh titles for volumes that sometimes comprised several stories, or whose original title was unpronounceable in English, or not usable for one reason or another (for instance, key words were used as the title of a subsequent book).

2. William B. Jones, "Off on a Comic: Jules Verne in Comic Books," *Extraordinary Voyages*, 21 (November 2014), 1-23; Brian Taves, *Hollywood Presents Jules Verne: The Father of Science Fiction on Screen* (Lexington, KY: University of Kentucky Press, 2015).

3. Walter James Miller and Brian Taves, "The Tribulations of Responding to a Publisher,"

and publishers began to concentrate on repeatedly issuing *Twenty Thousand Leagues under the Seas, From the Earth to the Moon, Voyage au centre de la Terre* (*Journey to the Center of the Earth*, 1864), and less frequently such titles as *L'Île mystérieuse* (*The Mysterious Island*, 1875) and *Michel Strogoff* (*Michael Strogoff*, 1876). In the two latter cases, their status was embellished by N.C. Wyeth illustrations, made many years before, but which had assumed a canonical status in their own right. Verne editions became vehicles to feature illustrators who were promoted as much—and in some cases more—than the author himself. The natural market forces that diminished possible sales of so many competing editions of a limited number of titles caused some to conclude that Verne was no longer commercial. At the same time, readers who wanted more than a half-dozen titles had to explore second-hand bookshops or the larger, more permanent libraries.

These were hardly promising conditions for a new generation of Vernians to pursue their hobby, but nonetheless the 1980s was a time of expanding contacts, sharing information that created a sense of community. In 1990, two of those who met through this correspondence, Stephen Michaluk, Jr. and I, devised *The Jules Verne Encyclopedia*, bringing together information about all English language Verne editions, previous associations of American Vernians, and such sidelines as Verne philately and the author on screen.[4] This was the first focus on the Anglophone experience of the author, and established precisely what Verne stories and plays had been published (and just as significantly, under what title)—and for the first time set forth "the work to be done," the works which remained to be translated.

This was a key expansion of the existing information about the author, which had begun with an article in the August 1936 issue of *Hobbies*, by Willis Hurd, which began the American Jules Verne Society, a group lasting into the 1950s.[5] Subsequently, however, efforts stalled, and bibliographies tended to be fragmentary, or geared toward booksellers promoting their inventories, rather than an impartial historical guide. This was also a matter of tradition;

Extraordinary Voyages, 15 (March 2009), 9-10.

4. The book was turned into Scarecrow Press in 1993, but due to the publisher's sale to Rowman & Littlefield, did not finally appear until 1996.

5. Hurd, Willis E. "A Collector and His Jules Verne." *Hobbies* (August 1936): 88-89.

academics usually leave bibliographies of editions to librarians and collectors.[6] Scholars understandably had largely reached for Verne in the original French, rather than delving into the bibliographic jungle that was the Anglophone Verne experience.[7] By contrast, *The Jules Verne Encyclopedia*, by establishing the various editions issued over time, indicated what had been overlooked, and in indicating the gaps, an agenda was set for translators. This also began sorting through the textual jungle that Hurd had first recognized, with most Verne works, in their own era and since, having multiple translations of varying merit.[8]

The first fruit of this effort appeared promptly. A personal friend, Evelyn Copeland, who had helped me with translations, became interested in one of those stories never previously in English, *Aventures de la famille Raton* (*Adventures of the Rat Family*, 1891). I secured the interest of Oxford University Press, and when the editor came to visit the Library of Congress, I showed her the original color engravings in the edition of *Le Figaro* that the Library held. *Adventures of the Rat Family* became the first time in literally decades that not only was a Verne tale published in English for the first time, but with all the original artwork from the original French edition.

This set a precedent for new editions. No longer need Verne books search for original art; it was already available from those French publications. So, too, *Adventures of the Rat Family* proved

6. Major urban libraries sometimes had an awareness of this problem. I recall, as an eleven-year-old, going to the main branch of the Los Angeles Public Library. I had just seen the recent reissue of the movie, *In Search of the Castaways* (1962), and had been trying unsuccessfully to find out what novel it was based on with the resources at hand in my smaller community library (which held some twenty Verne titles and a biography). A helpful librarian at the downtown library was aware of an informal cross-index that had been prepared over the years for such questions on Verne, and was able to direct me to an edition of *Captain Grant's Children* they had on the shelves as the source of the film in question. See the footnote above for the possible complexity of the answer on this volume in English translation.

7. One volume had a brief and partial overview of various translations and editions, but did not explore the topic; moreover, it was part of a series with almost entirely devoted to indexing critical studies on assorted topics. See Edward J. Gallagher, Judith A. Mistichelli and John A. Van Eerde, *Jules Verne: A Primary and Secondary Bibliography* (Boston, MA: G. K. Hall & Co., 1980).

8. Initial comparative evaluations of these translations was begun by Walter James Miller as part of an essay, "Jules Verne," in Jane M. Bingham, *Writers for Children* (New York: Charles Scribner's Sons, 1988), 591-598, and was treated more comprehensively by Arthur B. Evans, "A Bibliography of Jules Verne's English Translations," *Science Fiction Studies*, 32 (March 2005), 105-141.

By 1866, and the publication of his fourth novel, Verne's reputation as the father of science fiction was clearly evident.

that publishers would take little-known Verne books, not just new translations of familiar titles. Scholars could turn their energies toward titles unfamiliar to English readers. And so, by the beginning of the 21st century, Wesleyan University Press began a series of new Verne translations in critical editions, some of novels that had appeared before, but highlighting the four books in the "Voyages Extraordinaries" series that had not previously been published in English. And the series used all the original French engravings. Unfortunately that was not the case with the editions by University of Nebraska Press, although otherwise equally exemplary. Other presses from time to time have issued new translations of Verne stories, improving on the often shoddy 19th century renderings. Among these various editions, those of one Vernian deserves to be singled out: Norman Wolcott, whose Choptank Press series on Lulu brought some of the more elusive titles back into print, most with the engravings, including a critical edition of a Verne story set in the United States, *Le Testament d'un excentrique* (*The Will of an Eccentric*, 1899) previously only published in English a century before—but in Britain, not the US!

Yet, with all this activity, many of those titles not translated, delineated in *The Jules Verne Encyclopedia*, remained untouched, with no sign they would be tackled by the university presses. This was a task that the NAJVS was in a unique position to approach, while at the same time building upon the work of previous publications and scholars.[9]

One of these texts was *Voyage à travers l'impossible* (*Journey through the Impossible*, 1882), a science fiction play by Verne and his theatrical collaborator Adolphe d'Ennery, that had recently been rediscovered in French archives. Because of its genre, the North American Jules Verne Society decided to make this our first publication effort in 2003. It was a critical edition, with not only the original art but several additional new illustrations in the vintage style; Jean-Michel Margot and Roger Leyonmark were behind these aspects, respectively.

9. For instance, to fully appreciate *Fact-Finding Mission*, Jules Verne's beginning of a novel found in *Vice, Redemption, and the Distant Colony*, requires also reading *The Astonishing Adventure of the Barsac Mission*, which has appeared over the years in both hardback and mass market paperback (*Into the Niger Bend* and *The Ctiy in the Sahara*), and is therefore readily available on the second-hand market. *The Astonishing Adventure of the Barsac Mission* (originally serialized in 1914 as *L'Étonnante Aventure de la mission Barsac*), is largely the work of Jules's son Michel, incorporating his father's *Fact-Finding Mission*.

Ironically, the NAJVS edition was the first complete edition of the play in any language, and it would be adapted into the first complete French edition using the same critical material. Edward Baxter, who has translated Verne for New Canada Press, Wesleyan, and Nebraska, rendered the play into English.

Journey through the Impossible was underwritten by Edward D. Palik, Jr., a physicist who deserves a special place in the pantheon of Anglophone Vernians. He was one of those individuals encountered in that 1980s correspondence, and when I moved to Washington, D.C. to join the staff of the Library of Congress, we were able to meet on several occasions. We both shared an interest in those stories and plays that had never appeared in English, and discussed ways of possibly accomplishing this task.[10]

Ed took his interest the extra mile, donating funds yearly to the NAJVS publication fund, to translate texts not previously in English. In the last years of his life, Ed made two bequests to the society, one of them his highly valued collection of hundreds of Verne editions in various languages. This was to be sold to NAJVS members, with the proceeds going to the translation fund he had initiated. I fondly recall many Saturdays working with Mark Eckell on the catalog of Ed's collection; Henry Franke sometimes came by to help and the final auction was handled by Jean-Michel Margot.

Two other vital factors came into place: a publisher, and contributors. I had met Ben Ohmart of BearManor Media, who readily understood and agreed to the NAJVS aim, to publish a series of Verne books, never before in English, in critical editions profusely illustrated with art from Verne's own time. As well, BearManor agreed to a series including different forms: not just novels but short stories and plays. These will remain available on a long-term basis for book buyers, not the short-lived shelf-life too common among mass-circulation books.

Two translators immediately offered their services at this early point in the series. Edward Baxter stepped forth once more, along with Kieran O'Driscoll, who had recently completed a dissertation on Verne translations at Dublin University. Baxter and I had already

10. There remains, of course, the ongoing task of improving the original, largely 19th century translations of Verne, but as this project has already been undertaken by a variety of hands and a number of publishers over the years, Ed Palik's initiative, respected by the society, was to bring into English all those other stories and plays that continued to be overlooked.

discussed a number of stories that particularly piqued his interest and would inevitably be part of this series. The participation of both allowed the series to commence.

Gradually, others joined the task, as translators (Danièle Chatelain, Sidney Kravitz, Frank Morlock, George Slusser, Jean-Louis Trudel, Peter Schulman, Alex Kirstukas, Ian Thompson) and writers of critical material (Philippe Burgaud, Daniel Compère, Volker Dehs, Jean-Michel Margot, Walter James Miller, and Garmt de Vries-Uiterweerd), not to mention those who have contributed to this particular volume. All of these individuals have noted reputations and wide experience in the field, and Vernians from ten countries have been part of the Palik series.

The Palik series has completed the publication of all the short stories and novels that remained to be translated.[11] In addition, following the precedent of *Journey through the Impossible*, and with an encouraging publisher, we have included the principal plays; this was essential as the stage was a major part of Verne's writing career and a formative force in honing his literary techniques. More plays remain to translate, but they are of steadily diminishing interest, including many comic-operas, and in most cases with the original score no longer surviving. Many of these plays, too, were never staged.[12]

BearManor layout designer John Teehan has created volumes that are truly elegant in their look. He also facilitated creating a series of covers relying on 19th century European designs (most from France and the former Czechoslovakia), modified for the new titles, each book in the series using a different cover.[13]

We are particularly grateful to Bernhard Krauth of the German Verne organization for providing the largest share of our illustrations.

---

11. The exacting bibliographer will note that we did not include in the Palik series Verne's play, *Kéraban-le-têtu*, from one of the Extraordinary Journeys, but that was because an unpublished translation has existed for a number of years in private hands, that will hopefully see print, and NAJVS wanted to avoid any possibility of redundant effort (of the type that occurred in 2001 with the separate, simultaneous publication of two new, quality translations of *The Mysterious Island*).

12. However, there remains here room among these plays for additional research, and for a delineation, see the introduction by Jean-Michel Margot to the third volume in the series, *Mr. Chimp & Other Plays* (Albany, GA: BearManor Fiction, 2011).

13. And notice such details as only those with the words "Voyages Extraordinaires" as part of the design contain stories Verne intended for the series, even if rejected by his publisher Pierre-Jules Hetzel.

Many Vernians have graciously donated their services outright, allowing the NAJVS to stretch Ed Palik's gift to the limit. We are especially grateful to the City of Nantes and its Bibliothèque municipal, headed by Agnès Marcetteau, for their assistance with the Palik Series.

This final volume takes its title, *Worlds Known and Unknown*, from the subtitle of Verne's Extraordinary Journeys. In these pages, a number of rare texts are offered, some never translated, some in new translations, and others in rare translations of historical importance, all with critical material. "About the *Géant*," "Twenty-Four Minutes in a Balloon," and *Mona Lisa* have never appeared in book form in English before. "Recollections of my Childhood and of my Youth" is a fresh translation. "About the *Géant*" and "Twenty-Four Minutes in a Balloon" are ideally matched with "A Voyage in a Balloon," Verne's first "lighter than air" story, but in the original 1852 translation, reprinted for the first time—not the revised renderings of Verne short stories that comprised the 1874 collection, *Le Docteur Ox* (*Doctor Ox*), previously used by publishers. "Gibraltar" is, again, a unique translation, an effort of the very first American Jules Verne Society. By offering two 1890s renderings of "Frritt-Flacc," one of Verne's shortest stories, readers may see for themselves, in the pages of a single volume, how two responsible translators brought this incredible story into English. And finally, "The Humbug" has the unique status of probably the least-known Verne story of the United States, so is uniquely deserving of a place in this series. "The Humbug" was revised by Verne's son and literary executor, Michel Verne, and his initial series of stories, "Zigzags Through the World of Science," appears in English for the first time, completing the translation of all Michel's stories as well as those of his father, allowing comparison of their literary legacies.[14]

The Palik series has been a long journey. The books began appearing in 2011, and with this volume the series winds up nine years later with a dozen books. For details on the titles, see the society's website at najvs.org and the detailed description at the end of this volume. Some of these texts were only discovered in the second half of the 20th century, while others had long been known, some since the mid 1800s, but have been neglected for reasons that seem

14. See the upcoming book on Michel's writing and filmmaking, *Jules Verne's Ghost*, by Brian Taves.

incomprehensible today (most notably, *Le Comte de Chanteleine. Épisode de la revolution* [*The Count of Chanteleine: A Tale of the French Revolution*, 1864] the fourth volume in the Palik Series). More than half the books are aimed at the broad cross-section of readers, not just Verne devotees. The reader will find four novels, four novelettes, sixteen short stories, four articles, two forewords by Verne, eleven plays, and more. In terms of genre, you'll find narratives of humor, castaways, swashbucklers, science fiction, historical novels, social consciousness, melodrama, and colonial adventure, travelogue, mystery and gothic, and plays of every type and length. We've produced not only several books detailing the controversial posthumous father-son collaboration between Jules and Michel Verne, including the present volume as well as the novel, *Le Beau Danube jaune* (*Golden Danube*)—the version revised by Michel, *Le Pilote du Danube*, had previously been translated in 1967 as *The Danube Pilot*. The Palik Series also offers the first books on which father and son actually share a by-line (*Vice, Redemption and the Distant Colony* and the present volume). We've enhanced the use of the original engravings from Verne publications by including maps and historical views of the people and places described, particularly when the original French version was not itself illustrated, and the critical materials in each volume have their own illustrations. All of the Palik volumes are available in electronic form, and one as a professional audio book (*The Count of Chanteleine*), with others hopefully to follow.[15]

The only regret is that over time some important contributors have passed on. Ed Palik only lived to see the publication of *Journey through the Impossible*, but his family has enjoyed the other volumes in the series named for him, and understand the NAJVS gratitude and that of Vernians worldwide to this man whose generosity has made these volumes possible. I've been honored to be entrusted with editing this series, and am grateful to so many who have made it possible, relying on so many friends and making new ones along the way. NAJVS is made up of collectors, scholars, and pure readers, and as the Palik Series offers simultaneously the first editions, illustrated with vintage artwork of the time, and the highest quality translations and

15. See the BearManor Media website for the audible.com audiobook, read by Fred Frees, of *The Count of Chanteleine*: http://www.bearmanormedia.com/the-count-of-chanteleine-audiobook-a-tale-of-the-french-revolution-by-jules-verne-read-by-fred-frees?search=verne%20chanteleine

critical material, the series is significant on all of these levels. At last this closes the efforts to complete the texts that English readers had never been able to enjoy, so that Anglophiles may read *all* the tales of this master—and his son, such an important influence on his oeuvre. NAJVS and our collaborators are proud that the Palik Series has furthered this goal.

Part I

Autobiography

In this section are two items of Verne "autobiography" that are unique for having appeared in the United States, as well as France. "Souvenirs d'enfance et de jeunesse" ("Recollections of My Childhood and of My Youth") was first solicited by the American magazine, *The Youth's Companion*, in 1891, and was only subsequently published in French in 1974; it is offered here in a new translation.

"A La Nouvelle mariée Caroline" ("To the New Bride Caroline") is from the manuscript collection of the Pierpont Morgan Library in New York City, donated by Dr. Silvain S. Brunschwig in 1956. This unique item was twice sold by City Book Auctions. At a sale held on September 12-13, 1941 it was sold for $8, and again on May 23, 1942, this time for $12.[16] By then, this three page handwritten and autographed manuscript was enclosed in a half crimson morocco slipcase, with gilt paneled back and inner cloth wraps.

The poem was written when Verne's cousin Caroline had rejected his advances and married another. It occupies seven stanzas of ten lines each, and is dated April 27, 1847, when Verne was age nineteen. "To the New Bride Caroline" is a slightly different and more complete version of "Damoiselle et Damoiseau," published on pages 14-15 of the volume of collected Verne poetry, *Poésies inédites* (Paris, le cherche-midi éditeur, 1989). Seven lines are slightly different, or appear in "To the New Bride Caroline" but not "Damoiselle et Damoiseau."

16. For an analysis of original Verne manuscripts and autographs, and their value, see "The Autographic Legacy of Jules Verne" by Stephen Michaluk, Jr., in *Autographic Times*, Volume 3 (October 1996), 1, 26.

An additional manuscript version exists in Europe with minor word differences.

Altogether, these articles and poem offer a glimpse into the personal side of the author, beyond what may be discerned from only reading his stories and novels.

Recollections of My Childhood and of My Youth

by Jules Verne

Translated by Ian Thompson and Hélène Lamérant

There are two manuscripts of "Souvenirs d'enfance et de jeunesse." The oldest, which is in the collection of the Centre d'Etudes verniennes at Nantes, is full of corrections. The second one has few corrections and was sent by Verne to an American magazine, The Youth's Companion, *which had requested it. This magazine published it in 1891 in a poorly translated English version with the title "The Story of my Boyhood" in the issue of April 9, 1891, volume 64, page 211. This manuscript was bought by the Fondation Martin Bodmer, at Cologny near Geneva, and was published as a chapter in* Jules Verne *(Cahiers de L'Herne, 1974), with notes by Pierre-André Touttain. It is this version that has been used in the present translation.*

Men of my age should indeed be the ones to ask about recollections of their youth. Those memories are more vivid than what we have witnessed or achieved after reaching middle age. Halfway through its lifetime, our mind enjoys looking back to those early years. The images that it recalls are not of a kind that fades or loses their freshness: they are unalterable photos made even sharper by the passage of time. This vindicates the profound saying by a French author: "Memory is long-sighted." It extends with age, like a spyglass as its tube is pulled out, and it can make out the most distant features of the past.

The first draft and the revised initial pages of this article.

Are such memories likely to arouse interest? I cannot say. But the young readers of *Goalh's Companion* in Boston may learn with some interest how I got the calling to become a writer, which I still pursue well into my sixties.[17]

17. This is a commonly repeated error in French, where *Youth's Companion* is misprinted as

Souvenirs d'enfance et de jeunesse.

1.

Des souvenirs de leur enfance et de leur jeunesse ?... Oui ! c'est bien aux hommes de mon âge qu'il convient de les demander. Ces souvenirs sont plus vivaces que les faits dont nous avons été les témoins ou les acteurs à partir de notre maturité. Quand il a franchi la moyenne ordinaire de la vie, notre esprit se plaît à ce retour vers les premières années. Les images qu'il évoque ne sont point de celles qui se défraîchissent ou s'effacent : ce sont des photographies inaltérables et que le temps rend plus nettes encore. Ainsi se justifie ce mot si profond d'un écrivain français : « La mémoire est presbyte. » Elle s'allonge en vieillissant, comme une lunette dont on développe le tube, et peut distinguer les plus lointains linéaments du passé.

De pareils souvenirs sont-ils de nature à intéresser !.. Je ne sais. Mais peut-être les jeunes lecteurs du Youth's Companion de Boston apprendront-ils non sans quelque curiosité comment me vint cette vocation d'écrire que je poursuis au-delà des limites de la soixantaine ? Aussi, sur la demande du directeur de cette revue, j'allonge les tubes de ma mémoire, je me retourne et je regarde en arrière.

2

Et d'abord, ai-je toujours eu du goût pour les récits dans lesquels l'imagination se donne libre carrière ? Oui, sans doute, et ma famille a tenu en grand honneur les lettres et les arts. — D'où je conclus que l'atavisme entre pour une forte part dans mes instincts. Puis, il y a cette circonstance que je suis né à Nantes, où mon enfance s'est tout entière écoulée. Fils d'un père à demi-parisien et d'une mère tout à fait bretonne, j'ai vécu dans le mouvement maritime d'une grande ville de commerce, point de départ et d'arrivée de nombreux voyages au long cours. Je revois cette Loire, dont une lieue de ponts relie les bras multiples, ses quais encombrés de cargaisons sous l'ombrage de grands ormes, et que la double voie du chemin de fer, les lignes de tramways, ne sillonnaient pas encore. Des navires sont à quai sur deux ou trois rangs. D'autres remontent ou descendent le fleuve. Pas de bateaux à vapeur, à cette époque, ou du moins très peu ; mais quantité de ces voiliers dont les Américains ont si heureusement conservé et perfectionné le type avec leurs clippers

172

This is why, at the request of the director of this review, I extend the tubes of my memory, turn around and look back.

2

Firstly, have I always had a taste for tales in which the imagination is given free rein? Yes, probably, and my family held literature and the arts in high regard—hence my conclusion that heredity largely accounts for my instincts. There is also the fact that I was born in Nantes, where I spent most of my childhood. As the son of a half-Parisian father and a mother of Breton descent, I have lived in the maritime bustle of a large trading port, the point of departure and landing of many long voyages. I recall the river Loire, with its many branches connected by miles of bridges, its wharves cluttered with freight under the shade of tall elms, but not yet criss-crossed by the double railway track and tramway lines. Ships lay alongside the quays two or three deep. Others went up and down the river. No steamers at that time, or at least very few, but lots of those sailing ships of a type that has been retained and improved upon by the Americans with their clippers and three-masted schooners. In those days, we only had the heavy sailing ships of the merchant navy. They bring back so many memories! In my imagination, I was climbing the shrouds, clambering to the top mast, clinging to the trunk of their masts. How eager I was to walk across the shaky plank which connected them to the quay and to set foot on their deck. But with my childish timidity I did not dare. Was I timid? Yes indeed. And yet I had already lived through a revolution, the overthrow of a system of government, the establishment of a new monarchy, although I was only two at the time, and I can still hear the rifle shots in 1830 in the streets of the town where, as in Paris, the people fought against the king's troops.[18]

One day, however, I ventured to climb up the bulwark of a three-masted ship while the watchman was on duty in a neighboring bar. There I was on the deck. My hand caught a halyard and made it slip through its pulley block!… What fun! The hold covers open up!… I

"Goalh's Companion."

18. This is a reference to the abdication of the Bourbon monarch Charles X, as a result of a popular uprising in Paris, leading to the accession of Louis-Philippe from the Orléans family.

lean over the edge of the abyss... the strong smell rising from it goes to my head – the pungent smell of tar mingles with the aroma of spices!... I get up, I go back to the poop deck, I go in... It is full of scents from the sea which create an atmosphere reminiscent of the Ocean! Here is the wardroom with its anti-roll table, which unfortunately does not roll in the calm waters of the harbor! Here are the cabins with their creaking partitions where I would have loved to live for months on end and those hard narrow bunks where I would have loved to sleep for whole nights. Then it's the captain's room, the sole master on board under God... quite a different character in my opinion from any king's minister or lieutenant general of the kingdom! I come out, I go up onto the poop deck and there I am bold enough to give the helm a quarter turn... I feel as if the ship is going to leave the quay, to cast off with her sails covering the masts and I, an eight year-old helmsman am going to steer her out to sea!

The sea!... Well, neither my brother, who became a sailor a few years later, nor I had seen it yet! In the summer all our family stayed within the confines of the vast countryside fairly close to the banks of the Loire, amidst vineyards, meadows and marshes. We stayed with an old uncle, a former shipowner. He had been to Caracas and Porto Gabello![19] We called him Uncle Prudent and I gave this name to one of the characters in *Robur-le-Conquérant* (*Robur the Conqueror*, 1886) in memory of him. But Caracas was in America, a country which fascinated me already. So, since we were unable to sail at sea, my brother and I drifted around the open countryside, through the meadows and the woodland. For want of a mast to climb, we spent whole days in the treetops. We competed to build the highest crow's nest. We chatted, we read, we worked out travel plans while the branches, shaken by the breeze gave the illusion of pitching and rolling... What enjoyable free time!

3

In those days, people travelled little or not at all. Those were the days of street lamps, breeches with straps underfoot, of the National Guard and the tinderbox. Indeed I witnessed the arrival of phosphorous matches,

19. Uncle Prudent was a retired shipowner who lived on a farm in the hamlet of La Guerche some 15 kilometers south west of Nantes in the commune of Brain, of which he was mayor. Porto Gabello [sic] refers to Porto Cabello, Venezuela's largest port, 75 kilometers west of Caracas.

detachable collars, cuffs, letter paper, postage stamps, loose-fitting trousers, the overcoat, opera hats, button-up boots, the metric system, the steamers on the Loire, said to be "non-explosive" because they blow up slightly less often than the others, omnibuses, the railways, the tramways, gas, electricity, the telegraph, the telephone, the gramophone! I belong to the generation between Stephenson and Edison![20] And now I witness the astonishing discoveries with which America marches ahead, mobile hotels, sandwich-making machines, moving pavements, newspapers made of "puff pastry," printed with chocolate ink which are read first and eaten afterwards!

I was not yet ten years old when my father bought a property at the far end of the town, in Chantenay, such a pretty name! It stood on a small hill above the right bank of the Loire. From my small bedroom I could see the river winding over a length of two or three leagues through the meadows which were flooded in winter due to the rise in water level. Admittedly, in summer it is short of water and fine yellow sandbanks appear like an archipelago of moving islets. The ships find it hard to steer through those narrow channels, even though they are marked by blackened posts which I can still visualize. Ah! Although the river Loire cannot be compared to the Hudson, the Mississippi or the Saint Lawrence, it still is a major French river. It would probably just be a humble river in America. But America is not just a country, it is a whole continent!

However, as a result of watching so many ships go by, I became consumed by the urge to sail. I already knew the nautical terms and I understood the manoeuvres well enough to be able to follow them in the maritime novels of Fenimore Cooper, which I never tire of reading with admiration. Through the eyepiece of a small telescope, I watched the ships, ready to tack, letting out the jibs and hauling the square-rigged sails. But my brother and I had not yet tried our hand at sailing, not even on rivers!... The opportunity finally arose.

4

At the far end of the harbor, there was a man who hired out boats for one franc a day. It was quite expensive for us, foolhardy too on our part, for

20. George Stephenson (1781-1848) was a famous British engineer who built the first public railway in the world and whose rail gauge was adopted as the world standard.

those boats were not watertight and leaked like sieves. The first one we used had only one mast, but the second one had two and the third one three, just like the coastal *chasse-marées* and luggers.[21] We took advantage of the ebb tide and we sailed down river tacking against the west wind.

What a way to learn! False manoeuvres at the helm, steering errors, unfurling sheets at the wrong time, the shame of tacking with a rear wind when the swell disturbed the wide Loire basin in front of our Chantenay. Usually we went out on the ebb and came back with the flood tide a few hours later. And whilst our hired boat was sailing heavily between the banks, we cast such envious glances at the lovely pleasure yachts which lightly skimmed the surface of the river.

One day, I was on my own in a wretched yawl without a keel. Ten leagues downstream from Chantenay, some planking gave way causing a leak. It was impossible to staunch it! There was I, in distress. The skiff sank straight down and I just managed to jump onto an islet of tall, thick reeds with tufted tops swaying in the breeze.

Now, of all the books I read in my childhood, the one I particularly liked was *Der Schweizerische Robinson* (*The Swiss Family Robinson*, 1812), rather than *Robinson Crusoe* (1719). I am well aware that Daniel Defoe's work has a broader philosophical impact. It is about a man left to his own devices, a man on his own, who one day finds a naked footprint in the sand! But Wyss's book, with its wealth of facts and incidents, is more interesting for young minds. It is about the family, father, mother and children, and their various abilities. What a lot of years I have spent on their island! How eagerly I joined in their discoveries! How I envied their fate![22] No wonder I was compelled to introduce the Robinsons of Science in *L'Ile Mystérieuse* (*The Mysterious Island*, 1874), and a whole boarding school of Robinsons in *Deux ans de vacances* (*Two Year Holiday*, 1889).

21. A *chasse-marée* was a decked inshore sailing vessel specifically for the landing of fresh fish as close as possible to markets before the days of conservation. A lugger is a small square-sailed fishing boat.

22. Verne's admiration for *The Swiss Family Robinson* led him to write a sequel to this novel in later years, *Seconde patrie* (*Second Homeland*, 1900), just as he had published a "rational" conclusion to Edgar Allan Poe's unfinished novel *The Adventures of Arthur Gordon Pym* as *Le Sphinx des glaces* (*The Sphinx of Ice*, 1897).

Translation of the prefaces to both *Deux Ans de vacances* (*Two Year Holiday*, 1889) and *Second Homeland* were both published together for the first time in unabridged form as an appendix to a previous volume in the Palik series, *Shipwrecked Family: Marooned with Uncle Robinson* (Albany, GA: BearManor Fiction, 2011).

Meanwhile, on my islet, it was not Wyss's heroes but Daniel Defoe's hero who became embodied in me. I was already thinking of building a hut with branches, making a fishing rod with a reed and hooks with thorns, getting a spark like savages by rubbing two dry sticks together. Making signals? No way, they might be noticed too early and I would be saved sooner than I wanted. First of all, I needed to appease my hunger. How? My food supplies had disappeared in the shipwreck. Hunting birds? I had neither a dog nor a gun… Well, what about shellfish?… There weren't any. Finally, I got to know the pangs of abandonment, the horror of deprivation on a desert island, just like the Selkirks and the characters of *Naufrages celebres* who were not fictional Robinsons.[23] My stomach was crying out for food. It only lasted a few hours and as soon as the tide was low, I only had to wade ankle-deep to reach what I called the mainland, namely the right bank of the Loire. And I went quietly back home where I had to be content with the family dinner instead of the Crusoe-style meal I had dreamt of: raw shellfish, a slice of peccary and bread made with manioc flour![24]

Such was this hectic sailing, with head wind, leak, crippled vessel, everything a castaway of my age could wish for!

My books have sometimes been accused of inciting young boys to leave home to travel all over the world. This has not happened, I am sure of it. But if children were ever to embark on such adventures, let them follow the example of the heroes in the *Voyages Extraordinaires* and they are bound to arrive safe and sound!

5

At the age of twelve, I had not yet seen the sea, the real sea! No! I was still at the stage of imagining I was boarding sardine boats, undecked fishing boats, brigs, schooners, three-masted ships, even steamers—they were called *pyroscaphes* at the time—which used to sail towards the mouth of the Loire.

---

23. *Les Naufrages Célèbres,* by Frédéric Zurcher and Elie Philippe, described the deliberate shipwreck of Scottish sailor, Alexander Selkirk, after a dispute with his captain. He was marooned alone on an island for over four years. .

24. The peccary is a small pig-like animal widespread in the southwest United States and Central America.

One day at last, my brother and I were allowed to sail on board *pyroscaphe* no. 2!… What fun ! It was enough to make us lose our heads! So off we go. We pass Indret, the big state plant, completely streaked with black smoke.[25] On the right and on the left we leave behind landing places such as Couesron, le Pellerin and Paimbœuf.[26] The *pyroscaphe* cuts across the wide estuary of the river. Here is Saint Nazaire, with its embryonic jetty, its old church with its leaning slated steeple and the few houses or hovels that made up the village which was to grow so quickly into a town.

Rushing out of the boat, climbing down the seaweed-covered rocks to scoop some sea water into our hands and up to our lips, it was just a matter of a few leaps for my brother and myself….

"But it's not salty" I said, turning pale.

"Not salty at all!" he answered.

"We have been misled!" I exclaimed, in a tone tinged with the deepest disappointment.

We were such fools! The tide was low and it was just water from the Loire that we had scooped from a hollow in a rock. When the tide came in, we found it salty beyond all our expectations.

6

At last I had seen the sea, or at least the vast bay which opens onto the ocean between the extreme points of the river. Since then, I have sailed across the Bay of Biscay, the Baltic, the North Sea and the Mediterranean. On a simple fishing boat at first, then a sloop, then a steam yacht, I was able to do some coastal cruising for pleasure.[27] I even crossed the Atlantic on the *Great Eastern,* and I set foot in America where—I am ashamed to confess in front of Americans—I only stayed eight days. What could I do? I only had a return ticket for a week.

Anyway, I saw New York, I stayed in a Fifth Avenue hotel, I crossed the East River before the Brooklyn bridge was built, I went

25. The State engineering plant at Indret manufactured marine machinery.

26. Couesron is the old spelling of Couëron.

27. The boats cited are the three successive vessels owned by Verne all bearing the same name, *Saint Michel*: *Saint-Michel I*, *Saint-Michel II*, and *Saint-Michel III*.

Jules Verne at home in Amiens, France, in 1896.

up the Hudson river as far as Albany, I visited Buffalo and Lake Erie, I gazed at the Niagara Falls from the top of the Terrapin Tower while a lunar rainbow appeared through the spray of the cataract, and finally beyond the Suspension Bridge, I sat on the Canadian shore… then I was on my way back![28] One of my deepest regrets is to think that I shall

28. Verne is referring to his transatlantic crossing in the giant liner *Great Eastern* in 1867, accompanied by his brother Paul. For a slightly fictionalized account of the trip, see Jules Verne's *Une Ville flottante* (*A Floating City*, 1871).

never see America again, a country I love and any Frenchman could love as a sister of France.

But these are not memories of childhood and youth; they are memories of mature age. My young readers now know what instincts, what circumstances led me to write this series of geographical novels. I lived in Paris surrounded by musicians, some of whom have remained good friends, but with very little contact with other writers who hardly knew me. Then I made a few journeys in the west, north and south of Europe, far less extraordinary than those in my stories, and I retired to provincial France to complete my task.

This task consisted of painting the whole earth, the whole world, in the form of novels, by imagining adventures specific to each country, by creating characters peculiar to the environment in which they operate.

Yes indeed! But the world is very large, and life is very short.[29]

In order to leave behind a complete work, one would have to live for a hundred years.

Well I shall try to live that long, like Monsieur Chevreul.[30] But between you and me, it's not easy!

---

29. This expression appears to be a paraphrase of the line "L'Art est long et le Temps est court" from Baudelaire's *Le Guignon* in *Les Fleurs du Mal –Spleen et Idéal* (1857).

30. Michel-Eugène Chevreul (1786-1889) was a French chemist and physicist and the author notably of works on colors and light, who lived to the age of 103.

Caroline Tronson, courtesy of the Bibliothèque municipale of Nantes and Volker Dehs.

To the New Bride Caroline

by Jules Verne

Translated by Rhoda B. Miller

Edited by Stephen Michaluk, Jr.

Lovely little shepherdess
Bright as a flower,
Her fragrance
Is the fragrance of purity.
Simple in her excellence
From earliest childhood,
Oblivious to her beauty
Like a violet
Shrinking from this pleasing scent.

One day, one beautiful day,
A very gallant youth
Passed through the tiny village
And, hearing the lovely girl,
Walked in silence,
For fear she would flee
At the slightest presumptuousness,
So modest and proper was she,
Could a young man ask for more?

Seeing this charming, slender maiden,
Beguiled, not knowing why,
He turns and stops his palfrey.
The young man gazes at her
While his heart tries to resist,
But already cannot
When love sets our hearts afire,
Then our soul will not obey.

He comes back again and again,
Although his nerve fails him,
In his heart
He feels his ardor grow.
Finally, he stops her
"Lovely young lady,
"My love, will you accept
"The affection I feel for you
"Both at night and in the day?"

But the young girl blushes
With shame;
While feeling joy in her soul,
However she smiles
"My lord, she answers,
"As a damsel I am free,
"You are noble and good.
"Parents to me still
"But parents whom I honor,
"Grant permission!"

So lovely and charming was she,
And so generous was her liege,
A favorable response he longed
Would come to crown their vows.
What began only as a passing fancy
Gradually turned into serious love.
The more highly he thought of her,

The more beautiful he found her,
And every day he discovered
In her a new virtue.

But time drags on when in love,
Torment without end,
Tried to hasten the week,
The week of love.
Finally the fine day arrives.
The boat of love
Is already reaching the shore.
The maiden climbs aboard,
Letting go, the boat is untied.
Sail on, sail on forever!

La question des ballons.

The many attempts at lighter-than-air flight, from Verne's *Robur the Conqueror*, 1886.

Part II

First Flights: Three Aerial Pieces by Jules Verne

by Alex Kirstukas

When Jules Verne was launching his career as a writer, his country was floating in an atmosphere of balloon mania. France's affection for everything lighter-than-air, an ongoing romance that had begun with the Montgolfier brothers' ascents in 1783, was enjoying a fresh wave of interest in the 1850s.[31] The next step was to perfect a *dirigible* balloon, one that could be steered even against severe contrary winds. Numerous inventors jumped at the challenge, with its promise to transform aeronautics from a whimsical spectator sport to a practical means of transportation.

Verne rode this wave of interest with gusto, reveling in the dramatic history of aeronautics in his second published story, "Un Voyage en ballon" ("A Voyage in a Balloon").[32] It appeared in August 1851 in the Paris general-interest magazine *Musée des familles* (*Family*

31. Jean-Michel Margot, "Jules Verne et le rêve d'Icare," *Bulletin de la Société Jules Verne* 31, No. 121 (mars 1997), 40–46.

32. Jules Verne, "La Science en famille. Un Voyage en ballon. (Réponse à l'énigme de juillet)," *Musée des familles*, 18, No. 11 (août 1851), 329–336. Following a *Musée* custom, there had been a teaser for the story in the July issue in the form of a "scientific riddle" running as follows: "What kind of ship is afraid of water, achieves its victories without being armed for war, travels without oars or sails and with just one man for its crew, and yet moves at almost a hundred leagues per hour?" (Anonymous, "Enigme scientifique," *Musée des familles*, 18, No. 10 [juillet 1851], 320).

Museum), the previous issue of which had launched Verne into print by featuring his adventure tale "Les Premiers Navires de la marine mexicaine" ("The First Ships of the Mexican Navy").

"A Voyage in a Balloon" gave the young Verne a chance to test ideas and approaches he would later explore in more ambitious works—for example, Volker Dehs demonstrated compelling thematic parallels between "A Voyage in a Balloon," *Voyages et Aventures du capitaine Hatteras* (*Journeys and Adventures of Captain Hatteras*, 1866), and *Robur-le-Conquérant* (*Robur the Conqueror*, 1886), while Norman Wolcott and Jean-Michel Margot pointed out that the story lays the foundation for Verne's trademark blend of abundant contextual detail and suspense-laden storytelling bravado.[33] Verne himself, in an interview, noted that his story "about a madman in a balloon ... [was] the first indication of the line of novel that I was destined to follow."[34]

"A Voyage in a Balloon" is also a superb early demonstration of Verne's knack for weaving a memorable fictional story out of prosaic nonfiction sources. He was probably commissioned specifically to write about the history of ballooning; a footnote on the story's first page explained that "This article completes, in a dramatic form, the 'History of Balloons' in volume XVII, page 357."[35] Indeed, since the *Musée*'s illustrations for the story are historical engravings that exist "in-universe" within the text and are referred to directly, it is highly plausible that Verne was simply given the engravings and told to write

33. Volker Dehs, "Préface," in Jules Verne, *Un Voyage en ballon* (Amiens: Centre international Jules Verne, 2001), 6–9; Norman Wolcott, "Redactor's Note," in Jules Verne, "A Voyage in a Balloon" (Project Gutenberg e-text, 2005); Margot, "Jules Verne et le rêve d'Icare." Also worth reading are Frederick Paul Walter's comments in his "Introduction: Verne Takes Off," in Jules Verne, *Five Weeks in a Balloon* (Middletown, CT: Wesleyan University Press, 2015), xi–xxxi.

34. R. H. Sherard, "Jules Verne at Home," *McClure's Magazine*, 2, No. 2 (January 1894), 115–124.

35. The "History of Balloons" was the second in a series of three nonfiction articles, "Mémoires d'un maître d'école" (A Schoolmaster's Essays); the other two essays described lightning rods and compasses, respectively. The essays are sugarcoated in a humorous fictional backstory attributing them to Jean-Baptiste Gaspard, a recently deceased schoolmaster from a made-up town; some scholars have suspected Verne hiding behind a pseudonym. However, a far more likely author is the journalist-historian Camille Duteil (1808–1860), who is described in the framing material as Gaspard's legatee and the provider of the texts—a standard "literary agent" gimmick familiar in the works of Cervantes, Hawthorne, Poe, Dumas, and many others.

something to go with them.[36]

Verne's solution to this pedestrian assignment was to read up on the subject—probably in "Les Aérostats et les aéronautes," a dry 1850 popular-science article by Louis Figuier[37]—and then to transform it completely, furnishing the magazine with an original piece wildly different in genre, tone, and style than anything Figuier or the "History of Balloons" had been able to offer. Such was the alchemical power of Verne's creativity that, even at twenty-three, he seems to have known instinctively how to transform unpromising base materials into storytelling gold.

Meanwhile, while doing all this stretching of his writerly wings, Verne seems also to have used "A Voyage in a Balloon" as a chance to drop a hint toward his own thoughts on dirigible balloons. Though the story's protagonist remains hopeful about aeronautical experiments, the presence of a dirigible-crazed antagonist suggests a more pointed moral: controlled flight is an intoxicating goal, but relying on balloons is a path to madness.

Cinq Semaines en ballon (*Five Weeks in a Balloon*, 1863), Verne's first published novel, goes further. Its hero emphatically dismisses the future of dirigibles, relying instead on air currents to navigate the balloon *Victoria* on its perilous but blissfully described course across Africa. The pattern continues in Verne's later writings, such as the balloon travels in *L'Île mystérieuse* (*The Mysterious Island*, 1875) and *Hector Servadac* (1877): though Verne evokes the charms and dangers of flight with romantic intensity and lush background detail, he is careful never to imply a promising future for lighter-than-air designs.[38] Finally, in *Robur the Conqueror*, he addressed the issue head-on, pitting a misguided balloon-crazy establishment against a lone rebel who demonstrates the technological superiority of heavier-than-air flying machines.[39]

36. The *Musée* used exactly that strategy to commission Verne's short story "Martin Paz," written to accompany existing drawings by Ignatius Mérino. For more information, see Daniel Compère, "Introduction," in Jules Verne, *Bandits and Rebels* (Albany, GA: BearManor Media, 2013), 1–18.

37. Jacques Noiray, *Le Romancier et la machine*, Vol. 2, *Jules Verne—Villiers de L'Isle-Adam* (Paris: Corti, 1982), 20.

38. At Hetzel's suggestion, Verne even added a self-deprecating joke into *Hector Servadac* about using balloons as a plot device: "'A balloon!' exclaimed Captain Servadac. 'But they're pretty well played out, are balloons! Even a novelist wouldn't dare use one nowadays!'" (Part II, Chapter XVII). See Jean-Yves Paumier, "Pour un ballon d'essai… vernien, ce fut le coup de maître," *Revue Jules Verne* 37 (printemps 2013), 137–150.

39. For further discussion, see Alex Kirstukas, "Introduction," in Jules Verne, *Robur the*

Why this pattern? Because Verne's research, probably coupled with conversations with friends and colleagues in Paris, quickly convinced him against the practicality of steering balloons. A growing group of campaigners against dirigibles, including the viscount Gustave de Ponton d'Amécourt (1825–1888) and the writer Gabriel de La Landelle (1812–1886), looked toward heavier-than-air machines as the way of the future and the means of wiping out balloons for good.[40]

Five months after *Five Weeks in a Balloon* was first published, the aeronautical dispute took a new turn.[41] In July 1863, Ponton d'Amécourt and La Landelle visited Verne's friend, the celebrated photographer Nadar (born Gaspard-Félix Tournachon, 1820–1910), who had recently augmented his already considerable fame by photographing Paris from a balloon. The visitors had come to explain their plans for a propeller-driven aircraft—an early version of the helicopter—and to invite him to join them in founding a society for heavier-than-air experimentation.

Nadar, ever open to ambitious projects, was enraptured. Together, the three launched a "Société d'encouragement pour la locomotion aérienne au moyen d'appareils plus lourds que l'air" (Society for the Encouragement of Aerial Locomotion by Means of Heavier-than-Air Machines). Membership would include not only scientists and researchers, but also writers and artists. Verne was among the first to join the project, and was appointed finance director of the society; he reportedly fulfilled his duties diligently, and attended every meeting. Even the eminent Victor Hugo, one of Verne's idols, was on hand to lend his public support.

Even before the Society had its first meeting, Nadar began planning a huge publicity stunt to raise funds for the work. His idea was charmingly paradoxical. Why not sponsor heavier-than-air experiments, and bring about the downfall of balloons, by exhibiting the biggest balloon ever built? Why not design a balloon to be, literally, the lighter-than-air craft to end them all?

Conqueror (Middletown, CT: Wesleyan University Press, 2017), vii–xviii.

40. "Wiping out" is no exaggeration. As Henri Zukowski notes ("L'exception du ballon," *Revue des sciences humaines*, 71, No. 200 [décembre 1985], 45–90), many of the noisiest heavier-than-air partisans were obsessed with the idea of *destroying* balloons, invoking violent imagery to describe their quest to render lighter-than-air travel obsolete.

41. *Five Weeks in a Balloon* was published on January 31, 1863. The historical background that follows comes from Jean Prinet and Antoinette Dilasser, *Nadar* (Paris: A. Colin, 1966), 143–166, and Dehs, "Préface," in Jules Verne, *Un Voyage en ballon*.

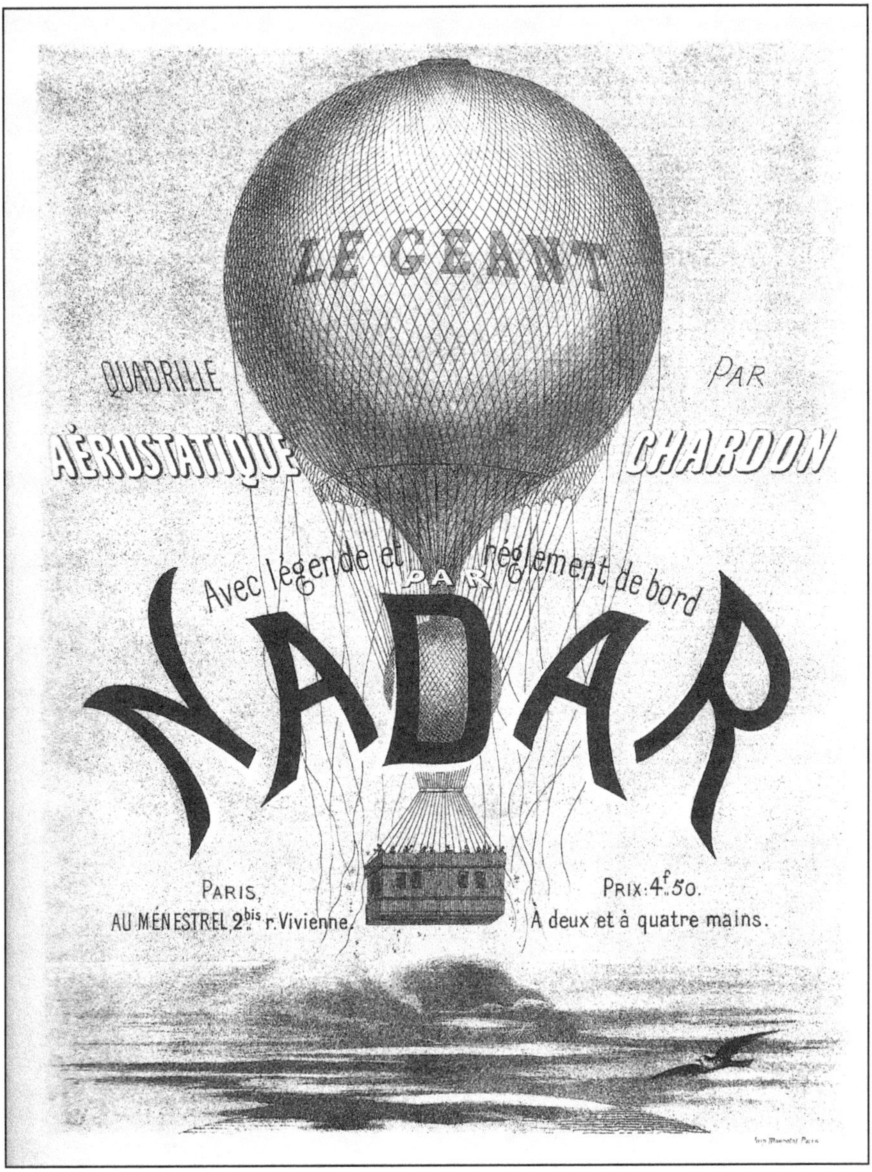

Nadar worked quickly, hiring the well-known aeronauts Louis and Jules Godard as designers and pilots of the enormous balloon. (And it *was* enormous: twenty-five meters in diameter, ten wider than Verne's fictional *Victoria*.) On October 4, the appropriately named *Géant* (*Giant*) began its maiden voyage. Verne intended to be one of the passengers, but he had to bow out at the last moment.

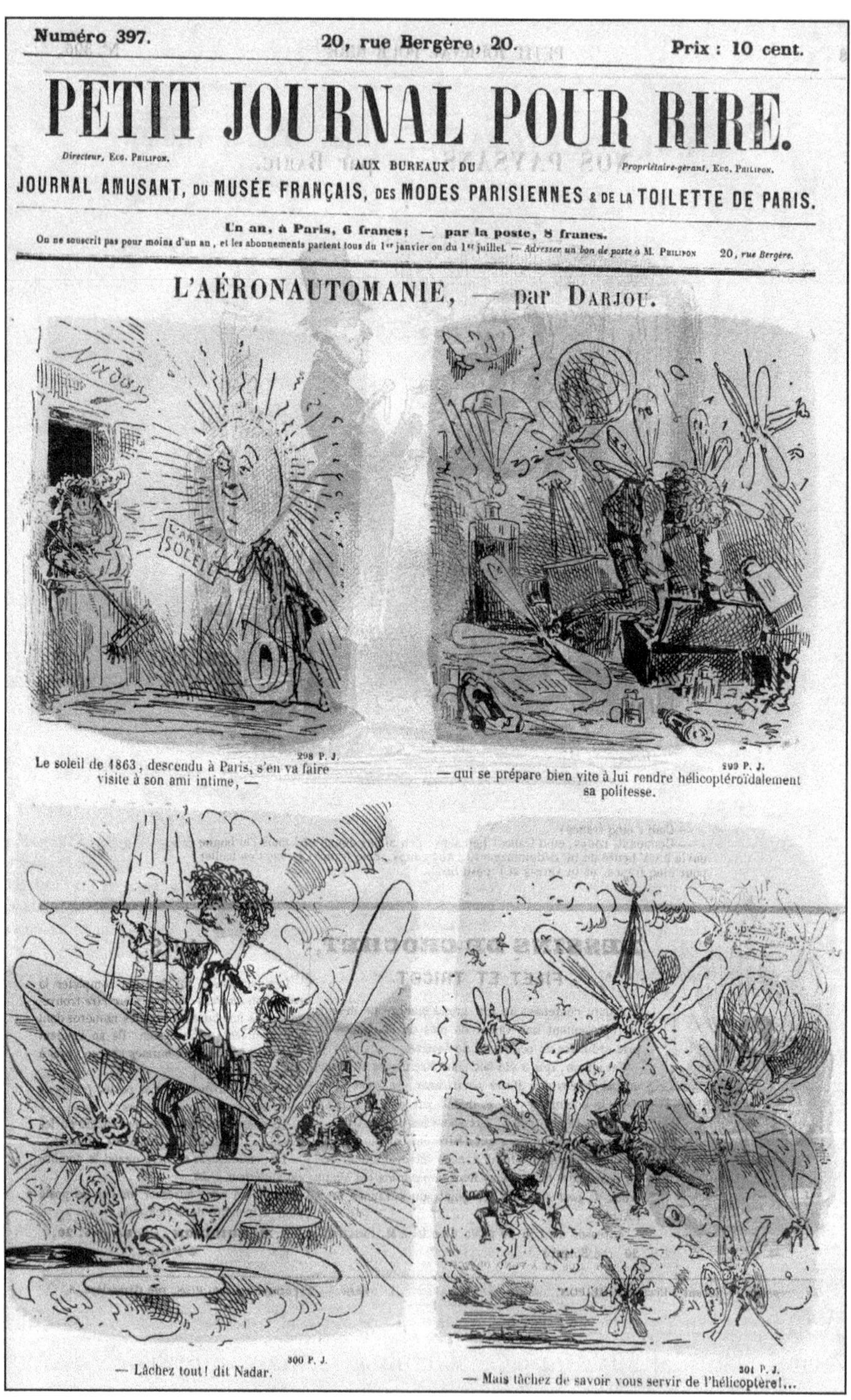

Numéro 397. 20, rue Bergère, 20. Prix : 10 cent.

PETIT JOURNAL POUR RIRE.

Directeur, Eug. Philipon. AUX BUREAUX DU *Propriétaire-gérant*, Eug. Philipon.

JOURNAL AMUSANT, DU MUSÉE FRANÇAIS, DES MODES PARISIENNES & DE LA TOILETTE DE PARIS.

Un an, à Paris, 6 francs; — par la poste, 8 francs.

On ne souscrit pas pour moins d'un an, et les abonnements partent tous du 1er janvier ou du 1er juillet. — *Adresser un bon de poste à* M. Philipon 20, *rue Bergère.*

L'AÉRONAUTOMANIE, — par Darjou.

298 P. J.
Le soleil de 1863, descendu à Paris, s'en va faire visite à son ami intime, —

299 P. J.
— qui se prépare bien vite à lui rendre hélicoptéroïdalement sa politesse.

300 P. J.
— Lâchez tout! dit Nadar.

301 P. J.
— Mais tâchez de savoir vous servir de l'hélicoptère!...

An 1865 cartoon by Darjou, mocking Nadar's support of helicopter experiments. Courtesy of the Robert Florey Collection.

The second ascent of the *Géant*, launched with nine passengers on October 18, began on a note of support: Napoleon III came in person to wish the voyage well (somewhat to the embarrassment of the left-wing Nadar). It ended in disaster, with a thunderstorm and a dramatic crash-landing in Germany. Though there were no fatalities, Nadar, his wife, another passenger, and the *Géant* itself were all seriously injured.

The time was right for an explanation—some kind of written piece that would put the accident in perspective and, in so doing, turn it into a selling point for the Society's heavier-than-air goals. Hugo, Nadar, and Verne each set to work on such a piece. Hugo's contribution, a poetic open letter to Nadar, was published in January 1864. Nadar's, a spirited and chatty book called *Memoires du Géant*, came out in September of that year.

Verne beat them both into print. In December 1863, two months after the accident, the *Musée des familles* published his short article "À propos du Géant" ("About the *Géant*"). The article appeared in the magazine's special end-of-year issue, the *Révue de l'année* (*Review of the Year*). An illustrator, Fellmann, contributed a large engraving of Nadar's balloon.[42]

It sounds like a perfect combination—Verne, fresh from his debut-novel success with *Five Weeks in a Balloon*, writes about a friend's harrowing adventures in a *real* balloon—and, indeed, the article is an effective piece of writing, as lucid as a didactic passage in a classic Verne novel.[43] However, despite the title and illustration, "About the *Géant*" is not really about the *Géant* at all. Instead of focusing on the balloon, Verne uses its notoriety to point readers toward two larger questions. Will the future of flight belong to lighter- or heavier-than-air machines? And, either way, what might those machines look like?

Ten years later, Verne finally got his chance to try flight for himself, under highly appropriate circumstances. The first paragraph

42. Jules Verne, "À propos du Géant," *Musée des familles*, 31, No. 12 (décembre 1863), 92–93.

43. La Landelle himself praised it in a later issue of the same magazine: "In his *Review of the Year* 1863, M. Jules Verne, the witty author of *Five Weeks in a Balloon*, consecrated to atmospheric navigation an article *about the Géant*. It could not have come from an abler or a kindlier pen." See Gustave de La Landelle, "Aviation ou navigation aérienne au moyen d'appareils plus lourds que l'air," *Musée des familles*, 31, No. 24 (mars 1864), 188–92.

of "A Voyage in a Balloon" mentions the French aeronautical star Eugène Godard (1827–1890), who had made his name at the Paris Hippodrome before launching a celebrated four-year American tour, returning to France for further ascents, and even working with Nadar on heroic ballooning efforts during the Siege of Paris in 1870–71. Godard built a whole carnival of music, spectacle, and general frolic around his ascents, and much of his family soon joined the excitement; the Godards who built the *Géant* were two of his younger brothers.[44]

By 1873, Godard was back on tour, with more than a thousand ascents under his belt. His 1,055th was scheduled to take place on Sunday afternoon, September 28, 1873, at the Place Longueville in Amiens. He could take two or three passengers with him, and Verne was literally just down the street, living at 44 Boulevard Longueville.[45] The occasion was propitious for Verne, then finishing *The Mysterious Island*, to travel with a balloonist he had first name-dropped more than twenty years before. The two set off, with a couple of other passengers and a monkey, amid a classic Godardian pandemonium of sack races, equestrian stunts, military band tunes, and other carnivalesque attractions.

Before getting into the basket, however, Verne had already promised to write about his experience. Verne's friend Théodore Jeunet edited the local newspaper, the *Journal d'Amiens*, and asked for a report. Verne wrote it up that night, and it was printed the next day in the *Journal* to accompany an anonymous article, "Ascension du *Météore*" ("Ascent of the *Météore*"). Verne had Jeunet republish the letter in pamphlet form the same year, titling it—with an impish nod to his first published book—*Vingt-Quatre Minutes en ballon* ("Twenty-Four Minutes in a Balloon").[46]

---

44. Richard Holmes, *Falling Upwards: How We Took to the Air* (New York: Pantheon Books, 2013), 98–100; Joseph Lecornu, *La navigation aérienne; histoire documentaire et anecdotique* (Paris: Librairie Vuibert, 1913), 142–59.

45. Now the Boulevard Jules Verne. The Place Longueville has also been renamed—it was christened the Cirque Municipal in 1889 by none other than Verne himself, in his capacity as town councilor. For this and the information that follows, see Jean-Michel Margot, *Jules Verne en son temps* (Paris: Encrage, 2004), 48–50, and Dehs, "Préface," in Jules Verne, *Un Voyage en ballon*.

46. "Chronique locale. Ascension du Météore," *Journal d'Amiens* 5109 (29–30 septembre 1873), 1–2; Jules Verne, *Vingt-Quatre Minutes en ballon* (Amiens: Imprimerie Jeunet, 1873).

Though far less dramatic than the balloon adventures in his novels, Verne's account could not be truer to form in style and themes. The aerial joys described are exactly those found in the calmer moments of *Five Weeks in a Balloon*: the contemplation of novel and imagination-stirring vistas; the security of traveling with a trusty guide; the pleasure of noting small details of time, location, and altitude; and, perhaps most importantly of all, the far-from-the-madding-crowd feeling of peace and tranquility. Similarly, the closing portrait of Godard could easily be one of Phileas Fogg from the previous year's *Le Tour du monde en quatre-vingts jours* (*Around the World in Eighty Days*, 1873), an unflappable traveler proceeding "mathematically" with bag in hand and plan in mind. Verne seems often to have seen his real-life voyages through the lens of others' writings—his travelogues on Scotland and Scandinavia both begin with thorough discussions of his preliminary reading—but in this case, it is his own fiction that is reflected. The wheel of literary influence came full circle a dozen years later when, in writing *Robur the Conqueror*, Verne found that his ascent gave him useful material for imagining the heavier-than-air flight of the *Albatross*.[47]

For this anthology, all three of Verne's short works on flight are presented together. "A Voyage in a Balloon" was in fact the first Verne story to reach the English-speaking world, thanks to an 1852 rendering by the prolific French-to-English translator Anne Toppan Wilbur (1817–1864).[48] Though George Makepeace Towle and Abby L. Alger also translated the story, Wilbur's rendering is the only version based on Verne's original two-chapter published text; Towle's and Alger's are both derived from "Un Drame dans les airs" ("A Drama in the Sky"), a one-chapter version modified for publication by Hetzel in the collection *Le Docteur Ox* (*Doctor Ox*, 1874).[49]

47. The travel accounts are *Voyage à reculons en Angleterre et en Ecosse* (*Backwards to Britain*, 1859–60) and the unfinished "Joyeuses Misères de trois voyageurs en Scandinavie" (*Joyous Miseries of Three Travelers in Scandinavia*, 1861). On the real-life and literary sources for *Robur*, see Kirstukas, "Introduction," *Robur the Conqueror*.

48. Jules Verne, "A Voyage in a Balloon," *Sartain's Union Magazine of Literature and Art*, 10, No. 5 (May 1852), 389–395. It appeared soon after in England, in *The Working Man's Friend and Family Instructor*, 2, No. 44 (July 31, 1852), 282–286. For more information on Wilbur, see Compère, "Introduction," in Jules Verne, *Bandits and Rebels*, which features Wilbur's other Verne translation, "Martin Paz," as an appendix.

49. Arthur B. Evans, "A Bibliography of Jules Verne's English Translations," *Science Fiction Studies*, 32, Part 1, No. 95 (March 2005), 105–141. The most striking differences between

Frontispiece of the Hetzel edition of *Doctor Ox* highlights the balloon story.

It is Wilbur's text that appears here, transcribed from its original appearance in *Sartain's Union Magazine of Literature and Art*. The text has a few eccentricities; for example, Wilbur renders "N. O." (an abbreviation of *nord-ouest*, northwest) as "northeast" or "N. E." each time it appears. Like many early Verne translators, Wilbur is also inconsistent about replacing French place names with their common English equivalents; thus, the area now known as Goetheplatz is left untranslated as *Place de la Comédie*, while the River Main is called "Maine" once and then reverts to Verne's spelling "Mein." Wilbur's original use of place names has been retained here, rather than updated to modern usage. By and large, though, Wilbur's text is a responsible and close rendering of Verne's French. This republication adds A. de Bar's engravings from the *Musée des familles* text, as well as those by Émile Bayard from the 1874 one-chapter revision.

Unlike "A Voyage in a Balloon," "About the *Géant*" has never been widely available in English. James C. Iraldi (1907–1989), an early Verne advocate and a member of the original American Jules Verne Society, began a translation around 1940, but it was left as a very rough draft and was never corrected or polished. The new translation that follows is based on the original *Musée des familles* text, including Fellmann's engraving. "Twenty-Four Minutes in a Balloon" is likewise a fresh translation, the first in print; Verne scholar William Butcher posted a translation in 2002 on his personal webpage, but so far it has only appeared online. The interested reader is encouraged to consult both.[50]

Here, then, are three little-known Verne pieces documenting his response to a memorable chapter of France's balloon mania—a response that ends up rejecting the future of balloons, but which celebrates the dream of flight and looks hopefully forward to other paths to the sky.

---

the 1851 and 1874 versions are mentioned in the footnotes that follow; the Hetzel text also includes a variety of smaller revisions, such as minor rewordings and new paragraph breaks.

50. Jules Verne, "Twenty-Four Minutes in a Balloon," translated by William Butcher, ibiblio.com. For this preface and all the following critical material, my sincere thanks go to Butcher, Jean-Michel Margot, Brian Taves, and the Jules Verne Forum for useful materials and fruitful discussions related to Verne's flight writings.

A Voyage In a Balloon

by Jules Verne

Translated from the French by Anne T. Wilbur

I.

My Ascension at Frankfort—The Balloon, the Gas, the Apparatus, the Ballast—An Unexpected Travelling Companion—Conversation in the Air—Anecdotes—At 800 Metres[51]—The Portfolio of the Pale Young Man—Pictures and Caricatures—Des Rosiers and d'Arlandes—At 1200 Metres—Atmospheric Phenomena—The Philosopher Charles—Systems—Blanchard—Guyton-Morveaux—M. Julien—M. Petin—At 1500 Metres—The Storm—Great Personages in Balloons—The Valve—The Curious Animals—The Aerial Ship—Game of Balloons.

In the month of September, 1850, I arrived at Frankfort-on-the-Maine. My passage through the principal cities of Germany, had been brilliantly marked by aerostatic ascensions; but, up to this day, no inhabitant of the Confederation had accompanied me, and the successful experiments at Paris of Messrs. Green, Godard, and Poitevin,[52] had failed to induce the grave Germans to attempt aerial

51. Wilbur (or her editor) adds a footnote: "A metre is equal to 39.33 English inches."

52. Charles Green (1785–1870), Eugène Godard (1827–1890), and Jean-Eugène (d.1858) and Louise Rosalie Poitevin (1819–1908), professional aeronauts, had all made recent

voyages.

Meanwhile, hardly had the news of my approaching ascension circulated throughout Frankfort, than three persons of note asked the favour of accompanying me. Two days after, we were to ascend from the Place de la Comédie. I immediately occupied myself with the preparations. My balloon, of gigantic proportions, was of silk, coated with gutta percha, a substance not liable to injury from acids or gas, and of absolute impermeability. Some trifling rents were mended: the inevitable results of perilous descents.

The day of our ascension was that of the great fair of September, which attracts all the world to Frankfort. The apparatus for filling was composed of six hogsheads arranged around a large vat, hermetically sealed. The hydrogen gas evolved by the contact of water with iron and sulphuric acid, passed from the first reservoirs to the second, and thence into the immense globe, which was thus gradually inflated. These preparations occupied all the morning,[53] and about 11 o'clock, the balloon was three-quarters full; sufficiently so;—for as we rise, the atmospheric layers diminish in density, and the gas, confined within the aerostat, acquiring more elasticity, might otherwise burst its envelope. My calculations had furnished me with the exact measurement of gas required to carry my companions and myself to a considerable height.

We were to ascend at noon. It was truly a magnificent spectacle, that of the impatient crowd who thronged around the reserved enclosure, inundated the entire square and adjoining streets, and covered the neighbouring houses from the basements to the slated roofs. The high winds of past days had lulled, and an overpowering heat was radiating from an unclouded sky; not a breath animated the atmosphere. In such weather, one might descend in the very spot he had left.

I carried three hundred pounds of ballast, in bags; the car, perfectly round, four feet in diameter, and three feet in height, was conveniently attached; the cord which sustained it was symmetrically extended from the upper hemisphere of the aerostat; the compass was in its place, the barometer suspended to the iron hoop which surrounded the

---

ascents when "A Voyage in a Balloon" was published.

53. In the Hetzel version, the passage from "The apparatus for filling…" onward is replaced with: "Illuminating gas, of perfect quality and great ascensional force, had been furnished me in excellent condition, and about 11 o'clock…" This topic recurs in "Twenty-Four Minutes in a Balloon," and is discussed in the first footnote to that article below.

supporting cord, at a distance of eight feet above the car; the anchor carefully prepared;—all was in readiness for our departure.

Among the persons who crowded around the enclosure, I remarked a young man with pale face and agitated features. I was struck with his appearance. He had been an assiduous spectator of my ascensions in several cities of Germany. His uneasy air and his extraordinary pre-occupation never left him; he eagerly contemplated the curious machine, which rested motionless at a few feet from the ground, and remained silent.

The clock struck twelve! This was the hour. My *compagnons du voyage* had not appeared. I sent to the dwelling of each, and learned that one had started for Hamburg, another for Vienna and the third, still more fearful, for London. Their hearts had failed them at the moment of undertaking one of those excursions, which, since the ingenious experiments of aeronauts, are deprived of all danger. As they made, as it were, a part of the programme of the fête, they had feared being compelled to fulfil their agreements, and had fled at the moment of ascension. Their courage had been in inverse ratio to the square of their swiftness in retreat.

The crowd, thus partly disappointed, were shouting with anger and impatience. I did not hesitate to ascend alone. To re-establish the equilibrium between the specific gravity of the balloon and the weight to be raised, I substituted other bags of sand for my expected companions and entered the car. The twelve men who were holding the aerostat by twelve cords fastened to the equatorial circle, let them slip between their fingers; the car rose a few feet above the ground. There was not a breath of wind, and the atmosphere, heavy as lead, seemed insurmountable.

"All is ready!" exclaimed I; "attention!"

The men arranged themselves; a last glance informed me that everything was right.

"Attention!"

There was some movement in the crowd which seemed to be invading the reserved enclosure.

"Let go!"

The balloon slowly ascended; but I experienced a shock which threw me to the bottom of the car. When I rose, I found myself face to face with an unexpected voyager,—the pale young man.

Monsieur, je vous salue bien ! me dit-il… (p. 103).

"Monsieur, I salute you!"

"Monsieur, I salute you!" said he to me.

"By what right?"—

"Am I here? By the right of your inability to turn me out."

I was confounded. His assurance disconcerted me; and I had nothing to say in reply. I looked at him, but he paid no regard to my astonishment. He continued:

"My weight will disturb your equilibrium, Monsieur: will you permit me—"

And without waiting for my assent, he lightened the balloon by two bags of sand which he emptied into the air.

"Monsieur," said I, taking the only possible course, "you are here,—well! you choose to remain,—well! But to me alone belongs the management of the aerostat."

"Monsieur," replied he, "your urbanity is entirely French; it is of the same country with myself! I press in imagination the hand which you refuse me. Take your measures,—act as it may seem good to you; I will wait till you have ended—"

"To—"

"To converse with you."

The barometer had fallen to twenty-six inches; we had attained a height of about six hundred metres, and were over the city; which satisfied me of our complete quiescence, for I could not judge by our motionless flags. Nothing betrays the horizontal voyage of a balloon; it is the mass of air surrounding it which moves. A kind of wavering heat bathed the objects extended at our feet, and gave their outlines an indistinctness to be regretted. The needle of the compass indicated a slight tendency to float towards the south.

I looked again at my companion. He was a man of thirty, simply clad; the bold outlines of his features betokened indomitable energy; he appeared very muscular. Absorbed in the emotion of this silent suspension, he remained immovable, seeking to distinguish the objects which passed beneath his view.

"Vexatious mist!" said he, at the expiration of a few moments.

I made no reply.

"What would you? I could not pay for my voyage; I was obliged to take you by surprise."

"No one has asked you to descend!"

"A similar occurrence," he resumed, "happened to the Counts of Laurencin and Dampierre, when they ascended at Lyons, on the 15th of January, 1784. A young merchant, named Fontaine, scaled the railing, at the risk of upsetting the equipage. He accomplished the voyage, and nobody was killed!"

"Once on the earth, we will converse!" said I, piqued at the tone of lightness with which he spoke.

"Bah! Do not talk of returning!"

"Do you think then that I shall delay my descent?"

"Descent!" said he, with surprise. "Let us ascend!"

And before I could prevent him, two bags of sand were thrown out, without even being emptied.

"Monsieur!" said I, angrily.

"I know your skill," replied he, composedly; your brilliant ascensions have made some noise in the world. Experience is the sister of practice, but it is also first cousin to theory, and I have long

Monsieur ! m'écriai-je avec colère. (p. 106).

"Monsieur!" said I, angrily.

and deeply studied the aerostatic art. It has affected my brain," added he, sadly, falling into a mute torpor.

The balloon, after having risen, remained stationary; the unknown consulted the barometer, and said:

"Here we are at 800 metres! Men resemble insects! See, I think it is from this height that we should always look at them, to judge correctly of their moral proportions! The Place de la Comédie is transformed to an immense ant-hill. Look at the crowd piled up on the quays. The Zeil diminishes. We are above the church of Dom. The Mein is now only a white line dividing the city, and this bridge, the Mein-Brucke, looks like a white thread thrown between the two banks of the river."

The atmosphere grew cooler.

"There is nothing I will not do for you, my host," said my companion. "If you are cold, I will take off my clothes and lend them to you."

"Thanks!"

"Necessity makes laws. Give me your hand, I am your countryman. You shall be instructed by my company, and my conversation shall compensate you for the annoyance I have caused you."

I seated myself, without replying, at the opposite extremity of the car. The young man had drawn from his great coat a voluminous portfolio; it was a work on aerostation.

"I possess," said he, "a most curious collection of engravings and caricatures appertaining to our aerial mania. This precious discovery has been at once admired and ridiculed. Fortunately we have passed the period when the Mongolfiers[54] sought to make factitious clouds with the vapour of water; and of the gas affecting electric properties, which they produced by the combustion of damp straw with chopped wool."

"Would you detract from the merit of these inventions?" replied I. "Was it not well done to have proved by experiment the possibility of rising in the air?"

"Who denies the glory of the first aerial navigators? Immense courage was necessary to ascend by means of those fragile envelopes which contained only warm air. Besides, has not aerostatic science

54. The Montgolfier brothers, Joseph-Michel (1740–1810) and Jacques-Étienne (1745–1799). Wilbur copies the *Musée* printing's misspelling of the name; the Hetzel version uses the correct spelling.

Ascension de Pilâtre des Rosiers et du marquis d'Arlandes, à la Muette.

made great progress since the ascensions of Blanchard?[55] Look, Monsieur."

He took from his collection an engraving.

"Here is the first aerial voyage undertaken by Pilatre des Rosiers and the Marquis d'Arlandes,[56] four months after the discovery of balloons. Louis XVI refused his consent to this voyage; two condemned criminals were to have first attempted aerial travelling. Pilatre des Rosiers was indignant at this injustice and, by means of artifice, succeeded in setting out. This car, which renders the management of the balloon easy, had not then been invented; a circular gallery surrounded the

55. Jean-Pierre-François Blanchard (1753–1809), pioneering balloonist and experimenter with heavier-than-air designs.

56. Jean-François Pilâtre de Rozier (1756–1785) and François Laurent, Marquis d'Arlandes (1742–1809).

lower part of the aerostat. The two aeronauts stationed themselves at the extremities of this gallery. The damp straw with which it was filled encumbered their movements. A chafing-dish was suspended beneath the orifice of the balloon; when the voyagers wished to ascend, they threw, with a long fork, straw upon this brazier, at the risk of burning the machine, and the air, growing warmer, gave to the balloon a new ascensional force. The two bold navigators ascended, on the 21st of November, 1783, from the gardens of La Muette, which the Dauphin had placed at their disposal. The aerostat rose majestically, passed the Isle des Cygnes, crossed the Seine at the Barrière de la Conference, and, directing its way between the dome of the Invalides and L'Ecole Militaire, approached St. Sulpice; then the aeronauts increased the fire, ascended, cleared the Boulevard, and descended beyond the Barrière d'Enfer. As it touched the ground, it collapsed, and buried Pilatre des Rosiers beneath its folds."

"Unfortunate presage!" said I, interested in these details, which so nearly concerned me.

"Presage of his catastrophe," replied the unknown, with sadness. "You have experienced nothing similar?"

"Nothing!"

"Bah! Misfortunes often arrive without presage." And he remained silent.

We were advancing towards the south; the magnetic needle pointed in the direction of Frankfort, which was flying beneath our feet.

"Perhaps we shall have a storm," said the young man.

"We will descend first."

"Indeed! It will be better to ascend; we shall escape more surely;" and two bags of sand were thrown overboard.

The balloon rose rapidly, and stopped at twelve hundred metres. The cold was now intense, and there was a slight buzzing in my ears. Nevertheless, the rays of the sun fell hotly on the globe, and, dilating the gas it contained, gave it a greater ascensional force. I was stupified.

"Fear nothing," said the young man to me. "We have three thousand five hundred toises of respirable air. You need not trouble yourself about my proceedings."

I would have risen, but a vigorous hand detained me on my seat.

"Your name?" asked I.

"My name! How does it concern you?"

"I have the honour to ask your name."

"I am called Erostratus or Empedocles,—as you please.[57] Are you interested in the progress of aerostatic science?"

He spoke with icy coldness, and I asked myself with whom I had to do.

"Monsieur," continued he, "nothing new has been invented since the days of the philosopher Charles.[58] Four months after the discovery of aerostats, he had invented the valve, which permits the gas to escape when the balloon is too full, or when one wishes to descend; the car, which allows the machine to be easily managed; the network, which encloses the fabric of the balloon, and prevents its being too heavily pressed; the ballast, which is used in ascending and choosing the spot of descent; the coat of caoutchouc, which renders the silk impermeable; the barometer, which determines the height attained; and, finally, the hydrogen, which, fourteen times lighter than air, allows of ascension to the most distant atmospheric layers, and prevents exposure to aerial combustion. On the 1st of December, 1783, three hundred thousand spectators thronged the Tuileries. Charles ascended, and the soldiers presented arms. He travelled nine leagues in the air, managing his machine with a skill never since surpassed in aeronautic experiments. The King conferred on him a pension of two thousand livres, for in those days inventions were encouraged. In a few days, the subscription list was filled; for every one was interested in the progress of science."

The unknown was seized with a violent agitation.

"I, Monsieur, have studied; I am satisfied that the first aeronauts guided their balloons. Not to speak of Blanchard, whose assertions might be doubted, at Dijon, Guyton-Morveaux,[59] by the aid of oars

57. Erostratus or Herostratus (fourth century BCE) was a Greek arsonist who burned down the Temple of Artemis, one of the Seven Wonders of the World, in a bid for fame. Empedocles (c.490–430 BCE) was a Greek philosopher-poet famous for naming earth, air, fire, and water the four elements; legend has it that he claimed to be a divine being, and that he killed himself by jumping into Mount Etna in an attempt to prove that he was immortal. Small wonder that the Hetzel version adds a line of narration: "This reply was not at all reassuring."

58. Jacques Charles (1746–1823), inventor of the gas balloon, known as the *Charlière* (as opposed to the Montgolfier brothers' hot-air balloon or *Montgolfière*).

59. Louis Bernard Guyton de Morveau (1737–1816) first attempted to steer a balloon in 1784.

and a helm, imparted to his machines perceptible motions, a decided direction. More recently, at Paris, a watchmaker, M. Julien,[60] has made at the Hippodrome convincing experiments; for, with the aid of a particular mechanism, an aerial apparatus of oblong form was manifestly propelled against the wind. M. Petin[61] placed four balloons, filled with hydrogen, in juxtaposition, and, by means of sails disposed horizontally and partially furled, hoped to obtain a disturbance of the equilibrium, which, inclining the apparatus, should compel it to an oblique path. But the motive power destined to surmount the resistance of currents,—the helice,[62] moving in a movable medium, was unsuccessful. I have discovered the only method of guiding balloons, and not an Academy has come to my assistance, not a city has filled my subscription lists, not a government has deigned to listen to me! It is infamous!"

His gesticulations were so furious that the car experienced violent oscillations; I had much difficulty in restraining him. Meanwhile, the balloon had encountered a more rapid current. We were advancing in a southerly direction, at 1200 metres in height, almost accustomed to this new temperature.

"There is Darmstadt," said my companion. "Do you perceive its magnificent chateau? The storm-cloud below makes the outlines of objects waver; and it requires a practised eye to recognise localities."

"You are certain that it is Darmstadt?"

"Undoubtedly; we are six leagues from Frankfort."

"Then we must descend."

"Descend! You would not alight upon the steeples!" said the unknown, mockingly.

"No; but in the environs of the city."

"Well, it is too warm; let us remount a little."

As he spoke thus, he seized some bags of ballast. I precipitated myself upon him; but, with one hand, he overthrew me, and the lightened balloon rose to a height of 1500 metres.

"Sit down," said he, "and do not forget that Brioschi, Biot, and

60. Joseph Julien (c.1815–1876) experimented at the Hippodrome in 1849 and 1850.

61. Ernest Petin (1812–1878) designed his multi-balloon dirigible in 1850.

62. *Hélice* is French for propeller.

Gay-Lussac,[63] ascended to a height of seven thousand metres, in order to establish some new scientific laws."

"We must descend;" resumed I, with an attempt at gentleness. "The storm is gathering beneath our feet and around us; it would not be prudent."

"We will ascend above it, and shall have nothing to fear from it. What more beautiful than to reign in heaven, and look down upon the clouds which hover upon the earth! Is it not an honour to navigate these aerial waves? The greatest personages have travelled like ourselves. The Marquise and Comtesse de Montalembert, the Comtesse de Podenas, Mlle. La Garde, the Marquis of Montalembert, set out from the Faubourg St. Antoine for these unknown regions. The Duc de Chartres displayed much address and presence of mind in his ascension of the 15th of July, 1784; at Lyons, the Comtes de Laurencin and de Dampierre; at Nantes, M. de Luynes; at Bordeaux, D'Arbelet des Granges; in Italy, the Chevalier Andreani; in our days, the Duke of Brunswick; have left in the air the track of their glory. In order to equal these great personages, we must ascend into the celestial regions higher than they. To approach the infinite is to comprehend it."

The rarefaction of the air considerably dilated the hydrogen, and I saw the lower part of the aerostat, designedly left empty, become by degrees inflated, rendering the opening of the valve indispensable; but my fearful companion seemed determined not to allow me to direct our movements. I resolved to pull secretly the cord attached to the valve, while he was talking with animation. I feared to guess with whom I had to do; it would have been too horrible! It was about three-quarters of an hour since we had left Frankfort, and from the south thick clouds were arising and threatening to engulf us.

"Have you lost all hope of making your plans succeed?" said I, with great apparent interest.

"All hope!" replied the unknown, despairingly. "Wounded by refusals, caricatures, those blows with the foot of an ass, have finished me. It is the eternal punishment reserved for innovators. See these caricatures of every age with which my portfolio is filled."

---

63. Carlo Brioschi (1782–1833), Jean-Baptiste Biot (1774–1862), and Joseph Louis Gay-Lussac (1778–1850). To this list the Hetzel version adds Jacques Alexandre Bixio (1808–1865) and Jean-Augustin Barral (1819–1884); since that duo reached only 5,500 meters, the rest of the sentence is changed simply to "went to the greatest heights to make their scientific experiments."

Miolan, Janninet et Bredin, caricature du temps.

I had secured the cord of the valve, and stooping over his works, concealed my movements from him. It was to be feared, nevertheless, that he would notice that rushing sound, like a waterfall, which the gas produces in escaping.

"How many jests at the expense of the Abbé Miolan! He was about to ascend with Janninet and Bredin.[64] During the operation, their balloon took fire, and an ignorant populace tore it to pieces. Then the caricature of *The Curious Animals* called them *Maulant, Jean Minet, and Gredin*."

The barometer had began to rise; it was time! A distant muttering of thunder was heard towards the south.

"See this other engraving," continued he, without seeming to suspect my manoeuvres. "It is an immense balloon, containing a ship, large castles, houses, etc. The caricaturists little thought that their absurdities would one day become verities. It is a large vessel; at the left is the helm with the pilot's box; at the prow, *maisons de plaisance*,

64. This failed ascension occurred in 1784. Biographical details on the aeronauts are scarce.

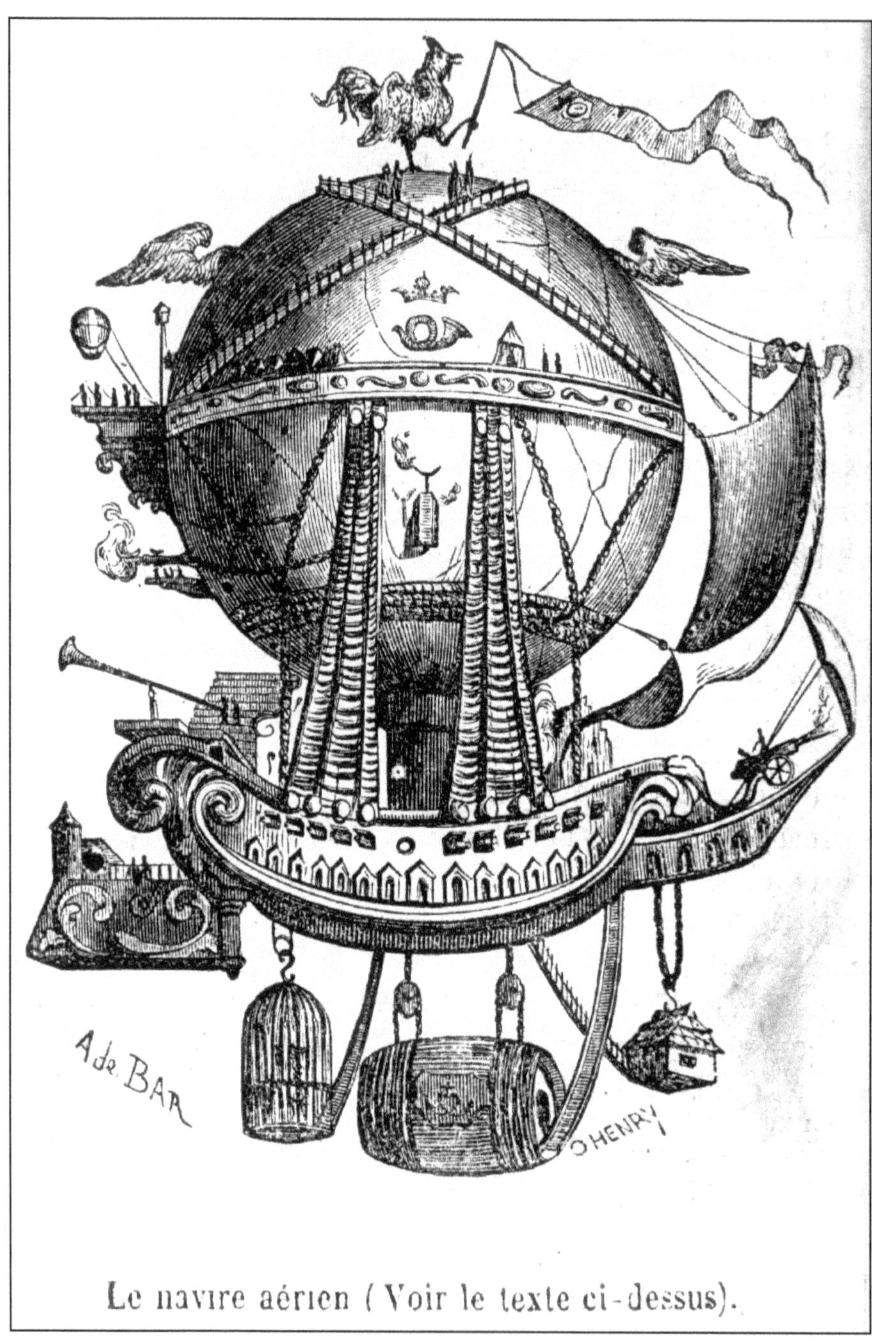

Le navire aérien (Voir le texte ci-dessus).

a gigantic organ, and cannon to call the attention of the inhabitants of earth or of the moon; above the stern the observatory and pilot-balloon; at the equatorial circle, the barracks of the army; on the left the lantern; then upper galleries for promenades, the sails, the wings; beneath, the cafés and general store-houses of provisions. Admire this magnificent announcement. 'Invented for the good of the human race, this globe will depart immediately for the seaports in the Levant, and on its return will announce its voyages for the two poles and the extremities of the Occident. Every provision is made; there will be an exact rate of fare for each place of destination; but the prices for distant voyages will be the same, 1000 louis. And it must be confessed that this is a moderate sum, considering the celerity, convenience, and pleasure of this mode of travelling above all others. While in this balloon, every one can divert himself as he pleases, dancing, playing, or conversing with people of talent. Pleasure will be the soul of the aerial society.' All these inventions excited laughter. But before long, if my days were not numbered, these projects should become realities."

We were visibly descending; he did not perceive it!

"See this game of balloons; it contains the whole history of the aerostatic art. This game, for the use of educated minds, is played like that of the Jew;[65] with dice and counters of any value agreed upon, which are to be paid or received, according to the condition in which one arrives."

"But," I resumed, "you seem to have valuable documents on aerostation?"

"I am less learned than the Almighty! That is all! I possess all the knowledge possible in this world. From Phaeton, Icarus, and Architas,[66] I have searched all, comprehended all! Through me, the aerostatic art would render immense services to the world, if God should spare my life! But that cannot be."

65. "The New and Fashionable Game of the Jew" was an early 19th-century dice game with a stereotyped-Jewish-moneylender theme. (Stephen Sondheim, who owns an antique copy of the game, once described it by saying that it "taught kids to be anti-Semitic." See Stephen Schiff, "Deconstructing Sondheim," *The New Yorker* 69 [March 8, 1993], 76–87.) The Hetzel version removes the reference to it.

66. In Greek mythology, Phaethon, son of Helios, borrowed his father's sun-chariot and was punished with death for his reckless flight; Icarus, a mortal, likewise met his death when he used artificial wings to fly too near the sun. Archytas was a real-life Greek philosopher (fourth century BCE) whose more modest flight achievement was to invent a mechanical dove that could appear to fly, most likely using pulleys.

Le jeu des ballons, d'après une ancienne estampe.

"Why not?"

"Because my name is Empedocles or Erostratus!"

II.

The Company of Aerostiers—The Battle of Fleurus—The Balloon over the Sea—Blanchard and Jefferies—A Drama such as is rarely seen—3000 Metres—The Thunder beneath our Feet—Gavnerin at Rome—The Compass gone—The Victims of Aerostation—Pilatre—At 4000 Metres—The Barometer gone—Descents of Olivari, Mosment, Bittorf, Harris, Sadler, and Madame Blanchard—The Valve rendered useless—7000 Metres—Zambecarri—The Balloon Wrecked—Incalculable Heights—The Car Overset—Despair—Vertigo—The Fall—The Dénouement.

I shuddered! Fortunately the balloon was approaching the earth. But the danger is the same at 50 feet as at 5000 metres! The clouds were advancing.

"Remember the battle of Fleurus, and you will comprehend the utility of aerostats! Coutelle, by order of the government, organized a company of aerostiers. At the siege of Maubeuge, General Jourdan found this new method of observation so serviceable, that twice a day, accompanied by the General himself, Coutelle ascended into the air; the correspondence between the aeronaut and the aerostiers who held the balloon, was carried on by means of little white, red, and yellow flags. Cannons and carbines were often aimed at the balloon at the moment of its ascension, but without effect. When Jourdan was preparing to invest Charleroi, Coutelle repaired to the neighbourhood of that place, rose from the plain of Jumet, and remained taking observations seven or eight hours, with General Morelot. The Austrians came to deliver the city, and a battle was fought on the heights of Fleurus. General Jourdan publicly proclaimed the assistance he had received from aeronautic observations. Well! Notwithstanding the services rendered on this occasion, and during the campaign with Belgium, the year which witnessed the commencement of the military career of balloons, also saw it terminate. And the school of Meudon, founded by government, was closed by Bonaparte, on his return from Egypt. 'What are we to expect from the child which has just been born?' Franklin had said. But the child was born alive! It need not have been strangled!"[67]

The unknown hid his forehead in his hands, reflected for a few moments, then, without raising his head, said to me:

"Notwithstanding my orders, you have opened the upper valve!"

67. The figures mentioned are Jean-Marie-Joseph Coutelle (1748–1835), Jean-Baptiste, Count Jourdan (1762–1833), Antoine Morlot (1766–1809), and, of course, Napoleon Bonaparte (1769–1821) and Benjamin Franklin (1706–1790).

La bataille de Fleurus. Le ballon lancé devant Charleroy.

Il resta sept ou huit heures en observation... (p. 112).

He remained taking observations for seven or eight hours.

I let go the cord.

"Fortunately," continued he, "we have still two hundred pounds of ballast."

"What are your plans?" said I, with effort.

"You have never crossed the sea?"

I grew frightfully pale, terror froze my veins.

"It is a pity," said he, "that we are being wafted towards the Adriatic! That is only a streamlet. Higher! We shall find other currents!"

And without looking at me, he lightened the balloon by several bags of sand.

"I allowed you to open the valve, because the dilatation of the gas threatened to burst the balloon. But do not do it again."

I was stupified.

"You know the voyage from Dover to Calais made by Blanchard and Jefferies.[68] It was rich in incident. On the 7th of January, 1785, in a northeast wind, their balloon was filled with gas on the Dover side; scarcely had they risen, when an error in equilibrium compelled them to threw out their ballast, retaining only thirty pounds. The wind drifted them slowly along towards the shores of France. The permeability of the tissue gradually suffered the gas to escape, and at the expiration of an hour and a half, the voyagers perceived that they were descending. 'What is to be done?' said Jefferies.—'We have passed over only three-fourths of the distance,' replied Blanchard 'and at a slight elevation. By ascending we shall expose ourselves to contrary winds. Throw out the remainder of the ballast.' The balloon regained its ascensional force, but soon re-descended. About midway of the voyage, the aeronauts threw out their books and tools. A quarter of an hour afterwards, Blanchard said to Jefferies: 'The barometer?'—'It is rising! We are lost; and yet there are the shores of France!' A great noise was heard. 'Is the balloon rent?' asked Jefferies.—'No! The escape of the gas has collapsed the lower part of the balloon'—'But we are still descending. We are lost! Everything not indispensable must be thrown overboard!' Their provisions, oars and helm were thrown out into the sea. They were now only 100 metres in height. 'We are remounting,' said the Doctor.—'No, it is the jerk caused by the diminution of weight. There is not a ship in sight! Not a bark on the horizon! To the sea with our garments!' And

68. John Jeffries (1745–1819), a Boston physician. The variant spelling "Jefferies," widely used in print, is favored by the *Musée*, *Sartain's*, and the Hetzel revision.

the unfortunate men stripped, but the balloon continued to descend. 'Blanchard,' said Jefferies, 'you were to have made this voyage alone; you consented to take me; I will sacrifice myself to you! I will throw myself into the water, and the balloon, relieved, will re-ascend!'—'No, no, it is frightful.' The balloon collapsed more and more, and its concavity forming a parachute, forced the gas against its sides and accelerated its motion. 'Adieu, my friend,' said the Doctor. 'May God preserve you!' He was about to have taken the leap, when Blanchard detained him. 'One resource remains to us! We can cut the cords by which the car is attached, and cling to the network? Perhaps the balloon will rise. Ready! But the barometer falls! We remount! The wind freshens! We are saved!' The voyagers perceived Calais! Their joy became delirium; a few moments later, they descended in the forest of Guines. I doubt not," continued the unknown, "that in similar circumstances you would follow the example of Doctor Jefferies."

The clouds were unrolling beneath our feet in glittering cascades; the balloon cast a deep shadow on this pile of clouds, and was surrounded by them as with an aureola! The thunder growled beneath our feet! All this was frightful!

"Let us descend!" exclaimed I.

"Descend, when the sun is awaiting us yonder! Down with the bags!" And he lightened the balloon of more than fifty pounds. At 3000 metres we remained stationary. The unknown talked incessantly, but I scarcely heard him; I was completely prostrated, while he seemed in his element.

"With a good wind, we shall go far, but we must especially go high!"

"We are lost!"

"In the Antilles there are currents of air which travel a hundred leagues an hour! On the occasion of Napoleon's coronation, Gavnerin[69] let off a balloon illuminated with coloured lamps, at eleven o'clock in the evening! The wind blew from the N.N.E.; the next morning at daybreak the inhabitants of Rome saluted its passage above the dome of St. Peter's. We will go farther."

I scarcely heard him; everything was buzzing around me! There was an opening in the clouds!

---

69. André-Jacques Garnerin (1769–1823). The *Musée* spells his name correctly; *Sartain's* does not.

Le ballon se dégonflait de plus en plus (p. 115).

Blanchard and Jefferies' balloon collapsed more and more.

"See that city, my host," said the unknown. "It is Spire. Nothing else!"

I dared not lean over the railing of the car. Nevertheless I perceived a little black spot. This was Spire. The broad Rhine looked like a riband, the great roads like threads. Above our heads the sky was of a deep azure; I was benumbed with the cold. The birds had long since forsaken us; in this rarefied air their flight would have been impossible. We were alone in space, and I in the presence of a strange man!

"It is useless for you to know whither I am taking you," said he, and he threw the compass into the clouds. "A fall is a fine thing. You know that there have been a few victims from Pilatre des Rosiers down to Lieutenant Gale,[70] and these misfortunes have always been caused by imprudence. Pilatre des Rosiers ascended in company with Remain, at Boulogne, on the 13th of June, 1785. To his balloon, inflated with gas, he had suspended a *mongolfier* filled with warm air, undoubtedly to save the trouble of letting off gas, or throwing out ballast. It was like putting a chafing-dish beneath a powder-cask. The imprudent men rose to a height of four hundred metres, and encountered opposing winds, which drove them over the ocean. In order to descend, Pilatre attempted to open the valve of the aerostat; but the cord of this valve caught in the balloon, and tore it so that it was emptied in an instant. It fell on the mongolfier, overturned it, and the imprudent men were dashed to pieces in a few seconds. It is frightful, is it not?" said the unknown, shaking me from my torpor.

I could reply only by these words:

"In pity, let us descend! The clouds are gathering around us in every direction, and frightful detonations reverberating from the cavity of the aerostat are multiplying around us."[71]

"You make me impatient!" said he. "You shall no longer know whether we are ascending or descending."

And the barometer went after the compass, along with some bags of sand. We must have been at a height of four thousand metres. Some icicles were attached to the sides of the car, and a sort of fine snow penetrated to my bones. Meanwhile a terrific storm was bursting beneath our feet. We were above it.

"Do not fear," said my strange companion; "it is only imprudence that makes victims. Olivari, who perished at Orleans, ascended in a mongolfier made of paper; his car, suspended below the chafing-dish, and ballasted with combustible materials, became a prey to the flames! Olivari fell, and was killed. Mosment ascended at Lille, on a light platform; an oscillation made him lose his equilibrium. Mosment fell, and was killed. Bittorf, at Manheim, saw his paper balloon take fire

70. George Gale (c.1797–1850), a professional aeronaut, was killed when a balloon landing went awry.

71. Verne evidently intended only the first sentence to be the reply; the rest of the paragraph is written in the past tense, i.e. as narration. But the *Musée* carelessly lumped the two parts together, and Wilbur, in an attempt to make sense of the result, simply converted the narration into present-tense speech. (The Hetzel version fixes the error by putting the narration on a separate line.)

in the air! Bittorf fell, and was killed. Harris ascended in a balloon badly constructed, the valve of which was too large to be closed again. Harris fell, and was killed. Sadler, deprived of ballast by his long stay in the air, was dragged over the city of Boston, and thrown against the chimneys. Sadler fell, and was killed. Cocking descended with a convex parachute which he pretended to have perfected. Cocking fell, and was killed. Well, I love them, those noble victims of their courage! And I will die like them! Higher! Higher!"[72]

All the phantoms of this necrology were passing before my eyes! The rarefaction of the air and the rays of tile sun increased the dilatation of the gas; the balloon continued to ascend! I mechanically attempted to open the valve; but the unknown cut the cord a few feet above my head. I was lost!

"Did you see Madame Blanchard[73] fall?" said he to me. "I saw her, I—yes, I was at Tivoli on the 6th of July, 1819. Madame Blanchard ascended in a balloon of small size, to save the expense of filling; she was therefore obliged to inflate it entirely, and the gas escaped by the lower orifice, leaving on its route a train of hydrogen. She carried, suspended above her car, by an iron wire, a kind of firework, forming an aureola, which she was to kindle. She had often repeated this experiment. On this occasion she carried, besides, a little parachute, ballasted by a firework terminating in a ball with silver rain. She was to launch this apparatus, after having lighted it with a *lance à feu*, prepared for the purpose.[74] She ascended. The night was dark. At the moment of lighting the firework, she was so imprudent as to let the lance pass beneath the column of hydrogen, which was escaping from the balloon. My eyes were fixed on her. Suddenly an unexpected flash illuminated the darkness. I thought it a surprise of the skilful aeronaut. The flame increased, suddenly disappeared, and re-appeared at the top of the aerostat under the form of an immense jet of burning gas. This sinister light projected over the Boulevard, and over the quarter Montmartre. Then I saw the unfortunate woman

72. The victims listed are François Olivari (c.1770–1802), Mosment (first name unknown; d.1806), Bittorf (first name unknown; d.1812), Thomas Harris (d.1824), James Sadler (1753–1828), and Robert Cocking (1776–1837).

73. Sophie Blanchard (1778–1819), professional aeronaut, wife of Jean-Pierre-François Blanchard. Verne also mentions her death in *Five Weeks in a Balloon* and *Robur the Conqueror*.

74. A *lance à feu* is a slow-burning fuse lighter on a stick, known in English as a portfire.

rise, twice attempt to compress the orifice of the balloon, to extinguish the fire, then seat herself in the car and seek to direct its descent; for she did not fall. The combustion of the gas lasted several minutes. The balloon, diminishing by degrees, continued to descend, but this was not a fall! The wind blew from the northeast, and drove her over Paris. There were, at that time, in the neighbourhood of the house No. 16 Rue de Provence, immense gardens. The aeronaut might have fallen there without danger. But unhappily the balloon and the car alighted on the roof of the house. The shock was slight. 'Help!' cried the unfortunate woman. I arrived in the street at that moment. The car slid along the roof, and encountered an iron hook. At this shock, Madame Blanchard was thrown out of the car, and precipitated on the pavement! She was killed!"

These histories of fatal augury froze me with horror. The unknown was standing upright, with bare head, bristling hair, haggard eyes.

Illusion was no longer possible. I saw at last the horrible truth. I had to deal with a madman!

He threw out half the ballast, and we must have been borne to a height of 7000 metres! Blood spouted from my nose and mouth.

"What a fine thing it is to be martyrs to science! They are canonized by posterity!"

I heard no more. The unknown looked around him with horror, and knelt at my ear.

"On the 7th of October, 1804, the weather had began to clear up a little; for several days preceding, the wind and rain had been incessant. But the ascension announced by Zambecarri could not be postponed! His idiot enemies already scoffed at him. To save himself and science from public ridicule, it became necessary for him to ascend. It was at Bologna! No one aided him in filling his balloon; he rose at midnight, accompanied by Andreoli and Grossetti.[75] The balloon ascended slowly; it had been rent by the wind, and the gas escaped. The three intrepid voyagers could observe the state of the barometer only by the aid of a dark lantern. Zambecarri had not eaten daring twenty-four hours; Grossetti was also fasting.

"'My friends,' said Zambecarri, 'I am benumbed with the cold; I am exhausted; I must die;' and he fell senseless in the gallery.

75. The companions of Francesco Zambeccari (1756–1812) were a Dr. Grassetti of Rome and Pascal Andreoli of Ancona.

"It was the same with Grossetti. Andreoli alone remained awake. After long efforts he succeeded in arousing Zambecarri from his stupor.

"'What is there new? Where are we going? In which direction is the wind? What time is it?'

"'It is two o'clock!'

"'Where is the compass?'

"'It has fallen out.'

"'Great God! The lamp is extinguished!'

"'It could not burn longer in this rarefied air!' said Zambecarri.

"The moon had not risen; the atmosphere was plunged in horrible darkness.

"'I am cold, I am cold, Andreoli! What shall we do?'

"The unfortunate men slowly descended through a layer of white clouds.

"'Hush!' said Andreoli; 'do you hear—'

"'What?' replied Zambecarri.

"'A singular noise!'

"'You are mistaken!'

"'No!—Do you see those midnight travellers, listening to that incomprehensible sound? Have they struck against a rower? Are they about to be precipitated on the roofs? Do you hear it? It is like the sound of the ocean!'

"'Impossible!'

"'It is the roaring of the waves!'

"'That is true!—Light! Light!'

"After five fruitless attempts, Andreoli obtained it. It was three o'clock. The sound of the waves was heard with violence; they almost touched the surface of the sea.

"'We are lost!' exclaimed Zambecarri, seizing a bag of ballast.

"'Help!' cried Andreoli.

"The car touched the water, and the waves covered them breast high. To the sea with instruments, garments, money! The aeronauts stripped entirely. The lightened balloon rose with frightful rapidity. Zambecarri was seized with violent vomiting. Grossetti bled freely. The unhappy men could not speak; their respiration was short. They were seized with cold, and in a moment covered with a coat of ice. The moon appeared to them red as blood. After having traversed these high regions during half an hour, the machine again fell into the sea. It was four o'clock in the morning: the bodies of the wretched aeronauts were half in the water, and the balloon, acting as a sail, dragged them about during several hours. At daybreak, they found themselves opposite Pesaro, five miles from the shore; they were about to land, when a sudden flaw of wind drove them back to the open sea. They were lost! The affrighted barks fled at their approach. Fortunately, a more intelligent navigator hailed them, took them on board; and they landed at Ferrara. That was frightful! Zambecarri was a brave

Son ballon s'accrocha à un arbre et sa lampe y mit le feu. (p. 120).

Zambecarri's balloon caught in a tree; his lamp set fire to it.

man. Scarcely recovered from his sufferings, he recommenced his ascensions. In one of them, he struck against a tree; his lamp, filled with spirits of wine, was spilled over his clothes, and they caught fire; he was covered with flame his machine was beginning to kindle, when he descended, half burned. The 21st of September, 1812, he made another ascension at Bologna; his balloon caught in a tree; his lamp set fire to it. Zambecarri fell, and was killed! And in presence of these high facts, shall we still hesitate? No! The higher we go the more glorious will be our death."

The balloon, entirely unballasted, we were borne to incredible heights. The aerostat vibrated in the atmosphere; the slightest sound re-echoed through the celestial vaults; the globe, the only object which struck my sight in immensity, seemed about to be annihilated, and above us the heights of heaven lost themselves in the profound darkness!

I saw the unknown rise before me.

"This is the hour!" said he to me. "We must die! We are rejected by men! They despise us! Let us crush them!"

"Mercy!" exclaimed I.

"Let us cut the cords! Let this car be abandoned in space! The attractive force will change its direction, and we shall land in the sun!"

Despair gave me strength! I precipitated myself upon the madman, and a frightful struggle took place! But I was thrown down! And while he held me beneath his knee, he cut the cords of the car!

"One!" said he.

"Mercy! O, God!"

"Two! Three!"

One cord more, and the car was sustained only on one side. I made a superhuman effort, rose, and violently repulsed this insensate.

"Four!" said he.

The car was overset. I instinctively clung to the cords which held it, and climbed up the outside.

The unknown had disappeared in space!

In a twinkling the balloon ascended to an immeasurable height! A horrible crash was heard. The dilated gas had burst its envelope! I closed my eyes. A few moments afterwards, a moist warmth reanimated me; I was in the midst of fiery clouds! The balloon was whirling with fearful rapidity! I felt myself swooning! Driven by the

Le fou avait disparu dans l'espace ! (p. 122).

The unknown had disappeared in space!

wind, I travelled a hundred leagues an hour in my horizontal course; the lightnings flashed around me!

Meanwhile my fall was not rapid. When I opened my eyes, I perceived the country. I was two miles from the sea, the hurricane urging me on with great force. I was lost, when a sudden shock made me let go; my hands opened, a cord slipped rapidly between my fingers, and I found myself on the ground. It was the cord of the anchor, which, sweeping the surface of the ground, had caught in a crevice! I fainted, and my lightened balloon, resuming its flight, was lost beyond the sea.

When I recovered my senses, I was in the house of a peasant, at Harderwick, a little town of Gueldre, fifteen leagues from Amsterdam, on the banks of the Zuyderzée.

A miracle had saved me. But my voyage had been but a series of imprudences against which I had been unable to defend myself.

May this terrific recital, while it instructs those who read it, not discourage the explorers of the routes of air.

Le ballon *le Géant* au champ de Mars. Dessin de Fellmann.

About the *Géant*

by Jules Verne

Translated by Alex Kirstukas

It seems the question of balloons has made new progress since Nadar's bold experiments. Aerostatic science had long appeared abandoned; and, to tell the truth, it had not made much progress since the end of the eighteenth century. The scientists of those days invented everything: the hydrogen gas to fill the balloon, the net to contain the taffeta envelope and support the basket, and finally the valve to let out the gas; the means of ascending and descending by removing gas or ballast were also discovered. And so, for eighty years, aeronautic art stood still.[76]

Is this to say that Nadar's experiments led the way to new progress? Perhaps; I am tempted to say, "undoubtedly." And here is why:

First, that brave and intrepid artist breathed fresh life into the forgotten question; he profited from his good standing in the press and with journalists to call public attention to the subject. At the beginning of great discoveries, there's always a man of that moral fiber, a seeker of difficulties, a lover of the impossible, who tries, tests, more or less succeeds, but finally gives the momentum. Then the scholars step in; they talk, write, calculate, and, one fine day, true success bursts into view for all to see.

That is what Nadar's daring ascents will bring about. If the art of rising and navigating through the air ever becomes a practical means of

76. This paragraph closely echoes a similarly expository passage from Chapter I of "A Voyage in a Balloon." In Wilbur's translation, the passage begins: "'Monsieur,' continued he, 'nothing new has been invented since the days of the philosopher Charles...'"

travel, then Posterity, if she is just, will be indebted to him for a large part of its understanding.

I will not narrate the voyages of the *Géant* here; others have done so, who, having accompanied it in its flight, were in a better position to see, and therefore to tell. I only mean to indicate in a few lines the direction that aeronautic science is tending to take.

First, according to Nadar, the *Géant* must be the last balloon; the difficulties surrounding its landings demonstrated superabundantly how dangerous such a large apparatus is to guide, how impossible to conduct.

So the wish arrived at is, quite simply, to do away with balloons. Is such a thing possible? M. Babinet believes so, as fully as if the idea had been his;[77] MM. de Ponton d'Amécourt and de La Landelle assert they have vanquished the difficulty and resolved the problem.

But before entering into the details of their invention, let us finish with balloons, and let me speak to you about M. de Luze's apparatus.[78] I have seen it work on a small scale, and it is very clearly the most ingenious thing done toward steering an aerostat, if an aerostat can be steered. Besides, the inventor has been very logical; instead of seeking to push the basket, he has sought to push the balloon.

To do so, he gave it the shape of an elongated cylinder; on this cylinder he has placed the blades of a propeller; he has linked the two ends of the cylinder to the basket by wires rolled on pulleys; these wires are intended, by means of some sort of motor, to rotate the cylinder, and the balloon literally screws through the air.

It is certain that the apparatus works, and works very well; it certainly cannot run against extremely strong winds, but in medium winds, I believe it will manage to steer; besides, the aeronaut will also have inclined planes at his disposal, which, when slanted to one side or the other, will permit him to run practically vertical courses.

His balloon must be constructed of copper, so as to avoid the loss of pure hydrogen gas, which happens very easily, and M. de Luze hopes to ascend and descend by means of a compartment placed inside the balloon, and in which he will retain air by means of a pump.

---

77. Jacques Babinet (1794–1872), an influential physicist and member of the Académie des Sciences, was an early supporter of the Heavier-than-Air Society.

78. "M. de Luze" was the prolific French inventor Pierre Jacques Carmien (1834–1907), who patented this dirigible in 1864. Contemporary reports refer to him as "M. Carmien de Luze" (i.e. Mr. Carmien from the commune of Luze), hence Verne's mistake.

That, very briefly, is his invention; plainly, what is most ingenious about it is that the balloon itself becomes the propeller. Will M. de Luze succeed? We shall see, for he intends to make a two-day flight over Paris.

But I return to the plan of MM. de Ponton d'Amécourt and de La Landelle; there is something of great import in it; but it remains to be seen if their idea is practicable with the mechanical means currently at their disposal.

You know those children's toys made of paddles, which are set at a lively spin by the quick unwinding of a string; the object takes flight, and glides through the air for as long as the propeller keeps gyrating.[79] If that movement continued, the apparatus would never fall; imagine a spring constantly in motion, and the toy would keep itself in the air.

It is on that principle that M. de Ponton d'Amécourt founded his helicopter. The air offers a point of support sufficient to the propeller, which hits it obliquely; all of this is physically true, and I have seen it work with my own eyes, on little apparatuses these gentlemen have made. A spring held back, then suddenly released, lifts up and takes the propeller with it.

But, of course, when the propeller drives an air column away, that air makes the apparatus rotate in the opposite direction. This inconvenience had to be removed, for such a midair waltz would soon make an aeronaut dizzy. Therefore, by means of two propellers, one atop the other, spinning in opposite directions, M. de Ponton d'Amécourt was able to provide complete immobility.[80]

With a third propeller, a vertical one, he steers his apparatus as he wishes. Thus, by means of the first two propellers, he keeps himself in the air; by means of the third, he pushes himself along as if he were in the water.

And so, theoretically, the solution has been found—the helicopter; but, practically, will it succeed? It all depends on the motor employed to move the propeller; it must be both powerful and light. Unfortunately, so far, the machines that use compressed air or steam, whether aluminum or iron, have not given completely satisfactory results.

79. This toy, called a *spiralifère,* had been a recent hit in French toyshops and remained popular through the rest of the nineteenth century. In his book *Aviation* (Paris: Dentu, 1863), 73, La Landelle points out the similarity between the toy and the helicopter. Verne returns to the comparison when describing the aircraft *Albatross* in Chapter VI of *Robur the Conqueror.*

80. James C. Iraldi notes in his manuscript: "Robur's Clipper was constructed on this very principle." And indeed, it is now widely recognized that the *Albatross*—nicknamed "the Clipper of the Clouds" in an early translation of that name—was based largely on Ponton d'Amécourt's helicopter.

I am very well aware that the experimenters have been working on a small scale, and that, to succeed, one has to work on a large one, for as an apparatus's volume increases, its relative weight diminishes. The fact is that one twenty-horsepower machine weighs much less than twenty one-horsepower machines. So we must keep waiting patiently for more decisive experiments. Inventors are learned and resolute people; they will get to the bottom of this discovery.

But they need money, perhaps a lot of money, and it is to get this money that Nadar has devoted himself heart and soul; that is why he summoned crowds to watch his daring ascensions. Spectators have not been numerous enough, perhaps because they thought only of present pleasures; if Nadar begins again, may the spectators think of future usefulness. If they do, the Champ de Mars will be too small to contain them.[81]

The question, plainly, is no longer to glide or fly in the air, but to *navigate* there.

One scholar said very humorously: "It's hopeless for man to try to turn himself into a bird; he will never be more than a turkey, and a stuffed turkey at that."[82]

So let us support the helicopter, and take for our motto that of Nadar:

Everything that is possible will happen.[83]

81. The *Géant* departed from the Champ de Mars in Paris on its first two ascents.

82. *Dindon à la farce* literally means "stuffed turkey," but is also used to mean the one who suffers, the victim of a practical joke, etc. The quote comes from "Navigation aérienne, avec ou sans ballon," an 1851 essay by the Jesuit physicist and journalist François-Napoléon-Marie Moigno (1804–1884). Verne may have seen it quoted in Ponton d'Amécourt's pamphlet *La Conquête de l'air par l'hélice* (Paris: Sausset, 1863), 5, where it is coyly attributed to "a man of science and merit" going by the pseudonym Théophile. According to Marguerite Allotte de La Füye's unreliable biography, Verne made a similar joke about stuffed turkeys during the writing of *Five Weeks in a Balloon* the previous year; see M. Allotte de La Füye, *Jules Verne* (Paris: Hachette, 1953), 89.

83. This motto, quoted on the same page of *La Conquête de l'air* as Moigno's turkey joke, comes from Nadar's "Manifeste de l'Autolocomotion Aérienne" (*La Presse*, August 7, 1864), 3. It sometimes appears in English in a more cautiously worded version—"All that is possible may be accomplished"—from Christopher Hatton Turnor's *Astra Castra: Experiments and Adventures in the Atmosphere* (London: Chapman and Hall, 1865), 339. As Christian Sánchez noted in a post to the Jules Verne Forum (June 3, 2000), the quote is also probably the source of a line that, from Allotte de La Füye onward, has often attributed apocryphally to Jules Verne: "What one man can imagine, another will someday be able to achieve."

Twenty-Four Minutes In a Balloon

by Jules Verne

Translated by Alex Kirstukas

Dear M. Jeunet,

Here are the few notes you requested from me about the flight of the *Météore*.

You already know the conditions planned for the ascent: the balloon, with its relatively small capacity of 900 cubic meters, weighing 270 kilograms with basket and rigging, filled with a gas excellent for lighting but, for that very reason, of only modest lifting power,[84] was to carry four people: the aeronaut Eugène Godard, and his three travelers, the lawyer M. Deberly, Lieutenant Merson of the Fourteenth Regiment, and me.[85]

When the time came to start, it was impossible to take all four of us. As M. Merson had already made balloon ascents in Nantes with Eugène Godard, he consented, whatever his own feelings, to cede his place to M. Deberly, who, like me, was making his first aerial excursion. The traditional "Let her go!" was ready to be pronounced, and we were just about to leave the ground…

But we were reckoning without Eugène Godard's son, a plucky little lad of nine, who clambered into the basket, and for whom we had

84. Verne's first-hand experience with illuminating gas may explain why it appeared the following year in the revised "A Voyage in a Balloon," taking the place of the original version's hydrogen.

85. Margot, in *Jules Verne en son temps*, identifies the first traveler as Albert-Léon Deberly (1844–1888). Merson's biographical details are more elusive; "Ascent of the *Météore*" notes that his regiment's band supplied the music for Godard's ascent.

to sacrifice two of our four ballast bags.[86] Only two bags left! Never had Eugène Godard gone ballooning in such conditions. The ascent could therefore not be of long duration.

We set off at 5:24, slowly and obliquely. The wind carried us southeast, and the sky was of incomparable purity. Only a few storm clouds on the horizon. By sending down Jack the monkey with his parachute,[87] we were able to rise faster, and at 5:28 we were sailing at a height of eight hundred meters, as the aneroid barometer revealed.

The view of the town was magnificent. The Place Longueville looked like an anthill full of red and black ants, the former military, the latter civilian; the cathedral's spire lowered slowly, marking our progress like a needle as we ascended.

In a balloon, no movement can be perceived, whether horizontal or vertical.[88] The horizon always seems to stay at the same level. It simply spreads out in diameter, while the landscape under the basket is sunk down like a funnel.[89] Meanwhile, absolute silence, the complete calm of the atmosphere, troubled only by the creaking of the wicker that carries us.

At 5:32, a sunbeam comes through the clouds burdening the western horizon. It strikes the balloon; the gas expands, and without any ballast thrown out, we are carried to a height of twelve hundred meters, the maximum altitude we will reach during the trip.

And here is what we can see. Beneath our feet, Saint-Acheul and its blackish gardens, contracted as if seen through the wide end of a telescope; the flattened cathedral, its spire seeming to mingle with houses on the outskirts of town; the Somme, a thin clear ribbon; the railways, a few strokes from a drawing pen; the roads, winding shoelaces; the floating gardens,[90] a mere market stall; the fields, one of

86. Eugène Godard *fils* (1864–1910) grew up to be an accomplished balloonist in his own right.

87. Jack's parachute stunts were a regular feature of Godard's ascents in the 1870s. The *Journal* included "the parachute descent of Jacques [*sic*] the monkey" in its announcement of Godard's visit: see *Journal d'Amiens* 5102 (21 septembre 1873), 2.

88. Compare "Nothing betrays the horizontal voyage of a balloon…" in Chapter I of "A Voyage in a Balloon."

89. This observation would serve Verne well for *Robur the Conqueror*, where it is alluded to in Chapters VIII and XIII.

90. Les Hortillonages, a once-marshy area of Amiens, was converted by medieval farmers into a complex network of boat canals and garden plots. The gardens flourished in

those varicolored boards of cloth samples that tailors used to hang at their doors;[91] Amiens, a heap of little grayish cubes; it is as if somebody had scattered a box of Nuremberg toys over the plain.[92] Then the surrounding villages, Saint-Fuscien, Villers-Bretonneux, La Neuville, Boves, Camon, Longueau:[93] so many big piles of stones, scattered here and there for a gigantic work of macadamization.

Just then, the inside of the balloon is lit up. I look through the appendix,[94] which Eugène Godard always keeps open. Inside, perfect transparency, with the alternating yellow and brown stripes of the *Météore* clearly visible. Nothing reveals the presence of gas, either by color or by smell.

Meanwhile, we are descending, for we are heavy. Some ballast must be thrown out to keep us aloft. The thousands of handbills tossed overboard indicate a stronger wind current in a lower zone. Longeau lies ahead, but before Longeau, a series of marshy hollows.

"Will we descend into the marsh?" I asked Eugène Godard.

"No," he replied, "and if we run out of ballast, I'll throw down my traveling bag. We absolutely must get past the marsh."

We are still falling. At 5:43, at five hundred meters from the ground, a strong wind seizes us. We pass over a factory smokestack, and our eyes look to the bottom; the balloon is reflected, by a sort of mirage, in the marsh water; the human ants, grown larger, run on the roads. A little meadow stretches out between the two lines of railway, in front of their junction.

"Well?" I say.

"Well, we'll pass the railway, and the village beyond it!" replies Eugène Godard.

The wind is strong. We can tell as much from the movement of the trees. We pass over La Neuville. Before us lie the plains. Eugène

---

Verne's lifetime, and a few gardeners (*hortillons*) still keep the practice alive.

91. Describing a flight over Zanzibar, *Five Weeks in a Balloon* (Chapter XII) features a similar passage in which fields become fabric samples and people shrink to insects.

92. Another observation adapted for *Robur the Conqueror* (Chapters VII–VIII), where landmarks seen from the sky are compared to Nuremberg toys, dice, and knucklebones.

93. All these villages still exist as communes, except La Neuville, which is now a district of southeast Amiens.

94. The tube at the bottom of a gas balloon, through which the envelope can be inflated and deflated.

Godard throws out his guide rope, 150 meters long, and then his anchor. At 5:47, the anchor hits the ground; a few puffs of gas are discharged from the valve; some curious passersby very obligingly rush up, seize the guide rope, and we are let gently down to touch the earth, without the slightest jolt. The balloon has landed like a big healthy bird, not like a game bird with a bullet in its wing.

Twenty minutes later, the balloon was deflated, rolled up, put in its wrapping, and placed in a cart, and a carriage brought us back to Amiens.

These impressions, my dear M. Jeunet, are brief but exact. Let me add that a simple aerial promenade, or even a long balloon voyage, can hold no danger in the hands of Eugène Godard. Bold, intelligent, seasoned, a man of great coolheadedness, with already more than a thousand ascents in the Old and New Worlds to his name, Eugène Godard never leaves anything to chance. He thinks of everything. Nothing can take him by surprise. He knows where he is going and where he will land. He chooses his stopping place with marvelous perspicacity. He proceeds mathematically, barometer in one hand, ballast-bag in the other. His instruments are in admirable condition: never a hesitation from the valve, never a fold in the envelope. A "breakage rope" allows him to split his balloon open, in case it should graze the earth and have to be emptied immediately to make landing possible. Eugène Godard, by his experience, coolheadedness, and power of sight, is a true master of the air that holds him up and carries him aloft. It is well known that no other aeronaut can be compared to him. In these conditions, a voyage through the air offers every security. In fact, such a thing is not even a voyage—it is something like a dream, but a dream that is always too short!

Sincerely yours,
Jules Verne

Part III

Comparing Translations—The Case of "Frritt-Flacc" by Jules Verne

by Jean-Michel Margot

VERNE'S POE-LIKE SHORT STORY, "Frritt-Flacc," has been the focus of several recent discoveries, revealing its widespread reception and various translations.[95] First was Andrew Nash's 2006 location of the first English translation, simultaneous with its initial French appearance in *Le Figaro illustré* for Christmas 1884. Then came Victor Berch's discovery of the 1890 pastiche, *Umberto*, by J. Fitzgerald Molloy, much longer than the original "Frritt-Flacc." Another, more direct translation of "Frritt-Flacc" was encountered using searches of the vintage newspapers online, and first appeared as "Dr. Trifulgas' Patient" in *The Washington Post*, on page 15, Sunday, July 9, 1893. Curiously, it adapts a title that first appeared in its British publication in the July 1892 issue of *The Strand Magazine*, where "Frritt-Flacc" was retitled "Dr. Trifulgas—A Fantastic Tale," yet the story itself was re-translated. While the *Strand* version has been often reprinted, the rediscovered 1884 and 1893 versions have only appeared in the pages of the North American Jules Verne Society's newsletter, *Extraordinary Voyages*.[96]

95. "Frritt-Flacc" has been adapted to the screen a number of times, and even enacted with puppets. Jean-Michel Margot, "Is Dr. Trifulgas a Puppet?," *Extraordinary Voyages*, 15 (December 2008), 9-10.

96. *The Strand Magazine* version has a footnote which says: "Published by special permission of Messrs Hetzel et Cie. All rights reserved." *Strand* renders the phrase "Frritt-Flacc" as "Swish! swash!"

Both are offered here, in book form for the first time, back to back. With the story's brevity (some 2400 words in French) there is room in this volume for these two versions, so readers may perceive for themselves the distinctions in two separate, almost simultaneous and up till recently, lost translatons. This reveals the wide dichotomies evident in Verne translations over the years, the differences, and distinctions in interpretations, and in many cases, varying degrees of fidelity to the original French. For further comparison, the *Strand* version is available online, and since the 1950s a number of new translations of "Frritt-Flacc" have appeared.

The first French publication was in *Le Figaro illustré* (Paris), "... only issue of the year 1884-1885." It was available for Christmas 1884. Vernians refer to such magazine publication as "pré-originale." The original edition is the small in-18 printing, without illustrations, published November 4, 1886. The first printing of the illustrated in-octavo edition is November 11, 1886, where "Frritt-Flacc" fills out the short novel *Un Billet de loterie* (*A Lottery Ticket*—serialized in the *Magasin d'éducation et de recréation* [*Magazine of Education and Recreation*] between January 1 and November 15, 1886). "Frritt-Flacc" came out in the *Magasin d'éducation et de recréation* on December 1, 1886. *A Lottery Ticket* was available as a single volume as well as a double volume with *Robur le Conquérant* (*Robur the Conqueror*). *A Lottery Ticket* was already translated into English in 1886 and published by Munro in America and by Sampson Low in England, but without "Frritt-Flacc." The illustrations from both *Le Figaro* and the *Magasin* versions of "Frritt-Flacc" are included here.

The first publication of "Frritt-Flacc" in English is special because it was published in Paris and the translation came out simultaneously with the French pré-originale edition. Advertisements in *The Scotsman* confirmed the publication of "The Christmas number of the French Illustrated monthly, *Le Figaro illustré* (London: Goupil & Co.) comes out, as in former years, in an English version."

"Frritt-Flacc" is the most intriguing Vernian text in respect of word invention and creation. As an example, here are three French words used by Verne in the short story: "craquelinier," "valvêtre," "lurtaine." The first one is a profession, the two others are fabrics used in clothing. A good English translation should keep the mystery behind the words and it would be the translator's turn to invent words whose pronunciation would recall a profession and pieces of clothing. For this fantastic tale, Verne also creates new French words: kerste, fretzer, verliche, balanze, craquelinier, camondeur, valvêtre, lurtaine. Most of them were not translated into English and the translators would use common English words instead. However, many of these words are German or French proper names (Verliche, Balanze, Fretzer). Another question which can be seen answered in different ways in the translations here is whether the original French title, "Frritt-Flacc," should be retained, as a sound effect, or some English equivalent formulated—or abandoned altogether in favor of a clearer descriptive phrase.

FRRITT-FLACC
PAR JULES VERNE

"FRRITT-FLACC"

I

Frritt!... whistles the rising gale.

Flacc!... beats the rain as it comes down in torrents.

Low sway the trees under the blast that sweeps the Volsinian shore and dashes its fury against the slopes of the mountains of Crimma. The rock-bound coast is rent and riven by the tempestuous billows that surge and foam along the vast Megalocrida Sea.

Frritt!... Flacc!...

In the depth of the bay nestles the little sea-port town of Luktrop. It boasts a few hundred houses with greenish miradors sheltering them from the winds of the main, and four or five steep streets that look more like the beds of a mountain-torrent than public thoroughfares. Not far off smokes the Vanglor, an active volcano, which by day belches forth thick volumes of sulfureous vapour and by night fitful floods of flame. This crater, seen fully one hundred and fifty kerstes out at sea, answers the purpose of a beacon and guides home to Luktrop the coasters, -felzanes, verliches or balanzes – that plough the troubled waters of the Megalocrida.

On the other side of the town are heaped up ruins of the Crimmerian era; while the suburb, of Moorish aspect, like a casbah or Algerian fortress, with its white walls, round roofs and terraces calcined by the sun, seems a huge pile of square stones thrown together at hap-hazard.

The whole mass looks like a cluster of dice, the dots of which have been worn away with age.

Among other peculiar structures may be seen an odd-looking building called the Six-Quatre from the number of its windows, six in front and four behind.

A steeple rises above the town, the square steeple of Sainte-Philfilène, with its bells visible through the open stone-work, and when these are swung (as they are at times) by the violence of the storm, it is accounted a bad sign, and the good people of the place are filled with fear at the omen. Such is Luktrop, with a few stray houses on the heath beyond, scattered amid the broom and furze, as in Brittany. Luktrop, however, is not in Brittany. Is it in France? I cannot say.

In Europe? I don't know.

At any rate it were useless to look for the place on the map, even in Steiler's atlas.

II

Toc! A discreet rap is heard at the narrow door of the Six-Quatre, on the left hand corner of the Rue Messaglière. A comfortable house this, if such a word is known at Luktrop, and one of the thriftiest of the place, if to earn on an average a few thousand fretzers a year be a sign of thrift.

A ferocious yelp, something between a bark and a howl, as from a wolf, has answered the rap, whereupon a window above the door of the Six-Quatre is thrown open and an angry voice bawls out:

"To the devil with all intruders!" A young girl shivering n the rain, with a sorry cape thrown over her shoulders enquires if doctor Trifulgas is at home.

"He is or isn't, - all depends."

"I come for my father who is dying."

"And where is he dying?"

"By the Val-Karniou, four kertses from here."

"And what's his name?"

"Vort Kartif."

"Vort Kartif,... the cracknel-master?"

"Yes, and if doctor Trifulgas would only..."

"Doctor Trifulgas isn't at home!"

And the window is brutally closed in the girl's face, while the

Frritts of the wind and the Flaccs of the rain outside mix their voices in a deafening din.

III

A hard man he, doctor Trifulgas, with but little feeling for a fellow-creature, and one who attends a patient only if well paid in advance for his services. His old dog Hurzof—a cross between a bull and a spaniel—would have more heart than he. The door of the Six-Quatre remains invariably closed to the poor and open only to the rich. He has, moreover, his scale of prices: typhoid fever, so much; brain fever, so much; so much for a pericarditis, and for as many more diseases as doctors choose to invent by the dozen. And Vort Kartif, the cracknel-maker is a poor man, with a penniless brood. Why, then, should doctor Trifulgas bedevil himself, and on such a night?

"They rousing me from my sleep," snuffled he, as he went to bed again, "is alone worth ten fretzers!"

Twenty minutes had scarce gone by than the iron knocker again woke the echoes of the Six-Quatre.

Grumbling, the doctor got out of bed, and from the window growled: "Who's there?"

"I'm Vort Kartif's wife."

"The cracknel-maker from Val-Karniou?"

"Yes, and if you don't come, he'll die."

"Well, then you'll be a widow?"

"Here are twenty fretzers…"

"What? Twenty fretzers to go to Val-Karniou, four kertses hence?"

"For God's sake, come!"

"Go to…"

And with an oath the window was again slammed. "Twenty fretzers!" Muttered he, what a windfall! Run the risk of catching a rheum or a lumbago for such a sum, when one has to attend tomorrow morning the gouty—but wealthy—Edzingov, at Kiltrens, whose ailment in worth fifty fretzers a visit.

With this pleasant prospect doctor Trifulgas sought his bed and went to sleep again as soundly as ever."

IV

Frritt!… Flacc!… and then, rap! rap! rap!

Three blows from the knocker struck with a firm hand have this time added their rattle to the noise of the storm. The doctor, startled from his sleep, got up in a towering passion. On opening his window the hurricane came in like a whirlwind.

"'Tis for the cracknel-master…"

"What, again that wretch!…"

"I am his mother."

"May his mother, wife and daughter all die with him!"

"Tis a fit…"

"Aye, and a right one, no doubt," chuckled the doctor.

"We have a little money," said the old woman, "an installment on the house sold to Dantrup, the drayman, of the Rue Messaglière. If you don't come, my grand-daughter will be without a father, my daughter without a husband, and myself without a son!"

It was heartrending and horrible to hear the old hag's voice, and to think that the wind froze the blood in her veins and drenched the very bones under her skin.

"A fit, say you? The fee is two hundred fretzers," rejoined the heartless leech.

"We have but one hundred and twenty."

"Good night, then!" And once more the window was closed.

On second thoughts, however, he came to the conclusion that, for an hour's trot and half an hour's attendance, one hundred and twenty fretzers made sixty fretzers an hour—one fretzer a minute! It was small profit at best, but not quite to be despised.

So instead of getting into bed, the doctor slipped himself into his velvet suit, hurried down stairs in a pair of thick waterproof boots, muffled himself up in a large overcoat, put on his gloves and sou-wester, and leaving the lamp lighted on the table near his Codex opened at page 197, pushed open the door of the Six-Quatre and appeared on the threshold.

The old cross was there, leaning on a stick, her frame emaciated by eighty years of misery.

"The money," said he.

"Here, and may God return it a hundred fold!"

"God! The money of God! Has any one seen its colour?"

The doctor whistled Hurzof, put a small lantern in the dog's mouth, and bent his steps towards the sea. The old hag trudged on behind.

V

Good heavens, what a weather of Frritts and Flaccs! The bells of Sainte-Philfilène sway to and fro under the headlong fury of the storm, an ominous portent, as we know, but doctor Trifulgas eschews all superstitious notions. The fact is he believes in nothing at all, not even in his own science, - except for what it brings him in. What weather to be sure, and what a road! Nothing but shingle and slag, the shingle slippery like sea-weed and the slag crisp as clinker. And no other light to see by, than a tremulous flicker from Hurzof's lantern. At times strange fantastic figures seem to toss and stir in the flames that swell from the mouth of the Vanglor. There is really no telling what lies hidden at the bottom of these inscrutable craters. Perhaps the souls of the underworld that volatilize on reaching our atmosphere.

The doctor and the old hag follow the line of coast that runs in and out of the small bays along the shore. The sea of a livid whiteness, and sparkles as its billows hurtle the phosphorescent fringe of surf that seems to pour waves on waves of glow-worms upon the beech.

Thus both walk on till they reach a bend in the road between two swelling downs, where the broom and sea-rushes clash their blades together like so many bayonets.

The dog has drawn nearer to his master and seems to say:

"Well, what think you? A hundred and twenty fretzers to place under lock and key in the safe! That's the way to build up a fortune! 'Tis another piece of ground added to the vine enclosure! Another dish added to the evening meal! Another bowl of wash for faithful Hurzof! Nothing like attending rich patients and loosening their purse-strings!"

At this point, the old woman stopped. She directed a finger which shook with age towards a red light some way off in the gloom: the house of Vort Kartif, the cracknel-master.

"There?" laconically put in the doctor. "Yes," responded the crone. "Hurrahwow-wow!" struck up Hurzof. Just then the Vanglor

vibrating to its foundations with a noise like thunder, threw up a mass of fuliginous flames that mounted to the zenith and rent the clouds. Doctor Trifulgas was thrown to the ground by the force of the concussion. Regaining his footing he swore like a Christian, and looked around. The beldam was gone. She must have fallen into the floating fog-clouds of the Ocean. The dog, however, was still there, upright on his haunches, his mouth wide open, and the light of the lantern blown out.

"Never mind; let's go on," mumbled doctor Trifulgas. The honest man had pocketed his one hundred and twenty fretzers and must needs earn them.

VI

A solitary light is alone visible in the distances half a kertse away. It is doubtless the lamp of the dying, or per chance, dead man, and yonder must be the cracknel-maker's house. There can be no mistake; the old hag pointed it out. And so saying, under the whistling Frritts and the driving Flaccs, with the noise of the storm in his ears, doctor Trifulgas hurries on towards the house, which, standing alone in the midst of a wide heath, is more distinctly perceptible as the wayfarer approaches.

It is a singular and note-worthy fact to observe how much the house of the cracknel maker's looks like the doctor's Six-Quatre, at Luktrop; there is the same arrangement in the front windows and the little vaulted door at the side. Doctor Trifulgas strides on as fast as the driving gusts of wind and rain will permit. He reaches the door, which is ajar, pushes it open, enters, and the blast closes it behind him with a bang. The dog outside howls or is silent by turns, like choristers chanting the verses of a Forty Hours' psalm.

How very strange! One might almost be led to suppose that doctor Trifulgas had come back to his own house. But this cannot be. He took no wrong turning on the road, nor did he lose his way. No, he is certainly at Val-Karniou, and not at Luktrop. Yet, how comes it his eye dwells on the same low, vaulted corridor, the same winding staircase, and the same massive wooden railing, hand-worn like his own! He ascends, and stops on the landing. A faint light comes from under the door, as at the Six-Quatre!

Is it a snare or a delusion? By the weak glimmer of the lamp he vaguely recognizes his own room; there, the yellow sofa; there, on the right, the old oaken chest; and there, on the left, the iron-girt safe, in which he had thought of placing his one hundred and twenty fretzers. Yonder is his armchair with its leather tassels, his table with its convoluted legs, and upon it, by the flickering lamp, his own Codex, open at page 197.

"What ails me?" murmurs the doctor. What ails thee? Why thou art palsied with fright. Thy eyeballs start from their sockets. Thy body contracts and dwindles in size. An icy sweat chills thy skin, on which nameless horrors seem to creep.

Quick, or the lamp for want of oil will go out, and the sick man die. Aye, the bed is there, - his own, with its pillars and baldaquin—a bed as long as it is broad, and the closed curtains with their large

inwrought flowers. Can this indeed be the bed of a poor cracknel-master? Trembling the doctor draws near, pulls the curtain aside, and peers within....

There outstretched on his dying bed lay the sick man, with his head outside the counterpane and motionless, like one about to breathe his last. The doctor bends forward ....

Ah! What ghastly scream is that which rends the air and is taken up by the dog outside with his sinister howling! It is not Vort Kartif, the cracknel-master, who is the dying man, but he, the doctor, doctor Trifulgas himself! He who is smitten down with brain-fever, he, and no other. Full well he knows the symptoms: it is cerebral apoplexy, with sudden accumulation of serosity in the cavities of the brain, and partial paralysis of the body on the side opposite that where the lesion exists. Aye, it was for him that assistance was besought, that one hundred and twenty fretzers were paid! He who, in the hardness of his heart, refused to attend the poor cracknel-master! It is he now that is dying!

Doctor Trifulgas raved like a maniac. The symptoms increased every minute. Not only were all the functions of relation dead in him, but the beatings of his heart were nearly gone like the breath of his lungs. Yet he had not lost all consciousness of his desperate strain.

What shall he do? Diminish the mass of the blood by bleeding? There must be no hesitation, or doctor Trifulgas is a dead man... Phlebotomy was still practiced in those days, and then as now the doctors rescued from apoplexy all those who were not to die from its effects.

Doctor Trifulgas seized his case of instruments, took his lancet, and punctured the vein on his duplicate self. No blood, however, spurted from the wound. He fractioned with all his might the chest of the dying one, but he found that the pulsations of his own heart diminished; he burnt the other's feet with hot bricks, but felt his own feet growing cold.

Suddenly his duplicate starts up in his bed, struggles wildly in the last throes of suspended breathing; a rattle is heard in his throat... And doctor Trifulgas, with all his science, falls back dead in his own arms. Frritt! Blows the wind; flacc! falls the rain outside.

VII

The following morning a corpse was found in the house known as the Six-Quatre, - that of doctor Trifulgas. He was placed in a coffin, and conveyed in great pomp to the cemetery of Luktrop, after the manner of the many he had already sent there.

As for old Hurzof. I am told the faithful beast may still be seen, with his lantern relighted, scouring the heath and howling for his lost master. If this be true or not, I cannot say; yet so many strange things do occur in this Volsinian country, especially round about Luktrop, that I see no reason to doubt the statement. At any rate, let me ask of you once more not to look for this town of Luktrop on the map. The best geographers are still uncertain as to its exact position in latitude—and even longitude.

Dr. Trifulgas' Patient

by Jules Verne

Adapted from the French by Mary J. Safford

I.

Whoo-oo-oo! roared the wind. Whi-i-ish! the rain was pouring in torrents. The fury of the gale bowed the trees on the Volsinian coast and beat upon the cliffs of the mountains of Crimma. The lofty rocks along the shore were gnawed by the waves of the vast Sea of Mégalocride.

Whoo-oo-oo! Whi-i-ish!

At the end of the harbor is the little town of Luktrop. A few hundred houses, four or five steep streets, which look like ravines, paved with pebble stones, and roughened by the scorim ejected by the neighboring volcano, Vanglor. During the day it emits sulphurous vapors, at night, ever and anon, huge tongues of flame. Like a lighthouse, the Vanglor shows the harbor of Luktrop to the coasters, whose keels cut the waves of the Mégalocride.

On the other side of the town are some ruins of the Crimmarian period. Then comes a suburb which recalls Arabian villages, with white walls, round roofs, and sun-scorched terraces, a heap of stones flung there hap-hazard, like a pile of dice whose angles were worn off by the steps of time.

Among other buildings is the Six-Quatre, a name given to an odd-looking structure with six windows on one side and four on the other.

A steeple dominates the town, the square belfry of St. Philfilene, with a chime of bells which are sometimes stirred by the tempest. It is considered a bad omen, and always inspires terror throughout the country.

Such is Luktrop. Then outside are scattered houses standing amid the broom and furze, as in Brittany. But it isn't in Brittany. Is it in France? I don't know. In Europe? I don't know that, either. At any rate, don't look for Luktrop on the map—not even on Stieler's atlas.[97]

II.

Tap! A timid knock was heard on the narrow door of the Six Quatre at the left angle of the Rue Messagliere. It was one of the most comfortable houses, if the word can be applied to Luktrop.

The knock was answered by savage barking, intermingled with howling, like the barking of a wolf. Then a window above the door opened. "Deuce take these troublesome people," said an angry voice.

A young girl wrapped in a shabby cloak, who stood shivering in the rain, asked if Dr. Trifulgas was at home.

"He is or isn't—acccording to circumstances."

"I've come to ask him to go to my dying father."

"Where is he dying?"

"On the coast of Val Karinon, four miles from here."

"What is his name?"

"Vort Kartif."

"Vort Kartif?"

"Yes, and if Dr. Trifulgas—"

"Dr. Trifulgas isn't in."

And the window closed abruptly, while the roar of the wind and the rush of the rain blended in a deafening noise.

97. The reference is to Adolf Stieler (1775–1836), a German cartographer, whose "Hand-Atlas über alle Theile der Erde und über das Weltgebäude" went through ten editions from 1816 to 1944 and was the leading German world atlas until the middle of the 20th century.

III.

This Dr. Trifulgas was a hard man. His old dog Hurzof—a cross between a bulldog and a spaniel—would have had more pity. His house, Six-Quatre, inhospitable to the poor, opened only to the rich. Besides, he had a regular scale of charges for his services—so much for typhoid fever, so much for a congestion, so much for pericarditis and other diseases which doctors invent by the dozen. Now, Vort Kartif was a poor man, a member of an insignificant family. Why should Dr. Trifulgas disturb himself, and on such a night?

"Just getting me up was worth ten fretzers," he muttered as he went back to his bed.

Scarcely twenty minutes had passed when the iron knocker again struck on the door of Six-Quatre.

The doctor in a rage again leaned out of the window.

"Who's there?" he shouted.

"I am Vort Kartif's wife."

"The man at Val Karinon?"

"Yes; and if you don't come he will die."

"Well, you'll be a widow."

"Here are twenty fretzers."

"Twenty fretzers to go to Val Karinon, four miles off! No, thank you! Deuce take me if I will."

And the window banged again. Twenty fretzers! A fine piece of business! Risk a cold or lumbago for twenty fretzers, especially when, the next morning, he was expected at Kiltreno, by the rich Edzingov, from whose gout he made fifty fretzers a visit.

With this agreeable prospect, Dr. Trifulgas slept still more soundly than before.

IV.

Whoo-oo-oo! Whi-i-ish! And then tap! tap! tap! This time three blows from the knocker, plied by a more resolute hand, blended with the noise of the storm. The doctor woke, but in what a temper! When the window was opened, the wind burst in like a bomb-shell.

"It is for Vort Kartif."

"That miserable fellow again."

"I am his mother."

"May his mother, his wife, and his daughter die with him."

"He has an attack of —"

"Well, let him defend himself."

"They have sent you some money," the old woman added, "an installment on the house which was sold to Dontrup on the Rue Messagliere. If you don't come, my grand-daughter will be fatherless, my daughter a widow, and I shall have no son."

It was pitiful and terrible to hear this aged woman's voice, to think that the wind was chilling the blood in her veins, that the rain was drenching her thin form!

"An attack of epilepsy is worth 200 fretzers," replied the heartless Trifulgas.

"We have only 120."

"Good evening!"

And the window shut again. But, on reflection, a hundred and twenty fretzers for a two hours' walk, including the visit, that was sixty fretzers an hour, a fretzer a minute. The profit was small, yet after all not to be despised.

Instead of going back to bed, the doctor slipped into his coat, put on his high boots, his thick overcoat, and his mittens, then leaving his lamp burning beside his Codex, open at page 197, he unbolted the door of Six-Quatre and stood upon the threshold.

The old woman was there, leaning on her staff, emaciated by her eighty years of poverty.

"The 120 fretzers?"

"Here they are, and may God increase them to you a hundred-fold."

"God! The money of the poor! Did anybody ever see the color of it?"

The doctor whistled to Hurzof, lighted a small lantern, hung it round his neck and turned toward the sea.

The old woman followed him.

V.

What a tempest of wind and rain! The bells of St. Philfilene began to ring. A bad omen! Pshaw! Dr. Trifulgas was not superstitious. He believed in nothing, not even his own science—except for the income it brought him. What weather, and what a road, too! Stones, slippery with sea weed; scories crunching under the tread. No light, except the faint, wavering rays from Hurzof's lantern. Sometimes

De son doigt tremblant, la vieille montra une lumière. (Page 194.)

With a trembling finger, she pointed to a light.

there was a burst of flame from the peak of Vanglor, amid which huge, grotesque silhouettes seemed to hover. We do not know what lurks at the bottom of these fathomless craters. Perhaps they are the souls of the underworld, which turn to vapor in rising.

The doctor and the old woman followed the curves of the little bays on the shore. The sea was white with a livid pallor—the whiteness of mourning—glittering with a phosphorescent light along the line of surf, which broke in shining waves upon the strand.

Both climbed to the bend in the road between the downs, where the broom and furze met like a thicket of bayonets.

The dog had come close to his master and seemed to say:

"Ha! A hundred and twenty fretzers for the strong box! That's the way to get rich! More land for the vineyard! Another dish on the supper table! Another bone for faithful Hurzof! Let us nurse the sick rich people and bleed—their pockets."

At this point the old woman stopped and, with a trembling finger, pointed to a ruddy light shining through the gloom. It came from Vort Kartif's house.

"There?" asked the doctor.

"Yes," replied the old woman.

The dog howled plaintively.

Suddenly the volcano, with a roar which seemed to shake it to its foundations, sent forth a sheaf of flames which appeared to touch the clouds. Dr. Trifulgas was thrown down by the shock.

Swearing like a trooper, he rose and looked around him.

The old woman was no longer there. Had she disappeared in some chasm in the earth, or was she concealed by the heavy mist?

The dog was standing erect on his hind legs, with his mouth wide open and the lantern out.

"Let us go on!" murmured Dr. Trifulgas.

The worthy man had pocketed his money. He must earn it.

VI.

There was only one glimmer of light—perhaps half a mile away. It came from the room of the dying or dead man. That was the house. The old woman had pointed to it. No mistake was possible.

Amid the roaring of the wind, the rush of the rain, the whole fury of the tempest, Dr. Trifulgas walked swiftly on. As he advanced, the house, standing alone in the fields, became more and more clearly visible.

It was strange how closely it resembled the doctor's residence, Six-Quatre at Luktrop; the same arrangement of the windows in front, the same little vaulted door.

Dr. Trifulgas hurried on as fast as the hurricane would permit. The door was ajar; he pushed it open and the gale banged it after him rudely. The dog, left outside, howled, pausing at intervals like the singers between the verses of a psalm.

Strange! One would think that Dr. Trifulgas had returned to his own home. Yet he had not grown bewildered, and made a circuit. He was really at Val Karinon, not at Luktrop. Yet, there was the same low, vaulted corridor, the same winding wooden staircase, with its wide railing, worn by the friction of many hands.

He went up to the landing. A faint light filtered under the door as at Six-Quatre. Was it a delusion? In the duck he recognized his own room, the bed with its yellow canopy, on the right the old pear-wood chest, at the left a strong box where he meant to deposit his 120 fretzers. There stood his leather-cushioned armchair, his table with its twisted legs, and on it near the dying lamp his Codex opened at page 197.

"What ails me?" he muttered.

What was it? A chill of fear crept through his veins. His pupils dilated. His body seemed to shrink. A cold perspiration came through the pores of his skin.

He must hasten. The lamp was going out for lack of oil. He must look at the dying man.

Yes, there was the bed—his bed, with pillars and canopy, closed by flowered curtains. Was it possible that that was a poor man's wretched pallet?

With a trembling hand he grasped the curtains, parted them, and glanced within.

The dying man, with his face in full view, lay motionless, as if about to draw his last breath. The doctor bent over him.

Oh! What a cry escaped his lips—answered by the mournful baying of the dog outside.

Oui, c'est lui qui va mourir! (Page 197.)

Yes, it is he who will die there!

The dying man was not Vort Kartif, but Dr. Trifulgas. It was he whom the congestion had attacked. A cerebral apoplexy, with a sudden accumulation of water in the cavities of the brain, with paralysis of the side of the body opposite to the seat of the injury.

Yes, it was he for whom a physician had been summoned. He, who in the hardness of his heart had refused to go to the poor man. He who was dying.

Dr. Trifulgas was like a mad man; he felt that the case was hopeless. The gravity of the symptoms increased every moment. The action of the heart and respiration were about to cease. Yet he had not wholly lost the consciousness of existence.

What should he do? Lessen the quantity of blood by means of bleeding? Dr. Trifulgas was a dead man if he delayed.

Bleeding was still practiced at that time, and, as at the present day, the doctors cured of apoplexy all who were not destined to die of it.

Dr. Trifulgas seized his case of instruments, took out a lancet, and cut the arm of his double. The blood did not flow. He rubbed the chest violently, the action of his own heart was failing. He put hot bricks to the feet; his own were growing cold.

Then the double started up in bed, struggled violently for breath, drew a long sigh. And Dr. Trifulgas, spite of all that his knowledge could suggest, died under his hands.

VII.

The next morning only a corpse was found in Six-Quatre—the body of Dr. Trifulgas. It was interred with great pomp in the cemetery of Luktrop, after numerous others, which he had sent there—according to the most approved formula.

As to old Hurzof, they say that since that day he has darted through the country with his lighted lantern, howling like a lost dog.

I can't vouch for the truth of the rumor, but so many queer things happen in this land of Volsinia, near the suburbs of Luktrop.

But I repeat, don't look for this place on the map. The best geographers have not yet agreed as to its situation in latitude or even longitude.

Portrait of Verne created by the American Jules Verne Society.

Part IV

Darwinian Echoes: "Gil Braltar" and "The Humbug"

Introduction by Brian Taves

"GIL BRALTAR"

The North American Jules Verne Society (NAJVS), that has brought to fruition the Palik series, was founded in 1993, to expand public knowledge of Verne. NAJVS was far from the first group of Verne enthusiasts. In 1921, in England at Dartmouth Royal Naval College, a group of students named themselves "Julians" and formed the Jules Verne Confederacy. Only in the wake of the achievements of the Jules Verne Confederacy was the Société Jules Verne formed in France in 1935, but their work would be interrupted by the war. Meanwhile, the American Jules Verne Society (AJVS) began a 20-year association. One of its members, James C. Iraldi, was still active in the late 1960s when Ron Miller and Laurence Knight began the second American Vernian group, the Dakkar Grotto, publishing two issues of a journal entitled *Dakkar*, after Captain Nemo's original Indian name.

The aims of the NAJVS built upon the Confederacy's achievements and some renderings of Verne's untranslated stories undertaken by AJVS. These had been led by Willis E. Hurd, who in 1944 retired as Chief of the Weather Bureau's Marine Section after a long government career.[98] Willis E. Hurd had published an article in 1936 recounting

98. This account of Hurd and the AJVS in indebted to the work of Stephen Michaluk, Jr. in a chapter of *The Jules Verne Encyclopedia* (Lanham, MD: Scarecrow Press, 1996), 23-31.

his discovery that most of Verne's novels available in English had received many different translations, under widely divergent titles.[99] Reading Hurd's pioneering analysis, a network of enthusiasts formed, becoming the AJVS in 1940, and endured into the mid-1950s.[100] While globally the time was not auspicious, the two years from 1940 to 1942 also saw the first books in English about Verne.[101]

A native of New Hampshire, Hurd had become interested in Verne at an early age, becoming so enthralled with *Vingt Mille Lieues sous les mers* (*Twenty Thousand Leagues under the Seas*, 1870) that he memorized entire passages to savor its phrases and incidents. This youthful enthusiasm allowed Hurd to write to his idol during the author's lifetime, and a facsimile of Verne's reply is included below, as contemporaneously translated for Hurd by Miss Georgia Wilcox (the original letter has been lost).

> Amiens, Aug. 1, '97
> Dear Sir:
>
> There is no use in asking if this little word in response to your letter will reach you, and in what New port you live, but I will write you just the same, and recommend to you the new romance, *Le Sphinx des Glaces* [*The Sphinx of Ice*, 1897], the first volume of which has just appeared. I have used for a foundation a romance of Edgar Poe, and I have dedicated this work to the

---

Steve and I coauthored the book, and we were among those who began, during the late 1980s, contacts among Vernians that would eventually bring about the formation of the NAJVS.

99. *Hobbies* was a magazine published in Chicago for a wide range of collectors. "A Collector and his Jules Verne" appeared on pages 88 through 89 in the August 1936 issue.

100. "Jules Verne Society Formed," *New York Times*, May 22, 1940, p. 21.

101. The AJVS had mixed reactions to these developments in Verne scholarship in the 1940s. Both James Iraldi and Nathan Bengis wrote reviews castigating Kenneth Allott's 1940 biography. Bengis's review was published in *Dime Novel Round-Up*, Vol. 14, No. 159 (December 1945), 1-3, and reprinted in Dakkar II, July 1968, pp. 55-56. They condemned Allott's reliance on the often inaccurate 1928 account, *Jules Verne, sa vie, son œuvre*, by Marguerite Allotte de La Fuÿe, as well as Allott's own errors in discussing the Extraordinary Journeys. Allott's absorption in 19th century literary trends, Iraldi noted, did not aid in elucidating Verne's works, and overlooked much of Verne's impact upon modern scientific achievements. By contrast, Bengis concentrated on George Waltz's 1943 book, *Jules Verne, the Biography of an Imagination*, praising Waltz, despite the volume's brevity, for a far more well-rounded approach to the author's life and books.

memory of your great poet, and also to my friends in America.
I think I may count you among them, and I am,
Your very devoted,

Jules Verne[102]

Hurd became interested in authoring English versions of some of Verne's last, untranslated stories. He had the goal of gathering every different Verne translation ever published. Unfortunately, most of Hurd's manuscripts were lost during the settlement of his estate and the acquisition of his collection by the Rare Book and Special Collections Division of the Library of Congress. However, a letter mentioning translating Verne's *Le Village Aerien* (*The Aerial Village*, 1901), in which Hurd gives it the title *The Village in the Treetops*, a title later also used by the I. O. Evans translation in the Fitzroy Edition of Jules Verne, may indicate that Evans and others benefitted from Hurd's efforts.[103] He noted that he had typed into English several of the short stories in the as-yet untranslated *Hier et Demain* (*Yesterday and Tomorrow*, 1910).

Hurd was not alone in the AJVS in leaving a legacy. Iraldi's collection was sold to Indiana University's Lilly Library. He also made two first translations, but in draft form rather than final product—an abridgement of "Edgard Poe and His Works," and "A propos of the

102. Copy of a letter from Jules Verne to Willis E. Hurd, contemporaneously translated for Hurd by Miss Georgia Wilcox, Newport, N.H., August, 1897. The original letter and the envelope in which it came were both written in Verne's own hand, as previously mentioned in *F.Mail* (issue of July, 1944) and other publications Hurd was associated with. Throughout the months of searching for the lost Hurd papers there was an ever present fear that this letter from Verne to Hurd was destroyed as an unfortunate consequence of the problems in closing out Hurd's Estate. However, in May of 1968 the letter was sold at auction for $120. It was described as: "With original holograph postmarked envelope. Two pieces. Remarkable literary letter, revealing Verne's interest in Poe, an interest which is reflected in Verne's writings. Very slightly soiled, otherwise in fine condition, accompanied by a full translation." The survival of this small letter allows a slight ray of hope that Hurd's other papers may have been salvaged. Unfortunately, the New York auction house where the letter was sold has changed location, and records for a sale of so long ago, for such a small item, seem to have been purged.

103. The copy of *Le Village Aerien*, which Hurd acquired from Iraldi, and now in the Library of Congress Rare Books collection, provides a clue as to the nature of Hurd's work: "This is a very distinguished volume in my collection of Verniana since its pages are those that I translated into American manuscript after my retirement from the Government Service at the end of May, 1944."

Balloon '*Le Géant*'" (the latter appearing in a new translation in this volume).[104]

The most concrete evidence of Hurd's activity in translation is provided by a unique special edition of Verne's short story "Gil Braltar." "Gil Braltar" first appeared in France with the 1887 volume, *Le Chemin de France*, but was left out when the book was translated and published the following year by Sampson Low as *The Flight to France*. The story is based on the famous Barbary apes who live high atop Gibraltar; according to legend, as long as they remain on the Rock, so too will the British. The unusual AJVS edition came into being in 1938 through a cooperative effort involving Ernest DeGay (a printer and native of France who died in Virginia in 1942), William Walling, and Hurd.[105] "Gil Braltar" was translated into English by DeGay, edited and arranged onto typed sheets by Hurd, and handbound by Walling into two copies, one for Walling, and the other for Hurd.[106] The last typewritten page of this little book displayed a literal translation of the letter Hurd received from Jules Verne in August of 1897. The volume was examined at the Library of Congress in their Hurd collection, and transcribed and published here for the first time.[107]

104. The first published English translation of the Poe article, and still the most comprehensive, was by I. O. Evans under the title of "The Leader of the Cult of the Unusual" in 1978 in *The Edgar Allan Poe Scrapbook*, edited by Peter Haining, published by the New English Library in England and Schocken Books in America.

105. William E. Walling's lifelong interest in Verne extended over 57 years by this point; he was a retired mail carrier and died in 1947. "Verne Group Has Member in the City," Minneapolis newspaper article (unidentified clipping) from May or June of 1940, provided courtesy of Mr. Eldred I. Walling of South Haven, Minnesota, William E. Walling's nephew, from the Walling Family Album.

106. The Library of Congress, Rare Books and Special Collections Division, Inscription page from Gil Braltar.

107. Hitherto, the only known translation was by I.O. Evans, first published in *Fantasy and Science Fiction* (*Magazine of Fantasy and Science Fiction* in England), in the July 1958 issue, reprinted in *The Best from Fantasy and Science Fiction*, 8th Series, in 1959, and included in Evans's edited *Yesterday and Tomorrow* as one of the stories he added to the Fitzroy edition of the anthology.

GIBRALTAR[108]

by Jules Verne

Translated by Ernest H. DeGay
Edited by Willis E. Hurd
Bound and designed by William E. Walling
1938

Introduction

Among the short fantastic stories written by the French master of extraordinary romances and simpler tales of quaint, amusing, and dramatic adventure, "Gibraltar" may well be classed as one of his most fantastic, not even excluding the whimsy of "Dr. Ox." The motif of "Gibraltar" is an attack by Barbary apes, which for centuries have dwelt in the higher fastnesses of the Rock of Gibraltar, upon the English garrison stationed at the fortress.

No one knows how the original apes came to the point of Spain. Tradition has it that they crossed from Africa, when a tongue of land connected the Rook, anciently known as Calpe, with Cape Spartel on the coast of Morocco. According to another legend, they immigrated to Europe through one of the natural tunnels said once to have existed beneath the Straight. More probably, they were introduced by the Moors or the Romans. However that may have been, Gibraltar is the only spot in Europe inhabited by apes in the natural state within historical times.

It is not known if this story has ever before been translated into English. In the original French it appears at the end of the romantic tale of the Franco-Prussian War—*Le Chemin de France*—written by Jules Verne in 1887 and published in the same year by the Paris House of Hetzel, from which were issued those splendid volumes, profusely illustrated, of "The Voyages Extraordinary."

108. While Hurd uses this geographical title, Verne's had been "Gil Braltar," used by I.O. Evans in his translation.

If the reader finds a quite apparent anachronism in one incident in the story, due to no fault in the translation, it is because the editor made no attempt to iron out an inconsistency in the incident which begins with the entry of the mad leader of the apes into the room of General Mac Kackmale.

Grateful acknowledgment is due to my good friend Ernest H. DeGay for making the original translation into English sense, in the preparation of which some delightful hours were spent by us together. Sincere appreciation is also due to William E. Walling—a fellow collector of the works of Jules Verne in original and translated texts—who generously offered to bind these sheets for me that I might thus add another, and unique, volume to my collection. My part in the result may be best seen in the textual style found in the following pages and in the arrangement of the text into final copied form. The pleasant efforts of the three of us form one of the most fascinating of adventurings as a Vernephile.

Willis E. Hurd
Arlington, VA
July 4, 1938

Chapter I

The Wildman and His Apes

There were at least 700 or 800 of them over there. They were of middle height, robust and agile, and so supple that they were capable of making prodigious leaps. They disported idly in the last rays of the setting sun ere it went down behind the mountains; which appeared uneven and serrated across the bay to the westward. The reddish orb soon disappeared, and darkness began to fall over the middle of the valley framed by the distant sierras of the Sonora and the Ronda, and the desolate land of the Cuervo.

Suddenly the troop mobilized, as its chief appeared on the back of an emaciated donkey standing silhouetted against the crest of the mountain. From the post of the soldiers on the extreme summit of the enormous rock, nothing could be seen of what was transpiring under the trees.

The chief, with lips puckered, uttered two intensely sharp whistles.

The whistles were instantly repeated in unison by the members of the queer troop.

Their chief was a peculiar being of great stature, clad in the skin of a monkey with the fur on the outside. His head was covered with a mop of bristly hair; his face was rough with a stubbly beard; his feet were naked and as horny on the soles as the hoof of a horse.

He dismounted from his donkey and, raising his right arm, pointed toward the smaller group on the mountain. Each one of the troop about him repeated the gesture like a marionette mechanically, but with military precision. He lowered his arm and they all lowered theirs. He stooped toward the ground and they bent over likewise. He picked up a stick and brandished it; they followed suit and swung their sticks in a similar manner. This whirling of the sticks is what is known as the "covered rose."

Then the chief of the band turned and, plunging into the herbage, began crawling under the trees. The troop followed him closely.

In less than ten minutes the mountain pathways, which had long been guttered by the rains, were being worn smooth by the silent passage of these hairy beings on the march.

A quarter of an hour later the chief came to a halt; his followers stopped likewise as though fixed, in position. Some 200 meters below them appeared the city, crouched beside the dark roadstead. Along the now darkened brow of the hill above them a great number of star-like lights confused the outlines of the group of houses, the villas, and the forts. Out beyond the lighted buildings were the warships, and the wet spiles glistening on the calm surface of the waters. Further, beyond Europa Point, the lighthouse projected its luminous beams out upon the Strait.

At this moment a burst of shot was heard. It was the First Gun Fire from one of the shore batteries. It. was followed by the rumble of drums and the shrill whistle of numerous fifes.

It was the hour of retreat—the hour for the return to the homes. No stranger was allowed after that to remain in the city, unless under personal escort of an officer of the garrison. All carriages were ordered inside the city before the closing of the gates. Every quarter hour the patrol was engaged in rounding up the belated ones and the sots. Then all was quiet.

General Mac Kackmale could now sleep in peace on both his ears.

It appeared that England had nothing to fear this night for her Rock of Gibraltar.

The garrison at Gibraltar from Verne's *Mathias Sandorf* (1885)

Chapter II

The Rock

We all know about this formidable Rock, 425 meters high, and situated on a huge base 145 meters wide and 4300 meters long. In appearance it is like an enormous crouching lion, with the head toward Spain and the tail dipping into the sea; its front showing the teeth—700 cannon planted at the embrasures. They are old teeth, to be sure, but they can bite hard upon sufficient provocation. England is solidly entrenched there, the same as at Perim, Aden, Malta, Poulo-Pinang, and Hong Kong. Some day the Rock, after the mechanics have done their work, will be a turning fortress.

Meanwhile, Gibraltar can assure the United Kingdom of an incontestable domination over the 18 kilometers of the Strait lying open between the Pillars of Hercules—Abyla and Calpe—where lie the profoundest depths of the Mediterranean.

Have the Spaniards renounced ownership of this piece of their peninsula? Yes, without doubt, as it appears to be untakable by land or by sea.

If there was a single person who had any idea of conquering this Rock, he was the chief of the band. We may even say of this strange being that he was a fool, as he had named himself Gibraltar, a title that in his mind foretold for him a patriotic conquest. His brain had never resisted the idea, and by all rights he should have been placed in an asylum. His troop knew him well, but until his appearance that evening, they had known nothing of his whereabouts during the past ten or more years. Perhaps he had been around the world? No, for in reality he had never left his patrimonial domain, but had dwelt as a troglodyte in the deep woods and in the caves, but mostly at the bottom of the inaccessible grotto of San Miguel. This grotto, it is still said, connects with the sea. They had believed him dead, but he still lived, yet like a madman deprived of all human reason and obedient only to the instincts of the animals such as those he led.

Chapter III

The Invasion

General Mac Kackmale slept well on his two ears, both of which were abnormally long. His arms were similarly out of normal proportion; his eyes were round, but deeply sunken under his shaggy eyebrows; and his scowling face was half hidden by a rough beard. With his projecting chin, his apelike manners and his extraordinary ugliness, even this great English general appeared like a real ape. He was a good soldier, nevertheless, despite his grotesque shape.

Yes, he slept in his comfortable habitation on Main Street, that thoroughfare that twisted through the city from the seaport to the gate of the Alameda. Perhaps he was dreaming that England would take Egypt, Turkey, Holland, Afghanistan, the Sudan, the country of the Boers—in a word, all points of the globe, at her convenience. And all this at a time when there was sudden risk of losing Gibraltar.

The door to his room opening with a bang.

"What is it?" demanded General Mac Kackmale, sitting straight up in bed.

"General," responded an orderly, as he burst into the room, "the city is being invaded!"

"By the Spaniards?"

"We do not know, but we think so."

"Would they dare!" cried the general furiously.

Then, without further speech or delay, he bounded from the bed, threw off the tight-fitting nightcap from his head, pulled on his trousers, drew on his coat, settled down into his boots, donned his military hat, buckled on his sword, and then asked:

"What is that noise I hear?"

"It is the sound of rocks rolling down in an avalanche upon the city."

"The little devils are numberless!"

"They must be," replied the orderly.

"Have all the bandits of the coast united in a plot to force the city—the contrabandists of the Ronda, the fisher men of San Roque, and the swarms of refugees in the villages?"

"I fear so, General."

"Has the Governor been informed?"

"No! It is impossible to join him at his villa on Europa Point. The gates are occupied and the streets are full of assailants!"

"And the fortifications at the seaport?" questioned Mac Kackmale.

"There is no way clear to get there. The artillerymen must have been shut into the fort."

"How many men have you?"

"About 20, General, of the Third Regiment, who have eluded the foe."

"By Saint Dunstan!" roared Mac Kackmale. "Gibraltar taken from England by those vendors of oranges! That shall not be! No, that shall not be!"

At this moment a strange being entered the doorway to his room and leaped upon the General's shoulders.

« Rendez-vous! » s'écria-t-il. (Page 216.)

"Surrender!" cried a coarse voice.

Chapter IV

General Mac Kackmale's Coup

"SURRENDER!" CRIED a coarse voice which had in it more of a roar than a human tone.

Several soldiers, now coming swiftly behind the orderly, were preparing to leap upon the invader, whom they recognized in the light of the room.

"Gibraltar!" they cried.

It was in fact that hidalgo concerning whom little had been known for a long time—the wildman of the Grotto of San Miguel.

"Will you surrender?" he shrieked again.

"Never!" cried General Mac Kackmale, struggling violently.

Suddenly, at this moment, when the soldiers had surrounded and seized him, Gibraltar uttered a long, shrill cry.

Hardly had the sound been uttered than the yard and the house itself became filled with an invading horde.

Can we believe it? They were the apes; they were the monkeys, for a fact. Had they come to retake from the English the Rock of which they were the original inhabitants; the mountain they had occupied long before the Spaniards; long before Cromwell dreamed of the conquest of Great Britain? Yes, it appeared so, and they were to be feared owing to their numbers, these monkeys without tails, with whom the garrison had long lived harmoniously upon the condition that they be allowed to prowl without hindrance. These beings, intelligent and daring, the soldiers had not cared to interfere with, lest they return after some unlucky visit, to take vengeance. This had sometimes occurred, in the rolling of enormous rocks down upon the city!

And now these apes were the soldiers of a madman—a fool as wild as they. This Gibraltar they had known, during the period of his lonely existence as a monkeyish William Tell, had concentrated his loneliness upon the idea of driving the strangers off the Spanish territory.

What a shame for the United Kingdom, if this lot should succeed! The English, victorious over the Hindus, the Abyssinians, the Tasmanians, the Australians, the Hottentots, and so many others—defeated by mere apes!

Should such a catastrophe occur, General Mac Kackmale could do no less than to blow off his own head. Who could survive so unparalleled a disgrace!

However, before the apes, called by the whistle of their chief, could invade the room, despite their agility, several of the soldiers had thrown themselves upon Gibraltar, after dragging him from the general's back. The madman had resisted with extraordinary power, and it was not without considerable effort that they had managed to conquer him. His borrowed skin had been torn from him during the struggle, and in a moment he sat nearly naked in the corner, so tied and gagged that he was without movement or speech. Shortly afterward, General Mac Kackmale emerged from his house, resolved to conquer, or to die according to military law.

But the danger had not, meanwhile, lessened outside. Undoubtedly a few soldiers had succeeded in coming together at the seaport and were then marching toward the general's house. Several shots were heard on Main Street and at the place of commerce. Nevertheless, the number of apes was so great that the garrison of Gibraltar appeared to be nearly on the point of surrendering. And then, provided the Spaniards would unite with the apes, the forts would be abandoned by the English; the batteries would be deserted; and, the fortifications would be without defenders. In such a dire event the English, who had made the Rock impregnable, would never be able to recover it.

Suddenly, however, everything was changed!

Unbelievable as it appeared, there, in the torch-lighted yard of the general, the apes were seen retreating. At the head of the band was their chief, flourishing his stick. Behind him, imitating his every movement of arms and legs, followed his motley crew, apparently thinking of nothing else than their present astounding actions.

Could Gibraltar have loosed himself from his bonds and escaped from the room in which he had been heavily guarded? It could no longer be doubted. But where was he now going? Was he on his way to Europa Point—on to the village of the Governor to fight him and demand his surrender, as he had previously done to the general?

No! The fool and his band descended Main Street. Then, having opened the gate to Alameda, all took an oblique path through the park and began reclimbing the slopes of the mountain!

An hour later there remained in the city only one of the invaders of Gibraltar.

What, then, had happened?

It was soon made known, when General Mac Kackmale appeared alone on the edge of the park.

It was he who had taken the place of the mad fool and had led the retreat of the band, after dressing himself in the skin of the prisoner. The brave warrior's resemblance to a quadrumanous beast was such

Tous remontèrent les pentes de la montagne. (Page 219.)

All climbed back again to the mountain.

that the apes mistook him for one of themselves. So he had only to come forth and entertain his followers. It was a simple idea, but that of a genius, which soon brought him the reward of the Cross of St. George.

As for Gibraltar, the United Kingdom gave the fool as a specimen to Mr. Barnum, who thereby made his fortune by traveling with him through the principal cities of the Old and New Worlds. Barnum rather broadly hinted that it was not the wildman of San Miguel that he had on exhibit, but the doughty General Mac Kackmale himself.

However, the adventure was a lesson to the government of Her Most Gracious Majesty, for it was realized that, although the Rock could not be taken by men, it was still at the mercy of monkeys. Therefore England very practically decided to send to this fortress thereafter only the most ill-favored of her generals, so that, if becomes necessary, the apes could again be deceived.

This action most certainly would assure forever her possession of Gibraltar.

"THE HUMBUG"

"**Gil Braltar" was only one** of a number of Verne tales dealing with evolution, as it was becoming understood during Verne's lifetime. Human kinship with the ape deeply fascinated Verne, in novels, short stories, and a play, becoming a recurring theme in his writing over more than fifty years. His Catholicism guided him one way, but he was also influenced by his study of the scientific journals of the day for story ideas.

The concept appeared as early as 1858, in *Monsieur de Chimpanzé* (*Mr. Chimpanzee*), a one act operetta written by Verne with Michel Carré, with music by Aristide Hignard.[109] This humorous play clearly foreshadowed Verne's "Voyages Extraordinaires" ("Extraordinary Journeys"), although the treatment of humans, apes, and evolution is placed in the framework of a musical comedy, with the unwelcome suitor of a scientist's daughter entering the savant's household by adopting a simian disguise. However, doubt is cast on scientific knowledge when the professor is unable to distinguish between man and beast. Most startling is the chronology; Verne's staging predates the November 24, 1859 publication of Charles Darwin's *On the Origin of Species by Means of Natural Selection, or the Preservation of Favoured Races in the Struggle for Life*, and in France, Darwin's ideas were not popularized and seriously discussed until 1871. A few years later, in

109. A translation and critical commentary is included in the Palik Series volume, *Mr. Chimp & Other Plays* (Albany, GA: BearManor, 2011), 75-104.

Like Verne's play *Voyage à travers l'impossible* (*Journey Through the Impossible*, 1882, published by the North American Jules Verne Society through Prometheus in 2003), *Mr. Chimpanzee* was considered lost for more than a century. At last, in 1978, both plays were discovered at the Archives nationales de Paris, in the archive of the Censorship Office of the Third French Republic. *Monsieur de Chimpanzé* was published in the *Bulletin de la Société Jules Verne*, no. 57 (1981). The music, however, is still lost.

the 1867 revision of *Voyage au centre de la Terre* (*Journey to the Center of the Earth*, 1864), Verne added a dream-like episode showing the discovery of a giant prehistoric man herding a herd of mastodons.

In "Gil Braltar," given above, both Gil Braltar and Mac Kackmale are introduced with an animalistic description, noting that the general is a bit of a monkey, although nonetheless an excellent soldier. Shortly after writing "Gil Braltar," Verne treated evolution in a more whimsical manner. Using the style of Swift's *Gulliver's Travels* (1726), Verne's *Aventures de la famille Raton* (*Adventures of the Rat Family*, 1891) is both a children's fairy tale and a parody as a close-knit family of rats is magically transformed into various forms of life, moving up and down the evolutionary ladder.[110] Their amusing incarnations include various lower forms, from mollusks to birds, finally making a metamorphosis into humankind.

Verne's treatment of evolution, however, could be far from humorous. The novel *Le Village aérien* (*The Aerial Village*, 1901) depicts a race of ape-men, although Verne disingenuously announced that the book should not be interpreted as an endorsement of Darwin, and discreetly chose the formula of a jungle adventure. The survivors of a lost safari find their surroundings ever more primitive, until they reach the city of a missing link between human and ape, the Waggdis, a tribe living in families and organized community amidst a giant forest. They evidence what Verne suggests is the uniquely human trait, religion, in which they are led by their own version of Gil Braltar / Mac Kackmale: Dr. Johausen, a European who, in attempting to study the Waggdis, has gone mad.

The most important presentation of evolution in Verne's writing, for American readers, was in the short story, "Le Humbug" ("The Humbug"), set entirely in the state of New York, and only published posthumously in 1910 in *Hier et demain* (*Yesterday and Tomorrow*). Probably because editors feared its unflattering portrayal of Americans, "The Humbug" was never translated in English until nearly a century after Verne's death, in the 1990s, and it still remains all but unknown to the readers in the nation for whom it inherently holds the most interest.[111]

110. *Adventures of the Rat Family* did not appear in English translation until a special critical edition with the original color engravings, translated by Evelyn Copeland, with an afterword by Brian Taves, published by Oxford University Press in 1993.

111. In translating the bulk of *Hier et demain* as *Yesterday and Tomorrow* (Wesport, CT: Asssociated Booksellers, 1965), I.O. Evans eliminatd both *Adventures of the Rat Family* and "The Humbug," labeling them unworthy, with no more justification than his subjective dislike of both stories. To make up for their absence, Evans had to re-arrange

Sketch of Verne and his family of Rats during their incarnation of fish, as drawn by Volker Dehs, reproduced by permission of the artist.

The United States fascinated him above all other countries, and the sincerity of Verne's interest is demonstrated by the fact that he had already used this country as a setting for stories even before he had gained a reputation in this country through translations. Indeed, Verne made his only journey to the United States in 1867, at a time when he was unknown here, although his books were popular in France.[112]

An apparent relation of the giant prehistoric man in *Journey to the Center of the Earth* is purportedly uncovered in "The Humbug," depicting a huckster, Meade Augustus Hopkins, who claims to have unearthed the ancient bones of a man some 120 feet tall. "The Humbug" is structured along a comparison between the old and new world, offering a French tourist as the first-person narrator, giving Verne the opportunity to directly highlight the contrasts between France and the United States he observes. These include the different roles of women, the role of slavery, and above all, American materialism. When two people are crushed to death in the rush to hear Hopkins's lecture on his fake discovery, their funerals become merely one more avenue for his advertising. Finally, Verne debunks American pride through his repeated, derisive echoes of Hopkins's own self-description as a "free citizen of the United States of America."

During Jules Verne's brief, intense visit to the United States, an unintended stopover may have served as the inspiration for "The Humbug." After arriving in New York City, Jules, traveling with his brother Paul, embarked on a paddle steamer up the Hudson, akin to the trip described in "The Humbug."[113] A thick fog delayed arrival in Albany, forcing the brothers to catch a train in the afternoon instead of the morning. This gave them time to explore the state capitol, and to visit the State Cabinet, precursor to the state museum established in 1870. Verne had probably heard about the Cohoes Mastodon, discovered not far away the previous autumn; the skeleton was remarkable for its condition, and was the second best preserved of its kind found at the time—and remains prominently displayed to this

much of the anthology's contents. Both *Adventures of the Rat Family* and "The Humbug" share in common the theme of evolution.

112. For a full account of Verne's American trip, see the appendix in the Palik Series volume, *The Castles of California* (Albany, GA: BearManor Fiction, 2016), 204-229.

113. Verne's general trip was fictionalized in *Une Ville flottante* (*A Floating City*, 1871), but while the same trip clearly inspired "The Humbug," Jules Verne made no attempt to publish "The Humbug."

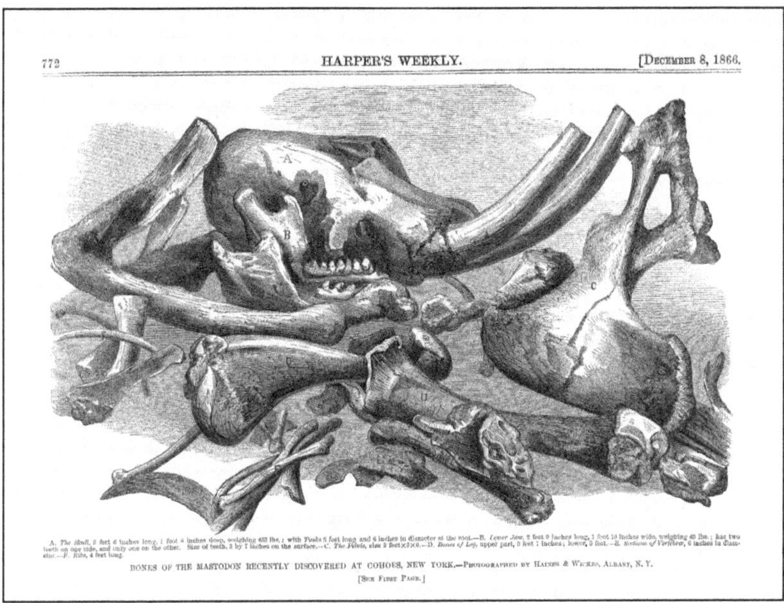

The Cohoes Mastodon, as Verne saw it in Albany; from *Harper's Weekly*, December 8, 1866.

day. However, at the time Verne saw it, the bones were piled in an apparent jumble, akin to the display Hopkins will offer of his discovery in "The Humbug."[114]

Subsequent accounts in the international press likely enriched the memory. The name, Meade Augustus Hopkins, may have derived from two individuals. Among those excavating the first mastodon skeleton had been Charles Wilson Peale (1741-1827), who painted numerous scenes of the diggings and prehistoric bones, and it may have been an intentional homage that Verne originally planned to name his humbug Charles Vincent ---- (the rest of the name has been crossed out and is no longer legible). However, if that was indeed the source of the name Verne first considered, his decision to change it is most understandable. Peale was one of the era's true renaissance men, equally at home in science, the arts, and politics. He was also a man with sufficiently advanced and eclectic views to be regarded as an American eccentric; for instance, he believed that man indeed

114. A sketch appeared in the December 8, 1866 issue of *Harper's Weekly*, one of the most widely-circulated journals of the time.

had a relationship to the monkeys. Realizing that the odd, enormous bones that had been given to him as curiosities would attract crowds, Peale opened a natural history museum in Philadelphia. The first mastodon skeleton ever assembled, whose excavation Peale had been closely involved with, was the centerpiece, and on one occasion a dinner was given beneath its massive frame. The carnival-like atmosphere of the museum, personally managed by Peale and his children, included motion-picture style light projections, such as Verne describes in "The Humbug," and was open in various places for over two decades.

Peale was not alone; Henry Augustus Ward (1834-1906) was a collector for natural history museums around the world, who had a successful business located in upstate New York from 1862, selling and exhibiting prehistoric bones, and his family said he met Verne in Paris while studying geology as he became known among specialists in the natural sciences. There is certainly a close resemblance between the final name Verne gave his character in "The Humbug," Meade Augustus Hopkins, and Henry Augustus Ward. Ward's grandson, Roswell Ward, became a member of the American Jules Verne Society, and indicated his grandfather's influence; Ward's Natural Science Establishment, Inc., continues to this day.

Henry Augustus Ward was in frequent contact with another individual, in Albany, whom Verne may have met or heard of during his visit. Professor James Hall (1811-1898), first head of the State Cabinet of Natural History and Geology, was as famous for his bellicose, quarrelsome, and egotistical manner as he was for his scientific expertise. He was New York's state geologist for fifty years, and was one of the most renowned national figures in the field. In 1869, he achieved unwelcome notoriety for believing in the "Cardiff Giant," the most direct inspiration for "The Humbug."

The Giant was one of the most extraordinarily successful hoaxes even in a time when they were common, in an America obsessed with ideas of the world before the Biblical flood. The creator of the Cardiff Giant, George Hull, was an atheist, a student of Darwin, and an inveterate rogue. Meeting a revivalist preacher in 1866, Hull argued with his fundamentalist beliefs and literal interpretation even the line, "There were giants in the earth in those days" (Genesis 6:4). To test the limits of gullibility, Hull decided to create his own giant, a naked

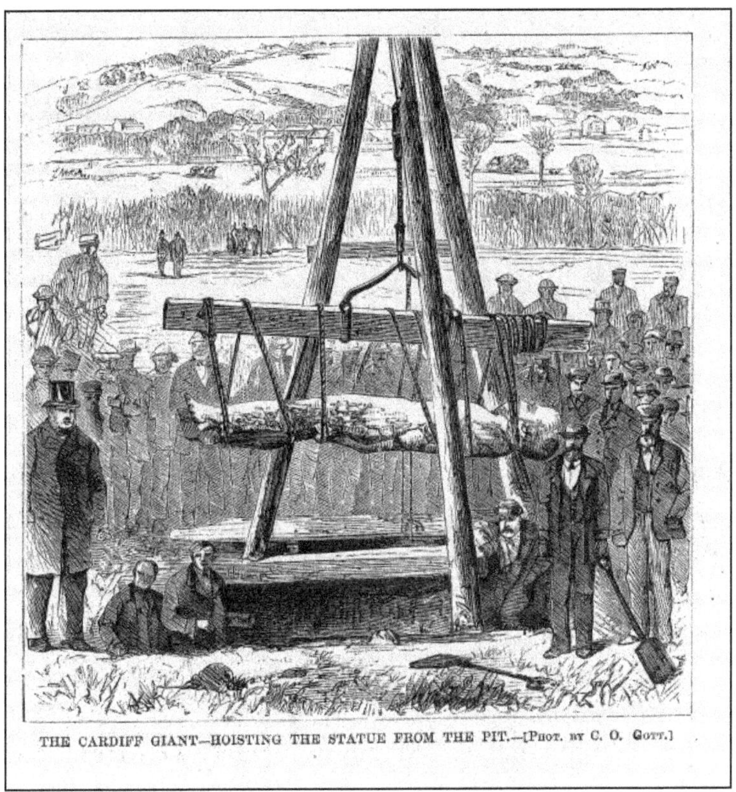
THE CARDIFF GIANT—HOISTING THE STATUE FROM THE PIT.—[PHOT. BY C. O. GOTT.]

Uncovering the Cardiff Giant, as depicted in the December 4, 1869 issue of *Harper's Weekly*.

man of gypsum, modeled after himself but ten and a half feet tall, and weighing 3,000 pounds. It was artificially aged and then buried under cover of night in a relative's farm in an area of Cardiff supposed to be rich in fossils and ancient relics.

Nearly a year later, according to plan, men digging a well on October 16, 1869 found the stone man. It immediately began to attract spectators and a large tent was placed over the excavation. The surroundings soon came to resemble a county fair, with the nearby roads crowded with buggies and 50 cents charged per person for admission; on one Sunday 2,600 tickets were sold. Bolstering the inclination of the faithful toward acceptance were statements that neighboring Indians told stories of giants who formerly roamed the Onondaga hills. Even those who realized that the supposed petrifaction that created the giant was impossible argued that instead it could be a

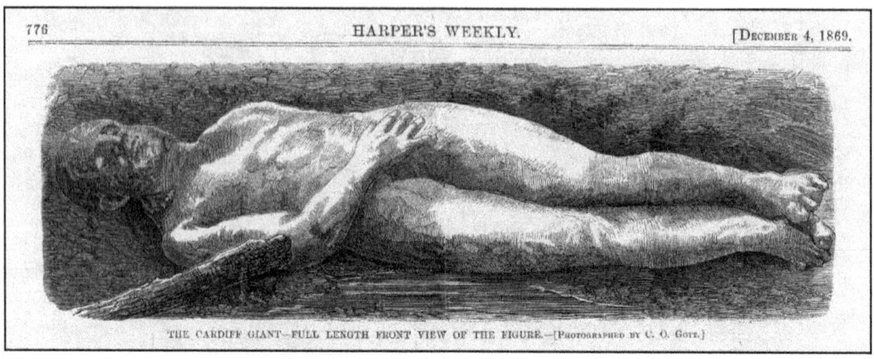

Sketch of the Cardiff Giant itself, from the same issue of *Harper's Weekly.*

statue.[115] Within a week of the giant being unearthed, Hull sold most of his rights, knowing the fraud would soon be recognized.

Yet one more model for the Humbug, P.T. Barnum (1810-1891), became involved with the Cardiff Giant. When it was taken to Albany for exhibition even as the truth about it was becoming known, Barnum, unable to buy it, simply had an imitation made. Soon the two giants were exhibited within a few blocks of each other in New York City, Barnum proclaiming that he had indeed bought the real one and what was being displayed by its owners was the fake. (A similar episode occurred at the end of the last chapter in "Gil Braltar;" P.T. Barnum exhibits the captured hermit who led the apes, not as the man who nearly conquered Gibraltar, but as the Englishman who saved the fort! [116]) Barnum's flair for showmanship prevailed, and it was at this point

115. Barbara Franco, *The Cardiff Giant: A Hundred Year Old Hoax*, (Cooperstown, NY: The New York State Historical Association, 1990), n.p.

116. Barnum's introduction into the narrative "Gil Braltar" should be no surprise; Verne himself included a brief passage in *De la Terre à la Lune* (*From the Earth to the Moon*, 1865), as Barnum tries to enlist Ardan in his traveling show, a prospect the Frenchman quickly declines. The 1874 Edward Roth translation of Verne's moon novels embellished Verne's two-sentence reference into a whole paragraph. Assuming Verne's authorial voice, Roth suggests an entire new possibility for Barnum, along with a political sentiment. "The Prince of Humbugs was withal so genial, so plausible, so insinuating that Ardan, finding it impossible to get angry with him, promised to accede to his demands on the return of the party from the Moon, if he, Barnum, would only join them in the trip. But the genial showman, knowing what a serious loss even his temporary absence would prove to the progress of the great Temperance movement in the United States, hastily declined the offer with many thanks, and started that very night for New York." Few if any Verne translators have exceeded Roth's audacity. This citation of Roth is from *From the Earth to the Moon, All Around the Moon: Space Novels by Jules Verne, Translated by Edward Roth* (New York: Dover, 1962), 164.

that the owner of the actual Giant, David Hannum, uttered the words later attributed to Barnum, "There's a sucker born every minute." When a lawsuit suit between the rival owners of the Giant loomed, Hull stepped forward to reveal the entire hoax.

In "The Humbug," Verne merges together the separate incidents that brought to light the Cohoes Mastodon and the Cardiff Giant and the hokum surrounding them.[117] Hopkins is a loud, pugnacious American who combines aspects of P.T. Barnum, James Hall, and George Hull. Ward and Peale may have rounded out the inspiration, despite their more commendable reputation. This was a time when men of science were also often commercial promoters, who served to promote the idea of evolution in a manner that facilitated Verne's treatment with both seriousness and satire.

117. Terrasse, Pierre, "A 'Humbug', Humbug et demi," *Bulletin de la Société Jules Verne*, No 71 (1984), 150–152; Olivier Dumas, "Afterword: 'The Humbug' in its Original Version," Translated from the French by Edward Baxter, in Brian Taves and Stephen Michaluk, Jr., *The Jules Verne Encyclopedia* (Lanham, MD: Scarecrow Press, 1996), 86; Brian Taves, "Jules Verne et le Humbug préhistorique," Translated into French by Jean-Marc Billaud, *Revue Jules Verne*, No. 15 (June 2003), 23-29.

LE HUMBUG (¹)
Roux

THE HUMBUG: THE AMERICAN WAY OF LIFE[118]

by Jules Verne with Michel Verne

Translated by Edward Baxter

On a March day in 1863 I boarded the steamboat *Kentucky*, which travels back and forth between New York and Albany.

Traffic between the two cities was heavy at that time of year, because of the large volume of merchandise arriving in the country. Not that there was anything unusual about this, for New York merchants are always in contact, through their agents, with even the most remote regions. This enables them to distribute goods imported from the Old World at the same time as they export domestic products to other countries.

My departure for Albany gave me a new opportunity to admire the hustle and bustle of New York. Travelers came flocking from all directions, some berating the porters who carried their numerous pieces of luggage, others walking alone, like true English tourists whose entire wardrobe can fit into one inconspicuous bag. Everyone was in a hurry to reserve passage on the steamboat, to which they all seemed to attribute the peculiarly American quality of elasticity.

The bell had already rung twice, spreading panic among the late-comers. The wharf groaned under the weight of the latest arrivals (who are inevitably the very ones whose journey cannot be postponed without the most dire consequences). Eventually, however, the whole crowd was accommodated. Parcels were piled up and travelers were

118. This translation of "The Humbug" is from its first published version, in 1910, for the collection *Hier et Demain* (*Yesterday and Tomorrow*), organized and partly rewritten by Jules's son, Michel. According to Olivier Dumas, Michel performed a useful task in replacing the semicolons by periods, by lightening the style and by modernizing the scientific terms. He corrected inaccuracies, and more importantly, the Biblical allusions. He also eliminated a sentence that would not be very pleasant for Americans: "Madame, you have the grace and the graciousness of primitive peoples," and censored a racist comment. However, Michel Verne also deleted an entire passage in which the narrator misses his absent friend, who had remained behind with a charming woman. This friend, Edouard Vaillant, was originally called Edouard Garnier, the name of an actual former friend of Verne. Dumas, "Afterword: 'The Humbug' in its Original Version," in Taves and Michaluk, 87.

packed together. The fire roared in the boiler tubes and the deck of the *Kentucky* shuddered. With a great effort, the sun broke through the morning mist, giving a little warmth to the March atmosphere, which makes you turn up your coat collar, shove your hands into your pockets, and say to yourself, "It will be fine tomorrow."

Since I was not traveling on business, since my portmanteau was big enough to hold everything I needed and a bit more, and since my mind was not preoccupied by speculative ventures or by business deals, I let my thoughts wander idly, trusting to chance, that intimate friend of tourists, to find me some source of pleasure and entertainment on the way. Suddenly I noticed Mrs. Melvil, standing not a dozen feet from me, smiling her most charming smile.

"Why madam!" I exclaimed, as surprised as I was pleased, "are you really braving the dangers and the crowds of a Hudson River steamboat?"

"I most certainly am, my dear sir," she replied, offering me her hand after the English fashion. "But I'm not alone. My trusty old Arsinoe is with me."

She pointed to her faithful black serving woman, who was sitting on a bale of wool and gazing at her affectionately. The word "affectionately" deserves to be underlined here, for no one but a black servant is capable of such a look.

"Even with all the help and support that Arsinoe can give you, madam," I said, "I consider myself fortunate to have the privilege of being your protector during this journey."

"If that's a privilege," she answered with a laugh, "I'll be under no obligation to you. But what brings you here? You told us you were not going to Albany for several days yet. Why didn't you tell us yesterday that you were leaving?"

"Because yesterday I didn't know that myself. I decided to go to Albany only because the ship's bell woke me at six o'clock this morning. You see how little it takes to change the course of events. If I had slept until seven, I might have gone to Philadelphia! But what about yourself, madam? Last night you seemed to be the most sedentary woman in the whole world."

"Indeed I did! However, the person you see before you now is not Mrs. Melvil, but the chief clerk of the New York merchant and shipowner Henry Melvil, on her way to Albany to supervise the arrival of a shipment of goods. That must be too much for you to understand, living as you do in the over-civilized countries of the Old World! Since my husband couldn't leave New York this morning, I'm taking his place. And you can be sure that the books will be just as well kept and the calculations every bit as exact."

"I've decided not to let anything surprise me anymore," I exclaimed. "But if such a thing were to happen in France, if wives carried on their husbands' business, husbands would soon be doing their wives' business, playing the piano, cutting flowers, embroidering suspenders."

Mrs. Melvil laughed. "You're not very flattering to your fellow countrymen."

"On the contrary! I'm assuming that their wives embroider their suspenders for them."

The bell rang for the third time. The last passengers rushed onto the deck of the *Kentucky*, amid the shouts of the sailors, who were picking up long gaffs to push the ship off from the dock.

I offered Mrs. Melvil my arm and took her a little farther astern, where the crowd was less dense.

"I've given you some letters of recommendation for Albany," she began.

"So you have. And for the thousandth time, I thank you for them."

"Not at all. They're of no use to you now anyway, since they're addressed to my father, and I'm on my way to see him now. Please allow me to introduce you personally and to offer you hospitality on his behalf."

"I see I was right in trusting to luck to make my journey a charming one. And yet we both came close to not leaving at all."

"Why do you say that?"

"There was one passenger, a man as eccentric as only the English could be before the discovery of America, who wanted to reserve the *Kentucky* exclusively for himself."

"Does he come from the East Indies, then, with a retinue of elephants and dancing girls?"

"Good heavens, no! I heard the argument that took place when the captain refused his request, and I saw no elephants taking part in the conversation. He's an odd individual, but he struck me as just a very jovial stout man who likes to have his own way. But look! There he is now. I recognize him. Do you see that man running up onto the dock, waving his arms around and shouting? He's going to delay us again, just when the boat is getting under way."

A man of average height, with an enormous head adorned by bushy, flaming red sideburns, and wearing a long double-collared frock coat and a broad-brimmed cowboy hat, puffed and panted his way onto the dock, just as the gang-plank had been taken down. He was gesticulating, stamping his feet, and shouting, completely oblivious to the laughter of the crowd that had gathered around him.

« Et mes colis, mille diables !.. » (Page 143.)

"Damn it to hell! What about my luggage?"

"Ahoy! *Kentucky*! Damn it to hell! I've booked my passage and paid my fare, and still I'm being left behind! Damn it to hell, captain, I'll hold you responsible before the High Judge and all his court."

"If people are late, that's their tough luck!" shouted the captain, climbing up onto one of the paddle-boxes. "We've got a deadline to meet, and the tide is starting to ebb."

"Damn it to hell!" bellowed the stout man again. "I'll sue you for a hundred thousand dollars at least. Bobby," he shouted, turning to one of the blacks who were with him, "look after the baggage and run back to the hotel, while Dacopa gets a boat going to catch up with that damned *Kentucky*."

"You're wasting your time," cried the captain, and he gave the order to cast off the last hawser.

"Get a move on, Dacopa!" said the stout man, to encourage his black servant.

Dacopa seized the rope just as the steamboat was dragging it past, and deftly slipped the end of it through one of the rings attached to the dock. At the same time, the persistent traveler jumped into a rowboat, to the applause of the bystanders, and, with a few strokes of the scull, drew abreast of the boarding ladder of the *Kentucky*. He leaped onto the deck, rushed up to the captain, and started shouting at him with the noise of ten men and the speed of twenty fishwives. The captain, unable to get a word in edgewise, and seeing that the traveler appeared to be possessed, decided not to worry about him. He picked up his megaphone and headed towards the engine. He was about to give the signal to leave when the stout man turned on him and shouted, "Damn it to hell! What about my luggage?"

"Well, what about your luggage?" retorted the captain. "Could that by any chance be it that I see coming now?"

Murmurs of protest arose from the passengers, irritated by this new delay.

"Why are you all blaming me?" demanded the newcomer, still undaunted. "Am I not a free citizen of the United States of America? My name is Augustus Hopkins, and if that doesn't mean anything to you…"

I have no idea whether this name carried any weight with most of the passengers, but in any case, the captain of the *Kentucky* was obliged to tie up again and take on the luggage of Augustus Hopkins, free citizen of the United States of America.

"I must admit," I remarked to Mrs. Melvil, "that is certainly no ordinary man."

"But not as extraordinary as his luggage," she replied, pointing to two carts that were approaching the dock, carrying two huge packing cases twenty feet high, wrapped in oilclcoth and tied up with a formidable network of cords and knots. The top and bottom were clearly identified in red letters, and the word "fragile," in characters a foot high, struck terror for a hundred yards around into the heart of everyone who was responsible for them in any way.

Despite the grumbling occasioned by the appearance of these enormous bundles, Mr. Hopkins used his hands, his feet, his head, and his lungs to such good effect that eventually, after much effort and considerable delay, they were deposited on the deck. At last the *Kentucky* was able to cast off, and she headed up the Hudson among the many different kinds of vessels that were plying its waters.

Augustus Hopkins's two black servants had taken up their positions near their master's packing cases, which were the object of intense curiosity on the part of the passengers. Most of them were crowding around, giving free rein to every weird fantasy that a foreigner's imagination is capable of. Even Mrs. Melvil seemed totally engrossed. I, on the other hand, as a true Frenchman, did my best to feign complete indifference.

"What a strange man you are!" said Mrs. Melvil. "You're not the least bit concerned about what may be in those huge structures. I'm consumed with curiosity."

"I must admit," I replied, "that all this holds very little interest for me. When I saw those two enormous objects arrive, I began making wild guesses as to what was in them. Perhaps there's a five-story house with all its occupants, I said to myself, or perhaps there's nothing at all. Neither of these two bizarre extremes would surprise me very much. However, madam, if you wish, I'll see what I can find out and I'll let you know."

"Thank you," she replied, "and while you're gone I'll go over these invoices."

I left my unusual traveling companion adding up figures with the speed of one of those Bank of New York cashiers who are said to be able to calculate the sum of a column of numbers at a single glance.

Still thinking about this singular business arrangement and about the double existence led by these charming American women, I made my way towards the man who had set every tongue wagging and on whom every eye was focused.

Although the forward part of the ship, and even the Hudson River itself, were completely hidden from view by the two packing cases, the helmsman steered the steamboat with absolute confidence and a complete lack of concern for obstacles. And yet, the obstacles must have been numerous, for no river in the world, not even the Thames, was ever traveled by more vessels than the rivers of the United States. At a time when France had no more than twelve or thirteen thousand ships and when England's total had reached forty thousand, the United States already had sixty thousand, including two thousand steamships plying the seven seas. These figures give some idea of the extent of commercial traffic, and also explain why accidents occur so frequently on American rivers.

It is true that these disasters, or collisions, or shipwrecks, are of little importance in the eyes of the intrepid traders. In fact, they even create new business for the insurance companies, whose profits would be very small if their premiums were not so exorbitant. Pound for pound, and volume for volume, a man is of less value and importance in America than a sack of charcoal or a bale of coffee.

The Americans may be right, but I would have given all the coal mines and coffee plantations in the world for my little French *demoiselle*. As we sailed full steam ahead through the obstacle course, I had some misgivings as to how our journey would end.

Augustus Hopkins apparently did not share my fears. He must have been one of those people who would jump off the rails or sink rather than miss out on a business deal. In any case, he paid not the slightest attention to the beauty of the landscape along the banks of the Hudson, as they disappeared rapidly behind us. For him, the distance between New York, our point of departure, and Albany, our destination, meant eighteen hours of lost time and nothing more. The delightful resorts on the bank, the villages clustered together in such a picturesque way, the wooded areas scattered here and there throughout the countryside like flowers tossed at the feet of a *prima donna*, the swift flow of the magnificent river, the first signs of spring—nothing could tear this man away from the speculations that preoccupied him. He paced back and forth from one end of the *Kentucky* to the other, muttering bits of sentences. Sometimes he would suddenly sit down

Les eaux du fleuve apparurent. (Page 103.)

The departure up the Hudson, from *Une Ville flottante* (*A Floating City*, 1970).

on a bale of goods and pull from one of his many pockets a large, thick wallet, stuffed with a thousand pieces of paper. I even saw him take this collection of every kind of red tape known to commercial bureaucracy and spread it meticulously out on the deck. He thumbed anxiously through an enormous pile of correspondence, unfolded letters mailed from every country and stamped with the postmarks of every post office in the world, and pored over the closely-written lines with a relentless determination that did not fail to attract attention.

I could see that it would be impossible to learn anything by speaking to this man. Several other curious passengers had tried in vain to strike up a conversation with the two blacks standing guard over the mysterious packing cases. The two sons of Africa maintained an absolute silence, quite out of keeping with their customary loquacity.

I was about to go back and give Mrs. Melvil my personal impressions when I found myself in a group of passengers standing around the captain of the *Kentucky*, who was holding forth on the subject of Augustus Hopkins.

"I tell you," he was saying, "this crack-pot keeps doing one stupid thing after another. This is the tenth time he's traveled up the Hudson from New York to Albany, it's the tenth time he's managed to arrive late, and the tenth time he's brought this kind of luggage with him. Where does it all go? I don't know. The rumor is that Mr. Hopkins is setting up some big enterprise near Albany and that people from all over the world are shipping merchandise to him without identifying it."

"He must be one of the principal agents of the East India Company," said one of the bystanders, "and he's coming here to open an office in America."

"He's more likely a millionaire who owns some goldfields in California," said another. "There must be some equipment involved…"

"Or maybe there's something up for tender that we can bid on," suggested a third. "The *New York Herald* has been hinting at that these past few days."

"Pretty soon," interjected a fourth, "we'll see shares offered for sale in a new company with a capital of five million dollars. I'll be the first in. I'll buy a hundred shares at a thousand dollars each."

"Why should you be the first?" someone else interrupted. "Maybe you've already been promised something in this deal. I'm ready to put up the money for two hundred shares, and more if I have to."

"That's if there are any left to buy after I'm finished," shouted someone on the far side of the crowd, whose face I could not make out. "What we're talking about here is obviously a plan to build a railroad from Albany to San Francisco, and the banker who got the contract to build it is my best friend."

"A railroad! What are you talking about? This Mr. Hopkins is going to lay an electric cable across Lake Ontario, and these big packing cases contain miles and miles of insulated wire."

"Across Lake Ontario? That will bring in a fortune," exclaimed several traders who had all caught the speculation fever. "Mr. Hopkins will have to tell us what kind of business he's in. I'm buying the first shares!..."

"For me, Mr. Hopkins, please!"

"No, for me!

"No, for me! I'll pay you a thousand-dollar bonus!..."

The offers and replies flew back and forth as the confusion increased. Although gambling on the stock market holds no fascination for me, I followed the group of speculators as they made their way towards the hero of the *Kentucky*. Hopkins was soon surrounded by a tightly packed crowd, on whom he did not even deign to cast a glance. Long rows of figures, and numbers followed by impressive series of zeroes, were spreading across his vast wallet.

Arithmetical calculations—addition, subtraction, multiplication, and division—flowed from his pencil. The millions streamed like a torrent from his lips. He seemed to be in the grip of a mathematical frenzy. Silence fell around him, despite the storms created in every American's brain by an obsession with business.

After an operation of tremendous proportions, during which he broke his pencil three times, Mr. Augustus Hopkins succeeded in tracing out a majestic figure 1, which commanded an army of eight magnificent zeroes. Finally, he pronounced these three ritual words:

"One hundred million!"

He quickly folded his papers, stuffed them back into his impressive wallet, and pulled from his pocket a watch adorned with a double row of fine pearls.

"Nine o'clock! It's nine o'clock already!" he shouted. "Is this damned boat not moving at all? The captain! Where's the captain?"

With this, Hopkins abruptly pushed his way through the three rows of people surrounding him. His glance fell on the captain, who was leaning over the engine room hatchway, giving orders to the engineer.

"You know, captain," he said pompously, "a ten-minute delay could cost me an important business deal."

"Who are you talking to about delay?" retorted the captain, taken aback by this criticism. "You were the one responsible for it."

"If you hadn't been so stubborn as to leave me behind," replied Hopkins, his voice rising in pitch, "you wouldn't have wasted valuable time—especially valuable at this time of year."

"And if you and your packing cases had managed to get here on time," the captain shot back in an irritated voice, "we could have left on the rising tide, and we'd be a good three miles farther on than we are now."

"That's no concern of mine. I've got to be at the Washington Hotel in Albany before midnight. If it's any later, I might as well not have left New York at all. I'm warning you! If that happens, I'll sue you and your company for damages."

"Just leave me alone!" shouted the captain, who was beginning to lose his temper.

"I certainly will not, not as long as you're so spineless and cheap with your fuel that you could make me lose a fortune ten times over. Come on, stokers, let's have four or five good shovelfuls of coal in your furnaces. And you there, engineer, just keep your foot on the safety valve of your boiler until we make up the time we've lost."

He took out a purse with a few shiny dollars in it and tossed it down into the engine room.

The captain flew into a violent rage, but his fanatical passenger bellowed even louder and longer than he did. I thought it best to hurry away from the scene of battle, for I knew that Hopkins's advice to the engineer, to make the ship go faster by holding down the safety valve and increasing the steam pressure, could very well cause the boiler to explode.

Needless to say, our traveling companions considered the advice very sound, and so I decided not to mention it to Mrs. Melvil. She would have laughed until she cried at my groundless fears.

When I rejoined her, she had finished her lengthy calculations, and the cares of business no longer furrowed her charming brow.

"You took leave of a businesswoman," she said, "and now you return to find a woman of the world, ready to listen to whatever you care to talk about—art, sentiment, poetry…"

"How can I talk about art, or dreams, or poetry, after what I've just seen and heard? I've caught the mercantile spirit, and all I can hear now is the jingling of dollars. I'm blinded by their glittering brilliance. To me, this beautiful river is now simply a route for moving merchandise. Its charming banks are just a highway for transporting goods. Those pretty little towns are nothing but a series of stores for selling sugar and cotton. I'm seriously thinking of building a dam

ET HOPKINS JETA DANS LA CHAMBRE DE LA MACHINE UNE BOURSE... (PAGE 151.)

He took out a purse with a few shiny dollars in it and tossed it down into the engine room.

across the Hudson and using the water to turn a coffee mill."

"Well now, except for the coffee mill, that's not a bad idea!"

"And why, may I ask, should I not have ideas, just like anyone else?"

Mrs. Melvil laughed. "So you've really been bitten by the industry bug, have you?"

"Listen, and judge for yourself."

I told her about everything I had seen that day. She listened attentively to my account, as any intelligent American would have done, and then began to ponder over it. A Parisian woman would not have let me tell the half of it.

"Well, madam, what do you think of this Hopkins?"

"He could be an investment genius starting up a huge enterprise, or he could be nothing but a bear trainer from the latest Baltimore fair."

I burst out laughing and the conversation turned to other matters.

Our voyage ended with no further incident, except that Hopkins tried to move one of his huge packing cases, against the captain's advice, and nearly dumped it overboard. The ensuing discussion gave him another chance to hold forth on the importance of his business dealings and the value of his cargo. He lunched and dined like a man whose aim is not to take on nourishment, but to spend as much money as possible. By the time we reached our destination, every passenger on board was singing the praises of this extraordinary character.

The *Kentucky* docked at Albany before the fatal hour of midnight. I gave Mrs. Melvil my arm, thinking myself fortunate to have disembarked safe and sound, while Mr. Augustus Hopkins, with considerable ado, got his two marvelous packing cases unloaded and made his triumphal entry into the Washington Hotel, followed by a large crowd.

Mr. Francis Wilson, Mrs. Melvil's father, greeted me with a grace and openness that made his hospitality all the more welcome. Nothing would do but that I must accept an attractive blue room in that honorable businessman's home. I cannot call it a hotel, for although it was an immense house, its spacious apartments were overshadowed by the enormous stores, crammed with merchandise from all over the world. The business establishments of Le Havre and Bordeaux are only a faint imitation of this city, with its swarms of office workers, tradesmen, clerks, and laborers. Although the master of the house had many demands on his time, I was treated like a king. I had no need to ask, or even to wish for anything. And as if this were not enough, I was waited on by black servants, and for anyone who has enjoyed that experience, nothing else will do.

The name Albany had always struck me as a charming one, and the next day I went for a walk in that beautiful city. I found that it had all the activity of New York, the same bustle of business, the same wide variety of interests. The businessmen's thirst for profit, the zeal with which they work, their need to extract money by every means that industry or speculation can discover, does not have the same repulsive aspect in the traders of the New World as it sometimes produces in their overseas counterparts. They act with a certain grandeur that is quite compelling. It is easy to understand why these people need to earn money in such large amounts, because they spend it on the same scale.

The conversations over our luxuriously served meals, and during the evenings, began in a very general way, but soon turned to more specific topics. We chatted about the city, its points of interest, its theater. It seemed to me that Mr. Wilson was very well informed about these worldly amusements, but when we got around to discussing the eccentricities of particular cities, a topic that has aroused considerable interest in Europe, he proved to be American to the core.

"Are you referring," he asked me, "to our attitude to the famous Lola Montès?"

"Of course," I replied, "only the Americans could have taken the Countess of Lansfeld seriously."

"We took her seriously because she acted like a serious person. It's the same in business. When serious matters are treated lightly, we don't attach the slightest importance to them."

"You must have been shocked," said Mrs. Melvil facetiously, "to learn that Lola Montès spent some of her time here visiting girls' boarding schools."

"To tell the honest truth," I replied, "that did strike me as bizarre. She is a very charming dancer, but not exactly a role model for our young ladies to emulate."

"Our young ladies," retorted Mr. Wilson, "are brought up along more independent lines than yours are. When Lola Montès visited their boarding schools, it was neither the Parisian dancer nor the Bavarian Countess of Lansfeld who made her appearance there, but simply a famous and very attractive woman. The curious children who saw her were not harmed in the least by her visit. It was a holiday, a bit of fun and amusement. Now what's wrong with that?"

"What's wrong is that great artists are spoiled by these extraordinary ovations. When they come home after a tour in the United States, they're completely impossible."

"What have they got to complain about, then?" asked Mr. Wilson abruptly.

"Nothing at all," I replied. "But how could Jenny Lind feel honored by European hospitality when here she sees the pillars of society clinging to her carriage during public festivities? How can hospital openings, which her impresario arranges for her, compete with that?"

"Now you're beginning to sound jealous," quipped Mrs. Melvil. "You resent the fact that such an eminent artist has always refused to perform in Paris."

"Absolutely not, madam. And in any case I wouldn't advise her to come to Paris, because she would find a very different reception from the one you gave her here."

"That's your loss," said Mr. Wilson.

"Not as much our loss as hers, if you ask me."

Mrs. Melvil laughed. "Well," she said, "you do lose some hospitals, at least."

After a few more minutes of banter, Mr. Wilson said to me:

"If you're interested in exhibitions and sales, you've come at just the right time. The first tickets for Madame Sontag's concert are going to be auctioned off tomorrow."

"Auctioned? Just as if they were auctioning off a railroad?"

"Exactly. And the buyer who seems ready to make the highest bid so far is an ordinary hatter from right here in Albany."

"He must be a great music lover, is he?" I asked.

"Him? John Turner? He absolutely detests music. He thinks it's the most unpleasant sound in the world."

"What's he up to, then?"

"He wants to improve his public image. It's an advertising stunt. People will talk about him, not only here, but in every state in the Union, and not just in America, but in Europe as well. People will buy hats from him. He'll ship his junk out to the whole world."

"I can't believe it!"

"You'll see tomorrow, and if you need a hat..."

"I won't buy one of his. They must be appalling."

"Oho!" said Mrs. Melvil, getting to her feet. "Listen to the fanatical Parisian!"

I took leave of my hosts and went off to ponder over these American wonders.

The next day I went to the auction of the famous first ticket to Madame Sontag's concert, with a serious look on my face that would have done justice to the most phlegmatic American in the whole country. All eyes were on John Turner the hatter, the hero of this new craze. His friends came up to him and complimented him as if he were the savior of his country's independence. Others were egging him on and laying bets on his chances of winning the honor, as against the chances of his competitors.

The bidding started. Soon the price of the first ticket had risen from four dollars to two hundred and then three hundred dollars. John Turner was sure his would be the winning bid. He never tried to outbid his competitors by more than a small amount, for an increase of a single dollar would have been enough to make him the lucky purchaser, and he was prepared to spend a thousand, if he had to, to acquire the precious ticket. The bidding rose rapidly to three, four, five, and six hundred dollars. The crowd's excitement rose to a fever pitch, and roars of approval greeted every reckless bidder. The first ticket took on an astronomical price in everyone's mind, and scarcely any thought was given to the others. It was, in short, a question of honor.

Suddenly, a longer cheer than usual rang out, as the hatter shouted in a stentorian voice:

"One thousand dollars!"

"A thousand dollars," repeated the auctioneer. "Any advance on a thousand? A thousand dollars for the first ticket to the concert. Do I hear another bid?"

In the silences between outbursts, a low rustling sound spread through the hall. In spite of myself, I was impressed. Turner, sure that victory was in his grasp, looked smugly at his admirers. He held in his hand a sheaf of bank notes from one of the six hundred banks that do business in the United States, and waved them about, shouting again:

"One thousand dollars!"

Then a new voice rang out. "Three thousand dollars!" I turned my head to see who had spoken.

"Hurrah!" shouted the excited crowd.

"Three thousand dollars," repeated the auctioneer.

In the face of such competition the hatter turned and fled with his head down, completely unnoticed in the excitement.

"Sold for three thousand dollars!" cried the auctioneer.

Up strode Augustus Hopkins in person, the free citizen of the United States of America. Obviously he was well on the way to becoming a famous man. All he needed now was to have anthems composed in his honor.

I escaped from the hall with difficulty and just barely managed to push my way through the ten thousand people standing at the door to greet the triumphant purchaser. As soon as he came in sight he was greeted with shouts of praise. For the second time since the previous evening, he was taken back to the Washington Hotel by the exuberant populace. He greeted them with a mixture of modesty and arrogance, and that evening, in response to popular demand, he made an appearance on the hotel balcony, to the applause of the delirious crowd.

"Well, what do you make of it?" Mr. Wilson asked me later, when I told him about the day's events.

"As a Frenchman and a Parisian, I think Madame Sontag will be kind enough to let me have a ticket without paying fifteen thousand francs for it."

"I think so too," said Mr. Wilson, "but if this Mr. Hopkins is clever enough, the three thousand dollars he spent may bring him a hundred thousand. A man as eccentric as that can make millions just by stooping down and picking them up."

"What kind of man can this Hopkins be?" wondered Mrs. Melvil. At that very moment, the entire city of Albany was asking the same question.

That question was answered by the events of the next few days. The steamboat from New York unloaded more packing cases, even more extraordinary in shape and size than the first. One of them, which looked like a house, carelessly (or carefully, depending on one's point of view) got stuck in a narrow street on the outskirts of Albany. It could go no farther, and there it had to stay, motionless as a block of stone. During the next twenty-four hours the entire population of

TOUTE LA POPULATION SE PORTA SUR LE THÉATRE DE L'ÉVÉNEMENT... (PAGE 160.)

At that very moment, the entire city of Albany was asking the same question.

the town arrived on the scene. Hopkins took advantage of the crowds to make fiery speeches, lashing out at the ignorant architects and even suggesting that he would have the plan of the streets changed to make way for his freight.

The feasible solutions were soon reduced to two. The packing case, whose contents were the object of widespread curiosity, could be broken open, or the tumbledown house impeding its progress could be demolished. The curious citizens of Albany would no doubt have preferred the first option, but Hopkins vetoed it. Still, something had to be done. Traffic in the neighborhood was blocked and the police were threatening to get a court order to have the packing case broken up. Hopkins solved the problem by buying the offending house and having it torn down.

This last little touch, as might have been expected, brought him to the pinnacle of his renown. His name and story made the rounds of every living room in town. He was the topic of conversation at the *Independent Club* and the *Union Club*. In the Albany cafés, wagers were laid as to what this mysterious man was planning to do. The newspapers indulged in the wildest speculation, temporarily diverting public attention from the problems that had recently arisen between Cuba and the United States. I believe it even led to a duel between a merchant and one of the town's offiicials, and that Hopkins's backer emerged victorious on that occasion.

When Madame Sontag gave her concert, which I attended with much less fanfare than our hero did, his presence all but changed the entire purpose of the gathering.

Eventually the mystery was explained, and soon Augustus Hopkins stopped trying to conceal it. He was simply a businessman who had come to set up a kind of World's Fair just outside Albany. He was planning to operate independently one of those colossal undertakings which up until then had been the monopoly of governments.

He had bought for this purpose a vast tract of uncultivated land about ten miles from Albany, with nothing standing on it but the ruins of Fort William, which at one time protected English trading posts along the Canadian frontier. He was already in the process of hiring workmen to make a start on his gigantic projects. His immense packing cases no doubt contained tools and construction equipment.

As soon as this news reached the Albany stock market, it aroused an unusually keen interest among the traders. They all wanted an option to buy shares from the great entrepreneur. Although Hopkins gave vague replies to all their questions, an artificial market soon sprang up for these imaginary shares, and from then on the affair began to snowball.

"This man is a very clever speculator," Mr. Wilson remarked to me one day. "I don't know whether he's a millionaire or a beggar, because you'd have to be either Job or Rothschild to undertake such a venture, but he'll certainly make a huge fortune."

"I don't know what to believe any more, my dear Mr. Wilson. And I don't know which to admire more, a man with nerve enough to embark on such an enterprise, or a country that supports and promotes it, and asks nothing in return."

"That's the road to success, my dear sir."

"Or to ruin," I replied.

"Well," retorted Mr. Wilson, "let me tell you that in America, a bankruptcy makes everyone rich and ruins no one."

My only arguments against Mr. Wilson were the facts themselves, and so I waited impatiently for the outcome of all the maneuvering and publicity, which I found extremely interesting. I collected every tidbit of news about Augustus Hopkins's venture, and every day I read reports of it in the newspapers. The first group of workmen had left for the site and the ruins of Fort William were beginning to disappear. The only topic of conversation was these construction projects, and what their ultimate purpose might be. Suggestions poured in from all sides, from New York and Albany, Boston and Baltimore. "Musical instruments," "daguerreotype pictures," "abdominal supports," "centrifugal pumps," "square pianos" were some of the guesses vying for attention, and the American imagination was going full speed ahead. It was stated as a fact that a whole new town would spring up around the Exposition. It was rumored that Augustus Hopkins planned to found a city that would rival New Orleans, and to name it after himself. Next came the theory that this city (which would of course be fortified because of its proximity to the Canadian border) would shortly become the capital of the United States! And so on, and so on.

While these and many other exaggerated ideas were circulating through every brain, the hero of the movement had almost nothing to say. He paid regular visits to the Albany Stock Exchange, made inquiries about business matters, took note of recently arrived shipments, but remained tight-lipped about his own extensive plans. It was surprising that such a powerful man had put out no actual publicity. Perhaps he considered himself above using everyday methods of starting up an enterprise and intended to do it purely on his own merits.

Developments had reached this point when, one fine morning, the *New York Herald* carried the following item:

> "As everyone knows, work on the Albany World's Fair is progressing rapidly. By now the ruins of old Fort William have disappeared and foundations are being dug for splendid new buildings. There is widespread enthusiasm for the project. The other day a workman's pick turned up the remains of an enormous skeleton that had evidently lain buried there for thousands of years. We hasten to add that this discovery will in no way delay work on what will be the eighth wonder of the world, right here in the United States."

I paid no more attention to these few lines than to any of the countless brief news items that clutter up American newspapers. Little did I suspect the use that would be made of them later. As Augustus Hopkins told it, the new discovery took on an extraordinary importance. He was now as free with his speeches, stories, theories, and deductions about the unearthing of this prodigious skeleton as he had been reluctant before to explain the plans that lay behind his great undertaking. It seemed as if all his speculations and money-making schemes were wrapped up in that one newly discovered item.

The discovery had come about, apparently, in a miraculous fashion. For three days, excavations had been under way, on Hopkins's orders, aimed at reaching the other end of the gigantic fossil, but still without results. No one could tell how big it might eventually prove to be. It was Hopkins himself, while he was supervising the excavation of a deep hole about two hundred feet from the first one, who finally made out the end of the cyclopean carcass. The news immediately spread with lightning speed, and the discovery, unique in the annals of geology, became an event of world-wide significance.

The impressionable Americans, with their tendency to revise and exaggerate, soon spread the news around, adding to its importance to suit their own tastes. People wondered about the origin of these huge remains and about the significance of their presence in the hitherto undisturbed earth. The *Albany Institute* undertook a study on the topic.

I must admit that this question held more interest for me than the future splendors of the Palace of Industry or the eccentric speculations of the New World. I began watching for every little incident related to it. That was not hard to do, for the press served it up in every possible way. I was even fortunate enough to learn about it in detail from citizen Hopkins himself.

Since his arrival in Albany, this extraordinary man had been sought out by the high society of the city. In the United States, where the merchant class are the nobility, it was only natural that such a venturesome speculator should be received with the honors due to his rank. And so he was welcomed in clubs and at family teas with characteristic eagerness. I met him one evening in Mr. Wilson's living room. Naturally, there was no talk of anything but the topic of the day, and in any case, Mr. Hopkins did not wait to be asked about it. He gave us an interesting, thorough, scholarly, but witty description of the discovery, how it had come about, and what its unforeseeable consequences might be. At the same time, he hinted that he was considering how he might make a profit from it.

"But," he told us, "our work has had to stop for the moment, because I have already put up some of my new buildings between the first and last excavations, where the two extremities of the skeleton were uncovered."

"But are you sure," someone asked, "that the two ends of the animal are joined together under the unexplored area?"

"There isn't the slightest doubt about that," Hopkins assured his questioners. "Judging from the bone fragments we have dug up so far, the creature must be gigantic—much, much bigger than the famous mastodon that was discovered in the Ohio valley some time ago."

"Do you really think so?" exclaimed a Mr. Cornut, who was a naturalist of sorts, and "did" science in the same way as his fellow citizens did business.

"I'm sure of it," replied Hopkins. "The monster's structure shows that it obviously belonged to the order of pachyderms, for it possesses all the characteristics so well described by Mr. de Humboldt."

"It's really a shame," I interjected, "that the whole skeleton can't be dug up."

"And what's stopping us?" Cornut asked excitedly.

"Why… the buildings that have just been put up…"

I had hardly uttered these words, which seemed to me nothing more than plain common sense, when I found myself surrounded by a circle of disdainful smiles. To these worthy merchants, it seemed a very simple matter to tear everything down, even the largest of buildings, in order to unearth a creature that dated from the time of the flood. No one was surprised, therefore, when Hopkins announced that he had already given orders to that effect. Everyone congratulated him heartily, and opined that fortune was right in favoring bold and enterprising men. For myself, I offered him my warmest compliments and promised to be one of the first to come and see his marvelous discovery. I even offered to go to *Exhibition Park* (a term that was by now in the public domain), but he asked me to wait until the excavations had been completed, for it was still too soon to estimate how huge the fossil really was.

Four days later, the *New York Herald* published new details about the gigantic skeleton. The carcass was not, the writer declared superciliously, that of a mammoth, or a mastodon, or a megatherium, or a pterodactyl, or a plesiausaurus. The remains of all the above-mentioned creatures belong to the third geological era, or to the second at the very earliest, whereas the excavations that Hopkins was directing went right to the primal layers of the earth's crust, in which no fossil had ever been discovered before. This display of science (of which the American merchants understood very little) aroused considerable excitement. What other conclusion could be drawn but that this monster—since it was neither a mollusk, nor a pachyderm, nor a rodent, nor a ruminant, nor a carnivore, nor a sea mammal—was a man? And that this man was a giant more than forty meters tall? No one could now deny the existence of a race of titans older than *homo sapiens*. If this were true (and everyone agreed that it was), even the best established geological theories would have to be changed, for fossils had been found well below the diluvian deposits, indicating that they had been buried there before the flood.

The *New York Herald* article created a tremendous sensation. It was reprinted in full by every newspaper in the United States. This topic of conversation was soon the order of the day, and the most complicated scientific terms were being pronounced by the prettiest lips in the New World. Great discussions opened up, leading to deductions that were highly flattering to America, for it was here, rather than in Asia, that the cradle of humanity was to be found. In conventions and academies, it was clearly proven that America, which had been inhabited since the beginning of the world, had obviously been the starting point of a series of migrations. The honors of antiquity passed from the Old World to the New. Voluminous dissertations, inspired by patriotic ambition, were written on this very serious topic. Finally, a meeting of scientists, the minutes of which were published and commented on by every newspaper in the United States, proved beyond all shadow of doubt that the earthly Paradise, bounded by Pennsylvania, Virginia and Lake Erie, occupied at one time the territory that is now the state of Ohio.

I must confess that all this daydreaming fascinated me beyond measure. I pictured Adam and Eve in command of packs of ferocious beasts that actually existed in America, whereas on the banks of the Euphrates not the slightest trace of them is to be found. In my mind's eye, the tempting serpent took on the form of a boa constrictor or a rattlesnake. But what surprised me most was the slavish and uncritical credence given to this discovery. It never entered anyone's mind that this famous skeleton might be a fraud, a bluff, or as the Americans say, a humbug. Not one of these keen scientists thought of going to see with his own eyes the miracle that was causing such a commotion in his brain. I mentioned this to Mrs. Melvil.

"Why bother?" she said. "We'll see our precious monster when the time comes. Everyone knows what it looks like, because you can't go a mile anywhere in America without coming across a picture of it in one form or another. Some of the pictures show a lot of imagination, too."

That was indeed the true genius of the speculator. Augustus Hopkins had been very close-mouthed about his proposed Exhibition, but when it came to planting the idea of his miraculous skeleton in the minds of his fellow Americans, he used all the zeal, inventiveness, and imagination at his command. He could do whatever he wanted, because his eccentricities had already attracted the attention of the public.

Before long, walls throughout the city were covered with colored posters showing the monster in a wide variety of shapes and forms.

Hopkins used every kind of poster known to man, and in the most striking colors. He plastered them on walls, on dockside parapets, on tree trunks along public walkways. On some, the lines were printed diagonally, on others, the message was spelled out in broad brush strokes, which no passerby could possibly miss. On every street there were men walking up and down, wearing jackets and coats bearing pictures of the skeleton. In the evening, immense transparencies projected its black outline against a brilliantly lit background.

But Hopkins was not satisfied with such everyday American publicity methods. Posters and page four newspaper advertisements were not enough for him. He devised a course of studies in "skeletology," in which he quoted Cuvier, Blumenbach, Backland, Link, Stemberg, Brongniart, and a hundred other paleontologists. His courses were so well attended and so highly applauded that one day two people were crushed to death at the door.

Needless to say, Mr. Hopkins arranged magnificent funerals for them. The flags in the funeral procession displayed, once again, the ubiquitous outline of the currently fashionable fossil.

All these publicity stunts worked very well in and around the city of Albany, but now the important thing was to expand the campaign throughout the entire country. When Jenny Lind was making her debut in England, a Mr. Lumley offered to give the soap manufacturers free molds, depicting the portrait of the eminent *prima donna*. The offer was accepted and produced excellent results, since people were now using the famous singer's face to wash their hands. Hopkins employed a similar method. He contracted with cloth manufacturers to have them produce material for clothing that would appeal to the good taste of customers by displaying an illustration of his prehistoric creature. It was printed on the inside of hats, and even plates were decorated with the outline of the amazing phenomenon! And so on, and so on. It was impossible to escape it. You could not get dressed, put on a hat, or eat dinner, except in this interesting company.

All this high-pressure salesmanship had a tremendous effect. And so, when newspapers, drums, trumpets, and volleys of musket fire announced that the miracle would shortly be put on display for public admiration, a cheer went up on all sides. Preparations were begun for building an enormous hall, large enough to hold, as the advertisements put it, "not only the myriads of enthusiastic spectators,

DES TRANSPARENTS IMMENSES PROJETAIENT LE SQUELETTE. (Page 168.)

In the evening, immense transparencies projected its black outline against a brilliantly lit background.

but also the skeleton of one of those giants who, according to legend, attempted to climb up to heaven."

I had only a few more days to spend in Albany. I was bitterly disappointed at not being able extend my visit long enough to attend the opening of this unique spectacle, but since I did not want to leave without seeing something, at least, I made up my mind to pay a secret visit to Exhibition Park.

Setting out one morning with my gun on my shoulder, I walked north for about three hours without finding any information about my desired goal, but five or six miles farther on, as I was looking for the site of old Fort William, I reached my journey's end.

I was standing in the middle of an immense plain, one small part of which had been disturbed by some recent, but not extensive, excavations. A fairly large area was tightly sealed off by a wooden fence. I had no idea whether this fence marked out the site of the Exhibition, but that fact was confirmed for me by a beaver hunter whom I met in the neighborhood as he was on his way to the Canadian border.

"It's here all right," he said, "but I don't know what's going on, because just this morning I heard a lot of rifle shots."

I thanked him and continued my search.

I saw not the slightest trace of any work going on outdoors. The unbroken plain, to which gigantic construction works were supposed to bring life and movement, lay wrapped in total silence.

Since I could not satisfy my curiosity without getting inside the fence, I decided to walk around it and try to find a way in. I walked for a long time without seeing anything that resembled a door, and had decided, in my disappointment, to settle for a crack or a hole that I could put my eye to, when I noticed, at a corner of the fence, some boards and posts that had been knocked down.

I quickly scrambled into the enclosure, and found that the ground under my feet had been completely torn up. Huge pieces of rock lay scattered wherever the gunpowder blasts had deposited them. The area was dotted with little mounds of earth that looked like waves on an angry sea. Finally I came to the edge of a deep excavation, at the bottom of which lay a large quantity of bones.

There, before my eyes, was the object of all the fuss and advertising. There was certainly nothing unusual about what I saw. It was a heap of bone fragments of every kind, broken into a thousand pieces. On some, the breaks appeared to be fairly recent. I did not recognize any major human bones which, according to the dimensions that had been announced, would have had to be of a tremendous size. With the help of a little imagination, I could have believed that I was in a boneblack factory and nothing more.

Needless to say, I was still very confused. For a moment I thought I had been on a wild goose chase. Suddenly, on an embankment covered with footprints, I noticed a few drops of blood. I followed the trail of blood back to the opening, and there I found more bloodstains that I had not seen when I came in. My glance fell on a scrap of powder-blackened paper lying beside the blood stains. It had probably come from the wad of a firearm. Everything fitted in with what the beaver hunter had told me.

I picked up the piece of paper and painstakingly deciphered a few of the words scribbled on it. It was a bill for materials supplied to Mr. Augustus Hopkins by a certain Mr. Barckley. There was nothing to indicate the nature of the items supplied, but I found more scraps of paper scattered here and there, which provided the missing information. In spite of my disappointment, I had to laugh. I was indeed in the presence of the giant and its skeleton, but it was a skeleton made up of very heterogeneous parts, which since time immemorial had roamed the plains of Kentucky under such names as buffalo, heifer, cow, and bull. Mr. Barckley was an ordinary New York butcher who had delivered enormous quantities of bones to the famous Mr. Augustus Hopkins. Those fossils had certainly never piled Pelion on Ossa to scale Olympus! Their remains owed their presence there to the efforts of the illustrious scam artist, who had known all along that he would discover them by chance in the course of laying the foundations for a palace that would never exist!

I had reached that point in my reflections, and my hilarity (which might have been more sincere if I had not, like my hosts themselves, been the victim of this incredible humbug) when I heard shouts of joy coming from outside the fence.

Hurrying back to the opening, I saw Mr. Augustus Hopkins in person running up, rifle in hand, obviously very pleased about something. When I walked towards him, he did not seem at all perturbed at finding me on the scene of his exploits.

"Victory! Victory!" he shouted.

The two black servants, Bobby and Dacopa, followed him at a distance. Experience warned me to be on my guard, in case the

« Victoire!.. » cria-t-il. (Page 171.)

"Victory! Victory!" he shouted.

audacious master of mystery should decide to use me as a target.

"I'm in luck," he said, "I have a witness to what has just happened to me. You see before you a man returning from a tiger hunt."

"A tiger hunt!" I mimicked, determined not to believe a word of it.

"And a red tiger at that," he added, "also known as the cougar, renowned for its cruelty. As you can see, the damned thing got into my enclosure. It broke through these gates, which up until now have kept out the curious public, and smashed my wonderful skeleton into a million pieces. As soon as I saw that, I decided to track it down and kill it. I caught up with it in a thicket about three miles from here. When I looked at it, it stared back at me with its two savage eyes and jumped. But it never finished its leap, because I dropped it with a bullet just behind the shoulder. That was the first time I ever fired a gun, by God! It will be quite a trophy for me. I wouldn't sell it for a billion dollars!"

"Now the millions will start to come back," I thought to myself.

Just then the two black servants came up, dragging the carcass of an enormous red tiger, an animal that is almost unknown in this part of America. Its coat was of a solid tawny color, except for its ears and the tip of its tail, which were black. It made no difference to me whether Hopkins had killed it or whether it had been supplied to him already conveniently dead (or maybe even stuffed) by some Barckley or other. What struck me was the carefree and indifferent tone with which my speculator friend talked about his skeleton. And yet, this whole affair must have cost him more than a hundred thousand francs.

Not wanting to let him know that I had stumbled onto the secret of his mystery—he would have been perfectly capable of giving thanks to Providence for it—I simply said, "How are you going to get out of this fix?"

"What the devil do you mean by 'this fix'? No matter what I do now, I can't lose. A wild beast has destroyed the wonderful fossil that would have won the admiration of the entire world, because it was absolutely unique, but it has not destroyed my prestige or my influence. I still enjoy all the advantages of being famous."

"But what will you say to your enthusiastic and impatient public?" I asked in a serious tone.

"I'll tell them the truth, nothing but the truth."

"The truth!" I exclaimed, wondering what he meant by that word.

"Of course," he explained, as calmly as could be. "Isn't it true that the animal got into my enclosure? Isn't it true that it smashed up these wonderful bones that I went to such lengths to dig up? Isn't it true that I tracked it down and killed it?"

"Now there," I said to myself, "is a whole host of things that I wouldn't want to swear to."

"As for the public," he went on, "What more can they expect? Now they'll know all there is to know about the affair. I'll even get a reputation for bravery. In fact, I don't see anything that I won't be famous for."

"But what good will it do you to be famous?"

"If I play my cards right, I'll be rich. A man who is well known can get away with anything. He can hope, he can dare, he can undertake whatever he likes. If George Washington had decided to put two-headed calves on display, after the battle of Yorktown, it's obvious that he would have made a lot of money."

"Perhaps," I answered seriously.

"There's no doubt about it," retorted Augustus Hopkins. "My only problem is to decide what I should put on display."

"Yes," I said, "it's a difficult choice. The tenors are worn out, the dancers are past their prime, and what's left of their legs is priced out of reach. The Siamese twins have had their day, and the seals, despite the best efforts of the distinguished professors who are teaching them, still can't talk."

"I won't concern myself with spectacles like that. No matter how worn out, exhausted, dead, or speechless the seals, Siamese twins, dancers, and tenors may be, they are still too good for a man like me, because I'm worth so much just for myself. I think, my dear sir, that I will have the pleasure of seeing you in Paris."

"Do you expect to find some cheap object in Paris," I asked him, "and make it famous on the strength of your reputation?"

"Perhaps," he replied seriously. "If I come across a doorman's daughter who has never been accepted by the *Conservatoire*, I'll turn her into the greatest singer in the Western Hemisphere."

On that note, we took leave of each other and I returned to Albany. That same day, the awful news came out. It was generally assumed that Hopkins was ruined. Large subscriptions were taken up for his benefit. Everyone went to Exhibition Park to assess the extent of the disaster, and this too put a goodly number of dollars in the speculator's pocket. He got a ridiculously high price for the pelt of the cougar that had brought him to such a timely ruin and thereby saved his reputation as the most enterprising man in the New World. As for me, I went back to New York and from there to France, leaving the United States richer (without knowing it) by one more superb humbug. And I brought back with me this conclusion: that artists with no talent, singers with no voice, dancers without a leg, and jumpers without a rope would have a dismal future before them if Christopher Columbus had not discovered America.

Part V

Jules Verne's Mona Lisa

Translated and with an introduction and annotations by Kieran M. O'Driscoll

THE FACT THAT JULES VERNE penned, in his early twenties, this short romantic comedy featuring as its two central characters the famous Renaissance artist Leonardo da Vinci and his most celebrated and enigmatic of subjects, Mona Lisa—real-life historical personages interwoven into an imaginary love story—is evidence of the surprising differences between the themes of Verne's early writings for the theatre and the types of stories of adventure, scientific anticipation and education for which he would eventually become famous. In a manner similar to the other two plays by Jules Verne which I have previously translated for the Palik Series, *Les Châteaux en Californie ou Pierre qui roule n'amasse pas mousse* (*The Castles of California*, 1852) and *Un neveu d'Amérique ou Les Deux Frontignac* (*A Nephew from America*, 1873) this is a romantic comedy; but unlike those two earlier renderings, *Mona Lisa* was written by Verne in verse in its original French language, and was not set in Verne's contemporary nineteenth-century France but rather in early sixteenth-century Renaissance Italy, in the workshop of da Vinci in Florence.[119]

In translating this play into English, I have respected the line breaks of the original and have occasionally achieved some matching

119. *The Castles of California* and *A Nephew from America* are in the Palik series volume collectively titled *Castles of California* (Albany, GA: BearManor Media, 2016).

rhyme, though this translation, in general, does not have rhyming lines to the same extent as its antecedent text. If I were to have provided the same amount of matching rhyme in my rendering, as exists in the source text, I would have had to distort original meaning to an unacceptable degree, whereas my priority as a translator is to achieve complete semantic fidelity to the original.

In this introduction to my translation of *Mona Lisa,* I shall firstly provide some historical background to this world-famous work of art, its mysterious subject and its creator, before going on, secondly, to discuss the plot, themes and characters of the play. Jules Verne took, as his inspiration and starting point for this piece, the world-famous masterpiece by the Italian Renaissance artist Leonardo da Vinci, known in Italian as *La Gioconda,* because the lady who is the subject of the portrait was the wife of the Italian nobleman Francisco del Giocondo, Lisa Gherardini; it is known in French as *La Joconde,* and in English as *Mona Lisa*. The portrait in question is a half-length portrait which has been acclaimed as "the best known, the most visited, the most written about, the most sung about, the most parodied work of art in the world."[120]

It was painted in oil on a white Lombardy poplar panel, and is believed to have been painted between 1503 and 1506, so that the action of Verne's play can be situated in 1506, though da Vinci may have continued working on this painting as late as 1517. Indeed, in this play, Verne portrays da Vinci as being a perfectionist who finds it difficult to complete to his satisfaction the various enterprises upon which he embarks, and is here depicted as finding it difficult to complete both *Mona Lisa* and *The Last Supper,* two of his most celebrated masterpieces. For instance, he is never completely happy with the expression he achieves for Mona Lisa in the former painting, nor has he yet found suitable models for Christ and Judas in the latter painting.

The painting of *La Gioconda* was later acquired by King Francis I of France and is now the property of the French Republic, where it has been on permanent display at the Louvre Museum in Paris since 1797, apart from occasional displays in other locations and attempts at theft. Over the past few centuries, this painting has been the subject of on-going study and fascination, due principally to the enigmatic expression of its mysterious subject and its novel artistic qualities.

120. <https://en.wikipedia.org/wiki/Mona_Lisa>, accessed April 22, 2016.

The title of the painting, *Mona Lisa,* comes from a description by Renaissance art historian Giorgio Vasari, who wrote "Leonardo undertook to paint, for Francesco del Giocondo, the portrait of Mona Lisa, his wife." *Mona* in Italian is a polite form of address originating as *ma donna,* similar to *my lady* in English, which became *Madonna*, and its contraction *mona*. Mona Lisa is commonly spelled in modern Italian as *Monna Lisa*, and indeed in the French original play by Verne, the spelling *Monna* is used, though in this translation the more usual English spelling has been used to translate the title of the play as *Mona Lisa*.

The model, Lisa del Giocondo, was a member of the Gherardini family of Florence and Tuscany, married to wealthy Florentine silk merchant Francesco del Giocondo. It is believed that the portrait was commissioned for their new home, and to celebrate the birth of their second son, Andrea. The Italian name for the painting, *La Gioconda*, means "jocund" ("happy" or "jovial"), or literally, "the jocund one," which is a pun on the feminine form of Lisa's married surname, Giocondo, and in French, the title *La Joconde* has the same sense of joviality or happiness.

Leonardo da Vinci began painting the *Mona Lisa* in about 1503 or 1504 in Florence, Italy, though there is some dispute over the exact dates. Da Vinci's contemporary, the art historian Vasari, said that da Vinci, "after he had lingered over it for four years … left it unfinished." Later in his life, da Vinci is said to have regretted "never having completed a single work," and indeed, this perfectionistic flaw in his character forms a central part of the comedy of Verne's play, which also makes much of the fact that he is having difficulty completing not only his portrait of *Mona Lisa*, but also that of *The Last Supper*.

In 1516, da Vinci was invited by King François I to work near the King's castle in Amboise, France. It is thought that he took the *Mona Lisa* with him and continued to work on it after his move to France, so that he probably continued refining and polishing the work until 1516 or 1517; indeed, as Verne depicts in this play, the Giocondo family, despite their commissioning of it and their waiting three years for it to be finished, never ultimately took delivery of it. Thus does Verne interweave much historical fact into his fictional romantic scenario of love between Mona Lisa and da Vinci.

From an aesthetic point of view, it has been noted that the Mona Lisa strongly resembles many Renaissance-era depictions of the Virgin Mary, who was at that time seen as an ideal of womanhood; indeed, in this play, da Vinci recognizes that his love for Mona Lisa represents love for an ideal woman, an ideal which can never be attained in reality. Mona Lisa's right hand is seen resting on her left, a gesture chosen by da Vinci to depict her as a virtuous woman and faithful wife; indeed, in this play, despite her being tempted, Mona Lisa ultimately does remain faithful to her husband when she realizes that a relationship with da Vinci is impossible. As regards the appearance of the real life Mona Lisa, it is considered that da Vinci probably painted his model faithfully, as her beauty is not regarded as being among the best, either by 16th century or 21st century standards. The painting was also one of the first portraits to depict the subject seated in front of an imaginary landscape; behind Mona Lisa, a vast landscape recedes to icy mountains, with little hint of other human presence.

The Background and Story of the Play

The source text from which this play has been translated into English is a 1995 publication by Editions de l'Herne, Paris, in which the play is published together with a short autobiographical text also written by Jules Verne, entitled "Souvenirs d'enfance et de Jeunesse." ("Recollections of My Childhood and of My Youth," 1910).[121] The 1995 publication formed part of a collection entitled *Confidences*, a collection of texts by French authors which aimed to provide formerly little-known writings by otherwise celebrated authors such as Verne himself, to a wider, more general readership, given that the selected texts in question had originally been written for, and published on a limited basis for, a restricted, special-interest, minority readership. The texts within this collection are, like this play, generally short, but many of them present their authors in a new, hitherto-unsuspected light, as is the case with this and other plays written by Jules Verne in his twenties, at the start of his writing career, and prior to his embarking on his epic life's work, the Voyages

121. Jules Verne, *Monna Lisa* (Paris: Editions de l'Herne, 1995). A new translation of "Souvenirs d'enfance et de jeunesse" is found at the beginning of this volume.

Extraordinaires (Extraordinary Journeys). As shall be seen in this Introduction and when reading the play itself, this piece, *Mona Lisa,* does indeed present a *nouveau visage* or "new face" to the authorial identity of Jules Verne.

It is a play which Jules Verne began in 1851 when he was 23 years old. At the time, its working title was *Léonard da Vinci,* subsequently altered to *Monna Lisa.* In a brief introduction to the 1995 French publication, Pierre-André Touttain described it as a comedy in the genre of the plays of the French author Musset. Verne apparently kept the unfinished play in a drawer over the subsequent years from his twenties, working on it occasionally over time. In a letter to his mother, dated 20th November, 1855, Verne stated that he intended to present the play, then called *La Joconde,* under another title, and he finally settled for the name *Monna Lisa.* One possible reason for the long delay in bringing this piece to fruition is that he was, at the time he began writing it, secretary of the Théâtre Lyrique in Paris and was extremely busy with several occupations (writing other plays, managing the theatre and practising law). He completed it many years later, and gave a public reading of it for the first time in 1874 to the Académie d'Amiens.

In the 1995 edition, the back cover provides the following brief synopsis, in French, of the play: "Leonardo da Vinci is painting the ravishingly beautiful Mona Lisa, wife of da Giocondo, an elegant Florentine nobleman. Tender and hitherto unacknowledged feelings begin to blossom between the painter and his model. But just as he declares his ardent love, Leonardo becomes distracted by a model in whom he recognizes his future "Judas" for his painting *The Last Supper.* He immediately dashes off in pursuit of this model, abandoning Mona Lisa" (my translation). Let us now examine the plot of this play in more detail.

The action of this short romantic comedy is set in Leonardo da Vinci's workshop in the city of Florence, during the period when he was painting *The Mona Lisa.* The play is set in the very early sixteenth century, most probably around the year 1506 which is when da Vinci most probably had his final sittings with his famous subject, Lisa Gherardini del Giocondo. In addition to the historically authentic, real-life characters of da Vinci himself, Mona Lisa and her husband Giocondo, Verne introduces two fictional characters in the persons of da Vinci's fictitious assistant Bambinello and the latter's lover, Pazzetta, who is also Mona Lisa's lady-in-waiting.

The opening scene of the play sees Bambinello ruefully reflecting that his station in life is markedly humble in contrast to that of his master, the great artist da Vinci, but even so, the artist's assistant concludes that his life is still a happy one overall, so that he is portrayed as a cheerful, optimistic fellow who is also enamoured with Pazzetta. Indeed, Bambinello and Pazzetta are currently engaged in a happy courtship. Their happiness in love stands in stark contrast to the uneasy relationship between Mona Lisa and Leonardo da Vinci, and between Lisa and her husband Giocondo. Pazzetta visits Bambinello at the start of the play, asking him whether his master da Vinci is at home, declaring with some urgency that "we need to seize this elusive butterfly," as her mistress Mona Lisa wishes to speak with him privately before that day's sitting for her portrait, which has been ongoing, at that stage, for the past three years. Bambinello makes reference to the many other distinguished occupations of the polymath da Vinci when he says that the latter may be

> on the meridian line,
> Contemplating some new wonders in the Heavens
> Or, lyre in hand, vanquishing his rivals
> Or perhaps even publicly defending some thesis or other
> Connected with medicine or canon law. (Scene II)

Thus, the reader is reminded that, in addition to being a painter, da Vinci was also an astronomer, medical doctor, architect, musician and theologian.

Pazzetta expresses her concern to Bambinello that her mistress Mona Lisa risks heartbreak as a result of her love for da Vinci, given that, according to Pazzetta, "such a man cannot possibly possess a tender heart … because he has a formidable intellect … and is not at all made for truly loving!" Though Pazzetta has tried to warn her mistress that she risks disappointment in the love she bears for da Vinci, Mona Lisa apparently refuses to heed her counsel, and Bambinello agrees that "She'll be simply wasting her time pursuing [da Vinci]!"

Just as Bambinello and Pazzetta are conversing on this topic (and enjoying some stolen kisses), Leonardo da Vinci arrives back in his workshop, his mind brimming over with a thousand different concerns at once, chief among which is the question as to whether or not Bambinello has yet successfully located a suitable model for the

Da Vinci's *The Last Supper*

figure of Judas in da Vinci's painting of *The Last Supper.* He enquires as to whether Bambinello has "found some brigands of sufficiently vile demeanor / To serve as models for ... Judas?" Unfortunately Bambinello's searches up to that point have all proved fruitless, but da Vinci peremptorily insists that his servant continue looking, as the great artist is

> being urged
> To finish my painting of the Last Supper[122]
> As soon as is humanly possible?
> And all that I'm missing is that Judas character! (Scene IV)

122. *The Last Supper* (known in Italian as *L'Ultima Cena* or *Il Cenacolo*) is a late 15th century mural painting by Leonardo da Vinci, and is, like his portrait of *Mona Lisa,* one of the world's most famous paintings, currently displayed in the refectory of the Convent of Santa Maria delle Grazie, Milan. The painting is presumed to have been begun around 1495 and was commissioned as part of a plan of renovations to the church and its convent buildings by Leonardo's patron Ludovico Sforza, Duke of Milan. The painting represents the scene of the Last Supper of Jesus Christ with his twelve apostles, as recounted in the Gospel according to John, 13:21. The precise moment during that meal which da Vinci sought to specifically depict in this painting was the consternation that occurred amongst the Twelve Disciples when Jesus announced that one of them would betray him. The painting specifically portrays the reaction of each individual disciple to this announcement by Jesus. Very little of the original painting remains today, owing to various environmental factors as well as intentional damage.

Bambinello delivers Pazzetta's message to his master, that Mona Lisa wishes to arrive before the time appointed for her sitting as she needs to speak to him urgently and privately, and then confides in da Vinci that "Mona Lisa is in love with you!" This unexpected news seems to momentarily distract and impress itself upon da Vinci, only to be supplanted a moment later by myriad other pressing concerns of his which cause him to instantly forget Mona Lisa and to exit the workshop, despite his servant's attempts to retain him there for Mona Lisa's requested meeting. This leaves Bambinello to ponder "Is he a man of flesh? Is he a man of ice?" Therefore, by the time Mona Lisa arrives at the studio, accompanied by Pazzetta, da Vinci has already left.

Lisa elects to wait as she wishes "to speak with him at my ease." She admits to Pazzetta that she is in love with da Vinci, upon which Pazzetta tries to dissuade her mistress from pursuing da Vinci romantically, telling her that "his mind is far too ethereal / To be bothered by such earthly concerns (as love)" and that continuing with this romantic attachment will ultimately lead to tears. Mona Lisa is, however, adamant that "Leonardo loves me; I can sense it quite clearly!" While this conversation between Mona Lisa and her lady-in-waiting is going on, Lisa's husband, Giocondo, suddenly and unexpectedly arrives at the workshop.

Giocondo wonders when the portrait of his wife—for which she has now been sitting for the past three years—will be completed, and insinuates to Mona Lisa that it is she herself who is deliberately prolonging the process of completing the portrait, through her ever-changing expressions. He also hints at his concern that romance may be blossoming between artist and subject, and echoes Pazzetta's objections to such a romance by arguing "[da Vinci] is incapable of loving anyone! … He possesses too much genius!" Mona Lisa disagrees, defending da Vinci by saying that "A man like that has an open heart … [and] can allow tender feelings." This tension between da Vinci (as an artist obsessed with his art and various branches of scientific accomplishment) and as a loving human being, represents a sort of duality which seems to be a leitmotif throughout this short comic play: there is, therefore, the dualism inherent in the conflict between da Vinci as an Artist and a Lover, together with the duality of Mona Lisa (the human being / object of romantic love for da Vinci and Giocondo) and the subject of a masterpiece of art. Da Vinci's flightiness in love is ironically self-referenced by him towards the end of the play when he comments "I follow, and enjoy following, far and wide, my wandering inclinations … I go where my heart desires, And, as my sole travelling companion, All I want is that wonderful ideal … That suits me better than reality."

The couple agree to disagree; Giocondo also gives his wife a precious bracelet, dating from Antiquity, as a token of his love for her. Realizing that Mona Lisa is indeed in love with da Vinci, Giocondo privately resolves that the only way to win her back is to allow her to see for herself that da Vinci is capable only of neglecting her and disregarding her love for him. Though he regrets that she will inevitably suffer a broken heart as a result of da Vinci's likely indifference, he nonetheless considers that this is the only means of saving their marriage: "Unhappy Mona! What causes her to forget me! This sad distraction of hers is being pursued to the point of folly! Oh, I ought to flee from her; but I love her! Her disabused heart must once again beat close to mine! […] Yes! I will leave her alone with Leonardo […] I want her to compare, then, When her ideal lover descends … from his pedestal … And she feels his neglectful love; She who had been accustomed to my tenderness…." Giocondo instructs Pazzetta to inform da Vinci of Mona Lisa's love for him.

Da Vinci returns to his workshop and is berated by Giocondo, who accuses him of "begin[ning] everything, but finish[ing] nothing!" Giocondo cites the example of the then unfinished painting of the *Last Supper,* which is still missing the figures of both Christ and Judas. He goes on to accuse da Vinci of being incapable of loving another human being, owing to selfishness and his all-consuming passions for art and science. Da Vinci argues that this is not the case: "I … defend Art against your system; Art complements Love, embellishes it, and even / A woman of wit must find, in their union, The ultimate form of passion." The name of Mona Lisa seems to hang tensely in the air between them throughout their protracted argument about the incompatibility of love with art and science. Just after Giocondo leaves, Pazzetta returns and passionately declares to da Vinci that "Mona Lisa loves you! … And your ungrateful heart doesn't even realize it!" This is the second time in the course of the play that da Vinci has been informed of Lisa's feelings for him, but on this occasion it truly registers and resonates with him: "If Dante were alive, he would write a poem / About the beautiful Lisa, for I love her! I love her!" Mona Lisa returns to the workshop for her sitting, to find that da Vinci is in raptures with his love for her, and has arranged for her to be surrounded by singers and musicians while she sits so that the courtly music of love performed by this troupe of performers may inspire the graciousness and beauty of her pose. The "villanelle," the particular type of love song which is sung in the play at this point by one of the choristers, often dealt with the theme of obsession, and indeed, it is notable that Verne, throughout his writing career, often dealt with various types of obsession. In this play, da Vinci has various artistic obsessions, such as his quest for the perfect Judas, and his obsessive perfectionism generally. In *Le Tour du monde en quatre-vingts jours* (*Around the World in Eighty Days*, 1873), Detective Inspector Fix (whose name may have been coined by Verne based on the expression *idées fixes*, or obsessive thoughts) is fixated on the idea of pursuing and bringing Phileas Fogg to justice (much like Inspector Javert's dogged pursuit of Jean Valjean in Victor Hugo's *Les Misérables* [1862]); in *Le Beau Danube jaune* (*Golden Danube*), the police inspector Karl Dragoch is obsessed with his pursuit of the master smuggler.[123] Indeed, throughout many of the novels in Verne's Extraordinary Journeys, central characters are quite obsessive in their pursuits of various goals. This has led me to speculate that Verne (who hinted at dark secrets in his life) may have himself suffered from some form of obsessive-compulsive disorder or ruminations, given that the trope of obsession and *idées fixes* is such a recurrent one throughout his lifelong corpus of work. This plot development of the *tableau vivant* with Mona Lisa at its centre was, in fact, an ingenious idea conceived by Jules Verne in order to interweave into the action of the play, the famous 1845 painting by Madame Brune-Pagès of Mona Lisa in da Vinci's workshop, surrounded by musicians and singers.[124]

123. *Golden Danube* was first translated into English for the Palik series by Kieran M. O'Driscoll and published by BearManor Media in 2014. It is the original Jules Verne version of *Le Pilote du Danube* (*The Danube Pilot*, 1908), rewritten by Jules's son and literary executor, Michel Verne.

124. Aimée Brune-Pagès was born in Paris on July 26, 1803 and died there on August 11, 1866. Throughout the nineteenth century, she was one of the most accomplished and respected female painters of her era. The diverse themes of her paintings represented an eclectic variety of subjects, including, notably, portraits, sentimental themes, religious paintings and historical subjects. The painting of Madame Brune-Pagès which is referred to here was first displayed in 1845, and depicts Mona Lisa in the foreground, posing for Leonardo da Vinci in his workshop, surrounded by musicians, singers and a page

Later, when Mona Lisa and Leonardo da Vinci are finally left alone in the artist's workshop, they declare their love for each other. However, when da Vinci suddenly notices the expensive, antique bracelet given to Lisa by her husband, he becomes enraptured of it, much to Lisa's disgust: she feels that da Vinci's true priorities lie with such material works of art and not with love of her: "Sadly," she muses, "a woman is not so wonderful, all in all, And does not date back to the early days of Rome! She cannot be purchased with gold! … Unlike this silly plaything … she is not a thing of metal or stone, either!" With these words, she crushes the bracelet underfoot. Though da Vinci continues to profess his ardent love for her, Mona Lisa now has doubts and anxieties, and begs to be released from his passionate embrace. But all is changed, changed utterly, when Bambinello suddenly arrives back at the workshop, with a local scoundrel in tow, whom da Vinci instantly recognizes as the perfect model for his Judas in his painting of *The Last Supper.* This causes him to dash out of the workshop in pursuit of the newly-found model, and to seemingly forget completely about his declarations of love for Mona Lisa, who in turn realizes that her feelings for the artist are destined to lead only to misery and disappointment. She tells her husband, who has by this time returned to the workshop, that her portrait has finally been completed, and asks her lady-in-waiting Pazzetta to have it taken away so that they may "take [their] leave of this hateful place!" Giocodo is there to support her in her heartbreak.

Da Vinci returns with a sketch of his newfound model for Judas, a drawing which Mona Lisa expresses ironic admiration for. Da Vinci apparently cannot make up his mind as to whether his portrait of Mona Lisa has been truly completed or not, and is comically portrayed throughout this play as being, despite his undoubted genius, a figure of

---

holding a bird, the whole tableau being based on the legend that da Vinci, to ensure that his model retained the graciousness of her expression throughout her sittings, arranged musical recreation for her. The young woman posing for her portrait in the artist's workshop resembles the original Mona Lisa very closely. Leonardo da Vinci is depicted as presenting his masterpiece, in the course of being completed, to his visitors, who apparently include the artist Raphael, though the historical authenticity of such a meeting having taken place is highly unlikely. I am indebted to French art historian Julie Martins for providing me with this information on the artist and the painting evoked here by Verne, and ingeniously interwoven by him into the subject matter of this play; indeed, when Verne began writing this play, the painting in question would have been very new and would have fed into contemporary (and continuing to the present day) fascination with da Vinci's enigmatic subject, Mona Lisa.

comic ineptitude who is constantly distracted by his myriad conflicting preoccupations and commitments, and as a perfectionist who is unable to complete works of art, begun by him, to his satisfaction. Da Vinci seems to realize, though, at the conclusion of this play, that he is indeed incapable of loving, and that there is now nothing to detain him in Florence, so that he now plans to go to Milan to finish his painting of *The Last Supper*. Also, Mona Lisa seems, at the end, to be no longer embittered by da Vinci's rejection, as she wishes for him the following: "May God speed you on your journey!" Though not explicitly stated, it appears that Giocondo and Mona Lisa do not ultimately take possession of her portrait from da Vinci, and this, as has been seen earlier in this Introduction, seems to accord with historical fact in that the artist is reported to have lingered over this painting for years before leaving it unfinished, and taking it with him to France years later; it does seem that Giocondo and Mona Lisa never did in fact take possession of the commissioned portrait.

Mona Lisa as Adaptation by Jules Verne

This play is, in essence, an adaptation of a seemingly unusual kind: the transposition of a famous work of art from its visual form (with all of the inherent mystery suggested by the subject and her background) into the form of a stage play, a recoding from the visual image into the printed word. Verne's idea of adapting a painting into a stage drama, in which fact is mingled with the playwright's imagination, seems highly original and creative; and, of course, as has been seen in this Introduction, not alone did Verne adapt his play from da Vinci's painting, *Mona Lisa;* he also used another, less famous but equally fascinating, painting to inspire his play, viz. the painting featuring da Vinci, Mona Lisa and a group of musicians painted by Brune-Pagès. This painting-to-stage adaptation may seem an unusual form of inter-semiotic transposition, but, as literary scholar Linda Hutcheon points out in her *A Theory of Adaptation:*

> If you think adaptation can be understood by using novels and films alone, you're wrong. The Victorians had a habit of adapting just about everything – and in just about every

> possible direction; the stories of poems, novels, plays, operas, paintings, songs, dances, and *tableaux vivants* were constantly being adapted from one medium to another and then back again. [...] Most of the work done on adaptation has been carried out on cinematic transpositions of literature, but a broader theorizing seems warranted in the face of the phenomenon's variety and ubiquity.[125]

Hutcheon goes on to define adaptation as follows:

> In short, adaptation can be described as the following:
>
> - An acknowledged transposition of a recognizable other work or works
> - A creative *and* an interpretive act of appropriation / salvaging
> - An extended intertextual engagement with the adapted work.
>
> Therefore, an adaptation is a derivation that is not derivative – a work that is second without being secondary. It is its own palimpsestic thing.[126]

This play meets the above criteria for an adaptation as defined by Hutcheon. It is based on recognizable pre-existing creations by da Vinci and Brune Pagès, which Jules Verne has extensively engaged with and appropriated in a highly creative manner, inscribing the play with his own fictional interpretation of a possible story behind the famous subject and her enigmatic smile.

Hutcheon also suggests that the pleasure which is felt by receivers of an adaptation is based on the interplay between the familiarity of the adapted entity or entities and the differences between the adaptation and the adapted artefact:

> Part of both the pleasure and the frustration of experiencing an adaptation is the familiarity bred through repetition and

125. Linda Hutcheon, *A Theory of Adaptation* (New York: Routledge, 2006), i.

126. Hutcheon, 5.

> memory. [...] As audience members, we need memory in order to experience difference as well as similarity.[127]

All in all, this play, translated into English here for the first time, seems to constitute an ingenious mingling of historical fact embroidered with a (presumably) fictional love story between the famous Renaissance painter and his most famous and enigmatic of subjects. It is Verne's unique interpretation and retelling or reshowing of the story, as imagined by him, behind two paintings of Lisa del Giocondo, which makes this play seem simultaneously familiar and different, old yet new, and thus deserving of our renewed attention to this little-known work by a young Jules Verne.

127. Hutcheon, 5.

Mona Lisa

List of Characters:

LEONARDO DA VINCI.
MONA LISA, wife of Giocondo.
GIOCONDO, a stylish, elegant nobleman from Florence.
PAZZETTA, Mona Lisa's lady-in-waiting.
BAMBINELLO, assistant to Leonardo da Vinci.

The action of this play takes place in Florence. The theatre stage represents Leonardo da Vinci's workshop, a wonderfully luxurious setting, full of picturesque piles of art-related objects, weapons, musical instruments, statuettes, paintings, maps, books and tapestries. To the rear of the stage, through a Gothic-style colorful stained-glass window, there is a view of vast gardens. At the back of the stage, there are doors on the left and on the right. On an easel, rests the famous painting entitled La Gioconda or Mona Lisa, which can be admired today at the Louvre museum in Paris.

Scene I

BAMBINELLO. (*He is vigorously scrubbing his master's palette.*)
I don't see anything wrong in the fact that Fate has given each one of us, here below, a role to perform in life;
But it does seem funny to me that one person should spend his life scraping the paint colours
With which the other paints Gods, women and flowers,
And dedicates his youth to that thankless task!
And to think that, of the two, I'm the one who's doing the scrubbing!

Aimée Brune-Pagès's depiction of da Vinci painting the *Mona Lisa*.

(*In a carefree manner.*) Bah! Despite what resentful people may say,
Life is still the best form of existence, day by day!

Scene II

BAMBINELLO, PAZZETTA.

PAZZETTA. Hello, Bambinello.

BAMBINELLO. Pazzetta – it's you!

PAZZETTA. Of course. Does that bother you?

BAMBINELLO. (*Trying to kiss her.*) Not in the least.

PAZZETTA. Kiss me, but listen to what I have to say!

BAMBINELLO. Why have you come so early today?

PAZZETTA. I've come to see whether your master is at home.

BAMBINELLO. Who knows?

PAZZETTA. But – you, better than anybody else, I should have thought! Is he here?

BAMBINELLO. Perhaps, Pazzetta, perhaps! Who can tell where my master might be?
Where resides the flash of lightning; where sleeps the storm?
Ah! What a desperado, what an outrageous creature,
Who, being always busy, can never stand still in one place,
And doesn't allow anybody to ever see his face!

PAZZETTA. Bah! So, when he wishes to converse, how does he go about it, pray?

BAMBINELLO. He speaks with three-quarters of his face towards you[128] and answers sideways.

PAZZETTA. (*Mysteriously.*) Nevertheless, we need to seize this elusive butterfly.

BAMBINELLO. *(Pointing to the garden.)* I saw him this morning, drawing pictures on the sand. But since then …

PAZZETTA. Well, in any case, my mistress would like to speak with him privately, before her sitting.

128. This would seem to be a humorous allusion to the *Mona Lisa* painting itself, which depicts the sitter in three-quarter profile, a form of representation which is similar to late 15th-century works by Lorenzo di Credi and Agnolo di Domenico del Mazziere. The sitter's general position can also be traced back to Flemish models.

BAMBINELLO. Privately! I understand, Pazzetta! Let her come,
For unless he is on the meridian line,
Contemplating some new wonders in the Heavens,
Or, lyre in hand, vanquishing his rivals,
Or perhaps even publicly defending some thesis or other
Connected with medicine or canon law,
She can count on Leonardo da Vinci's perhaps being here,
If he is not somewhere else!

PAZZETTA. But your master is a painter, I imagine?

BAMBINELLO. My word, but he's also a highly accomplished medical doctor!

PAZZETTA. But he is, above all, a painter!

BAMBINELLO. Of the most original kind,
One who constructs palaces and canals!

PAZZETTA. Oh! My poor mistress! Am I wrong in claiming
That such a man cannot possibly possess a tender heart
That because he has a formidable intellect, he is lacking in matters of the heart
And is not at all made for truly loving!

BAMBINELLO. A wise and prudent observation!

PAZZETTA. She pays no heed to it;
And loses her temper, in complete agitation!

BAMBINELLO. She'll be simply wasting her time pursuing *him*!

PAZZETTA. She shall lose her heart in pursuit of him!

BAMBINELLO. (*Catching her round the waist.*) Speaking of which—your own heart,
Do you still possess it, perchance?

PAZZETTA. Now, don't poke fun! And if I were to tell you—no?

BAMBINELLO. Just one sweet kiss, my beloved!

PAZZETTA. (*Slipping from his grasp.*) Another? Oh, but let's be sparing in our kisses! (*BAMBINELLO pursues her.*) I mean it! If someone were to see us
What on earth would they say?

BAMBINELLO. (*Holding her in his arms.*) They'd say: Those two are a real pair of lovebirds!
And isn't it true?

Scene III

BAMBINELLO, PAZZETTA, LEONARDO DA VINCI.

PAZZETTA. (*Breaking free from BAMBINELLO's embrace.*) My Lord Leonardo!

LEONARDO. What on earth is that Bambinello fellow up to now?

BAMBINELLO. Nothing, master; I was merely bestowing a few kisses
On this fair young lady's brow!

PAZZETTA. What? He was kissing me? What an indiscreet suitor!

LEONARDO. (*To BAMBINELLO.*) So, you get lots of fun out of that, do you?

BAMBINELLO. An enormous amount!

LEONARDO. So, you two are in love, I take it?

BAMBINELLO. In a way that is most right and fitting
Dear master, and the best way is always the final one,
For we don't make empty vows
And have the wit to find each other delightful.

(*LEONARDO begins to leaf through his sketches.*)

PAZZETTA. My mistress awaits me! (*To LEONARDO.*) My Lord!

(*LEONARDO doesn't seem to hear her.*) No answer.

BAMBINELLO. (*Shouting.*) Master, please listen! My master! (*To PAZZETTA.*) I give up!

PAZZETTA. So, stay here while I run to let my mistress know he's now at home.

BAMBINELLO. Very well. I shall make sure he doesn't roam.

(*She exits, and BAMBINELLO closes the door.*)

Scene IV

BAMBINELLO, LEONARDO.

LEONARDO. (*All the while preparing his sketches.*) So let's see, Bambinello: have you searched throughout the length and breadth of Florence
And found some brigands of sufficiently vile demeanour
To serve as models for my Judas?[129]

129. Judas Iscariot was one of Jesus Christ's Twelve Disciples, as recounted in the Gospels of the New Testament, and is the most notorious one of Christ's apostles, given that it was

BAMBINELLO. Hum! Not at all!
My searches have all been in vain!

LEONARDO. But don't you know that I'm being urged
To finish my painting of the Last Supper
As soon as is humanly possible?
And all that I'm missing is that Judas character!

BAMBINELLO. One could die trying
Before finding him, my master! The ruffians of our present century
Have all assumed the airs of fashionable gentlemen!

LEONARDO. No matter! Search and find!

BAMBINELLO. But where? Oh, where?

LEONARDO. (*Making his way towards the door.*) That is your affair!

BAMBINELLO. What! He's about to leave! I must hold on to him!
(*To LEONARDO.*) Lord Giocondo's wife is about to arrive…

LEONARDO. The second hour has only just finished;
I still have time.

BAMBINELLO. She wishes to arrive in advance of the time

---

he who betrayed his Master for thirty pieces of silver (identifying him to the Roman guards in the Garden of Gethsemane, thus ultimately paving the way for the crucifixion of Christ). In da Vinci's painting of *The Last Supper,* which is dealt with in the next footnote, Judas Iscariot forms part of a group of three at the table, together with fellow disciples Peter and John. Judas is wearing green and blue and is in shadow, looking quite withdrawn and nonplussed at the sudden revelation by Christ, during this Last Supper, of the treacherous plan of betrayal by one of the assembled disciples, i.e. Judas himself, though he is not identified by Christ at this point. Judas is clutching a small bag, which perhaps signifies the silver given to him as payment for betraying Jesus, but could also be an allusion to his role of treasurer within the twelve disciples. Judas is also portrayed in the painting as tipping over the salt cellar, an action which may be related to the near-Eastern expression "to betray the salt," meaning to betray one's master. It is also noteworthy that Judas is, as alluded to earlier in this footnote, depicted as leaning back into shadow, something which da Vinci apparently insisted on when completing this masterpiece.

appointed for her sitting;
Pazzetta has told me so, master, and propriety dictates that…

LEONARDO. (*Not listening to him; stopping in front of his easel.*)
This portrait interests me, and I like seeing it again!
But when shall it be completed? God only knows!

BAMBINELLO. (*Aside.*) Now he won't go out after all
And for good reason.

LEONARDO. The left hand does not have grace in its pose,
And it is not thus that God fashioned it!

BAMBINELLO. Master, what do you think of the beautiful Mona Lisa?

LEONARDO. I willingly allow that rich Nature
Shall never produce a more beautiful creature!
She has this exquisite turn, this graceful curve!
That beauty which satisfies both reason and vision!
Whether she is passing by, or stopping, getting up or sitting down, again to pose;
It is always an everlasting work of art which is presented by her;
Against those varied backdrops which are furnished by chance;
Her type is wonderful; it belongs to Art!

BAMBINELLO. (*Aside.*) There he goes again – he's back to his obsession with his subject, Mona Lisa!

LEONARDO. Oh, Greek painters! If only I had your genius!
It is said that, in ancient Greece,
The Athenian birds pecked at the grapes in Zeuxis' painting;[130]

130. Zeuxis was an innovative Greek painter who flourished during the 5th century BC. Although his paintings have, unfortunately, not survived, historical records state that they were known for their realism, small scale, novel subject matter and independent format. His technique involved creating volumetric illusion through manipulating light

I would aspire to worthier approbation;
And would wish to cast men of another era
Intoxicated and trembling, at the feet of this portrait,
To still talk to it of love in three thousand years!

BAMBINELLO. In the meantime, tremble and talk to it yourself!

LEONARDO. What did you say, Bambinello?

BAMBINELLO. Mona Lisa is in love with you!
She's on her way here to speak with you privately.

LEONARDO. (*Running away.*) Is this true? I don't have a single moment to lose.

BAMBINELLO. He's running away!

LEONARDO. (*Laughing.*) She's in love with me! Ah! What a tender soul is she!
But now, the Placers of Banners, those gonfaloniers, must be waiting for me![131]

---

and shadow, which, in a sense, seems to prefigure the importance of light and shadow in da Vinci's own work, especially in the two masterpieces which form the central themes of this Verne play, viz. *The Last Supper* and *Mona Lisa*. Zeuxis was born in Heraclea in 464 BC, probably Heraclea Lucania, in the present-day region of Basilicata in the southeastern "boot" of Italy. The incident which Verne refers to in this part of the play is one which is recounted in the *Naturalis Historia* of Pliny the Elder, according to whom Zeuxis and his contemporary Parrhasius (of Athens) staged a contest to determine which of the two of them was the greater artist. When Zeuxis unveiled his painting of grapes, they appeared so real that birds flew down to peck at them. This story was frequently cited in 18th- and 19th- century art theory to promote spatial illusion in painting. A similar anecdote recounts that Zeuxis once drew a boy holding grapes, and when birds, once again, tried to peck them, the artist was extremely disappointed, stating that he must have painted the boy with insufficient skill, as otherwise, the birds would have feared to approach. Perhaps Verne seeks to establish a link, here, between da Vinci and Zeuxis, in terms of both character and artistic inspiration. Da Vinci is portrayed as a perfectionist like Zeuxis, never completely happy with his artwork and hence finds it difficult to complete his masterpieces, when it comes to the final few finishing touches; this is evident throughout the play in his prolonged period of painting *Mona Lisa* and in the protracted searches for a suitably reprehensible Judas to complete the *Last Supper*.

131. A gonfalon is defined by the current edition of the *Oxford Dictionary of English* (2010) as "a banner or pennant, especially one with streamers, hung from a crossbar". The

Where are my maps? I must hasten, this instant, to the Duke.
Good heavens, I was forgetting about those plans for the aqueduct
That Julius the Second[132] wishes to construct in Perugia![133]
And my answer to the King of France, Louis the Twelfth![134]... She loves me! She loves me!

derived noun "gonfalonier" thus refers to a person employed to hang such banners. The English lexical item "gonfalon" originates from the Italian word "gonfalone" meaning "banner" and dates back to about the 16th century in English and French. The word "gonfalonier" exists in French as in English. The term "gonfalon" is described in more detail on wikipedia.org as a type of heraldic flag or banner, suspended from a crossbar in an identical manner to the ancient Roman vexillum. A gonfalon can include a badge or coat of arms. Nowadays, every Italian commune (municipal district) has its own unique gonfalon, which displays the district's coat of arms. The gonfalon has, over the centuries, been used for ecclesiastical ceremonies and processions, so that it has had strong religious significance in Europe over the centuries, since the Middle Ages. "Gonfalon" was originally the name given to a neighborhood meeting in medieval Florence, each neighborhood having its own flag and coat of arms, which eventually led to the word becoming associated with the actual flag.

132. Pope Julius II (1443-1513), nicknamed "The Fearsome Pope" and "The Warrior Pope," was born Giuliano della Rovere, and was Pope from 1503 to his death in 1513. His papacy was marked by an active foreign policy, ambitious building projects and patronage of the arts—for instance, he commissioned the destruction and rebuilding of St. Peter's Basilica and Michelangelo's decoration of the ceiling of the Sistine Chapel. What is evident throughout this relatively short play is that Verne seeks to combine a fictional tale of love with much historically authentic fact, just as his later *Extraordinary Voyages* combined fictional scenarios and characters with much scientific, historical and geographical fact and authenticity, for didactic purposes. In this way, both original writings such as Verne's (which provide an indeterminate mix of fact and fiction, as in this play) and rewritings, such as this translation, are influenced by history and collective, cultural memory and seek to preserve, rewrite and spread the memes of history (in the case of this play, artistic history which is of special significance to France and Italy, but also to art lovers worldwide). For a fuller discussion of memory, history and translation, readers are referred to a recently-published monograph on this topic: Siobhan Brownlie, *Mapping Memory in Translation* (New York: Palgrave Macmillan, 2016).

133. Perugia is the capital city of the region of Umbria in central Italy, crossed by the River Tiber. The city is also the capital of the province of Perugia. Perugia's history dates back to the Etruscan period, during which it was one of the major Etruscan cities. It is still a prominent university city, with several universities and smaller colleges including the Academy of Fine Arts. Perugia is a well-known cultural and artistic centre of Italy. The famous painter Pietro Vannucci, nicknamed Perugino, was a native of Perugia. Perugino was the teacher of Raphael, the great Renaissance artist who produced five paintings in Perugia and one fresco.

134. Louis XII of France (1462-1515) was a monarch of the House of Valois who ruled as King of France from 1498 to 1515 and King of Naples from 1501 to 1504.

Where do I have to go afterwards?
If only I had the time, how I would love her!
(*He exits, laughing.*)

BAMBINELLO. Is he a man of flesh? Is he a man of ice? (*Going towards the door.*) Here is Mona Lisa! I'll make way for her in a thrice! (*He flees.*)

Scene V

MONA LISA; PAZZETTA.

PAZZETTA. (*Calling.*) Bambinello! What's this? His Lordship Leonardo
Has already vanished? We've arrived too late!

MONA LISA. I'll wait, for I wish to speak with him at my ease.

PAZZETTA. Milady, could it be that you are enamored of that man?

MONA LISA. Pazzetta, could it be that he has no idea of my feelings for him?

PAZZETTA. Upon my word, his mind is far too ethereal
To be bothered by such earthly concerns!

MONA LISA. In your view, Pazzetta, love is a sedentary thing
And he who searches abroad for it, in the heavens,
Shall never find it.

PAZZETTA. I shall never go so high in search of it, in any case;
And risk falling to the ground, when it is so easy
Dear mistress, to be happy in one's own home!
Love dwells more usually on earth than in the heavens

And my eyesight is too poor to see it at such a distance!

MONA LISA. (*Sadly.*) His Lordship Leonardo isn't coming!

PAZZETTA: I imagine
That, as we speak, he's finishing work on some enormous machine
Which is occupying his mind in a thousand permutations
And which is of no interest to those who dwell in Lovers' Land.

MONA LISA. He isn't coming!

PAZZETTA. (*Bringing her to stand in front of the painting.*) So, let's admire your likeness! What a pity
It would be if he didn't finish this portrait!

MONA LISA. Pazzetta, do you think he loves it more than me?

PAZZETTA. I have no doubt that is the case;
It goes without saying.

MONA LISA. The same affection, in his heart, brings us together!
And tell me, Pazzetta, do you think it a good likeness of me?

PAZZETTA. Today… very good! But…

MONA LISA. But… is there something you cannot bring yourself to say?

PAZZETTA. But, Milady, tomorrow, if it is still to be an accurate likeness of you,
This portrait will have to shed tears, alas! And with good reason!

MONA LISA. But… shedding tears, Pazzetta, is that not something?

PAZZETTA. Shedding tears, Milady, is far too much,
Or it is nothing!

MONA LISA. And yet Leonardo loves me; I can sense it quite clearly!
I've been coming here to sit for my portrait for the past three years;
Yes, three years, throughout which period, at the same time each day,
I cross the threshold of his abode; I remain seated in reverie before him;
Three years during which the tiniest details are always apparent to me!
How many times has his gaze held me in its figurative embrace
And how many times, thrilled to be at the centre of his thoughts
Have I seen my heart and his
Come together, closely intertwined!
The passion within me breathed forth all its feverish flames
I no longer breathed but through *his* lips,
And then I would hear invisible kisses
Fluttering about, close to me, through the inflamed air!
The love of a great artist has nothing in common
With those vain pleasures he forsakes!
Such love is sensed and understood, but can't be explained.
It is not, therefore, susceptible to worldly error;
Its attraction is divine, its duration everlasting!
The artist is more than a man; he loves with genius!

PAZZETTA. Ah! Bah! Bambinello claims that intellect has nothing to do with happiness,

	And that you don't need all that much wit to be happy!
MONA LISA.	(*Sharply.*) He's coming!
PAZZETTA.	(*Going towards the door.*) It's Lord Giocondo in person!
MONA LISA.	My husband! But who has brought him here?
PAZZETTA.	Could this mean he suspects something?
MONA LISA.	(*Pointing to her portrait.*) He probably wishes to collect this picture, Once and for all!
PAZZETTA.	My God… well, I'm off to have a chat with Bambinello.

Scene VI

MONA LISA, GIOCONDO.

GIOCONDO.	(*In a very gentle, kindly tone.*) Oh, don't put yourself out on my account, darling, please! Well… And this portrait, full of flirtatiousness? When shall it be finished? For more than three years now, You've been displaying your most gracious features to the painter! I don't see any harm whatsoever in that And of course it's your own affair…
MONA LISA.	Yet you must admit, my dear Duke, That you are in a hurry to take home this portrait!

GIOCONDO. No, of course I'm not, and I'll happily wait;
What's the good of rushing? Leonardo has time!
Isn't his genius eternal,
And shall you not be eternally beautiful?

MONA LISA. You're in a delightful mood this morning!

GIOCONDO. (*Presenting her with an expensive bracelet.*) Dearest Mona, for me, these are days of happiness and good fortune,
When everything we try is a success, even our maddest ventures!
And please accept this jewel, found near Pozzuoli,[135] well!
It's pure Providence; it was a very good friend of mine
Who has just returned from his travels
Who presented it to me!

MONA LISA. What a delightful bracelet!

GIOCONDO. Accept it as
A precious work of our ancient Rome,
For it comes from the ruins of a temple in Serapis!

MONA LISA. (*Putting it on her arm.*) My heartfelt thanks.

GIOCONDO. Being a well-informed man, I render your thanks unto Fate;
Which will be sensitive to them;
Fate must be treated gently, for it can achieve the impossible!

MONA LISA. The impossible!

GIOCONDO. Undoubtedly, and Fate might even see to it
That today, your portrait shall at last be completed.

135. The Macellum of Pozzuoli, the marketplace or macellum of the Roman city of Puteoli (now known as Pozzuoli) was first excavated in the 18th century, when the discovery of a statue of Serapis led to the building being misidentified as the city's serapeum, the *Temple of Serapis*.

MONA LISA. In that case, Fate must be highly skilled,
I do proclaim!

GIOCONDO. All the more so,
Given that it would have to triumph over a woman!

MONA LISA. Ah! Really? That's not very kind of it.
Perhaps I'll understand you better if I sit down!
(*She sits.*)
And this woman is…?

GIOCONDO. None other than your good self!

MONA LISA. What a funny thing! So, you believe *me* to be the cause of these delays!

GIOCONDO. You, and you alone!

MONA LISA. It may be true!
But I don't at all follow your reasoning.

GIOCONDO. You don't understand! Perhaps it's because I'm standing. (*He sits.*)
Mona, your face is changing day by day,
Perhaps unbeknownst to you, but changing it is
And in a most peculiar way!
Oh! Truly, you are still most beautiful!
But with less tranquillity and simplicity than before!
For two years now, what's been most evident in your features
Is anxious ardor, a new fervor,
To sum it up in one expression, a complete transformation
Despite which you are still beautiful—but in a different way!
Though nobody, you understand, has a right to complain.
I'm merely explaining how Leonardo, in order to

paint you
Is, each day, forced to follow, step by step
That mobility which is never fixed,
Which never stays still!
So if you wish, Mona, that he finish this portrait,
Do not let your features change on a whim
And choose, once and for all, the type of beauty
You wish to bequeath to posterity, and to *him*.

MONA LISA. Your speech is shrewd, Sire, but do you think it's cloaking
Your secret desire to carry this painting away?

GIOCONDO. Who? Me? I'm the last person in the world…!

MONA LISA. So where's the harm?

GIOCONDA. Tis merely a copy; but *I* possess the original! (*Laughing hesitantly.*) Moreover, such a desire on my part could only be reasonable
Were Leonardo, so long impervious to your charms,
To allow himself to fall under your spell!
But, between ourselves, he is incapable of loving anyone!

MONA LISA. Incapable of loving!

GIOCONDO. He possesses far too much genius!

MONA LISA. You gifted artists! So maligned and slandered!
So how, pray, does he still manage
To belong to the ranks of humankind?

GIOCONDO. By the top of his head and three fingers of one hand,
As for a heart, essentially, he has only enough
For the modest and discreet use of a great man.

MONA LISA. And despite his love, his painstaking attention to detail,
His dedication;
In your view, a woman would seek in vain,
To be loved and understood by him!

GIOCONDO. And where, may I ask, might this woman be?
Come on, now! She can't be a mere mortal
And were she a goddess, she would still fail miserably!

MONA LISA. Explain to me the reason for this,
And your words shall be golden!

GIOCONDO. Here it is!
I don't believe it possible to combine art and love;
To each his own branch of expertise!
I can tell you quite categorically, when it comes to a painter and a lover,
That one is made for painting, the other for loving!
Witness them both! One sketches upon his heart
A thousand fleeting love affairs according to his whims
Which he quickly relegates to some dark corner
With his old paintings, facing the wall.
While the other, the man who is by nature a loving human being?
It is within his own heart that he frames yours;
He seeks to know neither the how, the why nor the wherefore of his guiding passion;
He simply loves! Judge for yourself, then,
What each one keeps deep within his soul;
And then you will agree, my dear, that a woman,
Instead of being an object of love for Leonardo's heart
Is nothing more than an object of art!

MONA LISA. Your distinction seems quite worthless to me;
The weak Omphale[136] has always triumphed over Hercules! Do we believe in the impossible,
We, who with a single word, can cast any man at our knees?
Truly, you forget that nothing or nobody can resist us,
My dear Duke; he's a man, after all, only an artist,
And, as such, he belongs to the ranks of those human beings
Whom we are able to bend with our weak, bare hands!
Lovers, by nature, possess this commonplace trait
That the song of their heart hardly becomes younger,
Whereas those such as Leonardo have their own lyrical outpourings
And he was not, yesterday, that which he is today.
You must believe, then, that a man like that has an open heart
That he can allow tender feelings,
And (I too can rhyme, dear Lord above)
Can unite the love of art with the art of love!

GIOCONDO. Very well! In the absence of any counter-arguments, I will no longer oppose
Your way of thinking! You are uncritically worshipful! You are idolatrous!
But if you secretly worship false gods, my dear,
Fortunately, that is by far the better portion!

MONA LISA. Why do you say that?

GIOCONDO. It is the prerogative of genius
To produce a bizarre effect of perspective
In that it loses, upon allowing itself to be closely scrutinized!

136. In Greek mythology, Omphale was a daughter of Iardanus, either a king of Lydia, or a river-god. Omphale was queen of the kingdom of Lydia in Asia Minor. The great hero Hercules was remanded as a slave to Omphale for a period of a year for his murder of Iphitus. After some time, Omphale freed Hercules and took him as her husband.

MONA LISA. Personally, I don't believe a word of all that!

GIOCONDO. My darling, if you were to talk to this man—this great man, this poet of yours—
For even a quarter of an hour at most, you would understand,
In spite of his lofty intellect, how different
The dream is from the reality!

MONA LISA. (*Sharply.*) The experiment, Your Grace, is, at the very least, a futile one;
And this discussion seems puerile to me!

GIOCONDO. But not at all!
I want to convince you, by your eyes!

MONA LISA. Let's not dwell on this matter any longer!

GIOCONDO. (*Laughing.*)Afterwards, we would love each other all the more!
It's pure egotism…

MONA LISA. (*Impatiently interrupting him.*) The more one reasons,
The more one argues, Duke, and the less one convinces anybody!
Let's leave the matter there; and, in order to agree,
Let's assume that, if I'm right, you're not wrong, you see! (*She rises and makes her way towards the door.*)

GIOCONDO. You're going out?

MONA LISA. Yes, I am! It'll be easier for me to breathe! The air is stifling
And this overcast weather weighs heavily upon me.

GIOCONDO. It's almost time for your sitting. (*He offers her his arm.*)

MONA LISA. (*Curtly.*) No, thank you! I'll be back later, and shall meet you here. (*She exits.*)

Scene VII

GIOCONDO. (*Alone.*) Unhappy Mona! What causes her to forget me!
This sad distraction of hers is being pursued to the point of folly!
Oh, I ought to flee from her; but I love her!
Her disabused heart must once again beat close to mine!
There's only one way—risky, yet decisive—left open to me
To destroy, in one day, this grievous frenzy
Yes! I will leave her alone with Leonardo,
Whose disturbed mind makes of him a singular fellow,
A peerless lover, one of the Chosen Few,
Living only on fresh air and poetry! I want her to compare, then,
When her ideal lover descends conventionally from his pedestal;
And she feels his neglectful love;
She who had been accustomed to my tenderness
To the indulgent attentions of an obedient heart
And not to the liberties of an insulting lover!
(*He remains overcome for a few seconds.*)
But suppose I were mistaken… no! It's not possible
I must be strong, invulnerable, unswayable!
I love her now more than I've ever loved her
And yet I would forsake her love?… Never!
(*PAZZETTA crosses the gardens.*) Pazzetta! Come here! (*PAZZETTA is seen coming back.*) Let's take Leonardo to task.

Scene VIII

GIOCONDO, PAZZETTA.

PAZZETTA. Here I am, Your Grace! Has my Lady gone out?

GIOCONDO. Yes. I must say, Pazzetta, I'm extremely unhappy with you.

PAZZETTA. But … what have I done, your Grace?

GIOCONDO. Come over here and look at me!
This morning, you received an order from your mistress
To artfully inform Leonardo of her sudden desire
To have a secret meeting with him.

PAZZETTA. Me! But no, Your Grace! I swear to you…

GIOCONDO. It would appear
That you accomplished the mission entrusted to you
Badly, very badly indeed
And that Mona found her tryst to be quite a dismal affair
As soon as she found herself alone at her trysting-place.

PAZZETTA. For the second time, Your Grace…

GIOCONDO. Between ourselves,
You know, nonetheless, the deep love, the worship
She bears for Leonardo, for she consults you;
And at times, Pazza, you take it into your head to rebuke her for it
And that is most improper.

PAZZETTA. But…

GIOCONDO. If it makes her happy to seriously love Leonardo,
Why should it matter to you! So, you're going to put matters right, and arrange for him
To learn, as quickly as possible, of this unexpected good fortune of his
So that he won't be unduly caught off guard!

PAZZETTA. What! You want to…

GIOCONDO. Of course, and without delay;
Begin by painting this love as endless!

PAZZETTA. But if he speaks of you,
What should I say in that case?

GIOCONDO. Of me? Say horrible things! Anything you like!
Spin yarns, embroider, malign, lie, exaggerate, invent!

PAZZETTA. Very well! His Grace shall be pleased with his servant!

GIOCONDO. (*Showing her the gallery at the rear.*) Wait for me in there! He's coming!

Scene IX

GIOCONDO, LEONARDO.

LEONARDO. My dear Duke, I must inform you
Of the greatest of the honors which are destined to be bestowed upon me!
In order to begin his military campaign,
Caesar Borgia wants me to go and lead his armies
From Rome! As you can see, this post
Is of the utmost importance!

GIOCONDO. You would leave Florence!... Do you have the time?

LEONARDO. The time to conquer Italy and Sicily!

GIOCONDO. Leonardo, your conquests are easily made... But if you accept this mission,
I'll be sorry that you'll have to renege on completing this portrait.

LEONARDO. (*Going to his easel.*) My dear Duke,
Only a tiny bit more work is required, a little touching up
Only to the hand and... and maybe to the mouth...

GIOCONDO. (*Stopping him.*) Leonardo, I've been listening to you
Speak like this for the past three years! Painting is your second-choice;
When you are unable to do anything else,
A craftsman weary of his craft,
You create masterpieces!

LEONARDO. (*Abruptly and heatedly.*) By Christ, then, am I such a master criminal? (*Calming down and preparing his paintbrushes.*) Yet art is patient, for it is eternal.

GIOCONDO. Eternal Art! Alright, I grant you that! Yet, whatever you may seek to do,
I am *not* eternal! No! The truth of the matter is that
You begin everything, but finish nothing!

LEONARDO. Yet what matter, my dear Duke,
Provided I get off to a good start!

GIOCONDO. In the past, you would certainly have driven Maecenas mad![137]

137. Gaius Maecenas (68BC-8BC) was an ally, friend and political advisor to Octavian (who went on to become the first Emperor of Rome as Caesar Augustus) as well as an important

For instance, in Milan, in your painting of the Last Supper,
How come the figures of Christ and Judas
Are still missing?

LEONARDO. I can't find them! To paint God,
He has to want it so, He has to come
And, with His hand, support and direct my own;
May He finally appear to me on His throne of fire!
'Tis not I who am late, but God!

GIOCONDO. And what about Judas, then?

LEONARDO. Ah! Judas! I do declare, my dear Giocondo,
That I'm worn out from searching for his likeness in this world!
Each evening, in Milan, I would go to the Borghetto[138], in the midst of the brigands and scoundrels,
To try to find my Judas, but in vain! 'Twas a wasted effort!
And here, Bambinello has been bringing me
The most hideous specimens of human nature
And yet, amongst all these good-for-nothings, these thieves,
I've failed to yet encounter those depraved features
That wretched and hypocritical face of the traitor
Who, for thirty pieces of silver, betrayed his Master!

GIOCONDO. Oh, ye eternal seekers! How right the heavens were
To limit to art your strange horizons

---

patron of such Augustan poets as Horace and Virgil. During the reign of Augustus, Maecenas' role was, effectively, that of a minister for culture to the Emperor. His name has become synonymous with a wealthy, generous and enlightened patron of the arts and provides the etymological root of the French word *mécène*, meaning "patron."

138. Borghetto Lodigiano is a municipality in the Province of Lodi in the Italian region of Lombardy, located about 40 kilometres southeast of Milan.

And to refuse you entry into those lands
Where dwell more simply other human hands.

LEONARDO. Do you believe us both to be nestled within a single, shared sentiment
With no hope of ever departing from it?

GIOCONDO. Luckily!

LEONARDO. Luckily! For whom?

GIOCONDO. For whom! For everybody
Who is in love, for example!

LEONARDO. Well! My dear Giocondo?

GIOCONDO. Well! I don't think…

LEONARDO. That we have good taste?

GIOCONDO. That you know how to love!

LEONARDO. Not at all…

GIOCONDO. Not at all!

LEONARDO. Yet the facts are consistent, my dear Duke;
I have a recollection
Of having, in times gone by, made Florence
What is it today; I was young, prodigious, ardent and, I guarantee,
If I was not loved, at least
Much love did come from me.

GIOCONDO. A love from which only you benefitted; without price,
Not love which involves sacrifice!

LEONARDO. But you are mistaken! I took love very seriously
To the point of sacrificing my mortal days…

GIOCONDO. (*Laughing.*) No! Only your nights!

LEONARDO. So you think it is not through my heart
That I exist?

GIOCONDO. No, certainly not…

LEONARDO. That the lover in me has been killed by the artist?

GIOCONDO. Without a doubt! Your heart is your whole workshop;
Full of friendly, familiar disorder,
Exquisitely tasteful works, marble sculptures and busts,
Precious vases, paintings and unpolished works.
There does distracted contemplation make poetry…
But there doth woman pose, not repose.

LEONARDO. Your pretentiousness beggars belief!
So you don't realize the intimate union of art and love, and how, here below,
Nothing would go right, if in harmony they did not go?

GIOCONDO. I doubt that…

LEONARDO. (*While painting.*) So listen, my dear Giocondo.
God became very tired after creating our world,
For it is said that he rested after six days
And has been resting ever since.
So God, to populate his solitary expanse,
Charged Art and Romance
To create in his wake,
And they've made this world what it is today.

Their mission is thus a sacred one;
Each person works and creates
In their own distinct genres, but helps their fellow human beings,
Generously and ceaselessly
And the word "friendship" has been invented for them,
Indeed, nowadays, as in Ancient times,
Love inspires poetic rhymes
And works of art. And Art gives love this ideal side
Which elevates it from tawdriness; except that, when one of the two
Takes precedence, it is called Gioot, Fabius, Zeuxis, Thimante, Appelle,
While the Other, if it wins the day,
Is named Laura,[139] Hero,[140] Cleopatra,[141] Phrynée,[142] Beatrice[143] and Sappho[144].
I therefore defend Art against your system;
Art complements Love, embellishes it, and even
A woman of wit must find, in their union,
The ultimate form of passion. (*Rising from his seat.*)
Yes! After God, artists are the creators of the world,

139. The name Laura means "victor," derived from the Latin "laurus" referring to the laurel plant which was a symbol of victory in ancient Greek and Roman mythology. The name Daphne has a similar meaning, Daphne being a mythological water nymph who attracted the romantic attentions of Apollo.

140. Hero: may refer to Heracles, a divine hero in Greek mythology, the son of Zeus; the word "hero" has its origin in the Greek word "heros" which has the sense of a warrior hero.

141. Cleo or Cleopatra (69-30BC) was the last active pharaoh of Ptolemaic Egypt.

142. Phryne was an ancient Greek courtesan, tried for impiety, who was born in 371BC.

143. Beatrice "Bice" di Folco Portinari (1266-1290) was a Florentine woman who has been commonly identified as the principal inspiration for *Vita Nuova* (1295) by the Italian poet Dante Alighieri (1265-1321), and is also commonly identified with the character of Beatrice who appears in Dante's *Divine Comedy* (1320). She is the incarnation of beatific love, which, as a symbol, is probably a significant choice by Verne within the context of this tale of love and the traditional purity associated with the image of Mona Lisa.

144. These are all references to various historical figures from antiquity. Sappho was a Greek lyric poetess, born on the island of Lesbos. Though most of her poetry—which was greatly admired through much of antiquity—has not survived, her immense reputation has endured through surviving fragments.

For He it was who populated Heaven, Earth and the oceans,
While the Other it was who brought forth wonderful masterpieces, high emotions!
Think of all this, my dear Duke, and you will understand
How a heart under the power of both, freely submits its hand
They are interlinked, and if, one fine day, some comet
Were to crush, with its mass, our world,
It could be recreated, with Art and Love unfurled.

GIOCONDO. That is most ingenious… as delusions go!
But experience, alas, gives the lie to theory!
Especially when genius is complex and seeks
To embrace Science and Art simultaneously!
It's time for the sitting… (*He makes his way towards the door.*)

LEONARDO. (*Stopping him.*) On the contrary… (*He detains GIOCONDO.*)

GIOCONDO. Your mind is always too easily distracted!
I'm going to fetch Mona Lisa.

LEONARDO. Please form a different opinion of us! And believe…

GIOCONDO. But, within you as a whole,
At least ten different people are struggling for your soul!
In the midst of such combat, how do you expect a woman
To tell which one is the lover… from the engineer, the painter, the doctor or the musician!

LEONARDO. Very well, then! Let them all love her!

GIOCONDO. Never! She would be deceived by it!

LEONARDO. I…

GIOCONDO. You are forever the kind of man who busies himself
With the veneer of a painting not yet begun!
You hasten the future at the expense of the past!
But the present wasn't created to be avoided
And the heart seeks not to be glossed over so quickly!

LEONARDO. You are mistaken, my dear Duke!

GIOCONDO. Please be so kind as not to detain me
And I'll be back presently!

LEONARDO. Even so…

GIOCONDO. (*Running away.*) No! I shall be back! (*He is seen at the rear of the stage speaking to PAZZETTA, while gesturing towards LEONARDO.*)

Scene X

LEONARDO. (*Alone.*) What a funny fellow that Duke Giocondo is!
So he imagines he's the only one in the world
Who has the right to be in love and the right to be loved?
In Heaven's name! So I'm just an inanimate being, am I?

Scene XI

LEONARDO, PAZZETTA.

PAZZETTA. (*COMING onstage, with a mysterious air.*)
Oh! My Lord Leonardo, please, please listen to what I have to say,

A single word, but it's truly sweet and tender,
A woman called while you were away,
A lover, and your eyes have seen nothing of her heart's surrender!
And your ungrateful heart doesn't even realize it!
Leonardo da Vinci! Mona Lisa loves you!
(*SHE runs offstage.*)

Scene XII

LEONARDO. (*Alone, becoming agitated.*)
She loves me! She loves me! And I had no idea!
Could it be true? So Bambino was right after all!
At last I understand all those trifling signs,
Those thousand little nothings…
The secret of her heart, the languidness of her pose
The fire in her eyes; and now, in the space of one single day,
For showing me so much love, I want to repay
The love of Mona Lisa, by dint of loving her!
Ah! If Dante[145] were alive, he would write a poem
About the beautiful Lisa, for I love her! I love her!

Scene XIII

LEONARDO, BAMBINELLO, SINGERS AND MUSICIANS.

BAMBINELLO. Here are your singers, Sire!

LEONARDO. (*Passionately.*) Ah, my friends! Come in! Come in! And may love be mingled
With the songs you shall sing!

145. Dante's *Divine Comedy* consists of three parts: the *Inferno, Purgatorio* and the *Paradiso.* The latter is an allegory telling of Dante's journey through Heaven, guided by Beatrice, who symbolizes theology. The poem in its entirety is an allegory for the soul's ascent to God.

BAMBINELLO. What's gotten into *him*, then?

LEONARDO. (*To BAMBINELLO.*) You must garland the stairwells and courtyards
With my most exotic flowers!

BAMBINELLO. Leave it to me, master!

LEONARDO. Bambinello! See to it that my lions are given extra-large rations
So that they may roar all the louder, pray!

BAMBINELLO. Your wish is my command: I hasten to obey!

LEONARDO. Bambinello! Let an escort worthy of her be prepared!

BAMBINELLO. Absolutely!

LEONARDO. Bambinello! See to it that today, the sun is halted in its course,
To prolong, upon the horizon, this most beautiful of all my days!

(*BAMBINELLO runs offstage.*)

Scene XIV

LEONARDO, MONA LISA, GIOCONDO, *musicians, singers.*

LEONARDO. (*Aside.*) There she is! No, never was she more beautiful
Her charm is fresh and her beauty new!

MONA LISA. (*Aside.*) Be still, my beating heart; I shall die!

GIOCONDO. (*Jokingly.*) You must admit, the daylight
Has never been made of more golden rays!
Painting shall surely be a pleasure
On a day like this day of days!

LEONARDO. (*To MONA LISA.*) A pleasure? An intoxication!
Nature has made of herself a joyous fascination!
And only Beauty has the right
To be painted in gleams of summer's light!

GIOCONDO. (*Sharply.*) Mona! (*Aside.*) I honestly thought that mine was the stronger soul!
And these singers! Come, now! (*In a low voice, to LEONARDO.*)
Is all this troop of people
Really so necessary to your inspiration
That you cannot paint without their congregation?

LEONARDO. Undoubtedly! (*To MONA LISA.*) Isn't that so?
Poetry and music—by giving my work a more poetic heart—
Chase, far from here, that inelegant and dismal grief
Which would soon weigh down your brow and eyes!

MONA LISA. These past three years, Leonardo, will count in my life!
I love seeing, each day, through your brush,
My joyful likeness emanate from your inspired fingers!

GIOCONDO. (*Brusquely.*) Are you going to start work with those brushes of yours, then?

LEONARDO. (*To MONA LISA.*) Just as soon as you wish!
For I feel happy! My hand is animated!

(*He seats MONA LISA in the middle of the singers and musicians, in a tableau vivant reminiscent of the painting by Brune-Pagès.*)

Please assume your customary pose
At the centre of this group, but with less awkwardness,
And let your arms become more gently rounded!
(*He goes to his easel and begins to paint.*)

(*Music.*)
(*A singer; he sings a villanellé.*)[146]

I wait in sweet anticipation
Of my nightly tryst
I lie in wait for my beautiful lady love!
The enamoured moon gives silvery sheen
To the sweet and bending grasses
As I wait in sweet anticipation!
Of such charming beauty,
My poor heart is a jealous snare!
I lie in wait for my lady fair!
From the languidly swaying trees
The shadows slip and slide in dreamy fascination
As I wait in sweet anticipation
In this grove of birdsong
No bolts are needed there!
As I lie in wait for my lady fair!
She hastens, trembling, to meet me
And I perish at her feet!
How I love my lady sweet!

(*The music stops; a long silence.*)

GIOCONDO. Come! I must leave! And yet I hesitate!
All are silent! Let us leave immediately; we must not wait!

146. A villanelle (also known as villanesque) is a nineteen-line poetic form consisting of five tercets followed by a quatrain. The villanelle is an example of a fixed verse form. The word derives from Latin, and later from Italian, and is related to the initial subject of the form being the pastoral. Despite its French origins, the majority of villanelles have been written in English, a trend which began in the late nineteenth century. The villanelle has been observed to be a form of poetry which often deals with the subject of obsessions, and one which appeals to outsiders; its defining feature of repetition prevents it from having a conventional tone.

(*He stands up; LEONARDO continues to paint.*)

I am off to the Royal Court.

MONA LISA. You're leaving?

GIOCONDO. A number of papal envoys are about to be presented
To His Grace, Duke Soderini;
I promised I'd be there.

MONA LISA. Very well…

GIOCONDO. In any case, I'll be back later to take you home! (*Aside.*) I have to do this! I have to! But I shall keep watch outside!

(*Going away, and watching LEONARDO, who continues working.*)

The poor lover! He doesn't even notice that I'm leaving!

(*He leaves; a drape falls at the back of the workshop, leaving LEONARDO and MONA LISA alone.*)

Scene XV

LEONARDO, MONA LISA.

MONA LISA. (*Looking at LEONARDO, who is contemplating her in a reverie.*) His brush no longer follows his secret thoughts. *(She goes to him).* So you've stopped painting? Has your hand grown tired?

LEONARDO. (*Looking round; speaking in an aside.*) Finally, we are alone! (*Aloud.*) I beg your pardon! I was in a world of my own!

I was dreaming!

MONA LISA. Dreams of the future, perhaps… ?

LEONARDO. This portrait is unworthy! I ought to destroy it at once!

MONA LISA. (*Aside.*) His hand is trembling! (*Aloud.*) So you no longer consider it, My Lord, to be a good likeness of me?

LEONARDO. No, Milady, and I feel I can do better.

MONA LISA. Wherefore hath the expression in thine eyes changed?

LEONARDO. I feel as though I'm returning to the days of my youth
It truly seems to me, Milady, that I've only come to really know you
This very day, just as a traveller
Does not truly know a foreign land, unless he penetrates
To its very heart!

MONA LISA. (*Aside.*) He loves me! Leonardo!

LEONARDO. Here we are, alone, just the two of us, Milady!

MONA LISA. (*A little troubled.*) There are at least three of us, and this portrait requires
Your attention…

LEONARDO. Here we are, alone, and I swear to you, here
That I like you better just as you are now, my dear!

MONA LISA. And why… Leonardo?

LEONARDO. You are more real
More simply pretty, more freely beautiful
Like an expensive painting placed within its frame!

MONA LISA. So what is new, then, in my expression?

LEONARDO. Love!

MONA LISA. *(Aside.)* Oh! My beating heart! (*Aloud.*) And whence doth proceed this love, pray?

LEONARDO. I do not know
If you yourself still do not know!

MONA LISA. But what is the object of this love?

LEONARDO. Alas, I do not know!
If you yourself, today, still do not know!

MONA LISA. (*Insistently.*) What is this sentiment?

LEONARDO. I still haven't come to realize what it is
But let Death itself appear! Milady, and I will do battle with it,
For just one word from you, or less than a word, a glance!
Even less than a glance!

MONA LISA. *(Aside.)* Oh! Thank you, Leonardo!
To anybody else but me, let this love appear
Too intense in its ardor, too swift in its rapture,
I want to know nothing of their opinion; haven't I observed it
Invading your heart, and almost unbeknownst to you!
I could give you a detailed, day-by-day account of it!

LEONARDO. Milady, do you believe in it?

MONA LISA. How could I not?

LEONARDO. You have read the pages of love within my heart
But I must now read your own, and from the very start!

MONA LISA. The book of my heart is indeed worth meditation
But you might read it with undue precipitation
And, in any case, everything is an obstacle to our love!

LEONARDO. (*Taking her hand in his.*) So, why can I not forever live like this?
Before your gaze, and care not for the hours thus spent
And unite my love with all your thoughts?
Why can't I see you, Mona, as I wish?
My quivering fingers plaiting your long tresses
Draping, in classical style, your finest dresses
Nurturing your poetic side
Making you sparkle under purest rays, heart's bride!

MONA LISA. Your words are such entrancing music!

LEONARDO. Your perfect charms need a different light!
Your gaze new horizons!
Put your hand in mine and let us talk,
Together, of this love I have for you!

MONA LISA. (*Seeking to refuse his outstretched hand.*) Leonardo…

LEONARDO. Oh! Give me your hand! (*He takes her hand in his and, just as he is kissing it, he notices the bracelet given to her by GIOCONDO.*) That wonderful pearl!
Such perfection! Such taste!
Truly, Antiquity has never produced anything to

surpass it! (*The bracelet comes loose and Leonardo remains in contemplation of it.*)

MONA LISA. (*Aside.*) Alas! Such an incredible blend of love and art!
Will he ever emerge from this strange ecstasy?

LEONARDO. Kings would have sought to acquire this Roman bracelet
At the price of all their treasures!
What exquisite workmanship!

MONA LISA. I want to destroy it with my abandoned hand!
(*Aloud.*) So, which of us two is thus captivating your thoughts?
And which of you will answer me: the artist or the lover?

LEONARDO. This pearl is perfect!

MONA LISA. (*Taking it back.*) Ah! Sadly, a woman is not so wonderful, all in all
And does not date back to the early days of Rome!
She cannot be purchased with gold! But what is more,
You should know, Leonardo da Vinci,
That, unlike this silly plaything, of such proud appearance,
She is not a thing of metal or stone, either! (*She crushes the bracelet underfoot.*)

LEONARDO. (*After a moment's silence.*) Milady, your pride should punish me
Were I the kind of man whose only occupation
Was to go about uttering romantic balderdash!
But I know nothing of the frivolous speech of such men;
My voice has not learned to lament in verse

And my tears are too proud to flow without sincerity!
I hate trite expressions and frozen phrases
On my honour, I know nothing of Aristotelian teachings!
I love you most ardently, but truly
And my love is well-matched with your dignity!

MONA LISA. You love me! About as much as this jewel!

LEONARDO. No! But Milady, you are glad to be loved…
As a woman!

MONA LISA. Alas!

LEONARDO. (*Falling to his knees.*) Oh! Please… I beg your forgiveness
For this moment of forgetfulness, neglect and confusion
Dear Mona Lisa, may God Himself be my witness!
Mona! I love you with an everlasting love!

MONA LISA. Leonardo! You love me! Leonardo!… I believe you…
And yet, my heart is struck with dread!
Some unknown force impels me into your arms
And our love can only be long martyrdom!

LEONARDO. (*Putting his arms around her.*) And why?
What unkind Fate has used you and your heart in this way,
Oh my dear Lisa,
And has thus used your life, forever in chains?

MONA LISA. (*Wanting to flee from him.*) I no longer belong to myself!

LEONARDO. (*Pressing her to his heart.*) But you do! For Destiny has,
Through your beauty, given you earthly freedom!

MONA LISA. Leonardo! Release me!

LEONARDO. Let your troubled heart
Rest in mine, my Mona!

MONA LISA. (*Horrified.*) No! Have mercy!

LEONARDO. My Lisa!

MONA LISA. Let me go!

LEONARDO. I worship at your feet…

MONA LISA. No!

LEONARDO. Do not reject my adoration!
I sense that my lips shall be unable to find the words of love
Needed to express my passions, desires and frenzies!
(*He holds her tightly – BAMBINELLO appears!*)

Scene XVI

LEONARDO, MONA LISA, BAMBINELLO, *a stranger.*

LEONARDO. (*Sharply.*) Who on earth is that?

BAMBINELLO. (*Proudly displaying the stranger to his master.*) Take a look!

(*A man dressed like JUDAS in the painting of the Last Supper, and looking exactly like that dreadful character, stops for a moment in front of the window. LEONARDO, taken by surprise, takes a couple of steps forward.*)

LEONARDO. My Judas! My Judas! That wonderful scoundrel!

(*The stranger moves on.*) Ah! Don't let him go! (*He dashes outside and disappears with BAMBINELLO.*)

Scene XVII

MONA LISA. Are my senses deceiving me? What on earth is happening?
Will that man come back here to complete the unfinished sentence
The word just begun today!
Oh! Let us escape this senseless love, without delay!
Let that man of genius love in his own way
My poor heart is filled with endless anguish today!
And my husband… I want… I beg his protection!
But do I really have the right to go back to him?

Scene XVIII

MONA LISA, PAZZETTA, BAMBINELLO.

(*BAMBINELLO passes by at the rear of the workshop, with his arm around PAZZETTA, speaking softly into her ear.*)

BAMBINELLO. (*To PAZZETTA.*) Till this evening, then.

PAZZETTA. Yes! My sweet love!

BAMBINELLO. My sweet love,
How long the hours shall seem until that magical time
When our joyous kisses shall once again combine!

Scene XIX

MONA LISA, BAMBINELLO, PAZZETTA, GIOCONDO.

MONA LISA. (*Speaking earnestly to her husband.*) My dear Duke! This portrait has finally been completed!

GIOCONDO. (*Aside.*) Poor Mona Lisa!

MONA LISA. (*Showing them her portrait.*) Pazzetta, have it taken away immediately!

PAZZETTA. Yes, Milady!

MONA LISA. And, with me, may my image take its leave
Of this hateful place! (*A valet carries the painting away.*)

GIOCONDO. (*Lovingly, to his wife.*) Dear Mona Lisa! (*Aside*). Her heart, ill-used by rough hands, has broken!

PAZZETTA. (*Aside.*) She has been weeping!

MONA LISA. My Dear Duke,
I now ask for your arm,
That we may leave!

GIOCONDO. Here it is!

PAZZETTA. The poor woman!

BAMBINELLO. (*Quietly.*) Till this evening, Pazzetta!

PAZZETTA. Oh! Always the gallant gentleman!

Scene XX

MONA LISA, BAMBINELLO, PAZZETTA, GIOCONDO, LEONARDO DA VINCI.

LEONARDO. (*A sketch in his hand.*) I've found my Judas! His eye is treacherous, arrogant!
With one hand he flatters,
While with the other he destroys!
He is truly a rogue of cowardly and base mien
Whom only a painter should be glad to find!

MONA LISA. I should like to have this drawing, to frame it!

LEONARDO. You like it?

MONA LISA. Very much! I find it magnificent,
And am truly indebted to Judas for this mark of esteem!

LEONARDO. (*Astonished.*) You! (*Aside, sadly.*) Oh! Damned head! Alas! My passion!

GIOCONDO. Judas has never performed a worthier deed!

LEONARDO. (*Graciously, to MONA LISA.*) Milady, we can, if you are willing to,
Complete this portrait! I have found inspiration anew!

(*He turns round and no longer sees the painting.*)

MONA LISA. (*Earnestly.*) It is already completed, my Lord.

GIOCONDO. Oh! Truly completed!

MONA LISA. It is, isn't it?

LEONARDO. (*Coming to a firm resolution.*) Yes! Milady is right… indeed
I could never have completed it… any further!
And yet, it is missing…

MONA LISA. What is it missing?

LEONARDO. In the face,
That proud expression which, for a moment,
Your own face wore.

MONA LISA. (*Looking at it*) Is it a fair likeness?

LEONARDO. (*TO GIOCONDO.*) I prefer it this way! See the difference! (*Aside.*)
If I were twenty years old,
I would have died upon seeing it!

GIOCONDO. And are you leaving Florence?

LEONARDO. Without a doubt! There is nothing to detain me here!
Moreover, as you know, my dear Duke, it is thus that I follow
And enjoy following, far and wide, my wandering inclinations.
I don't think I'm made to live in your world:
And so I take my leave, I go where my heart desires
And, as my sole travelling companion, all I want
Is that wonderful ideal which every poor poet,
To pay his heart's dues, carries in his head;

That suits me better than reality!
Ah! Laura and Beatrice! Your example has tempted,
More than once already, some beautiful but foolhardy woman
Who alas was unaware that, though Petrarch[147] and Dante
Never ceased to please you and to sing your praises
It was only because you took care never to exist!

MONA LISA. May God speed you on your journey!

LEONARDO. Let us go! I'm launching a campaign with the Borgia![148]
I shall travel through Rome, Sienna, Urbano,
Piombino[149], creating on my way
Rivers, cities, roads: but tomorrow,
Before acting upon that vast stage, I shall
Finish, in Milan, my painting of the Last Supper!

147. Francesco Petrarca (1304-1374), commonly anglicized as Petrarch, was an Italian scholar and poet in Renaissance Italy, and one of the earliest humanists. His sonnets were admired and imitated throughout Europe during the Renaissance and became a model for lyrical poetry.

148. The Borgia family became prominent in ecclesiastical and political affairs during the Renaissance in Italy, producing two Popes: Alfons de Borja, who ruled as Pope Calixtus III during 1455-1458, and Rodrigo Lanzol Borgia, who ruled as Pope Alexander VI, during 1492-1503. During the reign of Alexander VI in particular, the Borgias were suspected of many crimes, including theft, bribery and murder. Because of their grasping for power, they made enemies of the Medici, the Sforza and the Dominican friar Savonarola, among others. They were also patrons of the arts during the Renaissance.

149. Piombino is an Italian town of about 35,000 inhabitants in the province of Livorno (Tuscany). In the Middle Ages, it was an important port of the Republic of Pisa.

Part VI

Zigzags Through the World of Science

by Michel Verne

Translation and comments by Kieran M. O'Driscoll

Introduction

Upon the death of Jules Verne (1828-1905), the son of the author, Michel Verne (1861-1925), saw to publication many of his father's manuscripts, not only extensively revising them, but including several of his own works under the paternal byline.[150] This was not, however, Michel Verne's beginning as a writer—those were the much earlier works included in the following pages. Jules was so pleased with Michel's works that he told an interviewer a few years later that his son "writes ably on scientific subjects...."[151] While the possible paternal input on these pieces is unknown, they revealed a style that was both distinct yet also inculcated his father's example—to such a degree that the most successful would be mistaken for a product of his father's

150. These include, most notably, two works of science fiction, "L'Éternel Adam" (*The Eternal Adam*, 1910) and *L'Étonnante Aventure de la mission Barsac* (*The Astonishing Adventure of the Barsac Mission*, 1914).

The writing of Jules and Michel Verne has previously been partly the subject of two earlier Palik Series volumes: Jules Verne, *Golden Danube*, translated, with an introduction and notes, by Kieran O'Driscoll (Albany, GA: BearManor Fiction, 2014), and Jules Verne and Michel Verne, *Vice, Redemption and the Distant Colony*, translated, with an introduction and notes, by Kieran O'Driscoll (Albany, GA: BearManor Fiction, 2012).

151. R.H. Sherard, "Jules Verne at Home," *McClure's Magazine* (January 1894), 115-124.

Michel Verne.

pen. Moreover, Michel often styled his name Michel Jules Verne after his father, although his actual name was Michel Jean Pierre Verne.

Throughout the year 1888, Michel Verne published a series of scientifically-themed articles and short stories in the literary supplement of the French daily newspaper *Le Figaro*. The articles penned by Michel covered an impressive array of topics within the natural sciences, including astronomy, engineering, medicine, geology, the study of marine creatures and insects, human biology, electricity, telephony, photography, radiophony, the human digestive system, ornithology, anaesthesia and neuroscience. Such a bewildering diversity of topics, all drawn from the domain of the hard sciences, justifies Michel's collective title of this series of articles as "Zigzags à travers la science" ("Zigzags Through The World of Science"). In dealing at some length with the above varied branches of science, Michel certainly appears to have been following in his father's footsteps, given that Jules Verne's novels similarly deal with a comprehensive range of scientific themes, presented to his readers with a pedagogical aim, and incorporated within sometimes humorous, always thrilling fictional tales of exploration and adventure, which formed his lifelong corpus of work under the collective title of Extraordinary Journeys Into Known and Unknown Worlds. Michel Verne's Zigzags appear to have a similarly educational motivation, and are aimed at the general reader of "popular science." In addition, there is much humor to be found within each of these pieces, and—as we shall see from this introduction and through a reading of these articles—several rather controversial theses and observations which must surely have raised the hackles of more than one reader of *Le Figaro* in the late nineteenth century; female readers especially, perhaps.

These articles were republished in 1993 by the French Société Jules Verne, with copious annotations explaining the many historical references to various scientists and other historical figures, in their *Bulletin de la Société Jules Verne* (*BSJV*) and subsequently in the French journal *ETHUIN*. As part of the Palik Series of the North American Jules Verne Society (NAJVS), this series of scientific articles by Michel Verne is, here, translated into English in its entirety and for the first time (with the exception of "A Futuristic Express Train," which, though previously translated on several occasions into English, is here given a fresh 21st century retranslation). Let us now consider each of the nine "Zigzags" individually, in order to explore their themes, as well as investigating Michel Verne's frequent use of humor, a tone which is indeed common to all of these nine articles. Each article, though short (running to a few pages maximum) displays scientific accuracy and impressive research, qualities which also distinguished the *oeuvre* of Michel's father Jules.

The first, untitled article cleverly combines the apparently disparate topics of astronomy, telephony and engineering. It describes the construction of the Eiffel Tower which was, at that time, being erected in preparation for the World Fair of 1889, due to be held that year in Paris. It also discusses the potential of the Eiffel Tower to be used as a source of electricity facilitating the transmission of radiophone and telephone signals, and contains much of the trademark humor of Michel Verne. For instance, at the beginning of this first "Zigzag," Michel imagines two bewildered astronomers in their laboratory at Pontoise, outside Paris, being comically confounded by the distant sight of a high illumination which they mistake for some new comet. Michel then imagines the possibility of their overhearing speech signals transmitted by means of light, and radio signals, from the Tower to their laboratory. He goes on to discuss the role of beams of light in the operation of the telephone, referencing its illustrious inventor, Alexander Graham Bell. He also imagines a Parisian lover and his mistress having an illicit telephone conversation which is transmitted between the Eiffel Tower and the Trocadéro quarter of Paris, the telephone signals passing over the head of the "jealous husband enslaved on *terra firma* by severe, painful arthritis." Michel goes on to make the first of many jocose (though potentially offensive!) observations about women, such remarks being another feature common to practically all of these articles, asking whether women "really need (a telephone)" as "the eyes of an attractive woman are eminently electrified and highly-charged, and … can not only transmit the spoken word but, if necessary, replace it?" He then seeks to repair, albeit with that ironic tone which permeates "Zigzags," any offense which may have been caused to female readers of his columns, by observing that "yet again, … you, ladies, are top of the class in physics, as, indeed, in just about everything else." Towards the end of this article, Michel accurately anticipates the millions of tourists who now flock to the top of the Eiffel Tower each year to admire the spectacular views of Paris afforded thereby: "I am certain that a great many people shall ascend to the top of the Tower, to stock up on a little pure air. Many shall wish to gaze upon the superb landscape which, from the vantage point of that great height, shall unfurl over a radius of sixty kilometers around Paris!" His characteristically humorous conclusion is that many of those who ascend to the Tower's lofty summit will wish they could remain there on a permanent basis:

"devout Christians and poets: the latter wishing to live there in an idyllic, utopian setting … the former yearn(ing) to die a little closer to the heavens!" In marvelling at the great height of the Eiffel Tower, Michel mentions hot-air balloons, thus paying implicit homage to one of his father's earliest and most celebrated works, *Five Weeks in a Balloon*; indeed, throughout the subsequent eight articles, as shall be seen, much implicit, indirect homage is paid to the classic, best-known works of Jules Verne. Therefore, as this and other volumes within the Palik Series have been at pains to identify, the writings and even cinematic adaptations produced by Michel Verne as an artist in his own right illustrate that he was a competent writer (and adapter of his father's works) who is finally emerging posthumously from his father's shadow, thanks to the research of Verne scholars internationally, not least under the aegis of the Palik Series and within the Société Jules Verne.

The second article, again untitled, describes the construction and operation of military tanks from an engineering perspective, as well as describing the medicine antipyrine and concluding with a discussion of the composition of rubies. Another feature common to all of these articles is the ingenious means by which Michel Verne can appear to seamlessly glide (or *zigzag*) from one topic to several unrelated ones, so that readers are given a variety of science lessons even within one single piece of writing. Humor is once again to the fore in this second article; Michel compares a new military tank (with an ascending and descending gun turret) to "that toy which must certainly have afforded you hours of amusement in your childhood, that box from which, at the push of a button, a grimacing devil would shoot up with pointed tongue and outstretched arms?" In this piece, as in almost all the others, Michel Verne references a plethora of historical and contemporary figures, including, here, military engineers and chemists, as well as providing many other historical, cultural and (in other articles here) mythological references. The wealth of allusion which characterizes this series of newspaper columns has been usefully annotated by scholars of the *BSJV*, particularly Olivier Dumas and Volker Dehs, and the bulk of their footnotes have been rendered into English in this volume, due to their relevance in facilitating complete understanding and background knowledge on the part of the reader of these target texts.

The third piece, again untitled, offers a first departure from the usual "scientific article" genre of these columns, as it is, rather, a short story about a train journey from Boulogne in France, to Foulkestone on the southern English coast, the train travelling across an imagined bridge which has been constructed over the English Channel (a French engineer was, at the time of publication of this story, studying the possibility of building such a bridge). This story is thus one of scientific anticipation, justified by actual, then contemporary research on the feasibility of such a cross-Channel railway system, and foresees the subsequent, though much later, inauguration of the "Chunnel" (*le tunnel sous la Manche*) in the late twentieth century. Scientific *anticipation* and scientific *facts* (as opposed to the science *fiction* of, say, H.G. Wells), are thus seen to be hallmarks of the works of both Jules Verne and his son Michel.

In this short story, the first-person narrator boards the train from Boulogne to England, and shares his compartment with an aloof young woman whom he supposes to be a young English lady travelling the continent alone. When "a little bit of engine trouble" causes a temporary halt to the train, halfway across the Channel, the narrator and his attractive young "travelling companion" both find themselves stranded on the bridge when the train (from which they have alighted to admire the bridge and the sea view) continues on its journey and unwittingly leaves them behind. The young lady, a New Yorker (thus not English as the narrator had originally thought) is called Miss Georgina Waterford; she and the narrator decide to walk the rest of the way across the bridge to the English coast. Miss Waterford's character is jokingly portrayed by Michel Verne as idiosyncratic, every bit as eccentric as Phileas Fogg. Like Fogg, Georgina appears completely unperturbed by her various predicaments (unlike the extremely nervous male narrator). She also displays an impressive knowledge of the engineering and architectural principles underpinning the construction of this pre-Chunnel cross-Channel bridge *avant le jour* (before the day). Even when a fierce storm at sea seems to threaten their safety, the unflappable young woman remains perfectly calm, again unlike the more nervous male narrator. Finally, that narrator is witness to a surreal encounter on the bridge when, emerging from the fog, a young man appears. He turns out to be Percival, Georgina's fiancé, who has decided to walk across the bridge to meet his betrothed after failing to locate her at the terminus. Percival is equally as phlegmatic as his fiancée; both "exchange a solemn handshake" with the bemused narrator, and finally walk off, away from him, into the gloom, "side by side, with mechanical footsteps, mechanical footsteps ... gradually fading from sight in the darkness." Moreover, neither of them has even mentioned the raging storm.

Though this piece is in a genre markedly distinct from its predecessors (short prose fiction as opposed to a scientific column), Michel nevertheless takes the opportunity of inscribing, within the framework of this fictional narrative of scientific anticipation, much engineering detail on the bridge's structure. Some of the comic dialogue in this story recalls similar conversations occurring in Verne *père*'s *Une Ville flottante* (*A Floating City*, 1871).

In the fourth story, entitled "Oysters and Ants. A Scientific Judgement of Feminine Taste," the reader learns about the lives of oysters, through the bizarre device of an interview between the author and a "very elderly oyster whom I recently met on the shores of Cancale bay," a "distinguished personage who kindly agreed to grant me an interview." Similarly, mollusks would be one of the evolutionary stops in Jules Verne's only fairy tale, *Aventures de la famille Raton* (*Adventures of the Rat Family*, 1891), before his title characters are transformed into humankind. Though "Oysters and Ants" is couched in Michel's trademark humor, this article nonetheless discusses the very real threat of extinction which, even then, menaced the oyster population owing to their popularity as a gourmet dish, such a theme resonating with 21st century readers, given the contemporary urgency of questions of ecology, including the imminent extinction of many species, and the specter of climate change. Having "zigzagged" on to discuss edible ants (after the completion of his interview with the oyster), Michel concludes his piece with a discussion of our senses of taste and smell, noting that, when it comes to "sweet, bitter or salty flavors," women "detect these flavors ... with less sensitivity and sharpness than us," ending with the words "Women have a good nose—but a bad tongue!" Indeed, in several of these articles, Michel is seen to make humorous comparisons between women and men, comparisons often unfavourable to women. Though couched in irony, one wonders how late 19th century female readers, not to mention present-day ones, reacted to Michel's stinging observations, ironic or otherwise. Did his

Life found by the explorers in the center of the earth, from Jules Verne's novel, in a detail from the frontispiece of the 1867 Hetzel edition combining Verne's first two bestsellers, *Cinq Semaines en ballon* (*Five Weeks in a Balloon*, 1863) and *Journey to the Center of the Earth.*

pieces not sometimes provoke an outcry from outraged female readers of *Le Figaro*?

In article 5, entitled "Combined Photography. Electricity in the Home," the female characters in this story fare particularly badly. The narrator happens to run into an old friend of his, Anatole Passavent, a soldier stationed in Algeria. Passavent has recently married an older, middle-aged woman and has five stepdaughters "of marriageable age." He is far from happy: his spouse is an "electric woman" so that he often gets an unpleasant shock upon any physical contact with her. Her five daughters are most unflatteringly described as "monsters," and include one who is "hunchbacked, another bald, a third [who is] gap-toothed …" This story also takes the opportunity to discuss, in addition to the bizarre phenomenon of human electrification, the subject of "composite photography;" the five daughters, individually unattractive, seemed to be collectively angelic in appearance when their photograph was viewed by Passavent, the hapless spouse and stepfather, at a Parisian "matrimonial agency," because it was a composite portrait of the five young women, in which each one was photographed in the ordinary way, "in succession, but all on the same plate, the second being superimposed upon the first," etc.

Article number 6, "Under the Earth," is very evidently influenced by one of Jules Verne's most famous and most-acclaimed novels, *Voyage au Centre de la Terre* (*Journey to the Center of the Earth*) and also by the less well-known *Les Indes Noires* (*The Black Indies*, 1877). The article by Michel seems to present, in a much-condensed form, some of the most salient scientific facts, tropes and theories from the above two novels, especially the former. Michel's article first discusses the composition of the substrata lying beneath the Earth's surface, and evaluates the various successive theories purporting to explain what lies beneath the ground on which we walk, from the center of the Earth upwards. It also muses on the possible prehistoric creatures, human and animal, which in Jules Verne's *Journey to the Center of the Earth* were found to exist underneath the surface of the globe. It goes on to discuss the mining industry and the possibility of piercing a great hole to the very center of the Earth, concluding with a less than flattering reference to the theatrical adaptation of Emile Zola's novel *Germinal*. *The Black Indies*, in which themes of mining and mines played a central part may be regarded as having had a significant influence on this specific article by Michel Verne, given that he also produced a cinematic adaptation of this work by his father, an internationally successful feature film also entitled *Les Indes Noires* (1917).[152]

Article number 7, "A Futuristic Express Train," has, on several previous occasions, been translated into English, under the title "An Express of the Future." For the purposes of this volume, I decided to retranslate it afresh—though previous renderings in English seem accurate, there were instances of less than idiomatic language use or of occasional unnatural grammatical structures. This is another short story, reminiscent of the other railway-themed story in this collection (Zigzags number 3). In this instance, the railway in question is (like the Chunnel, which this story seems also to anticipate) an underwater system which travels from Boston to Liverpool, under the waves of the Atlantic Ocean. The article goes into some detail in its explanations of the engineering principles and design of this "futuristic express train," but the narrator is suddenly woken by drops of rain and gusts of wind, from what turns out to have been a dream. However, the dream was caused by his reading of a newspaper article discussing the proposed project of such a train system.

---

152. For a detailed analysis of this movie, see the book by Brian Taves on Michel's filmmaking career and its impact, *Jules Verne's Ghost*.

"Humans and Animals" is the title of the eighth and penultimate article in "Zigzags." This biologically-themed article discusses the human digestive system. There is some scatological humor on the part of Michel Verne when, having described the "journey" made by food as far as the stomach or indeed "lower down than the stomach," he wryly observes that "to recount the rest of the journey, I'd need the Gallic writing skills of that humorous, cheery storyteller Armand Silvestre and, unfortunately, I simply don't have those kinds of skills." (See the relevant footnote to this article for a comparison with similarly scatological humor as displayed by Jules Verne in his early writing). Finally, Michel displays his customary verve in switching or zigzagging from one topic to a completely different one within the same article, when he concludes by discussing the way in which birds, especially the woodcock, are able to heal their own wounds; both human biology and ornithology feature, then, in one and the same article.

"Intelligence and Pain: An Anglo-Chinese Anaesthetic" is the title of the final article, number 9 in the series. This article discusses the findings by anthropologists and neurologists that human (and other mammalian) intelligence is related to the size of the brain. Once again, Michel Verne proves less than complimentary to women, provocatively declaring that "I am sorrowfully forced to admit their inferiority. Women have less grey matter than us men." He also refers to the alleged lesser intelligence of "les paysans" (farming folk, country folk in general) and to the lesser growth of the cranium in the "working classes," such a phenomenon being "nothing but the normal order of things." He also propounds the thesis that higher intelligence leads to higher sensitivity to suffering, mental and physical (this, indeed, is a common theme of present-day discussions about the drawbacks of having an extremely high Intelligence Quotient or IQ, especially in regard to emotional suffering). The notion of physical pain provides an ingenious means of then zigzagging to the topic of the power of anaesthesia to deaden all pain by rendering patients unconscious during operations. He briefly sketches the history of anaesthesia, from its contemporary use in modern medicine, back to its supposed origins in the Middle Ages, and, finally going back much further in time, he traces its true beginnings back to Chinese medicine in the third century AD, as well as mentioning mythological references to an anaesthetic-like "liqueur" in the *Odyssey* in about 1300 BC. It was apparently Chinese physicians who first used a preparation containing hemp as an anaesthetic; this fact allows Michel Verne to conclude with a humorous reference to the alleged use of hemp "on a daily basis" by "our friends, the English."

Conclusion

To conclude, the most salient features of Michel Verne's "Zigzags Through the World of Science" are, first, its provision of abundant, well-researched scientific detail (across many of the natural sciences), all with a pedagogical purpose; second, the inscription of these weekly "science lessons" within a contemporary and sometimes fictional framework and, third, the pervasion of a humorous, ironic tone, with women often being the subject of Michel's wit. His articles discuss both contemporary and older, historical scientific facts and theories. They also offer much "scientific anticipation," as, for example, in the article about the imagined train across the English Channel or the piece concerning those supposed submarine, sub-oceanic trains furrowing a passage to and fro across the Atlantic between the USA and the UK.

Many of the foregoing characteristics of "Zigzags," especially their goal of scientific education, often combined with fictional stories within which these scientific instructional texts are framed, clearly show the influence of the writer's father. As for possible misogyny within Michel Verne's writings, it is noteworthy that a similarly misogynistic vein has sometimes been identified by commentators on the works of Jules Verne. The latter's novels are certainly characterized by—in general—a notable absence of leading, strong female characters and by exclusively, or heavily, male-dominated environments. Twenty-first century readers of this first translation into English of his entire series of scientific articles, first published in 1888 in a weekly newspaper column, may now draw their own conclusions.

Special thanks are due here to Verne expert Volker Dehs, who has transcribed the original Zigzags articles from their original appearance, and composed extensive annotations, many of which have been adapted for this translation.

I.[153]

"Well, my dear colleague, what do you make of this comet?" asked the astronomer of his fellow researcher, who was engaged in his own scientific operations close by him.

"It's impossible to understand a single thing about it! It's at exactly the very same spot as it was yesterday at the same time! It's enough to make you want to tear your hair out in frustration!" exclaimed the second astronomer, who would, however, have been unable to achieve phenomenal exploits of that nature, given his marked absence of luxurious tresses.

"It's the most extraordinary thing! It would almost lead you to believe that we've made some kind of mistake! Could it be, by any chance ...?"

"A comet? With a tail like that? ... Come on, now!"

And the two astronomers looked at each other in dismay.

"Anyway! Let's get back to work!" went on the first astronomer, after a moment's silence.

"Indeed, let's get back to work, my dear colleague," replied the second, affixing his eye once more to the lens of his telescope.

Such is undoubtedly the scene which would have been most delightfully enacted, in the year of Our Lord 1889, by two astronomers from the Pontoise observatory, catching sight, for the first time, on the southern horizon, of the top of the Eiffel Tower, mounted by its electric searchlight.[154] Yes! It is in this way that their surprise would have manifested itself, had the preparations for the World Fair been better kept secret. Unfortunately, given the freedom of the press, those things which are the easiest to conceal – and wasn't this among the easiest of all? – become widespread public knowledge, appallingly quickly. Thus, the above scene shall not take place. And that is really a great pity, for, after their initial reaction of surprise, can you just

153. This short story was originally published in *Le Figaro. Supplément littéraire*, 14th year, No. 20, May 19, 1888, p. 78. Republished in *BSJV*, No. 106, 1993, pp. 10-14 and in *ETHUIN*, pp. 15-21, under the title "The Eiffel Tower."

154. The Eiffel Tower, which was the crowning centerpiece of the World Fair of 1889 in Paris, was constructed between January 1887 and March 1889.

imagine the astonishment of our two learned men of science if one of the beams of light striking their lens, suddenly bursting into speech, had unexpectedly brought to them something akin to the confused echo of a faraway conversation:

"Exhibition ... open ... splendid ... stronger than the captive balloon ... superb ... Eiffel Tower ..."[155]

Our good astronomers would certainly have had good reason to believe that they were hallucinating. And yet, however impossible such a thing might appear, it would have been, well and truly, a reality.

Indeed, it has already been some time since Mr. Alexander Graham Bell, the renowned inventor of the telephone, discovered certain most remarkable phenomena, in whose production luminous beams of light play a significant part.

Believe me, I'm not concocting any dastardly plans to turn this column into a series of lectures on chemistry, physics, physiology, or any other branches of science which, though equally sublime, are profoundly impenetrable to anybody who hasn't learned them at an age when one can digest "x"-es without upsetting one's stomach. No, what this column is, rather, concerned with, is, simply, some zigzagged meanderings through the world of science.

However, without going into details which are far too technical, I really must say a few words about that device invented by Mr. Bell, to which he has given the name of the *Radiophone.*

It basically consists of a thin sheet of Muscovy glass, on which beams of light fall at an angle. At the exact point at which these rays of light begin to converge—through the successive action of the luminous sheet of glass which reflects them, and then of a lens and a concave mirror—a piece of selenium (a metalloid which doesn't come from the moon, as its name might lead one to believe, though scientific terminology does tend to include absurdities of this nature) is introduced into the circuit of an ordinary telephone. And the next thing is that a strange phenomenon occurs: the resistance offered by the selenium to the passage of the electrical current is inversely proportional to the intensity of the light which is beamed towards it.

155. Constructed by Henri Giffard (1825-1882), a "captive balloon" of 25,000 cubic meters and with a passenger capacity of 40, was exhibited in the Tuileries district of Paris during the World Fair of 1878.

After these tedious explanations, it is easy to understand that, if you speak from behind the sheet of Muscovy glass, that sheet will start to vibrate, and that at times it will expand, while at other times it will retract. As a result, it will send variable amounts of light to the selenium, which will lead to a varying intensity of electrical current within the telephone, the membrane of whose receiver will, by this means, in turn begin to vibrate, thereby faithfully transmitting the words spoken.

* * *

Thus do I find myself obliged to confess that, a short time ago, at the start of this article, my imagination had gone into overdrive. The Pontoise astronomers would still not have been forewarned and would thus not have been able to equip themselves, beforehand, with a telephone embellished by the said selenium. Furthermore, is it currently possible for us to produce light rays which can travel a distance of fifty kilometers? Probably not, but at the rate at which things are progressing, am I not entitled to presume that, between now and next year, some means will have been found to dispense with selenium and telephones, to entrust light beams with the task of transmitting the spoken word on their own, and to increase their power, to enable them to carry speech at a distance of fifty kilometers, if not more? Who's to say that, one day, we might not even be able to *radiophone,* in this way, the inhabitants of other planets in our solar system?

* * *

But for the moment, all of this talk is pure idiocy. In actual fact, it is neither a question of two planets, nor of Pontoise. The only single issue is to conduct experiments between the Trocadero and the Eiffel Tower, with the help of that powerful source of electricity for which the self-same Tower will be like a gigantic candelabra. I can already imagine two lovers exchanging romantic messages from those two points. Ah! Just imagine the sweet nothings which would thus fly back and forth through the atmosphere, passing each other, occasionally colliding, pecking each other as they went on their merry way, passing shamelessly over the head of the jealous husband enslaved on *terra firma* by severe, painful arthritis. Although, come to think of it, do lovers, particularly of the female gender, really need a device of this kind, and aren't they the real inventors of a principle to which Mr. Bell has, at the end of the day, merely given a practical and ingenious application? Has it not been a recognized fact, since time immemorial, that the eyes of an attractive woman are eminently electrified and highly-charged, and that they can not only transmit the spoken word but, if necessary, replace it?

Which only goes to prove, yet again, that you, ladies, are top of the class in physics, as, indeed, in just about everything else, and that the old saying will always remain true: "There is nothing new under the sun."

* * *

Even if lovers don't feel the urge to climb the Eiffel Tower, either to *radiophone* each other or to try to find a little bit of their dreams, since they carry their dreams within themselves, this 300-meter-high pylon will, nevertheless, not be short of visitors. For it will still enjoy the patronage of those whose hearts are free and unattached, which is most certainly the majority of people. Indeed, Mr. Eiffel must be firmly counting on this, for he is pressing ahead with his construction work at a rate so steady that it augurs well for the future.

Moreover, the admiration of all and sundry must surely be sufficient to encourage him and stimulate his determination. Each day, squashed up against the barriers of the construction site, crowds flock to see what progress is being made by Eiffel Tower Limited.

It's certainly a spectacle which is well-worth taking a look at.

But it is inside the construction site, on the other side of the barriers, that there is a multiplicity of interesting details to be observed. An example? The raising of the metal girders, carried out a short time ago.

Let us sketch this picture.

The girders lie dormant, heavily spread out on the ground, ready to be pressed into action: chains then descend and seize them. From on high, steam begins to hiss and the massive bulks begin their upward movement and slowly slot into the spaces which have been provided for them. But what's this? A space has remained empty between their extremities and the steel columns which, four by four, form the pillars of the monument! What's to be done? Everything has been provided for, everything has been calculated. In a cavity, for which space has been expressly made at the foot of each column, the piston of a hydraulic press is inserted. Then, a pump starts up. Girders are raised, and are slotted in to the required place. They are riveted together, and the job is completed. These girders, weighing almost one hundred tons, have now been permanently installed.

I don't know if I'm deluding myself, but I would dare to suggest that there is a certain elegance to the serene manner in which such a colossal structure is being raised upwards to its lofty heights.

* * *

Do you want some figures? They are poetic in their eloquence. The weight of the completed Tower, for example? 7,500,000 kilos! The number of individual pieces of iron used? 12,000! I have even read somewhere that, if you were to place, end to end, the holes which had to be pierced in the cast-iron, you would end up with a seventy-kilometer-long tube! Was I wrong in claiming that these figures have a poetry of their own? Why, it's *mathematical* poetry!

But it is, above all else, an ode to *height* which this imposing, grand architectural creation shall be able to sing to us. And, for us, is there anything more fascinating than height?

Human beings, indeed, cramped and restricted as they are on their globe which they have travelled in every direction, have taken *Excelsior* as their motto.[156] Human beings ceaselessly aspire to climbing ever higher, and a monument is made all the more appealing, the more it thrusts its summit upwards into the azure heavens. It is an intoxicating sensation to rise, higher and higher, and to be able to embrace in one sweeping, panoramic view, a slightly less miniscule fragment of this earthly domain to which we are tied.

When I used to sail on the rolling waves, and when, in order to get a glimpse, a few seconds sooner, of the so eagerly-anticipated shore, I would heave myself up to the top of the masts, I would certainly have wished that those masts too could have been three hundred meters

156. *Excelsior* (Ever upwards!) is the Latin motto of the State of New York. It was also the motto of Dr. Fergusson, one of the central characters in Jules Verne's 1863 novel *Five Weeks in a Balloon.*

high! And later, in Calcutta, when, standing on tiptoes, I used to try (in vain, as it happens) to make out, in the distance, the snow-capped Himalayan mountain tops, what wouldn't I have given to share those uncommon dimensions!

May he attain those dimensions, then, that iron giant![157] May he force his steely brow ever upwards in his assault upon the clouds, where electricity shall spark the flame to light great fires! I am certain that a great many people shall ascend to the top of the Tower, to stock up on a little pure air. Many shall wish to gaze upon the superb landscape which, from the vantage point of that great height, shall unfurl over a radius of sixty kilometers around Paris! And indeed, many are they who shall wish they could remain up there, even if it's only devout Christians and poets: the latter wishing to live there in an idyllic, utopian setting, far from the noise of trains and buses, of newspaper vendors and the tiresome ho-hum of politics; whereas the former shall yearn to die a little closer to the heavens!

II.[158]

Cedant arma togae, or *May weapons yield their authority to the power of the toga:* Cicero may well have uttered those words in times gone by, but in this day and age, he would be well and truly obliged to do an about-turn on his argument as contained within that apophthegm and reverse it, turning the argument round in the opposite direction.[159]

For the fact is that questions relating to armies and war occupy the foremost place in the current concerns of the general public. From the top rung of the ladder right down to the bottom, everybody seems to have an axe to grind on matters military, holding forth, arguing, risking criticism, proposing reforms and approving of such and such a measure

157. It is somewhat ironic that Michel Verne here refers to the Eiffel Tower, which was at the time of his writing this article, obviously still in the process of construction, as an "iron giant," ascribing male gender (he) to it, given that Parisians subsequently christened their iconic monument *La Dame de Fer*, or the *Iron Lady.*

158. This short story was originally published in *Le Figaro. Supplément littéraire*, 14th year, No. 22, June 2, 1888, pp. 87-91, and later in *BSJV*, No. 106, 1993, pp. 15-19, and *ETHUIN*, pp. 23-29, as well as in *Textes et Langages: Jules Verne* (University of Nantes, 1984), 4-8.

159. An apophthegm is a concise saying, maxim or aphorism uttered by a wise person. This saying by Cicero expresses the desire to replace military power by civil government.

while disparaging another. Some lay into the good General Boulanger tooth and nail, whereupon his defenders counter-attack by means of assorted, multi-coloured cannonballs. Some people recommend adopting that system known as *the provision of covering troops,* while others prefer ("and greatly so, kind Sir!") the convergence of troops on the borders. The most modest and unassuming of citizens, the most peace-loving and conventional middle-class householders each have their plan (infallible, I hasten to add) which they fervently expound.

"They ought to do this! ... Why don't they do that? ... Ah! If only *I* were the Minister for War!"

Far be it from me to even think about jesting on such a topic. This fervor has its roots in noble sentiments, and, what's more, some well-informed people assure me that it is by his inordinate urge to cut up his fellow creatures into little pieces that one truly recognizes a civilized European.

Patriotic and civilized! There you have two fine descriptors of which I am, by Jove, just as deserving as the next man! Let us therefore talk battle, if you please.

The tour of inspection recently completed by General de Freycinet lends to these questions an even more urgent topicality and relevance, making of them the burning issues of the hour.[160] Following this tour, you must all have read, with concern, journalistic evaluations of the degree of potential resistance offered by the revolving steel gun turrets of assault tanks, to new missiles made of meninite.[161] According to some, those turrets would be in smithereens in the event of an attack by such missiles. Naturally, the constructors of those turrets have registered their protest.

Without wishing to be seen to come down on one side or the other in this debate, I will dare to put forward the following audacious suggestion, that steel armor-plating would, in any case, be in much

160. Charles Louis de Saulces de Freycinet (1828-1923) formed part of the National Defence government of France in 1876 as prefect of the Tarn-et-Garonne region, and later served the government as a war commissioner, appointed by Gambetta in 1870-71. He was a senator in 1876, subsequently a minister, head of cabinet on four separate occasions, and Minister of Defence dealing with war in 1888. In this capacity, he inspected military fortifications and implemented a border-defence policy.

161. Meninite was an explosive which was patented by the chemist Eugène Turpin (1848-1927) in 1885 and adopted by the French government in 1887. In 1896, Turpin instituted legal proceedings against Jules Verne for slander for the novel *Facing the Flag* (*Face au drapeau*, 1896).

better health if it hadn't been struck by shells and shrapnel. That is, of course, a truism, but far be it from Yours Truly to weigh in with any practical inferences of his own!

Fortunately, people other than myself have resolved this part of the problem. Over the past ten years, indeed, several gun turrets have been devised which can be raised and then lowered into their tanks. One of the most ingenious of these turrets, both in its principle and in the simplicity of the equipment which it calls for, is, undoubtedly, that of Colonel Souriau.[162]

The armor-plated turret invented by him is based on the scientific principle of the neutral equilibrium of bodies which have been plunged into liquid. Instead of resting on the ground like previous versions, it is supported by a hollow cylinder which acts as a float. This cylinder, submerged in a tank, is of such dimensions that the water displaced by it counterbalances the weight of the turret, by which it is surmounted. In such conditions, it takes only four men to cause the whole contraption to move, either round in a circle, or vertically.

Once the cannon has been aimed, shots are fired and the gun turret instantly goes back inside the shelter of the tank, out of sight. The enemy returns fire, but its efforts prove quite harmless and ineffective. While this is happening, targets are once again searched for, the turret rises once more, and, bam!, a fresh discharge of gunfire is followed by another descent of the gun turret. This system is, it appears, capable of allowing for the unlimbering of guns twice a minute.

Doesn't all that remind you of that toy which must certainly have afforded you hours of amusement in your childhood, that box from which, at the push of a button, a grimacing devil would shoot up with pointed tongue and outstretched arms?

Colonel Souriau's idea is to provide protective enclosures for our military fortifications by means of these toys. In times of peace, the Jack-in-the-box shall remain sealed. However, in wartime, the devil shall spring up out of the ground, as though from Hell itself. He shall have (to give you an idea of his appearance) arms which arc infinitely longer and an incomparably more pointed tongue than his miniature

162. François Auguste Souriau (1832-1897) was a military engineer in Orléans. His project was examined in 1888 but not proceeded with as the slightest crack in the water reservoir would have risked the breaking down of his invention.

model, and he shall make, and cause to be made, grimaces altogether uglier than those which used to entertain you while you were still at that happy age when you weren't yet civilized.

I hope that many years may pass before Colonel Souriau's gun turrets have to prove themselves, but can we reasonably hope for this? With the arrival of spring, rumblings of war are renewed like Nature's green shoots. True, up to now, these haven't gotten any further than the stage of threats, just like simple Homeric heroes. But if you keep playing with fire, you'll eventually get burnt! ...

It is difficult to live eternally in peace, when one is surrounded by one's enemies, and the Germans are hardly sparing us the marks of their reluctance. After Lagny, Vexaincourt, after Vexaincourt, antipyrine ... and then a fresh incident ... this time, of a therapeutic nature.[163]

"Antipyrine?" I hear you ask.

"Antipyrine is a simple alkaloid, derived from tar, wherein it was first discovered by Doctor Knorr, a German medic."

"So it's a kind of medication, then?"

"Absolutely. Which is prescribed for fevers, neuralgia, etc."

"A type of medication ... which actually *cures* people? Now *that* seems quite unlikely!"

Whatever the case may be, consumption of this product is increasing daily, and French factories have been set up to produce it. Which has drawn complaints from our kind neighbors.

"Don't touch our antipyrine!" they cry in unison. "Antipyrine is a German invention over which the German people have a monopoly."

"Are you joking?" our doctors reply. "Your antipyrine is badly made, impure, and we have no intention of finishing off our patients with products other than those whose nature *we* can control!"

This is met with silence on the part of the Germans, who, feeling extremely chagrined to be unable to poison us through retail channels, are waiting until they are at liberty to kill us *wholesale.* But, changing their line of attack, they quickly launch a fresh charge upon us with utterly Teutonic rage.

"You're manufacturing this medication, that's as may be! We'll settle for that, since we can't do anything to prevent it. But in that case,

163. *Antipyrine* or *phenazone* possesses analgesic and antipyretic properties, but its use has been banned from modern medicine owing to its toxicity—it carries the risk of allergic reactions and of haemolytic (relating to the disintegration of red blood cells) anaemia.

change its name—that's *our* trademark!"[164]

So here we are, holding sovereignty over a substance to which it's impossible to give a name. A competition is then launched to come up with an official name for this poor disinherited entity. In the meantime, the Académie Française, faithful to wise parliamentary traditions, has set up a special commission to decide on the date of baptism.

The distressing aspect to this whole affair is that this meeting of godfathers, obliged to choose an alternative designation for their antipyretic goddaughter, is probably going to choose a truly scientific name. And you know what that means. There are already suggestions of adopting (shudder!) the name Dimethyloxiquinizine! A name like that is enough to give you several splitting headaches, and I consider that our excellent neighbors, by reducing us to these cruel, dire straits, are already well and truly giving us ample justification for many future reprisals.

* * *

While our doctors were patriotically defending the stomachs of their compatriots against German poisoning, our chemists were in a chivalrous mood, chivalry being another French quality. Indeed, are Messrs. Frémy and Verneuil not extremely chivalrous, given that they are the very ones who, marshalling their scientific learning in the service of the feminine concern for stylishness, have transformed their laboratory into an inexhaustible mine of rubies?[165]

The issue of rubies has several aspects.

The drunkard wears them on his nose, and produces them at will through his absorption of that liquid so dear to Bacchus.[166]

For you, my dear ladies, rubies are blood-red stars, whose value is equal to and often greater than that of diamonds, by means of which

---

164. Ten years later, German researchers from the Bayer laboratories were to discover aspirin. This very useful medicine—over which Germans also wished to preserve their monopoly—enjoys special conditions of use in France, obtained in 1919 following the signature of the peace treaty.

165. Auguste Verneuil (1856-1913) worked, from 1883 onwards, as assistant to the chemist Edmond Frémy (1814-1894) with whom he began his research into the mineralogical synthesis or fusion of the ruby in 1886. This subject is reminiscent of the manufacture of an artificial diamond in the novel *L'Étoile du sud* (*The Star of the South*, 1884) which Jules Verne published based on a manuscript by Paschal Grousset (1844-1909).

166. Bacchus is a god of wine in ancient Greece and Rome.

you enhance the snow-white complexion of your fair hands, arms and shoulders.

As for the scientist, he or she sees in rubies only the most beautiful variety of corundum, a gemstone. If a Buddhist were to come to him and tell him the tale that rubies are made from the tears shed by the beautiful Yasodhara on being abandoned by her much-loved spouse, Siddharta, the future Buddha, the scientist would smile and, examining the stone through a magnifying glass, would have the diligence to discover that its shape was rhombohedral.[167] Then, casting it into a crucible and analysing it, he would find nothing of the components of tears, but quite simply aluminia, or crystallized aluminium oxide.

This composition of the ruby had already been known for a long time. Despite this, all of the methods employed to bring about the artificial crystallization of aluminia had produced only negative or incomplete results. In a vain attempt to coax this stubborn substance to allow itself to be crystallized, it had been presented with the most unctuous, ingratiating alloys, the most persuasive salts and the most silver-tongued acids. Being the unyielding virgin that she was, she had reserved nothing but chilliness and scorn for all of these bashful lovers. And such would still be the case to this very day, if Messrs. Frémy and Verneuil, applying themselves to this challenging task where so many others had failed, had not had the idea of enclosing her with only that seductive barium fluoride for company in her prison cell. What a sorry state of affairs! That bold libertine succeeded where so much platonic wooing before it had failed. That courtly fluoride proved more forward than his predecessors; indeed, one could even say that he was downright insolent! To such an extent that Milady Aluminia, staggered by such behaviour, ended up succumbing to his bold advances and thereby finally becoming … crystallized.

Twelve years of labor and effort have been spent on this undertaking, which I've recounted here in only a few lines. But Messrs. Frémy and Verneuil's achievement was magnificent, bringing about as it did this mineralogical fusion, the scientific impact of which has been considerable.

It is important to note that this isn't merely some more or less perfect imitation, nor even a spinel nor indeed a common *balas ruby*.[168]

167. Rhombohedral is a crystal, trigonal shape.

168. The *spinel*, a glassy mineral, an aluminiate of magnesium, coloured pinkish-red, has

No, this is the genuine article, the natural gemstone in all its glory, the quintessential Oriental jewel, consisting only of aluminia, and tinged by slight traces of chromium.

This is a result of which Messrs. Frémy and Verneuil can deservedly be proud. Not to mention happy, when you think of all those pretty feminine mouths which shall call down blessings from Heaven upon their heads. What excuse, I ask you, shall husbands now have for refusing rings, bracelets and other jewellery and finery? And not only rubies, but topazes, sapphires, and emeralds too, for he who can do more can do less, as the old proverb has it! And, in all seriousness, is it rash to suppose that those two learned chemists will even, in the near future, be able to reproduce humbler varieties of corindon, since they are already able to produce, at will, from the self-same corindon, that dazzling King, he who is the altogether fitting consort of a future *Topaz Queen*?[169]

III.[170]

On September 25, 1895, at the Boulogne railway station, I took the 6:45 p.m. fast train to London. A three and a half-hour journey, one of which is taken up with the crossing of that much-lauded bridge, thirty-seven kilometers in length, which connects France to England.

An exceedingly pretty young woman, probably English, was already occupying the compartment which I entered. Remaining supremely indifferent to my entrance, she kept her gaze steadfastly fixed on the guidebook to the bridge which she was studying, not

---

nothing in common with the actual ruby. Furthermore, the *balas ruby* (a light wine-coloured gemstone).is not commonplace; its name—which has nothing to do with the French word *balai* (a sweeping brush)! – refers only to its origin (Samarcand, in Central Asia). The world's most beautiful rubies come from Birmanie.

169. The *Topaz Queen* is a reference to Victor Massé's (1822-1884) comic opera, based on a text by Lockroy and Battu. Massé was a friend of Jules Verne.

170. This short story was originally published in *Le Figaro. Supplément littéraire.* 14th year, No. 24, on June 16, 1888, p. 20. It was subsequently republished under the title "The Crossing of the English Channel in 1895" in *La Confiance* (Paris), 10th year, No. 33, on September 6th, 1888, p.1. Even though, in this second publication, it was still credited to "Michel Jules Verne," the anonymous author of the introduction attributed the text to "the vivid imagination of that 'brilliant writer' *Jules* Verne." That second version was republished in the *BSJV*, No. 103, 1995, pp. 9-13, and in *ETHUIN*, pp. 31-38 ("The Bridge over the English Channel"). Here, the original version has been reproduced, but includes the principal variations.

bothering to waste her time giving so much as a mere glance in my direction. One of those young English ladies, no doubt, who travel round Europe in the manner of a bachelor.

There is nothing to report of the journey until we reached the Gris-Nez cape, which is where the "airborne" segment of the trip begins. We're travelling along above the waves.

My female travelling companion still persists in studying her guide book.

As for me, I'm leaning out of the window, and, for more than half an hour, I look out. A magnificent sight! In the fog, the French coast has disappeared from view. At my feet, the waves are doing eternal battle with one another, under an ominously grey sky through which ragged clouds sail like wings. The weather seems as though it's about to turn nasty. The north-west wind seems to be freshening and a storm is brewing.

Hold on a moment: what's going on now? The train has stopped and everybody is getting out. I follow suit and head off to find out what's going on.

A little bit of engine trouble is the cause of this halt. Nothing serious. A delay of a quarter of an hour, nothing more. Let's go and kill these fifteen minutes.

So off I go, strolling idly along the railway track. The coastline has become completely obscured in the fog. I am surrounded by nothing but vast, open space, at which I gaze, lost in contemplation …

Half past seven! Goodness, no! I mustn't let the train leave without me.

But no sooner have I taken a few steps than a large red eye begins to blaze through the twilight and moves forward at speed. Whistle blows pierce the air … God in Heaven! It's my train!

"Stop! Stop!"

Bah! It has disappeared in a gust of wind: gone with the wind! Engines, carriages, coaches fly past and disappear from view in the gathering shadows. And so I find myself alone!

* * *

Alone? But no! An indistinct shape forms a confusing blur at a hundred paces from where I'm standing. I approach it, and no, what a pleasure, I find myself in the company of my pretty travelling companion of a short time ago. She too must have forgotten the time, absorbed as she was in the study of her guide. I do declare! This is no time to stand on ceremony. So I approach her, and somewhat abruptly engage her in conversation:

"Here we are, Miss..." I say to her.

"Excuse me, Sir—your name?"

Taken aback, I tell her my name, in exchange for which I am given her own: Miss Georgina Waterford, from New York, an American and not an Englishwoman as I had thought. Well now! This is perfect! We've introduced ourselves to each other in accordance with the rules of polite society. We can now converse. I continue:

"We find ourselves, Miss, in a sorry situation."

"Why so?"

"Why, indeed! The train has left us in dire straits, it seems to me!"

"Fair enough," she calmly replies, "but haven't we each got a pair of legs?"

"Walk?" I timidly ventured. "It's necessary, that much is obvious. But in which direction? Back towards France, in my opinion."

"No," protests Miss Georgina. "We're only sixteen kilometers from the English coast. It's the Warne which is underneath us."

"The Warne? But that reef isn't, to my knowledge, situated between Folkstone and the Griz-Nez cape."

"So I take it you aren't aware," she replies to me, "that the construction firm responsible for the building of this bridge, Messrs. Hersent and Schneider, rather than building it in a straight line, instead followed the line of the shallowest sea depths, which vary from a minimum depth of six meters to a maximum of fifty?[171] There are two bends in the bridge, the first one at Clobart, which we've already passed through, the second at the Warne, over which we're now standing."

Good grief! She's well up on this subject, that's for sure!

Without waiting for me to respond, she has continued walking. Leave her alone? Impossible, with the bad weather which is currently threatening to unleash its fury. I run to catch up with her, at that

171. Hildevert Hersent (1827-1903) was a French engineer who was, in fact, in 1888-89, studying the proposed project of constructing a bridge over the English Channel, with the company Schneider and Co., having previously overseen the construction of several famous bridges, as well as having worked on the regularization of the course of the River Danube, in Vienna, between 1869 and 1875, and having contributed to preparatory work on the Panama Canal, from 1881-1883.

protective railing which she is striving, in vain, to climb over. To my great astonishment, I see a wide highway where I had presumed I would encounter nothing but empty space. I express some surprise at this.

"The bridge has four railway lines and one road for carriages," comes the reply.

"So how wide is it?"

"Thirty meters."

She knows all her information off by heart, that's quite obvious: this one certainly knows her stuff.

With much effort, we manage to clear the barrier at the edge of the track, and land on the highway. On the other side, there is another protective railing, which I go over to, resting my elbows on it.

Down below, as though in the very depths of an abyss, the waves crash with thunderous roars. No gently rippling undulations are these; nothing but an almighty crashing of towering, angry waves. The sea seems to be boiling with anger.

"Upper oolitic terrain," my travelling companion laconically declares. "A shallow stretch, hence this swirling water."[172]

I look at her in astonishment. This young woman is a fount of knowledge! And, truth be told, there would be nothing in the least unpleasant about gazing into the depths of this particular fountain!

Once again, I lean over to look down on the waves. Shrieks, moans, howls emanate from the watery depths, intermingled with the whistle of the wind as it rings in my ears, a wind which is growing ever stormier. Stirred by the rising storm, the waves are becoming ever squallier, crashing angrily against the pillars of the bridge. How can this bridge still be standing? How come it hasn't been swept away by these raging waters which batter it incessantly? I rather naively express this fear to my companion.

"Impossible," replies Miss Georgina, with a slight shrug of her shoulders. "Haven't I already told you that it is oolitic terrain on which the foundations of this bridge have been laid, foundations made from compressed air, and thus solidly fixed, indestructible. What's more, the pillars, whose shape is elliptical, and which have been constructed so as to be directly in line with the current, have an unlimited capacity to resist pressure. Moreover, there is no obstacle to the passage of

172. Oolitic: made of spherical pieces of limestone.

the water. At this spot, the reach of the protective metal girders is about eighty meters, but further on, where the sea is at its deepest, it increases to between four hundred and five hundred meters. In such conditions, all of the bridge's supports combined don't reach one tenth of the section of the strait. A negligible amount."

As for me, I'm quite willing to be neglectful!

* * *

We've started walking again, chatting as we go. I ask Miss Georgina: "So, has it been long since you left New York?"

"Five months."

"So you're travelling alone?"

"By chance," comes her reply to me. "The person who was supposed to come with me became suddenly indisposed."

"Anything serious?"

"A heavy cold."

"Ah!" By now, night has fallen, while the storm is growing ever fiercer. The difficulties in seeing where we're going are rendered greater by the pitch dark of this black night enveloping us. Suddenly, I am blinded by a dazzling light. At each pillar, a powerful electric reflector has been switched on, sprinkling the sea waters with cartloads of glimmering sparks. To our right, to our left, like some enormous iron snake, blazing, inflamed rings seem to be unfurling along the length of the bridge. It's a magical sight. Transfixed by admiration, I stand and stare, motionless.

"How beautiful it is!" I exclaim.

"Yes, not bad," Miss Georgina replies with a disdainful pout. "But what's really needed is a bridge to be built between America and Ireland."[173]

173. This stretch of dialogue is reminiscent of a similar conversation occurring in Jules Verne's novel *A Floating* City, on the subject of "that admirable Niagara Falls," in which a European perspective comes into similar confrontation with an American viewpoint:

> "Isn't this beautiful! Sir," I said to him, "isn't this admirable!"
> "Yes," he replied to me, "but what a waste of mechanical power, and what a windmill one could power with such a waterfall!"
> Never have I felt a fiercer desire to throw an engineer into the water! (Chapter XXXIX, my translation).

I disagree: "But the cost alone of such an undertaking would be prohibitive. This bridge must have already cost a pretty penny."

"Pooh! A billion, perhaps! 350 million for the concrete superstructure, 550 for the metalwork, sixty to connect the railway lines. Multiply that sum by a hundred, that's all."

She speaks with an easy authority.

* * *

Looking at my watch, I see that it's now 8 p.m. Lights are beginning to appear from all sides. Lighthouse beams flash on the horizon, beating their rays down upon us like the watchful eyes of surveillance cameras. Below us, more lights, as the sidelights of ships glide underneath us, red, green, white, over the sea, like fireflies of the grasses, waving in the breeze, in this green oceanic prairie.

Yes, hundreds of ships! At each moment, they sail along underneath the arches of the bridge, ships sailing swiftly onwards towards the ocean, steamers spewing out smoke. Viewed from this height, they seem positively miniscule, appearing, then vanishing, as though swallowed up whole by the darkness.

The storm, at its height, is roaring. Great birds wheel and whirl round in the air above us, swept along helplessly by the gale. Others, attracted by the reflectors, end up having their heads dashed against the metal barriers. You hear a thud, and then: *splash*!

Despite the distance, we are covered in sea spray. Miss Georgina has had to accept my offer to place her arm in mine, but even walking together side by side, we have difficulty in making headway.

Suddenly, to our right, a great ship appears, sailing under its bare poles, rear wind. Driven by the gale through the strait, swept along by towering waves, it looks like a gigantic battering ram which has been launched straight at us.

Nervously, I grasp my companion's hand.

"There's nothing to be frightened of," she says calmly to me. "At this point, the reach of the protective metal girders is five hundred meters and their height is fifty-five. There's enough space for even the

---

Michel revisited this idea of harnessing the power of the Niagara Falls in his short story, "In the Year 2889."

biggest of ships to pass safely through this strait."

This time, however, she is to be proven wrong.

Because, at the moment when, with lightning speed, the ship arrives, a gigantic wave seizes it, lifting it upwards like some mere plaything. A dreadful crunching sound is heard. The top of the mast is smashed against the metal girder. The bridge is strewn with fragments of the shattered mast. I rush to Georgina's side.[174]

But, signalling to me to stop, cupping her hands and peering through them as if through an eyeglass:

"Its royal mast has been broken," she reports, in a supremely dispassionate tone.

What a night! Exhausted, soaked to the skin, bone-tired, we continue to drag ourselves wearily forward. By a stroke of good fortune, the wind has at last died down. No matter! I had really thought we would never reach our destination safely.

Finally, at almost one o'clock in the morning, we're approaching the shore. But then, suddenly, a shadow comes into view, and a voice begins to speak, saying:

"Is that you, Georgina?"

"Yes," replies my American lady.

"I went to meet you at the train terminus of the bridge on the date we'd agreed when you left New York, but when I couldn't find you on the train, I supposed you had come here on foot."

What's more, no mention is made of the storm.

By now, the shadow has come right up to us and has taken shape: a red-haired young man, well-dressed in black, exchanges a perfunctory handshake with Georgina.

Turning towards me, my astonishing travelling companion says: "Percival, my fiancé."

Upon which both of them exchange a solemn handshake with me.

Nothing more. Then, while I stay there, bemused, they turn round on their heels and, side by side, with mechanical footsteps, they walk off, gradually fading from sight in the darkness. Their voices, fainter and fainter, reach my ears:

---

174. In place of these few lines, *La Confiance* offered a less dramatic version:

> "And indeed, the ship, swept along by terrifying waves, rapidly crossed the wide bay.
> "So you see," Georgina said to me, with a supreme lack of emotion."

"When did you leave Paris?" asked Percival.

"Three months ago," replied Georgina.

"Three months! So what have you been doing in all that time?"

"I've been travelling around the world. And what have *you* been doing since I left New York?"

"Me? I've been recovering from my cold."

IV.

Oysters and Ants.
A Scientific Judgement of Feminine Taste.[175]

"Waiter! A dozen Ustend oysters!"

That's an utterance which, possibly very soon, only Rothschild shall be able to utter without trembling in fear for the fatness of his purse. For the fact is that the number of oysters is diminishing (and it pains me to say it), while individual oysters are getting fatter.

At least, this is what has emerged from the information recently confided to me by a very elderly oyster whom I recently met on the shores of Cancale bay. Upon my request, this distinguished personage kindly agreed to grant me an interview, which I wrote down for you, and which I've faithfully transcribed hereunder.

* * *

Dispensing with any unnecessary preface, let's go straight to the most interesting part of the interview.

ME. Your sisters, however, dear Madam, are so great in number that they're surely driving any mother of a large brood to distraction.[176]

175. This gastronomically-themed piece was first published in *Le Figaro. Supplément littéraire.* 14th year. No. 26, June, 30, 1888, p. 103. It was republished in *BSJV*, No. 106, 1993, pp. 21-25 and in *ETHUIN*, pp. 39-45.

176. In the original French, Michel Verne writes about driving "la mère Gigogne" to despair. This source text culture-specific reference is to a French puppet character representing a large lady surrounded by children, who are so numerous as to be falling from her skirts—this character has become proverbial and symbolic within French culture. It was decided not to reproduce this French culture-specific reference in this translation, given its likely unfamiliarity to many readers of this target text; instead, I have simply replaced it with the explanatory "mother of a large brood," together with this explicatory footnote.

THE OYSTER, manifesting deep, intimate pride. That's true. Each of us lays between fifty and sixty thousand eggs per year. Just imagine how many oysters that produces in the space of ten years.

ME. Please excuse me. The fear of a splitting headache is the beginning of wisdom. But how, with such a prolific rate of fertility, can that beautiful oyster family be in danger of extinction?

THE OYSTER, raising her valves to the heavens. Alas! We have so many enemies!

ME, with interest. Enemies? But who are they?

THE OYSTER. Why, first and foremost, *yourselves*, cruel humans!

ME. Do you really think so? After all, we love you so …

THE OYSTER. Too much! … Ugolino loved his children too, didn't he?[177] A love like *that* couldn't possibly be to the liking of the person loved! Why don't you try a love like that on your own womenfolk? As for oysters, we're unable to make any protest. We must dumbly submit to that all-consuming affection which, in Paris alone, gobbles up one hundred million of my sisters each year, who end up inside the bellies of overly-zealous, impassioned oyster worshippers.

ME, feeling sorry for her. But what about when you're in the depths of the ocean, my ill-fated mollusc?

THE OYSTER. Here, we've only got even more enemies! Starfish, for instance, which slowly entangle us in their deathly embrace. In vain, we close our valves. But as this could lead to us dying from suffocation, we soon have no choice but to spread them open again. And through the gap thus formed in the oyster, the starfish, inserting his extendable tongue, greedily sucks up his victim's flesh. And there are so many others! … Here! Winkles: they're like those honorable gentlemen of yours who force open safes; those little wretches, no bigger than a bean, use a sort of brace with which cruel Mother Nature has endowed them. With the aid of this tool, they pierce our shells, and pump out the nourishing juices we've gathered so painstakingly. We oysters, powerless and paralyzed, can only sit and helplessly watch this odious misappropriation of our life's savings.

ME. Indeed, you can't even flee these attackers.

THE OYSTER. Only in our youth are we gifted with the power of movement. I myself didn't stay very long in the bosom of she who

177. Ugolino lived in 12th century-Pisa, and was a tyrant who inspired Dante's damned hero who apparently ate his own children, in the *Divine Comedy*.

conceived me.

ME. Ah, the recklessness of youth!

THE OYSTER. Tell me about it! We're hardly born when we're off on our adventures. Blissfully unaware of the dangers which lie in wait for us, we travel over a great stretch of underwater terrain, opening our curious eyes on everything, stocking up on memories for that day, near at hand, when old age shall constrain us to paralysis.

Should an obstacle present itself, we ask the locals for information, and if the area is to our liking, we settle down there, without moving on any further.

ME. And what does it need to have in order to be to your liking?

THE OYSTER. Only one thing: cleanliness. From her earliest childhood, the oyster is a sensitive, refined creature. Far superior in that regard to your own offspring, of whom the same couldn't be said. If a potential dwelling place isn't immaculate, off we go again, searching further. Very often, such searches are in vain, on these coasts, polluted as they are by rivers of waste matter!

ME. So what happens then?

THE OYSTER. The poor wayfarer grows weary of her pursuit of an unattainable ideal of spotlessness; she becomes exhausted, old age paralyzes her and, gradually sinking into the mud, she dies.

ME. Just as the poet, who has journeyed forth in conquest of some ideal state, falls, broken, onto the ground.

My honorable interviewee seems flattered by the comparison.

"If, on the other hand," she went on, "we find a lodging which is to our taste, we remain there, we lose our locomotive organs and, now doing nothing more than merely fattening up, we are considered worthy, four years later, of going to meet our death on your dining tables: and what a death!"

"But such relative happiness is rare!"

"Believe me, Sir, when I tell you (speaking from the experience of an elderly oyster whose shells have become whitened with age) that our cruellest enemy is the dirtiness of these shores. Add to that, all those who devour us during the wanderings of our youth, and those who eat us when we've reached maturity, a state about which I've only told you a very limited amount, and you will understand the threat of extinction of such a populous race."

And with those words, I politely took my leave.

And as I went on my way, I do declare that I was astonished by only one thing: that, in the midst of so many perils, a single oyster can still find its way to our lemons on the dinner table.

* * *

The day will come, I fear, when such astonishment will have become a thing of the past, when we shall be able to sell, by weight, all our three-pronged forks, which will have been rendered obsolete.

But will that really constitute irreparable damage? After all, there are plenty of other delicacies in the sea! The world is vast enough to provide us, for a long time to come, with hitherto unknown victuals. Haven't we already imported swallows' nests from China? Who is there to prevent us, I ask you, from making a fresh foray into the territory of exotic gastronomic delights?

What would you say to a dish of white ants, for instance?

Is that a grimace of disgust I see you making? So you're unaware, then, that in Central Africa and on the Indian Archipelago, entire races are nourished by that insect?

"That's all very well!" I hear you object, "but how do you cook it? That's one recipe you won't find in the *Householders' Cookbook*."[178]

That doesn't make an ounce of difference! As I am practically a walking cookery book, an augmented human version of that worthy tome, I can search for the ingredients right before your very eyes.

First of all, let's go hunting, because, as the above-mentioned cookery book author wisely recommends, in order to make a stew, you've first got to go catch a hare.

White ants are winged insects. To capture them, a lit lamp is placed above any vessel filled with water. Attracted by the light reflected by the sheet of water, the ants dive headfirst into Eternity.

Once they've been captured, and their wings torn off, they are mixed with flour which is moistened with butter, dripping, oil, or some other similar ingredient, and a cylindrical-shaped cake is made from this combination. It is skewered, and roasted. This is the native method of preparing this dish, which is, I'm assured, exquisite.

178. A classic French cookery book, whose French-language original title is *Cuisinière Bourgeoise* (*The Middle-Class Cook*), first published in two volumes in 1746, under the pseudonym (the real name of the author has never been revealed) Menon.

Moreover, the primitive peoples from whom (obviously) I've gotten this information, are true gourmets. Not content with roasting insects, these epicures equally enjoy bees. The latter, rolled with honey in an aromatic leaf, are grilled on hot coals.

Soup: Chinese-style swallows' nests. *Roast:* Ant supreme. *Dessert:* Unseasoned bees. There you have, it seems to me, a most splendid menu for a three-course dinner.

Pooh! I hear a sceptical reader mutter, a truffled cock is much more to *my* liking.

* * *

Agreed. I would even willingly proclaim that this marriage of the truffle with the cock is a most charming one, if I weren't afraid of acquiring an unfortunate reputation for gluttony. Since I began writing this article, each time I open my mouth, I want to fill it with food. Imagine forgetting myself for so long, writing and thinking about cooking! You must think I'm some cordon bleu chef starving for literature. I think it's about time I headed to the living-cum-dining room.

Bah! Is it really necessary? Even if male readers disparage my choice of subject, female readers can, at least, being the good housewives that they are, only approve of my choice (may I say this at the risk of offending them?). Indeed, I doubt very much that they'll be offended, as I consider them ever so slightly fond of their food.

Do I hear you protest at this?

Alright! Alright! I've consulted the authors who are my sources, and I'm merely repeating what Science has told us, through the voices of Messrs. Balley and Nicholls. Numerous experiments conducted by these gentlemen have shown, indeed, that women's taste buds are keener and more developed than those of their bearded counterparts.

The only exception is in the case of savoury flavors, in which case it is men whose taste buds have the upper hand.

Doesn't this detail, which seems totally insignificant, open new horizons to you? Now we know why dressmakers' bills are so salty! It's quite simply lack of perception on the part of our women!

By way of conclusion, allow me to briefly object to this word "taste," which means little or nothing. Nine times out of ten, "sense of smell" would be a more accurate term. Our olfactory organs are, in fact, the means by which we perceive most of the sensations which are incorrectly attributed to the sense of taste.

A little experiment will show you what I mean. Blindfold your eyes, hold your nose, and then eat (or drink, as the case may be) veal, beef, water, wine, mutton, chicken, etc. Afflicted with an artificial head cold, you will be unable to distinguish these foodstuffs and drinks from each other.

Only sweet, bitter or salty flavors are perceived by the tip and sides of the tongue, leaving our sense of smell in perfect peace.

What a fine thing is Science: it explains everything. Indeed, doesn't it teach us that women detect these flavors, and particularly the latter, with less sensitivity and sharpness than us?

Conclusion: Women have a good nose … but a bad tongue!

So, as I was saying …

V.

Combined Photography. Electricity in the Home.[179]

The other day, as I was walking along the boulevard, I recognized, among the evening strollers of the so-called "green hour," one of my former friends, who was wearily traipsing and trudging along in a most solitary and dejected manner.[180] Passavent, Anatole Passavent: a former fellow solider from my military days, now living in exile on the edge of the Great Desert of Biskra.

What was this Algerian doing here in Paris? And most importantly, why the face as long as a wet week? Feeling curious, I approached him.

Once the initial outpourings of delight at seeing each other again had been gotten over with, and both of us had seated ourselves comfortably at the terrace of a café, I began asking him a series of questions about himself.

179. This story was first published in *Le Figaro. Supplément littéraire.* 14th year. No. 29, July 21, 1888, p.114; it was republished in *BSJV*, No. 106, 1993, pp. 26-30, and in *ETHUIN*, pp.47-52.

180. The "green hour" is the name given to the popular custom of going to cafés to drink absinthe at 5 p.m.

"It's quite a story," he replied to me, not needing much persuasion on my part to tell it.

"Tell me all," I said to him encouragingly, as I lit a cigar.

"Whatever! I'll start by letting you know that I've got married."

"Now that *is* sad, I grant you. So when did this marriage take place?"

"I've been married for the past five months."

"Five months already! And … any hope of a forthcoming baptism?"

"I've got five daughters to marry off," he replied without blinking an eyelid.

"Holy smoke! One per month! Well done!"

"What can you expect!" he sighed. "Life in Biskra is a little lonely, one feels a bit lost. That's how the idea came to me of finding a wife. I thought to myself that a wife might liven up my solitary existence. So I put in a request for leave, which was granted; I arrived in Paris. But whose door was I to knock on? I don't know anybody here. So I went to a matrimonial agency, whose manageress, as soon as we'd finished discussing her fee, spread out a whole series of lovely portraits before my eyes. One in particular. It would be pointless to try describing it to you: the face of an angel. I settled on that one. "Ah! You'll have plenty of choice there," the matchmaker said to me: "That's a composite portrait of five young women of marriageable age."

"Hold your horses!" I said to Passavent. "I don't follow. What do you mean by a composite portrait?"

"The very question I was asking myself at that very moment. At the time, I was just as blissfully ignorant as you. But since then … ! A composite portrait, my dear chap, is a portrait of several people—five young women in this case—from the same family, or at the very least, the same race, photographed in the ordinary way, in succession, but all on the same plate, the second being superimposed upon the first, the third on the second, and so on."

"The result must be horrifying!"

"It seems not. Great care is taken to place the subjects of the photo in an exactly identical manner. The portraits are superimposed, without distorting one another, and a single print is obtained; the average, the round-up of the family or of the race; in a word, the composite portrait."

"I say! *That's* quite a curious thing!"

"It was a portrait of that kind which was shown to me. Why had such a system been chosen? For cost-cutting reasons, I presume. Whatever the case may be, the people who peddle this system must be quite the smooth talkers, given the amount of profit they're making! I had no hesitation and, inflamed with the ardor of love, I went off to introduce myself to the family. Ah! My friend! …"

"So what happened?"

"There were indeed five young women to be married off. But what a cruel reality after such a beautiful illusion! One was hunchbacked, another bald, a third was gap-toothed, a fourth …"

"Okay, okay, I get the picture! In a word, monsters."

"Yes, monsters, when taken individually; but an angel, collectively. As for the photo, it was the spitting image of the mother, to whom none of the daughters, however, bore the slightest resemblance. Isn't that strange?"

"Yes and no. All in all, it's natural for girls to resemble their mother. This resemblance, which can often be concealed by the particular expression of each face, or even by a very prominent personal feature, exists nonetheless, and logically, it has to become evident in this combination of the entire group of offspring. But, come to think of it, that photograph, didn't you tell me it was charming?"

"Indeed it was!"

"Well then, since it was an exact likeness of the mother, the mother must have been …"

"Charming, as you say."

"So, therefore …"

"Haven't I already told you: I got married?"

"Ah! My goodness!"

"Yes, I'm only too well aware; she *is* a bit on the mature side, the mother; in her forties, but still beautiful; and somewhat wealthy, which always sweetens the pill. What's more, I'm hardly in the first flush of youth myself … To cut a long story short, two weeks later, I was married. Ah! That wedding day! There were torrential downpours of rain, and it had been raining thus for the previous two weeks, non-stop. There I was, squelching through mud, escorted by my five daughters, the bald one, the hunchback …"

"The gap-toothed one, etc. Yes, I see."

"Finally, when night had fallen, I sneaked away a few minutes after my bride. In the marital bedroom, I found my wife stretched out by the fire on a silk-covered *chaise longue*. But listen to what happened next, because it's important. I went over to her, and, with a romantic gesture, I took her hand. But no sooner had I touched her than an unpleasant electric shock forced me to let go of her hand. I tried again, once, twice, three times … Always with the same result. My terrible predicament can be summed up in one phrase: I'd married an electric woman!"

"What on earth is that?"

"You haven't heard of electric women?"

"My God! I'm not positive about them. Like everybody else … at the fairground … the so-called torpedo women …"

"No, you've got the wrong end of the stick. If you were a regular newspaper reader, you'd be familiar with that extremely strange phenomenon: the spontaneous electrification of a woman, observed by M. Féré, and on which he gave a scientific paper to the Biology Society.[181] What I was witnessing that night was a fresh manifestation of that phenomenon."

"How come you hadn't noticed it before uttering those fatal words 'I do'?"

"Well you may ask! My wife's electrical propensities (I only found this out later, you understand) are non-existent on rainy days: and it rained the whole time I was courting her! It only becomes apparent in dry weather, which it is even capable of forecasting."

"A walking barometer!" I laughed. "Handy, that!"

"What's more, the only reason I'd got an electric shock was because of our respective positions; my wife, as I've told you, was stretched out on a silk covering, silk being an electrical insulator, while I, on the other hand, was on the wooden floor, wood being a good conductor. When both of us are in the same conditions, in the street for example, I don't feel anything."

"So, what are you complaining about?"

"What am I complaining about? I must say, you're being very high-and-mighty! For starters, on the "electrical" days as I call them,

181. Charles Féré (1852-1907), a French doctor, studied under Achille Flaubert (brother of French novelist Gustave) and was private secretary to Jean Martin Charcot. He is the author of numerous publications on medicine, psychology, sexuality and criminality.

my wife can't get undressed without assistance. Her clothing sticks to her skin, producing a most distinctive luminous crackling. I'm obliged to help her …"

"And you get electrified … by influence?"

"Precisely. But here's the unfortunate aspect of the whole situation. On those evenings, my wife is like a bear with a sore head."

"By the deuce! Impossible to 'combine yourselves with each other,' so to speak …"

"And that's not all. Often, at night, her hair stands on end, so if I accidentally bring my finger near to her chignon in the latest style, sparks fly out of it."

"A female night-light, you might say!"

"And the last aspect, though this one is not so troublesome: would you believe that my wife's fingers attract light objects: ribbons, paper, and so on, just as a magnet attracts iron?"

"Now that's not at all extraordinary," I said, in contradiction of his argument. "In my youth, I met lots of very nice people whose fingers could attract ribbons, lace, and especially paper … as printed by the Bank of France … with absolutely exceptional power!"

"I forgot to mention," he went on, "that my idle daughters are gifted, or cursed, with the same paradoxical power as their mother. On one occasion, I was foolish enough to bring my entire family to a concert. The next day, things were absolutely intolerable. They had to admit to me that music exacerbated their electrical condition. In the meantime, the phenomena I've told you about have taken a distressing turn. It seems that dreadful itchiness of the legs has become a further related ailment. In my home, everybody is itching themselves from morning to night; whereas from night-time to the following morning, they're dancing! Those goddamned itches are an excuse for parties and non-stop dances. My nerves are on a knife's edge… If my wife was, at least, a pleasant person … But a filthy temper, my friend, oh, what a filthy temper!"

"That's quite natural."

"Why?"

"My God! The application of the power of extremities. You're well aware of lightning conductors. We learnt about them in secondary school."

"I don't see the connection …"

"Yet it's quite clear. Since your wife is constantly producing electricity, it would have ended up making her feel uncomfortable, if Nature, in its foresight, hadn't facilitated its passage from her system, by giving her a touchy disposition."

"Get away out of that, you blackguard!"

And with those words, we left the café.

"Come to think of it!" he asked me, just as we were saying goodbye, "You couldn't give me any advice, could you?"

"But of course," I said to him. "Since your wife isn't electrified in rainy weather, go and live in some wet region. Rouen, for example, or Brest. Whereas in Biskra ..."

"In Biskra, the weather is always fine!" he said, pitifully completing my sentence.

We exchanged a final handshake.

"Bah," he concluded; "At least there *is* one redeeming feature to this whole sorry saga. Thanks to my wife's electricity ..."

"What of it?"

"I've been completely cured of my rheumatism ..."

VI.

Under the Earth[182]

To offer a delicious piece of Dutch cheese to a starving, absolutely famished person, subject to the proviso that he shall only be allowed to nibble the rind, would, most certainly, constitute a joke of most dubious taste. And yet, it is precisely this type of prank which the Most High played upon us when he cast us poor human beings onto this great lump of Dutch cheese which is this Earth of ours. Ours are the outer limits, with the exception, however, of the North and South Pole and diverse other points, ours is the rind of the cheese! As for the delicious, succulent marrow which must surely lie concealed within its interior, we are condemned to desiring it from afar, just as elusive freedom is craved by contemporary household pets.

182. This piece was originally published in *Le Figaro. Supplément littéraire.* 14th year, No. 33, August 18, 1888, p.130; subsequently published in *BSJV*, No. 106, 1993, pp. 31-34 and in *ETHUIN*, pp. 53-58.

Stimulated by an overweening desire for the acquisition of knowledge, we have, throughout the last hundred thousand years (for this is the approximate age of humanity, according to scientific reckoning) been making continuous efforts to distance ourselves, in one direction or the other, from this terrestrial surface devolved upon us by Divine contract. But how meagre are the results obtained thus far!

Thanks to the invention of hot air balloons, which were surely not envisaged by the heavenly chief who keeps us on such a tight leash, we've been able to travel a bare eight kilometers to the zenith of our earthly capacities, and even less towards the lowest point attainable.

One thousand meters: this is, in fact, the depth of the new mine shaft of the Poirier Mining Company, forced by the scant expanse of its mining territory to gain, vertically, what it was refused horizontally, and this depth is, I believe, the longest stride ever made by humankind in its descent into the Underworld.[183]

The mines of Kitz-Bahl (Tyrol) and of Wutemberg (Bohemia) do, it is true, sink to a depth of fourteen hundred meters into the bowels of the earth,[184] but, if you deduct from this measurement the altitude at which their mine shafts open, you find their true depth to be severely reduced.

* * *

A humble kilometer! There you have it, then, the greatest distance achieved by humankind when it aspired to *descending* into the earth's interior. Truth be told, it's very little, and couldn't possibly be sufficient

183. Though the original French text by Michel Verne describes humankind as striding towards the *descensus averni*, the quote should read, more accurately, *Facilis descensus Averno* (*Easy is the descent towards Averno*). As Jules Verne made the same mistake in Chapter 23 of *Journey to the Centre of the Earth*, it seems likely that in this instance, as in others (see the next note), Michel was referring directly to his father's above-mentioned novel, one of his most famous. Thus, in the original French of this article, Michel Verne describes the descent towards the underworld as the "descent towards Avernus," Avernus being a lake near Naples which fills the crater of an extinct volcano and which was described by Virgil and other Latin writers as the entrance to the underworld. I have translated this reference to Avernus by the less culture-specific "the underworld," while noting Avernus and its meaning in this note, given that the reference may be obscure to many 21st-century readers of this translation.

184. More accurately, the mines of Kitzbuhel (Austria) and Kuttenberg (Czech Republic). Jules Verne, in the same chapter of his novel previously cited the preceding footnote, makes the same mistake when he writes: "We had already overtaken by six thousand feet the greatest depths attained by humankind, such as the Kitz-Bahl mine in the Tyrol, and those of Wuttemberg in Bohemia" (my translation).

in giving us an exact knowledge of the composition of the core of our terrestrial spheroid.

Despite the constant, unremitting onward march of scientific progress, we are thus reduced, nowadays, just as we were in the past, to mere conjecture.

However, there can be no question of depriving ourselves of the possibilities of such conjecture!

Without mentioning those illusionary hypotheses, now discredited, which saw our globe as an enormous, air-filled balloon, in which two stars, Pluto and Proserpine,[185] distributed light to subterranean regions; without mentioning the even more unusual conception of Professor Kircher,[186] who likened the Earth to a living entity, generously endowing it with lungs, arteries, veins, etc.; what diversity is nonetheless to be found in the less fanciful, more orthodox theories which, each in their turn, have prevailed and had their day, like simple political parties!

To this question: what actually *is* down there, underneath the Earth's surface?

"Water," replies Woodwart [sic], forgetting that if such underground oceans existed, they would be subject to the laws of tidal forces, just like any other ocean, and would thus cause us to experience the pleasant distraction of repeated earthquakes.[187]

---

185. See *Journey to the Center of the Earth*, chapter 30: "I then remembered the theory put forward by an English captain, who likened the Earth to a vast, hollow sphere, at the interior of which the air remained luminous as a result of its pressure, while two stars, Pluto and Proserpine, there described their mysterious orbits." (my rendering). Jules Verne had, in this reference, amalgamated two separate theories: that of the *American* captain John Cleves Symmes (1780-1829) on the hollow sphere, and that of the *English* physician Sir John Leslie (1766-1832) on the presence of the two planets, Pluto and Proserpine, at the center of the Earth.

186. Athanasius Kircher (1602-1680), a German Jesuit, professor of Mathematics and scholar of world renown with an impressive volume of published work on every possible subject, but whose research outputs were, admittedly, criticized for superficiality, often bordering on the arcane. Michel is here referring to Kircher's work *Mundus subterraneus* (Amsterdam, 1884). For his supposed influence on Jules Verne, see Irene Zanot's Italian-language article: "Through a geography of the magical: Athanasius Kircher's *Mundus Subterraneus* as the foundation of Verne's *Journey to the Center of the Earth*," in *Rivista di letterature moderne e comparate*. Pisa: Pacini, Vol. 64, No. 2, 2011, pp. 115-134 (my rendering from Italian of the article's title).

187. Several English geologists shared this surname. Michel is referring to John *Woodward* (1665-1728), a doctor and naturalist who, according to Larousse, "was most famous for his *Essay on the natural history of the Earth* (London, 1696), a geological text in which he

"Fire," say Descartes, Leibnitz and others, neglecting, however, to inform us how, without oxygen, such fire burns, or what it burns.

"Rock," states Humphrey Davy, "like that upon which our feet tread."[188]

According to the latter scientist, the idea of heat at the center of the earth is only what appears to be the case, but actually is not the true picture. Accumulated and stored since the dawn of the Earth's existence, this heat was apparently produced by chemical compounds close to the surface, by the combustion of certain elements such as potassium and sodium, which have the property of ignition upon contact with air or water, and of which the Earth, in his opinion, was almost exclusively composed.

It is indeed an attractive theory which has been propounded by that illustrious English physician! If he was accurate in what he said, what obstacle should there be to prevent M. de Lesseps, in time (lots of time, admittedly, but after all, he *is* so young!) from piercing a hole through the Earth?[189] My God, just look at how many people are doing just that every day to the moon, whose diameter is, after all, only four times smaller! Now that would be very handy! I can already hear the announcement made by an employee of the Central Tube Company (Limited):

"Next train for the Antipodes now boarding: please take your seats!"

How pioneering such a journey would be, if, confirming former hypotheses, it were to reveal to us that the interior of our planet harbored extinct races of early humans and animals! What exciting relations we could forge with these brothers of ours: our fathers! What uncharted territory, hitherto uncultivated land, would become available to our tourists and our hunters! Can you just picture the display windows

imagines the Earth's core to contain an immense mass of water which, having emerged from the abysses at the voice of God, apparently flooded the Earth at the moment of the Biblical Deluge, sweeping along with it billions of zoophytes and marine flora and fauna which are found all over the Earth's surface." (*Grand dictionnaire universel du XIXe siècle*, volume 18 [1876], p. 1373). (My translation of the quote from Larousse.)

188. It is worth recalling that, sixty years earlier (in 1825), the illustrious Humphrey Davy (1778-1829) had paid a Jules Verne-imagined visit to the fictional Professor Lidenbrock (*Journey to the Center of the Earth,* chapter VI).

189. He was actually 82 years of age in September 1888. At the time, Lesseps was on the brink of failure with his project for the Panama Canal, a planned enterprise for which bankruptcy was declared in February 1889.

of the famous Parisian caterers Potel and Chabot, decorated with the hides of the Mastodon and the woolly mammoth?[190] And can you imagine the astonishment of these peoples, buried within the center of the earth for so many centuries, at the sight of Krupp canons and Level rifles, given that those poor people had, hitherto, only ever known the stone axe!

* * *

Unfortunately, modern Science no longer considers it possible to make these kinds of dreams come true. Following theories of a great void, of water, fire or rock, this ball which, according to more recent theories, carries us along through space, launched by remarkably strong arms through the bowling alley of Infinity, is now seen as being filled with molten iron. Then, above this central iron mass, one perceives, through the optic of a geologist, a circular ocean of liquid silicate, itself enveloped by the solid rock which constitutes the ground we walk on.

The idea of transforming this subterranean world into the Promised Land of anaemia sufferers is, it has to be admitted, a bizarre one, and yet it is supported (oh! just like the ideas which preceded it!) by figures, those flawless advocates which are equally eloquent in all cases.

The fact is that if one deducts, from the Earth's radius, the forty kilometers of thickness attributed by scientists to the Earth's crust, this radius is reduced (average radius) to 6,328 kilometers, in round figures. From which, methodical minds immediately deduce the volume of the Earth's core, which we shall continue, for the time being, to presume to be iron-bearing, to be, namely: 1,061,385,574,357 cubic kilometers. A neat little figure indeed, one which the likes of Cavendish and Baily have helped us to arrive at, and very flattering to our terrestrial pride![191]

Knowing as we do the average density of the globe (5.67 according to experiments conducted by Cavendish and Baily) and that of its surface (2.5) you therefore get, for the innermost core, a density very close to that of iron, which is, on average, 7.8.

190. *Elephas primigenius* was the original name given by German naturalist Blumenbach (1752-1840) to the woolly mammoth.

191. Henry Cavendish (1731-1810) had discovered carbon gas and hydrogen; his verification of the average density of the Earth dates from 1798. In order to calculate the Earth's density, astronomer Francis Baily (1774-1844) used the same method as Cavendish, the result of which deviates only by 0.6% from the figure which is currently accepted.

Flawless reasoning, if (for there is always an *if* in science, and that's what lends it such great charm) a small objection was not easily made.

The fact is, it has been observed that heat increases by one degree approximately, for every thirty meters of depth. The source of this heat being supposed to be at the center of the Earth, this progression in temperature ought to remain constant, so that the temperature at the very center of the Earth would, in this case, rise to about two hundred thousand degrees Centigrade.[192] In that scenario, the iron would not be merely liquefied but well and truly volatilized, and you can only wonder, without knowing the answer, how the thin shell of this enormous egg which we are forced to "swallow whole" could resist the pressure of the gases which would thereby have been caused to expand to such an extraordinary level.

I certainly won't be the person answering that question. Nor you, I presume?

Most fortunately, the Poirier Company offers us the opportunity to enable everyone to reach agreement. Thanks to that company, and given that one kilometer has already been pierced, there no longer remain but six thousand, three hundred and sixty-five kilometers before we reach the very center of the Earth.[193] It's a trifling distance, not even worth speaking about!

I am therefore now imploring the above-mentioned Company to cease forthwith its operations of coal extraction, and to resume the drilling of its wells, for scientific purposes.

True, the intensity of heat may constitute an insurmountable obstacle, for, up to now, it has followed the trajectory generally agreed upon. It is inside a veritable sauna, heated to thirty-five degrees, and which powerful ventilators struggle to maintain at a cool temperature, that miners (those employees amongst whom our future Caesar has recruited his most loyal soldiers) work. But who can say that,

---

192. Far from reaching the center of the Earth, Lidenbrock and his two companions had arrived at a depth of 160 kilometers (40 leagues) before being expelled from the globe's interior by an eruption of the Stromboli volcano.

193. It will be remembered that Paschal Grousset proposed that a pit of approximately 1,500 meters be dug into the Earth, for the World Fair of 1900. This proposal, officially made in March 1895, was not ultimately accomplished. See Volker Dehs: "Le Trou de Grousset" (The hole proposed by Grousset) (containing an unpublished letter written by Jules Verne) in *Spiridon. Bulletin de la SGDL*, No. 10, June 2016, pp. 2-3.

having increased to a certain limit, this heat will not diminish, thus corroborating Humphrey Davy's theory?

Only time can provide the answer to this question.

However, I must not conceal from you the fact that my appeal has little chance of being heard. In spite of my pleas, it is likely that miners shall persist in piling, each morning, into cages, in which, in the space of two minutes, they make that alarming drop of one thousand meters. Then, once they've arrived at their destination, they will continue, continue to plough their furrows, like oversized dust mites on some huge epidermis, and, no doubt, for a long time to come, the dark blood of the Earth shall continue to flow in heavy drops under the bites of these dust mites.

I could write countless pages on this subject; it certainly lends itself to detailed exposition. But what good can possibly come from speaking about miners? That's simply flogging a dead horse, after *Germinal*![194] Everybody is familiar with those human moles, knowing them as well as the parliamentarian M. Basly himself, since the discovery, on the site of the Châtelet, of new, but rather meagre coal deposits and coalmines, whose opening was attended by large crowds.[195]

That day, unfortunately, the ventilators, still badly operated I presume, proved to be way too generous.

The miners got a decidedly frosty reception.

194. A reference to the theatrical adaptation of Zola's novel, published in 1885, produced by the novelist himself in collaboration with William Busnach. *Germinal* (the novel and play center round a miners' strike in northern France in the late 19th century), in its adaptation for the theatre, was staged on 21st April, 1888, at the Châtelet theatre, and was a resounding flop.

195. Emile-Joseph Basly (1854-1928) had worked as a miner in Anzin, where he became involved in the organization of the strikes of 1880. Having been dismissed, he went on to work with the miners' union and was elected as a deputy for Paris, from 1885 to 1889.

[VII].

A Futuristic Express Train[196]

[I].

"Be careful!" my guide warned. "Mind the step!"

Having gone down that step which had so fortunately been pointed out to me, I entered a vast room, illuminated by blindingly

196. This story was originally published in *Le Figaro. Supplément littéraire.* 14th year, No. 35, September 1, 1888, pp. 138-9; it was republished under the title "Forgotten pages / - / An Express of the Future," credited to M. Jules Verne, in *Annales politiques et littéraires*, 11th year, No. 531, dated 27th August, 1893, pp. 139-40, and, in slightly amended form, under the title "An 'express' of the future," credited to Jules Verne, in *Le Petit Parisien. Supplément littéraire et illustré.* 7th year, No. 339, dated 4th August, 1895, pp. 243-44. The French-language source text of this translation used—as did the *BSJV*, No. 106, 1993, pp. 35-38, and *ETHUIN*, pp. 59-64—the version which appeared in the *Figaro*, while nonetheless pointing out several variations in the final publication (abridged as *PP*), which reveals some of the stylistic features characteristic of Jules Verne (including a proliferation of semicolons, which Michel tends to avoid). In that version, this text was subdivided into four chapters, which we have here numbered within brackets. During the lifetime of both authors, and from 1890 onwards, this article was translated into numerous languages and always attributed to Jules Verne, not Michel, and has often been anthologized.

The first English translation appeared as "An Express of the Future" in *The Strand Magazine* (London), Vol. X, November 1895, pp. 638-40, with illustrations by A.J. Johnson in the November 1895 number of *The Strand Magazine*. After Jules's death, an altered version of the story appeared. The *New York Journal* was a newspaper owned by William Randolph Hearst, with a color Sunday supplement entitled *The American Weekly* that often carried sensational or pseudo-scientific articles. "30 Miles a Minute: The Last and Most Marvelous of All His Scientific Conceptions," was the new title given Michel's story when it was published there on April 30, 1905, p. 12, with an uncredited half-page illustration (reproduced in this volume). In those pages the assertion was made (falsely) that no posthumous works have been announced by the Verne estate, suggesting that the story "is probably the only message from him to his millions of readers that remained to be delivered." The editor added, "The executors have just now permitted the publication of a most interesting and characteristic sketch, showing the general design of a tale which Verne was planning at the time of his death." The article, it was noted, suggested how current Verne's thinking was with the problem of reducing travel time between America and Europe, and gave insight "into Jules Verne's method of fixing both his scientific ideal and the style of his narrative in one brief outline. There is evidence of the same scrupulous exactness in dealing with figures and natural phenomena that made Jules Verne almost the only writer of this sort of fiction who enjoyed the respect of scientists." The story was sufficiently retold in this journal to be a distinct variation from Michel's text, just as the work of his father often appeared in translations distant from the French. This version, in turn, was abbreviated as "A great transatlantic subway" in the June 19, 1955 issue of the same magazine in the *New York Journal and American*.

bright electrical reflectors, a room whose silent solitude was disturbed only by the sound of our footsteps.

Where was I? What was I doing here? Who was this mysterious guide?

Questions which all remained unanswered.

A long walk under cover of darkness, iron gates which were opened and then noisily closed behind us, stairways which seemed to me to sink deep into the ground; all that was as much as I could remember.

Moreover, I didn't currently have the leisure of thinking about any of this.

"You're probably wondering who I am?" my guide went on. "Colonel Pierce, at your service. And where are you? In the United States, in Boston, in a railway station."

"A railway station?"

"Yes, the station of the Boston to Liverpool Pneumatic Tubes Company."

And, with a gesture by way of explanation, the Colonel pointed out two long iron cylinders to me, each of about one and a half

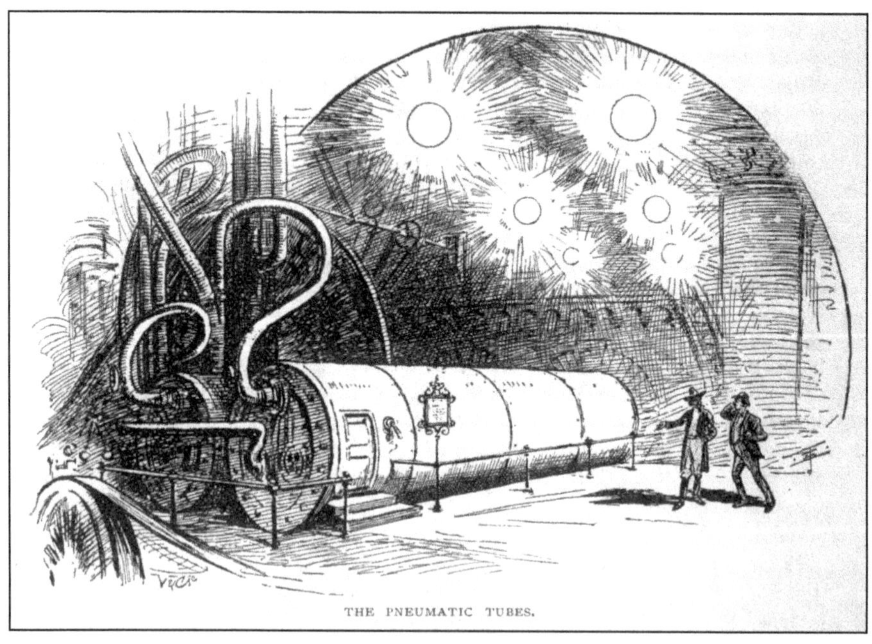

THE PNEUMATIC TUBES.

From "An Express of the Future," *The Strand Magazine*, November 1895.

meters in diameter, which lay on the ground a few steps from where we stood.

I looked at those two cylinders, which disappeared to the right into a mass of concrete masonry and stonework, and which, on the left, ended in enormous metallic obturators, from which a mass of pipes climbed upwards, disappearing into a very high ceiling, and, all at once, I understood.

For had I not read, just a short time previously, in an American newspaper, an article describing this extraordinary project: that of linking Europe to the New World by means of two gigantic underwater tubes? An inventor had been located who claimed to be in the process of doing just that. And that inventor, Colonel Pierce, was the man who now stood before me.

In my mind, I mentally reviewed the contents of that newspaper article.

The reporter who had written the article had obligingly provided a detailed description of the enterprise. He described just how much iron was necessary: more than sixteen hundred thousand cubic meters weighing thirteen million tons, and stated the number of ships necessary for transporting all this material: two hundred vessels each weighing two thousand tons, and each making thirty-three voyages. He depicted this scientific *Armada* bringing the steel to two master ships, on board which the ends of the tubes were held. He then showed those tubes themselves, ever-extending in length underneath the waves, in individual sections of three meters, all screwed to each other, held securely in the powerful grip of a triple net of resin-coated iron meshes.

The article then went on to discuss the question of the trains' operating system, in which the tubes, transformed into two enormous blowpipes, were filled with a series of passenger coaches, swept along, together with their passengers, by means of powerful currents of air, much in the manner of those telegrams which circulate throughout the city of Paris by means of a pneumatic "sucking up" followed by a discharge of the messages in question.

The article concluded by drawing a parallel between this system and our existing railway network, and the author enthusiastically enumerated the advantages of this boldly innovative project. Within the tubes (if he was to be believed) there would no longer be any annoying juddering experienced by passengers, thanks to the burnished steel coating of the interior walls; there would also be an evenness of temperature, with currents of air whose level of heat could be regulated according to the seasons, and train tickets which would command improbably cheap fares, explained by the economies of scale which would be achieved in the construction and operation of this new underwater rail system. And, on this subject (forgetting that, despite the sixteen hundred and seventy kilometers which their daily rotation causes them to travel every hour, bodies situated along the Equator are still subject to the laws of gravity; forgetting that, in order to allow them to break free from the Earth's gravitational pull, they would need to travel at a speed seventeen times greater) did he not go so far as to claim that the proposed trains, owing to their extremely high speed and the curvature of the Earth, would tend to remove themselves from the forces of gravity according to the tangent of the Earth's surface, and that this would cause those vehicles to suffer only slight friction on the outer surface of the tubes? And, as a result, did he not conclude that the planned transport system would not suffer from any wear and tear, and was thus guaranteed to last eternally?

All those details were now coming back to me.

[II].

So, had this utopian vision become reality, and were these two iron cylinders which I now saw unfolding at my feet, travelling beyond the Atlantic to fuse together on the coast of England? Despite the evidence, I failed to be convinced. Even though tubes had been laid (I accepted that much) I could never accept that human beings could ever travel by this route: ever!

Moreover, wouldn't it be impossible to obtain a current of air of that length? I expressed this opinion aloud to the Colonel.

"On the contrary, nothing could be easier," he protested. "All that is needed to produce that current of air is a large number of steam bellows, similar to those found in smelting furnaces. The air is discharged by them with a level of power which is, so to speak, unlimited, and our coaches and passengers, swept along in a fearful whirlwind, itself propelled by a train speed of eighteen hundred kilometers per hour, eat up, in two hours and fourteen minutes, the four thousand kilometers separating Boston from Liverpool."

"Eighteen hundred kilometers per hour!" I cried.

"Not one kilometer less. And the consequences of such speed are so extraordinary! Because Liverpool time is four hours and forty minutes ahead of our U.S. time, a passenger who leaves Boston at nine o'clock in the morning arrives in England at six minutes to four in the afternoon. Isn't that truly a day which passes very quickly? But in the other direction, on the contrary, our coaches, under this latitude, travelling nine hundred kilometers an hour faster than the Sun, will beat that morning star hands down, and, leaving Liverpool at midday for example, the train will arrive in this station at 9:34 in the morning, that is, before it has even left! Eh! Eh! Now there you have something darned fantastic! Before it has even left! One can hardly travel faster than that, it seems to me!"[197]

I didn't know what to think. Was I dealing with a madman? Or should I believe in his sensational theories, even though all sorts of objections were crowding into my mind?

"Well, perhaps!" I said. "I'm willing to accept that passengers may make this insane journey, and that you may obtain this incredible speed. But how do you manage to break that speed and slow down the trains? Surely, when they come to a halt, everything must be smashed to smithereens!"

"Not in the slightest," replied the Colonel with a shrug of his shoulders. "Between our tubes, one of which is used for the outward journey, the other for the return journey, and through which air currents travel in opposite directions, there is a communication system in the area around each shore. If a train is approaching, an electric spark warns us of it, and flies to England to paralyze the force which propels that train. Left to its own devices, as it were, the train continues its journey because of the speed it has built up, but we only have to operate a valve to make the opposite current of the parallel

197. This trope of the effects of different time zones on global travellers is somewhat reminiscent of the journey round the world of Phileas Fogg in Jules Verne's *Le Tour du monde en quatre-vingts jours*,(*Around the World in Eighty Days*, 1873), in which spatio-temporal and geographical realities finally enable Fogg to reach the Reform Club just in time to win his wager, despite his having at first believed that he had arrived a day late. He has, in fact, gained a day in his circumnavigation of the world, due to his travelling through different time zones, and due to the 360 degrees of the Earth's circumference over which he has journeyed. However, Fogg's "phantom day" can hardly compete with Michel Verne's notion, in this story, of arriving at one's destination before one has even set out.

From "An Express of the Future," *The Strand Magazine*, November 1895.

tube rush to meet it, and, slowing it down little by little, the current ultimately acts as a cushioning buffer, absorbing the final impact."

"But anyway, what use are all these explanations?" he concluded. "Wouldn't it be a hundred times better to actually *experience* the system in action?"

And without even waiting for me to reply, Colonel Pierce suddenly pulled on a brass handle which shone brilliantly at the side of one of the tubes or tubular-shaped trains. A panel slid sideways within the tube's system of sliding doors, and through the opening thus provided, I observed a succession of seats, upon each of which two people could comfortably have sat side by side.

"Your carriage awaits," declared the Colonel grandiloquently, by way of explanation. "Come on – let's go!"

I followed him like an obedient lapdog, and the sliding door immediately closed behind us.

[III].

I began to examine my surroundings with curiosity, by the light which was shining downwards from an Edison lamp attached to the ceiling. Nothing could be simpler in design. A long cylinder with slanting corners, comfortably padded on all its interior surfaces, throughout which fifty seats, attached in pairs, were set out in twenty-five parallel rows. At each end was a valve regulated to a tension of one atmosphere, the one at the back allowing breathable air to enter the tube, while the one at the front allowed the air to be discharged as soon as it exceeded normal pressure.

After spending several minutes examining my surroundings, I began to grow impatient.

"Well!" I asked, "Aren't we going to set off anytime soon?"

"Set off? But we've already set off!" cried the Colonel.

So we had left, just like that, without any shaking sensation?

Was such a thing truly possible?

I listened carefully, trying to perceive any type of noise which might have enlightened me as to my situation. If we had indeed set off, if the Colonel hadn't deceived me in speaking to me of a speed of eighteen

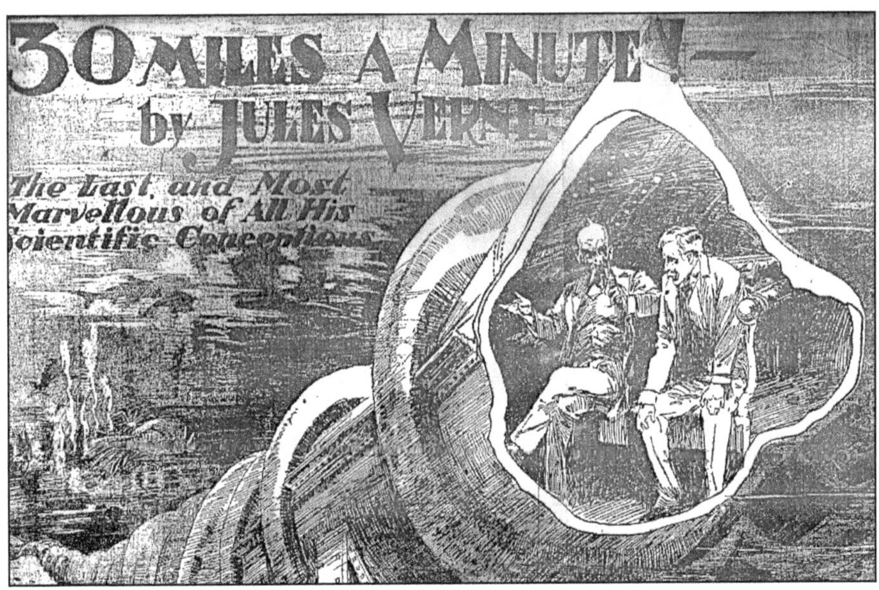

From the retitled version in *The American Weekly*, April 30, 1905.

From "An Express of the Future," *The Strand Magazine*, November 1895.

hundred kilometers per hour, we must already be far away from all and any *terra firma*; we must be underneath the waves. Above our heads, the crests of waves collided noisily, and perhaps even at this very moment, whales, imagining it to be some monstrous serpent of an unknown species, were battering our long iron prison with all their might!

However, I could hear nothing but a muffled rumbling sound, probably produced by the wheels of our train, and, plunged into a state of limitless astonishment, unable to believe in the reality of all that was happening to me, I silently allowed the time to pass.

[IV].

About an hour had passed in this manner when a sudden blast of fresh air to my forehead abruptly pulled me out of the torpor into which I was gradually sinking. I brought my hand to my face: it was damp.

Damp? Why was this the case? Had the tube thus burst under the pressure of the water, a level of pressure which had to be tremendous, since it increases by one atmosphere for every ten meters of depth? Was the ocean about to invade the train?

I was gripped by fear. Frantic with terror, I wanted to call for help, to yell, and …

And I found myself in that haven of tranquillity which is my garden, liberally drenched by driving rain, whose large drops had woken me from my slumber.

I had quite simply fallen asleep while reading that article which an American reporter had devoted to the incredible projects of Colonel Pierce, who, I very much fear, must himself have been dreaming!

VIII.

Humans and Animals[198]

Those inventors who wrack their brains in their quest for perpetual movement have always seemed to me to be curiously naïve. Isn't their own individuality the living proof of the futility of their efforts, and doesn't it clearly show them that everything here on Earth needs to seek its sources of energy from outside itself? If it were deprived of its provision of coal, would a locomotive be able to pull its train of carriages? And isn't it a similar necessity which, within the human mechanism, has introduced that particular "cog" which is cordon-bleu cuisine?

The human mechanism, did I say? It's exactly the right term. Our human organism is, indeed, an actual machine, but one which functions, and which therefore consumes sources of energy on a permanent basis. Only one thing can shut down that machine: death.

In order to consume, to *spend* energy, as it were, it's pointless to perform labor, like workers (when they aren't on strike, that is!) or to reflect, like philosophers. No, for that, it is enough to simply *live*, even if only through sleeping, as idle persons do, and even Harpagon himself, that famous miser, couldn't possibly object to *that* expenditure of energy.[199]

198. This article was first published in *Le Figaro. Supplément littéraire*, 14th year, No. 37, on September 15, 1888, p. 147, and was reproduced in *BSJV*, No. 106, 1993, pp. 39-42, and in *ETHUIN*, pp. 65-70.

199. Harpagon is a fictional miser who was the lead character in Molière's play *L'Avare* (*The Miser*, 1668).

Through the lungs, the pores of our skin, and by yet other channels which I won't go into here, particles which have been used up are relentlessly eliminated from our system. This is an operation which impoverishes the tissues, to such an extent that, in the end, some tissues calling out for nitrogen, some for carbon and others for fat, and being the fierce, exacting creditors that they are, they ultimately turn, as a last resort, to their eternal debtor: blood. The latter accedes to their requests, as much as it possibly can; but there comes a moment when, finding itself in its turn deprived of sustenance, it becomes necessary for it to make application to the stomach, its cashier. Alas! There are currently no funds remaining in the account! And …

And it is thus that Sir, speaking to Madam, grumbles, with an extremely sullen countenance: "But, my good woman, what on earth are you thinking of? Aren't we having any dinner today? I'm so hungry I could eat a horse!"

* * *

Let's not get annoyed. Dinner has been served and, seated in a circle round the table, Sir, Madam and Baby settle down with gusto to the task of clearing the contents of the said table into their stomach. Sir's teeth (veritable piano keys), Madam's pearly whites and Baby's milk teeth, all these try to outdo each other, and so begins that noble undertaking: the process of digestion, so revered by epicures.

To the question: "What *is* digestion?" one could reply: "Digestion is a task divided into three stages."

First: the act of *mastication* or chewing, a pleasant activity, and one which is, moreover, necessary.

The fact is that living organisms cannot ingest the materials providing sustenance and nutrition unless they are first liquefied; hence the need for those materials to be initially dissolved, an operation which is facilitated by chewing, as it divides food up into smaller pieces and allows the digestive juices to make their way into the foodstuffs we consume.

This operation is needed most of all when it comes to digesting vegetables, in which the edible components are covered by a tough coating which must therefore be broken. It is for this reason that animals who are herbivores spend more time chewing than their carnivorous counterparts, and is the reason why some of them, ruminants, those who chew the cud, even chew their food twice. Perhaps you used to accuse them of gluttony? Pure defamation of character on your part!

Once the food has been crushed, the second stage of the digestive process gets underway: that of actual *digestion* itself.

Several different liquids act as agents of this process.

First of all, there is *saliva*, one of whose components, *Ptyaline*, transforms insoluble starchy food into dextrin, and then into glucose (sugar), which is a soluble substance. The next liquids to come into play are the gastric or digestive juices, which are changed into *peptone* and dissolve fibrin, casein, albumin, etc. Digestion is finally completed in the duodenum and small intestine, where *bile* and *pancreatic* and *intestinal* juices pour forth, these being liquids which all have, as their main mission, the task of emulsifying (liquefying) fat and allowing it to be absorbed.

Having started off in the mouth, here we are, already, lower down than the stomach. In the space of a few minutes we have travelled a distance which food takes, on average, three hours to cover. Let's not go any further. In order to recount the rest of the journey, I'd need the Gallic writing skills of that humorous, cheery storyteller Armand Silvestre, and, unfortunately, I simply don't have those kinds of skills.[200]

In any case, the above description is sufficient for our purposes. For it is precisely within the duodenum and the small intestine that countless radicles end in intestinal veins and chylous vessels which, through a process of endosmosis, seize upon those substances required by this "digestive economy." And it is there that the third and final stage is largely accomplished: that of *absorption*.

Our three diners, whom we met a short time ago, have now reached this final stage. They've finished their meal. And, in a voice as friendly as it was grumpy before, Sir, distractedly stirring the black brew of his coffee with his small spoon, lethargically tells Madam: "Good God! My little darling, I've dined like a king!"

What has brought about this change? What cause has brought the marital barometer to this happy point on its gauge?

---

200. Armand Silvestre (1837-1901), an art critic and humorous writer. Here, Michel Verne employs scatological humor, similar to that occasionally exhibited by Jules Verne, in such stories as *Jédédias Jamet, or The Tale of an Inheritance*, first translated, and with a preface and annotations, in the Palik Series volume, *The Marriage of a Marquis* (Albany, GA: BearManor Fiction, 2011).

Quite simply, it's down to the fact that the tissues have been satisfied, while it's the blood that has paid the check!

And it is always thus. Atoms, leaving our system, constantly go away and are constantly being replaced. To such an extent that, after a certain amount of time, the organism has completely renewed itself. In the past, it was thought that seven years constituted the period needed for such complete renewal; but more accurate calculations have infinitely reduced this time period, and it is now estimated that two months are all that are needed for the atoms comprising the human body to be completely replaced.

This theory, which is completely accurate, does indeed have bizarre consequences! Picture a sailor making for the French shore: he's no longer the same being who, three years earlier, had set off to sea from that same shore, and his wife could be forgiven for failing to recognize him!

Those elected members of the National Assembly who, as soon as they've been elected and have assumed office, neglect to spread the butter promised by their electoral manifestos on the electoral slice of toast, can rightfully retort: "That manifesto? By Jove! It wasn't *me* who signed it!"

I could go on! That shy maiden to whom you, presumptuous young man, give yourself completely and defencelessly, is not the same person whose charms captivated you only three months ago. Nothing remains of that charming waist she had when you began courting her, and that young woman you are about to marry *is not the same person you originally chose*!

But what of it? Bah! What does it matter! So your fiancée has changed? She'll change even more. Indeed yes! A woman! Every two months you shall thus have a new female companion; this is the virtuous solution to that issue of an eminently social nature: for you've got a harem at a bargain price!

* * *

But faithful lovers must not use the foregoing information in order to condemn their lady-loves to a perpetual starvation diet. In such a case, they could be truly certain that the woman they loved was always the same, but on the other hand, this would be a bad way to round off feminine curves, things which are essential to a harmonious marital household. It's better to attach greater importance to physical appearance, and less to fidelity.

Eat your fill, then, you young married couples, as if it didn't matter an iota, and, I dare to add (parodying a famous saying): Fatten yourselves up!

Or at least do so as much as you can, for there *are* sometimes cases…!

Such as that of X, a man who recently came to Paris to seek a medical consultation with the *princes of science.*

He was afflicted with a raging hunger which he was, however, unable to satisfy following a blockage of the oesophagus, and this sick man was literally wasting away, like a latter-day Tantalus, tormented by the most mouth-watering dishes.[201] To overcome this hurdle, everything had been tried, but without success, and despite the best efforts of a veritable Tanner, X, in despair, was getting thinner and thinner and withering away.[202] He seemed doomed to imminent death when Doctor Terrillon brought him salvation through an act of severing with his surgical knife.[203]

That eminent surgeon quickly managed to open an artificial mouth in the wall of his patient's stomach, a tube was adapted to fit into this "mouth" and, ever since, X has been eating and digesting his food through this passage, just like you and … No, better than me, or at least I hope so, for his sake.

* * *

That daring operation is certainly a great credit to the skilful surgeon who performed it. But at the end of the day, Dr. Terrillon *did* study medicine, and I don't think I'm going too far in presuming that his

201. Tantalus was a figure in Greek mythology, who is most famous for being condemned by the gods to eternal punishment in a place called Tartarus. For having stolen ambrosia and nectar to bring back to his own people, and for having revealed the secrets of the gods, he was condemned to standing eternally in a pool of water, underneath a fruit tree with low branches, with the fruit perpetually out of his reach, and the water always receding before he could take a drink. His name provides the etymological root of the verb "tantalize," meaning to sorely tempt and thus torment.

202. Adam Tanner (1572-1632) was a Jesuit and German theologian, and was opposed to the witch hunts of his era. Michel's allusion to Tanner, and what exactly he is referring to in this reference, are not clear.

203. Octave Terrillon (1844-1895) was a surgeon in several Paris hospitals, and is considered to have pioneered surgical asepsis (the exclusion of bacteria during surgery).

education must have cost his family a great deal of money. If we go into raptures about his surgical skills, just think how much admiration we should have for the surgical knowledge of birds!

Our feathered friends don't have the benefit of colleges, schools or lectures, and yet there are winged creatures, especially the woodcock, that could certainly teach a thing or two to more than one descendant of Hippocrates.

What a sad life the woodcock leads! She's simply too *kind*, that's her only failing, and it gets her into so much bother! Some biped or other is constantly hot on her heels, following a dog and shouting himself hoarse. From time to time, the biped raises a rifle to his shoulder, and… bang! … Missed!

Such is the routine lot of the woodcock.

Sometimes, however, (for such strokes of bad luck do occur) a piece of lead goes astray, and there you have a broken leg.

However, our woodcock doesn't worry too much about it. With the aid of her beak, she's well able to apply a plaster to her wound, and even to make herself a perfect ligature which keeps the fractured member rigid until the callus (a broken bone) has completely healed. A real surgeon couldn't do any better.

The skill of these birds who bandage themselves in this way has often been admired by hunters. True, on other occasions, poorly-healed fractures have been observed, and it has had to be recognized that, in such instances, the woodcock has made some kind of mistake.

But isn't that just something else they have in common with *non*-feathered physicians?

IX.

Intelligence and Pain
An Anglo-Chinese Anaesthetic[204]

An English physician, Doctor Venn, recently gave an interesting paper to the Anthropological Institute of London, and the echoes of this

204. This article was first published in *Le Figaro. Supplément littéraire*, 14th year, on November 3, 1888, pp. 174-175; it was subsequently republished in *BSJV*, No. 106, 1993, pp. 43-47; and in *ETHUIN*, pp. 71-77.

presentation have reached us here in France.[205]

This doctor took the trouble to measure the heads of 1,095 students of the University of Cambridge, and, following his patient research undertaking, he has reached the following conclusions:

1. That the largest brains belong to the most intelligent and hard-working students;

2. That, amongst those young people who are engaged in intellectual pursuits, the brain increases in volume right up to the age of twenty-five years, whereas, within the bulk of the population, it stops growing at the age of nineteen.

However original this research paper may appear, it doesn't really contribute any truly novel fact to scientific knowledge. If it is correct to state that there is a positive link between the measurement of one's degree of intelligence and the size of the brain, it is neither today nor yesterday that this correlation has been observed. Numerous observations have indeed established this fact, and not only in relation to human beings, but, in fact, also in relation to *all* animals. By 1840, hadn't Doctor Leuret already discovered that the weight of the encephalon relative to the body is in a ratio of 1 to: 5,668 for fish, 1,321 for reptiles, 212 for birds, 186 for mammals and 36 for human beings?[206] And that, amongst mammals, the cat comes in first place, the dog second, the horse in seventh place, behind the donkey, who – oh, how shameful! – comes in sixth place? And that the heaviest brains, in absolute terms, have been allotted to the dolphin, whose brain weighs in at 1,800 grams, to the elephant and the whale (1,550) and, finally to the human being, whose brain weighs, on average, 1,334 grams, apart from exceptions such as Cuvier and Byron, whose brains exceeded, in size, those of dolphins?

205. John Venn (1834-1923) was a mathematician and logician. His paper "Cambridge Anthropometry" was presented by him on 24th April, 1888, and published in the *Journal of the Anthropological Institute* (London), Vol. 18, 1889, pp. 140-154. See <http://galton.org/criticism/10-14-02/venn-1889-j-anthro-cambridge-anthropometry.pdf>.

206. François Leuret (1797-1851) was an anatomist and psychiatrist famous for his research into the comparative anatomy of the brain, undertaken in collaboration with the anthropologist Louis Gratiolet (1815-1865), his student, and whose work *De la physionomie et des mouvements d'expression* (Hetzel, 1865) was a significant influence on Jules Verne.

As for women, I am sorrowfully forced to admit their inferiority. Women have less grey matter than us men; this is a fact; one which is admittedly difficult to accept, yet undeniably true. On the encephalic scale, their position is lower down in the pecking order than that of men … but oh! It is higher, at least, than the scatter-brained linnet![207]

Don't these already long-existent findings illustrate the truth of the matter? Aren't men, however stupid they may be (and they certainly *are*, on occasions!) nonetheless superior to parrots? Don't women, however futile you may presume them to be, have somewhat superior intellectual value to … the sole, for instance, to which, in other aspects, women bear such an unfortunate resemblance?

Certainly.

The existence of a close correlation between the size of the brain and the level of intelligence is thus obvious. This is a conclusion further reinforced by the example of idiots, whose brain drops abruptly to a weight of 1,000 grams, compared with 1,334 for the fully-formed human being, in possession of all of his or her intellectual faculties.

As regards the gradual growth of the encephalon, neither is there anything very new in Dr Venn's thesis with respect to this question. That, too, has been an incontestable fact for a long time. It is well-known that the cranium, composed, not of a mere single bone as one might have imagined, but of eight, possesses a certain power of growth. So much so that, among the intelligent classes, the head continues to swell (just as the body grows among all classes) until about the age of forty-five, and not nineteen.

If, among the working classes, such growth is a little less pronounced, that is nothing but the normal order of things.

Indeed, the brain behaves just like any other of our organs. If left idle, it goes into decline, it wastes away, or, at the very least, doesn't advance intellectually. If, on the other hand, it is maintained in an active state, then that intellectual exertion, a form of mental gymnastics, makes the brain grow, just as doing physical gymnastics causes the biceps to increase in size.

However, it shouldn't be concluded from this that all persons of learning must inevitably end up suffering from hydrocephalus. Like everything else, brain growth has its limits. Limits which are

207. In French, the expression "avoir une tête de linnot" (to have a linnet's head) means "to be scatter-brained."

sometimes accorded little respect, though. Hasn't it even been claimed that Napoleon, following each of his battles, found himself obliged to wear a new hat, the previous one having become too small?

That seems like an exaggeration to me.

* * *

But, at the end of the day, is it really so desirable to be in possession of a heavy brain and, as a result, to have an extremely high level of intelligence? Is that faculty of superior intelligence really such a valuable possession, given that it is one which, despite the rare joy which it bestows, causes us so much suffering? Suffering of all kinds. Mental, certainly, but also physical.

You don't really see the connection? It exists nevertheless. Just look at farmers and country folk in general. They are renowned for their stoical characters. Would you try to claim that they derive their stoicism from the study of philosophical maxims? They are unaware of the very existence of such teachings. No, the fact that rural dwellers don't complain, like us, about the slightest cut or bruise, ache or pain, is actually because their sensitivity is less acute than ours. To truly suffer, one must understand what pain and suffering are. And how could those country people understand it, when their brains hardly even function?

Let's take another example. Could a carter endure, for six months, the blows which he so liberally rains down on his horses, without dying from the cruel experience? Obviously not. And that is only because, though carters may often very well be ferocious brutes, they are still—hard as it is to believe—intellectually superior to their victims.

But of what use are these arguments? In order to accept a certain connection between sensitivity and intelligence, we only have to consider that, if the brain governs that latter faculty, it also regulates the former; it is the brain which perceives all of our physical sensations, be they pleasant or not, in the same way as our mental and emotional sensations.

This theory, which may seem paradoxical, is proven by an infinity of facts, not least of which is the observation that a wound suffered in such and such a part of the encephalon, deadens, numbs all feeling in the corresponding part of the human organism.

Thus, when one imagines that one feels pain here or there, it's merely an illusion. The suffering is inside the head, in every case.

To tell the truth, the brain acts like a mirror. It reflects sensation. Even though such feelings are, in reality, actually perceived by the brain, the sensation finds itself virtually transferred to the part of the body where it has originated. Sometimes even further than that. Like a person who has had their leg amputated, but who complains of pain in the foot which he or she no longer possesses.

However, such distinctions are ultimately futile. Whether it is felt in the brain or elsewhere, pain is no less unpleasant for all that. That horrible goddess of pain is not any milder or kinder for all that, she to whom the nails, hair, cartilage and skin, indeed every part of the body, except part of the encephalon itself, are blindly subjected.

What horrible tyranny! Suffering is the only truly terrible thing here below, in our mortal realm. Death, in sum, is nothing but a somewhat affected joke, a piece of humor which is a little ... forced.

Thus, what gratitude we should feel towards those who have struck that word "suffering" from our dictionaries: how grateful we should be to those kindly geniuses, the inventors of anaesthesia!

Alas for our forebears, anaesthesia is practically a present-day discovery. Though it was back in 1799 that Humphrey Davy declared that nitrogen protoxide possessed anaesthetic properties, and in 1818 that Faraday made the same declaration in relation to ether; though it was in 1832 that Soubeiran[208] obtained chloroform through the distillation of alcohol mixed with an aqueous solution of calcium chloride and caustic lime; and, though it was shortly afterwards that Flourens[209] discovered the stupefacient properties of that new product; despite all these facts, it was yet only in 1844 that the chemist Jackson and the dentist Morton,[210] both American, proved, through practical

208. Eugène Soubeiran (1797-1858) was a pharmacist and assistant professor of physics in Paris, who discovered chloroform at the same time as the American Samuel Guthrie (1782-1848) and the German Justus von Liebig (1803-1873), though it was Soubeiran who was the first to publish his findings.

209. Pierre Flourens (1794-1867), a physician and biologist, is considered to be one of the founders of experimental neuroscience, yet he was the target of a great deal of negative criticism for his work *De la longévité humaine et de la quantité de vie sur le globe* (1856), a work which is mocked by Jules Verne in *Paris au XXe siècle* (*Paris in the 20th Century*, 1863).

210. Charles Thomas Jackson (1805-1880), of Harvard University, had been one of William Thomas Green Morton's (1819-1868) professors; Morton came into conflict with Boston doctors because he was a dentist rather than a doctor. However, in the end, his method

demonstration, the reality of the power of ether, and in 1847 that Doctor Simpson[211] of Edinburgh rendered the same service to chloroform.

These days, nitrogen protoxide, chloroform and ether are all very commonly used as anaesthetics. It would be superfluous to recall, here, the wonderful results obtained from them, despite the fact that their mode of action on the organism remains somewhat uncertain.

We are, of course, told that anaesthetic "sleep" is caused, just like natural sleep, and just like asphyxia, by cerebral anaemia. To prove this point, we are given the example furnished by Nélaton.[212] That great surgeon, having anaesthetized a patient whose heart then suddenly stopped beating, did not hesitate to turn him upside down, thus bringing him back to life through those heroic means.

That's as may be! But they've forgotten to tell us by what mechanism chloroform actually chases the blood from the brain. "By acting on the nerve centers," the men and women of science explain to us. That's all very vague, though. Wouldn't it be better to just admit that they don't know?

* * *

I mentioned earlier in this article that anaesthesia was a modern discovery; however, that is not entirely accurate.

For didn't Helen of Troy, in the fourth Ode of the *Odysey*, pour into the cups of Télémachus and Pisitrate, son of Nestor, a certain liqueur which wiped away all troubles of the heart and soul? Well, that event took place in something like 1300 BC. So that piece of information is hardly hot off the presses.

Furthermore, do we not read in the writings of Pliny that the Ancients credited the plant mandrake with the same soporific properties?

And if somebody were to point out to me that it was necessary to "ingest" those drugs, which therefore classifies them, rather, as narcotics, I would reply that a thirteenth-century physician, Hugues de Lucques,

---

of proving the anaesthetic properties of ether through inhalation, was accepted.

211. James Young Simpson (1811-1870) was a Scottish obstetrician who was the first to administer chloroform during childbirth.

212. Auguste Nélaton (1807-1873) practised medicine as both a physician and a surgeon between 1851 and 1867, the year in which he became personal physician to Napoleon III.

used to render his patients unconscious by having them "inhale" the combined juices of mandrake, morel, henbane, etc.[213] The origins of actual anaesthesia *per se* could thus be dated back to that mediaeval historical period … were it not for the existence of the Chinese.

Admit it, you would have been very surprised if the inevitable Chinese person wasn't to be found somewhere within this story, given that the Chinese learned and invented everything before we did; the printing press, canon powder, the wheelbarrow, etc. It's perhaps the same Chinese person who discovered or invented all of the foregoing, who also discovered anaesthetics; always the same, like the armored cavalryman in a line of inspected soldiers.

Don't worry, on this occasion the Chinese have once again proven faithful to the cause. The fact is, it has just been discovered that, in the third century of the Common Era, sixteen hundred years before Bismarck (at a time when we were wallowing in barbarity, whereas nowadays … !) one of China's then physicians, who bore the harmonious-sounding name of Hoa-Tho, used to employ, in his operations, a certain preparation of hemp, which rendered his patients as unconscious as a corpse![214] There you have the first real anaesthetic that we know about.

The earliest in date, obviously, but also the most powerful first known anaesthetic.

You doubt this? Just take a look at our friends the English, among whom hemp is used on a daily basis. In England, nobody has ever complained of having suffered, even after the most major of operations.

Hemp is indeed a notorious anaesthetic, in the hands of the London executioner!

---

213. Ugo Borgognoni, known as *de Lucca*, a surgeon in Bologne, revolutionized the treatment of wounds.

214. "Finally, in the Far East, we witness the Chinese physician Hoa Tho, under the Wei dynasty, from 220 to 230 AD, who gave the name *Ma-yo in its Konkin-i-tong* to what was probably a preparation containing hemp, which rendered the patient unconscious, plunging him or her into a sort of intoxicated state which seemed to deprive him or her of all signs of life … It was thereby possible to carry out incisions, amputations and sutures, without the patient feeling a thing." (Jules Stanislas, *Proceedings of the Académie des sciences*, Paris, 1849, t. XVIII, p.195) from Emile Dutertre: *Des anesthétiques dans l'antiquité*. A. Davy, 1885, p.12.

Illustrations

One of the challenges in the Palik Series is selecting illustrations. They are either derived from the first French publication of Verne stories and plays in the 19th century, or are selected from sources of the time depicting actual historical locales, persons or events.

For illustrations from the original publications of Verne, the North American Jules Verne Society is indebted to Bernhard Krauth, chairman of the German Jules-Verne-Club. He has been deeply involved in a project to digitize the illustrations, more than 5,000 in all.

Additional illustrations were provided by Verne bibliographer, Stephen Michaluk, Jr., and renowned Verne biographer Volker Dehs.

The cover is a design from an early Czechoslovakian edition, and the scan was provided by Jan Rychlík especially for this Palik series volume.

Acknowledgements

The Palik Series, while spearheaded by the North American Jules Verne Society, represents a cooperative effort among Vernians worldwide, pooling the resources and knowledge of the various organizations in different countries.

The City of Nantes (France) and its Municipal Library have placed all Jules Verne manuscripts online. They helped make this publication possible, and the Society would like to thank the City of Nantes and its Bibliothèque municipale (especially Agnès Marcetteau and Claudine Sainlot) for their ongoing assistance with the Palik Series.

The Society is grateful for research assistance to Frédéric Jaccaud, curator of Jean-Michel Margot's Verne Collection at the Maison d'Ailleurs (House of Elsewhere) in Yverdon-les-Bains, Switzerland.

Verne scholar Volker Dehs has offered invaluable advice and assistance throughout the Palik series.

Stephen Michaluk, Jr.'s research made available the publication here of "Gibraltar," from the sole surviving copy in the Rare Book collection of the Library of Congress. Michaluk also provided the transcriptions and translation of the versions of "To the New Bride Caroline."

Hélène Lamérant collaborated on the translation of "Recollections of My Childhood and of My Youth." Patricia French and Anna Jean Mayhew assisted with the introduction of "Comparing Translations—The Case of 'Frritt–Flacc' by Jules Verne."

Andrew Nash first discovered the simultaneous English first appearance of "Frritt-Flacc," initially reprinted in the pages of the NAJVS newsletter, *Extraordinary Voyages.*

Transcriptions were made by Dennis Kytasaari of "Gibraltar," and by Julia Mastro of "Dr. Trifulgas' Patient."

Contributors

Edward Baxter translated *Bandits & Rebels*, *The Count of Chanteleine: A Tale of the French Revolution*, and "The Marriage of Mr. Anselme des Tilleuls" for *The Marriage of a Marquis* in the Palik Series. Baxter is a graduate of Mount Allison University and the University of Toronto, and has also studied at the University of Lausanne. He taught French for nearly thirty years at Ontario secondary schools. From 1977 until retiring in 1986, Baxter was Head of Modern Languages at Don Mills Collegiate Institute in North York, where he was appointed for a one-year term in 1980 as the city's first Poet Laureate. Baxter has translated several hundred articles for the *Dictionary of Canadian Biography*, along with eight books. These include two distinguished new versions of Verne's *Family without a Name* (1982) and *The Fur Country* (1987), both sponsored under the auspices of the Canada Council, published by the New Canada Press. After translating "The Humbug" for *The Jules Verne Encyclopedia* (Scarecrow Press, 1996), Baxter contributed a series of new Verne translations for several publishers: *The Invasion of the Sea* (Wesleyan, 2001), *The Golden Volcano* (Nebraska, 2008), and the 1882 play *Journey Through the Impossible* (2003), copublished by Prometheus and the North American Jules Verne Society.

Alex Kirstukas is a trustee of the North American Jules Verne Society and the editor of its peer-reviewed newsletter, *Extraordinary Voyages*, and has also translated Verne's *Robur the Conqueror* for Wesleyan University Press.

Jean-Michel Margot authored critical commentary for *The Marriage of a Marquis, Mr. Chimp & Other Plays*, and translated the introductions for *Around the World in 80 Days—The 1874 Play* and *Bandits & Rebels* for the Palik Series. Margot is an internationally recognized specialist on Jules Verne. He served as president of the North American Jules Verne Society and has published several books and many articles on the author. Margot edited Verne's theatrical play *Journey Through the Impossible* (Prometheus, 2003) for the North American Jules Verne Society; a volume of 19th century Verne criticism, titled *Jules Verne en son temps* (Encrage, 2004); and provided the introduction and notes of Verne's *The Kip Brothers* (Wesleyan University Press, 2007).

Rhoda B. Miller received her M.A. in French Language and Literature from George Washington University, and was a Fulbright Scholar at the University of Dijon. Her long career as a professional translator includes two decades as an interpreter with the United States Department of State.

Kieran M. O'Driscoll also translated *The Castles of California*; *Golden Danube*; *Vice, Redemption and the Distant Colony*; and *Jédédias Jamet or The Tale of an Inheritance* in *The Marriage of a Marquis* for the Palik Series. O'Driscoll was awarded his Ph.D. in Verne literary translation, by Dublin City University, in 2010. His doctoral thesis was entitled *Around the World in Eighty Changes: A Diachronic Study of Six Complete Translations (1873-2004), From French to English, of Jules Verne's Novel, Le Tour du Monde en quatre-vingts jours (1873)*, and explored the multiple causes of Verne retranslations. The monograph version was titled *Retranslation through the Centuries: Jules Verne in English*, published in 2011 by Peter Lang Ltd. Kieran holds a B.A. in Applied Languages (French and Spanish) with International Marketing Communications (2003) from Waterford Institute of Technology, and an M.A. in Translation Studies (2005) from Dublin City University, both degrees with First Class Honors. His Master's dissertation focused on the translations into French of J.K. Rowling's Harry Potter series. He has lectured in French at third-level, and in Advanced English as a Foreign Language, and currently lectures in English for Academic Purposes at Griffith College Dublin. Before entering academia, Kieran worked for almost twenty years in Irish local government, and also holds academic qualifications in Public Administration, Law and Music (Pianoforte).

Ian Thompson is the author of *Jules Verne's Scotland: In Fact and Fiction* (Luath, 2014). Thompson graduated from the Universities of Durham and Indiana. He has held lecturing posts in the universities of Leeds, Southampton and Miami University in Ohio before being appointed to the Chair of Geography at Glasgow University in 1976. He is an Honorary Life Fellow of La Societe de Geographie (Paris) in 2003 and promoted to the rank of Commandeur dans l'Ordre des Palmes Academiques by the French Government in 2005. He was for many years President of the Alliance Française Francaise de Glasgow.

Additional vintage translations included are by Anne T. Wilbur, Mary J. Safford, and Ernest DeGay.

Palik Series editor **Brian Taves** (Ph.D., University of Southern California) was an archivist in the Motion Picture, Broadcasting, and Recorded Sound Division of the Library of Congress for over a quarter century. He is the author of more than 100 articles and 25 chapters in anthologies, and has written books on P.G. Wodehouse and Hollywood; director Robert Florey; the genre of historical adventure movies; and fantasy-adventure writer Talbot Mundy, in addition to editing an original anthology of Mundy's best stories. In 2002-2003, Taves was chosen as Kluge Staff Fellow at the Library to write the first book on silent film pioneer Thomas Ince, published in 2011. In 2015, Taves's *Hollywood Presents Jules Verne: The Father of Science Fiction on Screen* was published by University Press of Kentucky. His upcoming *Jules Verne's Ghost* examines the career of Michel Verne, especially his filmmaking and its impact over the years. Taves was coauthor of *The Jules Verne Encyclopedia* (Scarecrow, 1996), and editor of the first English-language publication of Verne's *Adventures of the Rat Family* (Oxford, 1993), before becoming editor of the Palik series.

The Palik Series

THE LAST TWO DECADES have brought astonishing progress in the study of Jules Verne, with new translations of Verne stories, including the discovery of many texts. Still, there remain a number of Verne stories that have been overlooked, and it is this gap that the North American Jules Verne Society seeks to fill in the Palik series.

The North American Jules Verne Society (NAJVS) was formed in 1993, and a decade later, underwrote *Journey Through the Impossible*, the first complete edition in any language of Verne's 1882 science fiction theatrical spectacle, *Voyage à travers l'impossible.* With this experience, and thanks to the generosity of the Society's late member, Edward Palik, a series was commenced to bring to the Anglophone public a series of hitherto unknown Verne tales, published by BearManor Fiction.

Edward D. Palik (1928-2009) was a physicist who had a special enthusiasm for bringing neglected Verne stories to English-speaking readers, and this will be reflected in the series that bears his name. In this way the Society hopes to fulfill the goal that Ed's consideration has made possible, along with the assistance of a variety of Verne translators and scholars from around the world. The volumes in the Palik series will reveal the amazing range of Verne's storytelling, in genres that may surprise those who only know his most famous stories. We hope to allow a better appreciation of the famous writer who has, for more than a century and a half, been the widest-read author of fiction in the world.

Editor of the Palik series is Brian Taves.

Previous Volumes in the Palik Series

The Marriage of a Marquis

Foreword by Brian Taves; Introduction by Walter James Miller; *The Marriage of Mr. Anselme des Tilleuls* translated by Edward Baxter, with a preface and notes by Jean-Michel Margot; Afterword by Edward Baxter; Appendix: *Jédédias Jamet, or The Tale of an Inheritance* translated, with a preface and annotations, by Kieran M. O'Driscoll.

Jules Verne is the acclaimed author of such pioneering science fiction as *Twenty Thousand Leagues under the Seas* and *Journey to the Center of the Earth.* Yet he also wrote much more, and foreshadowing such classics as *Around the World in Eighty Days*, this inaugural volume focuses on two of Verne's earliest humorous stories, *The Marriage of Mr. Anselme des Tilleuls* and *Jédédias Jamet, or The Tale of an Inheritance.* Mr. Anselme des Tilleuls, in the featured story, is a ridiculous young man seeking a bride, following the advice of his Latin tutor to utilize the maxims of that language in his courtship. Translation is provided by Edward Baxter and Kieran O'Driscoll, two of the leading Verne experts; critical commentary by Jean-Michel Margot, Walter James Miller, and Brian Taves examine both stories, and why some of the author's tales were overlooked for so many years.

Shipwrecked Family: Marooned with Uncle Robinson

Translated by Sidney Kravitz; Introduction by Brian Taves.

Castaway by pirates on a deserted island … without tools or supplies to survive … a mother and her children have only a kindly old sailor to help. But what explains the strange flora and fauna they find?

The second volume in the Palik series was rejected by Verne's publisher, so rather than finish it, he began to rewrite it with new characters—and that became the classic, *The Mysterious Island*, where Captain Nemo made his last appearance. Here, then, is Verne's first draft of that novel, one which is very different from the book that it became.

Translation is provided by Sidney Kravitz, also translator of the definitive modern edition of *The Mysterious Island* (Wesleyan University Press, 2002). The introduction by Brian Taves discusses the influence of the Robinsonade on Verne's oeuvre, while an appendix comprises Verne's own prefaces to two of his novels in the genre, describing the influence of the form on his writing.

Mr. Chimp & Other Plays

By Jules Verne with Michel Carré, Charles Wallut, and Victorien Sardou; Translated by Frank Morlock; Introduction by Jean-Michel Margot.

Long before Verne stories had formed the basis for such movies as *Around the World in 80 Days*, many of his plays were theatrical blockbusters on the 19th century stage, including several from his novels. Even as he became a novelist, the stage remained crucial to Verne. In this volume, expert scholarly research by Jean-Michel Margot introduces four of Verne's plays written early in his career, from 1853 to 1860. The four plays are translated by Frank Morlock, one of the most prolific modern translators of 19th century French drama. Included in this volume are: *The Knights of the Daffodil* and *Mr. Chimpanzee*, coauthored by Verne with Michel Carré; *An Adoptive Son*, co-authored by Verne with Charles Wallut, and *Eleven Days of Siege*, co-authored by Verne with Charles Wallut and Victorien Sardou. The works range in content from romantic comedies to a scientist's discovery that there may not be much difference between human and ape after all!

The Count of Chanteleine: A Tale of the French Revolution

Translated by Edward Baxter; Introduction by Brian Taves; Notes and maps by Garmt de Vries-Uiterweerd; Afterword by Volker Dehs.

This adventure, first published in France in 1864 but never before available in English, is for everyone who has thrilled to *The Scarlet*

Pimpernel, *A Tale of Two Cities*, or *Scaramouche*. A nobleman, the Count of Chanteleine, leads a rebellion against the revolutionary French government. While he fights for the monarchy and the church, his home is destroyed and his wife murdered by the mob. Now he must save his daughter from the guillotine. This exciting swashbuckler is also a meticulous historical re-creation of a particularly bloody episode in the Reign of Terror.

Commentary by an international team of experts including Garmt de Vries-Uiterweerd, Volker Dehs and Brian Taves explores the historical background, composition, and generic context of *The Count of Chanteleine*, translated by Edward Baxter.

The Count of Chanteleine is also available in a full-length professional reading by the noted vocal artist, Fred Frees, on audible.com.

Vice, Redemption and the Distant Colony

By Jules Verne with Michel Verne; *Pierre-Jean*, *The Somber Fate of Jean Morénas*, and *Fact-Finding Mission* translated, with an introduction and annotations, by Kieran M. O'Driscoll.

Literary fraud or filial devotion? This is the question at the heart of a firestorm that erupted when manuscripts and letters were discovered proving that Jules Verne's son, Michel, significantly revised over a dozen of the stories published posthumously under his father's name, and even originated some himself. It was a collaboration that had begun while both were still alive, and continued as Michel was his father's literary executor.

In this volume will be found two different versions of a story, as written by Jules (*Pierre-Jean*), and expanded by his son (into *The Somber Fate of Jean Morénas*)—a tale Michel even made as a full-length movie in 1916. Also in these pages is the first English translation of a novel Jules began, *Fact-Finding Mission*, but which his son finished, and hitherto has been only available in the completed version by Michel Verne.

The English rendering and notes are by a leading Verne translator and expert on the history of Verne translations, Kieran O'Driscoll.

Around the World in 80 Days—The 1874 Play

By Jules Verne and Adolphe d'Ennery; The original translation commissioned by the Kiralfy Brothers; Introduction by Philippe Burgaud, with Jean-Michel Margot and Brian Taves; Afterword: "The Meridians and the Calendar" by Jules Verne, translated and annotated by Jean-Louis Trudel; Appendix: The Play on Screen, by Brian Taves.

Jules Verne's most famous novel was originally conceived as a play—and immediately after writing the novel, Verne himself adapted his story into a stage hit. Running for thousands of performances in many different countries, including the United States, here is the original playscript, translated directly from the French by the producers of the original Broadway presentation, and only issued in the most limited form in 1874. Like filmmakers after him, Verne understood the need to make changes for the stage, and in collaboration with Adolphe d'Ennery created a distinct variation, a play with many different characters and episodes than are in the novel, *Around the World in Eighty Days*. Included in this volume are an introduction about how the play was created and staged, together with the first translation (by Jean-Louis Trudel) of Verne's 1873 essay, "The Meridians and the Calendar," explaining how Phileas Fogg accomplished his feat. Background on the production of the play, especially its staging in the United States, is provided by Philippe Burgaud, Jean-Michel Margot, and Brian Taves, along with an appendix on films of the play.

Bandits & Rebels

"San Carlos" and *The Siege of Rome* translated by Edward Baxter; With "Future of the Submarine;" Introduction by Daniel Compère, translated by Jean-Michel Margot with Brian Taves; Appendix: *Martin Paz, or The Pearl of Lima*, the 1852 translation by Anne T. Wilbur of the original French magazine edition.

Captain Nemo's *Nautilus* in *Twenty Thousand Leagues under the Seas* was not the first undersea craft imagined by Jules Verne! A decade earlier, the prophetic author wrote "San Carlos," imagining a Spanish smuggler who utilizes a vehicle capable of diving beneath the surface of the waves. This newly-discovered story is published here in English for the first time—together with Verne's final words before his death on the future of the submarine as an instrument of war. Also in this volume is another never-before-translated tale, *The Siege of Rome*, a historical adventure of love and betrayal as Garibaldi's revolutionaries are defeated in 1849. Sorbonne professor Daniel Compère introduces the expert translations by Edward Baxter.

Since *Bandits & Rebels* emphasizes two Verne stories written early in his career, but remained unpublished during his lifetime, this volume also includes *Martin Paz*, another story of the same genre but which did appear in the 1850s, in both France and the United States. Reprinted here for the first time from the original translation, this preserves in unvarnished form Verne's own first version of *Martin Paz* to American readers. Previously, only the more polished version rewritten in the 1870s has appeared in book form.

Golden Danube

Translated, with an introduction and annotations, by Kieran M. O'Driscoll.

Jules Verne's "Extraordinary Journeys" often used the travelogue mode, and here the author offers a voyage down the entire length of the Danube, from Germany to the Black Sea. However, rather than the placid "blue" Danube of classical conception, the author offers one which is golden, in multiple ways. Smugglers are operating along the river, with the police in pursuit, and the hero is a champion fisherman who is abducted and forced to prove his courage.

The English rendering and notes are by a leading Verne translator and expert on the history of Verne translations, Kieran O'Driscoll.

A Priest in 1835

Translated with an introduction and notes by Danièle Chatelain and George Slusser.

Here is not only a treasure, but a literary revelation—the very first novel by Jules Verne. Finished by the age of 20 and under the influence of Edgar Allan Poe, *A Priest in 1835* was composed before Verne encountered any editors to hone his storytelling skills. Yet this tyro effort is a masterpiece, a novel told in a modernist style with a nonlinear narrative. This first English translation, with extensive critical commentary, redeems *A Priest in 1835* from the neglect and misunderstanding of French critics, who mistook its contemporary approach for an unfinished work. Instead, Verne reveals that he had not only the prophetic skills that would render him the father of science fiction, but a technique that would win him a place among the vanguard of 21st century authors.

Danièle Chatelain (University of Redlands) and the late George Slusser (University of California, Riverside) are renowned translators and scholars of the early history of science fiction.

Castles of California

Two plays by Jules Verne, *The Castles of California* and *A Nephew from America*, Translated with an introduction and notes by Kieran M. O'Driscoll; Appendix: "Jules Verne's Trip to America" by Brian Taves.

Two of Jules Verne's plays have long piqued the interest of American readers, and are included in this volume in translation for the first time. Both feature Frenchmen, recently returned from the United States, discovering the ephemeral nature of wealth. In *The Castles of California*, the Frenchman has come from the California gold fields—has he struck it rich, or has he had the bad luck that befell most of the "Forty-niners"? In *A Nephew from America*, an unattached ladies' man suddenly discovers that his late brother had a son in America, who is now an adult. And his new nephew is in love, and needs his uncle's assistance. Will true love, and kinship, win out?

Accompanying the two plays is an afterword on Verne's 1867 trip to the United States, and its lasting inspiration; some one-third of the author's stories would include American characters, settings, or themes.

The book is profusely illustrated with original engravings from Verne's time. Translation is by Kieran O'Driscoll, a leading expert on Verne in the English language, who is also translator of other Verne short stories and novels, and author of a study of more than a century of different translations of Verne's *Around the World in Eighty Days*.

Sheherazade's Last Night and Other Plays

Three Plays by Jules Verne, *An Excursion at Sea*, *The Thousand and Second Night*, and *Le Guimard*, Translated with an introduction and notes by Peter Schulman.

Jules Verne, before he became the famous novelist we know today from *Around the World in 80 Days*, learned his profession writing for the stage. Many of those youthful plays have been discovered for the first time, and three are translated into English for the first time in *Scheherazade's Last Night and Other Plays*. In *An Excursion at Sea*, Verne offers a humorous account of a nautical adventure interrupted by pirates, foreshadowing many of his classic stories. In *La Guimard*, he relates a love affair between the dancer, and the painter Jacques-Louis David, creating a realistic historical background as well as a deeply-felt romance. And in *The Thousand and Second Night*, Verne draws upon the world of the Arabian Nights to tell how the Sultan and the story-telling Scheherazade are finally united in marriage.

The book is illustrated with many scenes from Verne's novels echoing the the plays, along with engravings of the time of the subjects involved. Translator Peter Schulman is Professor of French and International Studies at Old Dominion University, and previously translated Verne's invisible man novel, *The Secret of Wilhelm Storitz* (Bison Books, 2011).

In 2003, the North American Jules Verne Society also co-published (with Prometheus) the Verne play, ***Journey through the Impossible***. A tale of fantasy and science fiction, *Journey through the Impossible* ran for 97 performances in Paris in 1882 and 1883. In three acts, the characters go first to the center of the Earth, then under the sea, and finally into outer space to the imaginary extrasolar planet Altor. Characters from *Journey to the Center of the Earth, From the Earth to the Moon, Twenty Thousand Leagues under the Sea*, and *A Fancy of Doctor Ox* appear again in *Journey through the Impossible*. The players include Captain Nemo, the lunar travelers Barbicane and Michel Ardan, Doctor Ox, and Professor Lidenbrock, after his trip to the center of the earth. Translation of *Journey through the Impossible* is by Edward Baxter, with introduction and notes by Jean-Michel Margot, along with reviews from the play's first presentation. Roger Leyonmark provides new illustrations in the style of the 19th century woodcuts that first illustrated French editions of Verne works, and the original engravings from the play are also featured. This is both the first complete edition in any language and the first English translation of a surprising work, by the popular Frenchman whose writing continues to delight readers—and audiences—to this day.

For additional details, reviews, and links to order the books, see the North American Jules Verne Society's website, najvs.org.

The North American Jules Verne Society

Jules Verne was a Frenchman, born in Nantes in 1828, who lived most of his life in Amiens, where he passed away in 1905. Despite his nationality, Verne has always had an exceptional popularity among English-language readers, one which the North American Jules Verne Society celebrates today as the successor to previous organizations.

The first group of Verne enthusiasts was formed, not in Verne's own France, but in England. The Jules Verne Confederacy began in 1921 at Dartmouth Royal Naval College, publishing *Nautilus*, a literary magazine in tribute to Verne and his son Michel, with whom they were in regular contact until Michel's death in 1925. The most permanent legacy of the Confederacy came with the publication of the Everyman's Library edition of *Five Weeks in a Balloon and Around the World in Eighty Days* in 1926, reprinted as late as 1966. Not only did it contain some of the first new, corrected translations, but the introduction by members of the Confederacy offered one of the earliest thoughtful critical overviews and bibliographies of Verne.

In France, the Société Jules Verne was formed in 1935, but their work would be interrupted by war and did not resume until 1967. Meanwhile, the American Jules Verne Society began a 20-year association. It was initiated when Willis E. Hurd penned an article, "A Collector and His Jules Verne," for the August 1936 issue of *Hobbies*, recounting his discovery that most of Verne's novels available in English had received many different translations, under widely divergent titles. A number of enthusiasts read Hurd's pioneering analysis, and a network formed. Hurd's retirement allowed him to take an interest in authoring English versions of some of Verne's untranslated stories. His collection would be willed to the Library of Congress and the volumes of another American Jules Verne Society member, James C. Iraldi, were deposited at Indiana University's Lilly Library. Iraldi was still active in the late 1960s when Ron Miller and Laurence Knight began the Dakkar Grotto, publishing two issues of a journal entitled *Dakkar*, after Captain Nemo's original Indian name.

In 1993, the North American Jules Verne Society (NAJVS) formed, and has steadily grown with annual meetings and a peer-reviewed newsletter, *Extraordinary Voyages*. Although founded largely by collectors, the group now includes scholars and readers generally, to span all types of Verne admirers. In 2003, NAJVS undertook its first book publication, Verne's science fiction play, *Journey through the Impossible*, with the Palik series of first-time translations commencing seven years later.

The Society is a not-for-profit corporation with these goals and objectives:

- To promote interest in Jules Verne and his writings.
- To provide a forum for the interchange of information and materials about and/or relating to Jules Verne and his works, such as annual meetings with workshops and presentations.
- To stimulate Jules Verne research.
- To publish a newsletter, *Extraordinary Voyages*, with articles about Jules Verne and Society related issues.

Information on membership and activities, along with various educational activities, may be found at the society's website, najvs.org, as well as on Facebook.

www.ingramcontent.com/pod-product-compliance
Lightning Source LLC
LaVergne TN
LVHW010934100826
845153LV00001B/34
9781629333915